BLIND MICE BITE

A MATT LOOSE MYSTERY

ELLE ANDREWS PATT

BLUE BEECH
PRESS

Cover Design: Elle Andrews Patt

ISBN (EBK): 978-1-960974-06-8

ISBN (PB AZN): 978-1-960974-07-5

ISBN (PB D2D): 978-1-960974-96-9

ISBN (HB): 978-1-960974-08-2

Published by BLUE BEECH PRESS 5923 Kingston Pike #161, Knoxville, TN 37919

Blind Mice Bite/A Matt Loose Mystery/ Book 1 -- 1st ed. December 2023

Publisher's Note: This is a work of fiction. Names, characters, places, and incidents are a product of the author's imagination. Locales and public names are sometimes used for atmospheric purposes. With the exception of public figures, any resemblance to actual people, living or dead, or to businesses, companies, events, institutions, or locales is completely coincidental. Any historical personages or actual events depicted are completely fictionalized and used only for inspiration. Any opinions expressed are completely those of fictionalized characters and not a reflection of the views of public figures, the writer, or the publisher.

ALSO BY ELLE ANDREWS PATT

NOVELS

GHOST: An Andrea Kelley Mystery
(The Archivist Book 1)
SPIRIT: An Andrea Kelley Mystery
(The Archivist Book 2)
WRAITH: An Andrea Kelley Mystery
(The Archivist Book 3)

SHORT FICTION

MISSING: PRELUDE TO A MURDER CONVICTION
The Prometheus Saga: MANTEO
The Prometheus Saga 2: REMUDA
Return To Earth: SOMEDAY LOYAL
The Masters Reimagined:
REGARDING MR. BULKINGTON
The Masters Reimagined 2:
AMONG THE BLUE HORSES

For Ruthy Charlot, our Ebonbird.
I hope you are flying wild and free in heavenly skies.

ACKNOWLEDGMENTS

As lonely a pursuit as the act of writing is, no book is ever produced in a vacuum. First and foremost are the readers, who are the cheerleaders and peanut gallery in the back of the writer's mind before they ever lay eyes on the pages of a completed book. Between the writing and the completion, many people—seen and unseen, named and unnamed, in person and through digital means— help the writer along a story's journey.

I began writing this story several years ago. Time, reflection on the story puzzle, and a team of gracious and generous writers, readers, and editors have finally enabled me to write, "the end." They have helped me convey Matt Loose and Lucinda Troy's personalities, love story, and evolutions back into and out of the world, respectively, in the way I intended.

Thank you so much to the Daytona Fiction Writers, especially the Harts, Michael J., and Chris McKenna. Thank you to first reader Kelley Rebori. Thank you to my adventurous beta readers, Brenda C. Krygowski, Cate Bronson, Penny Zang, Morgan Fleming, and a couple of anons, you know who you are! My ARC readers proved invaluable. Thank you all! Extra thanks to LaDonna Millman, Liz Janairo, Lorraine Hudson, and Caroline Thompson for the extensive feedback you offered.

Thank you to The Time Turners and Shakespeare Sisters for your endless support through the daily trudge. Thank you to my immediate and extended family for the continued enthusiasm for my work. My husband and daughters practice a great amount of patience as I pick my way through the words of each novel and they know this one has been particularly time-consuming.

Thanks is owed, in many ways, to Paul Stevens. Thank you for your honesty and thoughts regarding this story and these characters. Thank you for pointing out that primary sources are both fallible and only as good as their interviewers. You have been a great guide for my publishing adventure. I wish you luck on your new path.

Final thanks are owed to you, the reader. Thanks for giving this story a go. Thank you for your support. Thank you for your reviews and for sharing my stories with others. I truly appreciate you.

~ Elle

BLIND MICE BITE

PROLOGUE

"Can you tell me your name again?" the quiet voice said.

In the dark, Matt lay still on the cot, not aware until then of having spoken. What name had he given her?

"Could you please confirm your name out loud?"

Everyone was forever asking his name here, even after they checked his wristband. But he was leaving soon. Going to—

"I need your name."

"Yeah," he said, hearing the slow in his voice, tasting it on his tongue.

Daytona. That's where he was going.

He had a different name there. But not even the company knew that cover. He'd never said the name out loud. That wasn't who he was right now.

"Your name?"

"My name is Matt Loose."

"Are you married, Matt?"

"Divorced." Anna left him two years ago for an investment banker. That's what he got for moving back to New York. This line of questioning seemed familiar to him, but he couldn't remember anyone else asking about Anna since he'd been here.

"Kids?"

An image rose in his mind's eye. Dakota spinning around to greet him, dark brown hair swinging over her shoulder, big brown eyes shining, a grin spreading across her freckled face that broke his heart with happiness. God, he wanted to wrap his arms around her and bury his nose in that hair, snuffle up her scent of baby shampoo and little kid sweat and crayons and horse and her. "A daughter."

"Tell me about your daughter."

No words would come. How could he describe her? "She reminds me of my sister."

"And your sister is . . .?"

"Lily." Lily would be coming to get him soon. To take him to Daytona Beach, let him adjust.

"Your nephew?"

Did he say he had a nephew? "Ethan."

"How old is Ethan?"

He had to think about it, but Ethan was born a year before Dakota. "Nine."

"When was the last time you saw him?"

"When he was three."

"Has your daughter met him?"

Dakota knew she had a cousin, but Lily couldn't afford to fly up and they didn't have the time to fly down. Anna's job was as busy as his own. Though that was different now, wasn't it? It wasn't like he had a job anymore. Not that he could watch Dakota anyway.

"Matt?"

"No. Maybe next summer."

"Does your daughter live with you?"

He lifted his right hand, opening his fingers wide, only then aware that both his hands had been fisted on his stomach.

"What?" the woman said, sounding honest-to-god curious about what he might be thinking.

"No," Matt said, letting his hand indicate his condition and his tone convey his irritation. "She lives with her mother."

"You could learn to care for her."

He let his hand drop onto his chest. "Maybe."

"When was the last time that you saw her?"

"Her eighth birthday." He'd brought her a chocolate cake from a little bakery near his place in Tribeca and a cross-eyed stuffed unicorn. Anna's boyfriend banker had been away somewhere on business. After candles and cake, Dakota fell asleep sprawled across the couch, trying to anchor herself to both of them at once. When he came back from tucking her in, Anna had a glass of bourbon in her hand.

She tilted her head in invitation, and Matt plopped down beside her.

They'd finished watching The Little Mermaid for the umpteenth time, taking turns adding random lines between the dialogue and sipping from the one glass like they used to before Anna left him. He'd gone back to his apartment instead of staying, but it had been a near thing.

Matt rolled his lower lip under, tasting the ghost of Anna's cherry-cola chap stick under the gentle scrape of his teeth.

"What's your daughter's name?" the woman asked.

"Her mother named her. I was deployed."

"How old is Dakota now?"

"Who?"

"My mistake. What's your daughter's name again?"

"I wanted to name her Sophie, but she'd have hated that. She's a tomboy, through and through."

"How old is she now?"

"She likes horses, you know? She takes riding lessons in Central Park."

"When will you get to see her again?"

"Soon, I hope. I have to get better first. And I'll have to wait until a school break."

"Okay, Mark—"

"Matt. My name's Matt."

"*Seguro que te llamas Matt?*"

What?

"Matt?"

"I, uh, Spanish isn't my strongest language. Are you asking for my name? It's Matt. Loose."

"Okay, Matt. I know you're tired. You're relaxed. Your eyelids are heavy."

His muscles were heavy, too. His head hurt in a vague way. He let his eyes close.

"When I count backwards from three," the woman said, "you'll sleep until I wake you, okay?"

"Sure."

"Three, two, one."

"Is he out that fast?" a man said, too loud, too deep, too close.

Matt tried to close his fingers in his shirt, hold on to himself.

"Hang on," the woman said.

The words distorted, pulling at the edges of him.

Cool fingers closed on his, stilled his scrabbling hand, stilled his mind.

"You've done," the man said, each syllable stretching and stretching as Matt hung on to them, "a remarka—"

Matt fell into the silent darkness where he'd been living for too long. Fell and fell and fell.

CHAPTER
ONE

2017 ~ DAYTONA BEACH

Matt Loose lay in the dark, listening to cicadas buzz at one other in the meager landscaping outside his apartment. At nearly one a.m., he'd normally be nestled within the ordered intensity of the Daytona Beach Racing and Card Room, pouring drinks for the regulars who muttered their orders at the bar girls in smoke-grizzled voices. But Ed only let him work ten nights on, before he made him leave for two.

He noticed the cars first, three in a row, coming in the complex entrance that lay beyond his second story window. Just after the cicadas picked up their rhythm again, two more rolled in. Matt waited for the slamming of doors, the alcohol fueled voices that would signal a party in the making, but neither came.

He sat up, his foot hitting the laptop he'd left near the middle of the bed. The slight odor of cheese pasta lingered in the humid air. He felt around in the folds of his duvet and found his cell phone. A thud echoed up from the other side of the single apartment-wide building, near the stairs. And then boots were coming up the stairs, several sets, sounds familiar from Matt's Marine Corp days.

A raid maybe. There'd been a couple of drug arrests in the parking lot in the past couple of weeks. He set his cell phone on the shelf above his bed and lay back down, glad he'd not yet fallen asleep, prepared to hear what he could hear. It wasn't just a couple of men, it was a team. The boot steps hit the top of the stairs and passed his door, but stopped even with his bedroom wall, waiting out there on the other side of his closet as others continued pounding up the stairs. They must have been lining up along the walkway, waiting for the full team to make the second floor before they continued past. Why anyone thought they were safe behind wood framing and drywall was beyond him.

There was a pause, a held breath, and then a resounding crash from his living room that catapulted Matt straight up again, heart thumping. A woman shouting, but he couldn't tell what over the rush of blood in his ears. Were they really in his apartment? He scrambled over, his hand brushing over the holster attached to the side of his bed.

"Police, police, police," a man yelled in the hall outside Matt's closed bedroom door.

Cops. Matt drew his hand back.

Another voice, hollow, from his bathroom. "Clear!"

Swinging his legs over the side of the bed, Matt stumbled up, the blanket catching his leg.

"On your knees, on your knees, on your knees," the first man yelled again as Matt's door burst open, bouncing off the stop as men rushed into the room, filling it with the fury of their movement, rank sweat, leather, gun oil, shouting, "Down, down, down."

Matt fell to his knees, bringing his hands up behind his head, elbows out. Hands grabbed him, dragging him forward, pushing him face-down onto the musty carpet.

"Stay down," the first man said, although another had a knee planted in the small of his back. The man sitting on him yanked Matt's right hand out and down, snapping the cuff against his wrist bone hard enough to bruise and then grabbed the other.

Unable to breathe, a chilling wave of familiarity crashed into Matt's chest, and he tensed, resisting the pull on his wrist.

The man above him snapped, "Don't. We're cops. Police. *Policia*."

Matt closed his eyes tight, fighting the instinct to roll, lay this man flat out on the floor before he could stop Matt from doing it. He hitched in a stifled breath and then relaxed his shoulders, let the guy tug his arm down to his lower back.

―――――――――

DETECTIVE LUCINDA TROY STRODE FORWARD, alert for trouble as more men disappeared into the bedroom. In the doorway, she fetched up against the SWAT team leader's back. From inside the room, she heard a quiet grunt and the unmistakable sound of cuffs being closed.

"Clear," someone said.

She peered over Latham's shoulder into the dark room. His acne-scarred cheek caught the reflection of his men's hooded flashlights before he hit the light switch to his right. He turned sideways, swinging his right arm back to both invite her in and let her by.

In a glance, she registered that the bedroom was as spare as the rest of the small apartment. Boxy headboard with built-in bookcase, bare except for a handful of stacked CDs, half a bottle of water, a cell phone. No lamp. Laptop sitting half-buried in the crumple of dark red sheets and beige comforter. Three-drawer dresser. No mirror. Nothing on the walls. A hat rack looking thing that held a button-down shirt, slacks, a dark jacket, a tie, and a single pair of black dress shoes.

A blonde bulldog of a white man in boxers and a black tee shirt lay on his belly on the beige wall-to-wall carpet, arms cuffed behind him, face turned away from her. From what she could see, he matched the description of their suspect. That was a good start.

SWAT team giving way, Cin crossed the small room to the foot of the bed and crouched down to address the man. "Doug Moultrie?"

"No."

"Excuse me?"

". . . loose."

"No, sir, I can't do that. Are you Doug Moultrie?"

"No."

Sighing, Cin looked up at Latham. "You ready to hand this over, let my team find out who he is?"

Latham leaned back a little to look down the hall. "Already flipping the living room."

"I'm Matt Loose," the bulldog said.

"Excuse me?" she said again.

"Is my tongue not working?" He lifted his head. "My name is Matt Loose."

"You're not Doug Moultrie?"

He pressed his forehead down onto the carpet and growled.

"This guy for real?" she said to Latham.

Latham shrugged.

She sighed. Their witness, one of her CIs, a criminal informant, had sworn up and down the man they wanted for the murder of a local drug dealer lived here and was headed out of town. He'd provided a bloody shirt for DNA evidence and said their suspect had taken drugs and the murder weapon from the scene.

After cursory checks and speaking with the lab, she'd convinced the judge on duty to sign out an arrest warrant for murder on Doug Moultrie as a flight risk and a no-knock premises warrant in search of Moultrie, electronics, weapons, and drugs before they could be destroyed. Her CI had proved reliable, but he'd been jumpy on this one. "Where's your ID, Matt?"

"Kitchen drawer," he said into the carpet. "Closest to the hall."

Latham turned to retrieve it without being asked.

Talking to the back of Matt's head, she said, "You know James Shad? Jimmy?"

Silence.

"Got it," Latham announced. He pulled a card from the top of a small wad of cash held together by a rubber band. "Florida ID card. Matthew Anthony Loose. Got a carry permit here, too."

"You don't drive?" Cin asked. After another moment of silence, she leaned forward. Matt's eyes were closed. She frowned at him. His breathing was rapid, and his jaw clenched. Sweat beaded in his hairline. "Sit up," she said, looping her arm through his.

Latham stooped to grab Matt's other elbow and help him kneel upright before they steadied him as he maneuvered around to sit cross-legged. Latham stepped back as Matt took a deep breath. Cin let go of him but remained crouched at his side. "Little tense there, Matt," she said. And he was ripped under that tee. "Your name's not on the lease."

"I sublet."

They always had a pat answer. "Want to look at me?"

He shook his head slightly, but opened his eyes, turning his face to her. His brilliant blue eyes stared through her, unfocused.

"You take something, Matt?"

He took another deliberate breath and swallowed before he said, "Panic attack."

She looked up at Latham. He shrugged. Stepping to the side, he keyed his mike and asked dispatch to run the ID for outstanding warrants.

Charlie, the other detective on Cin's team, stepped into the room. "Nothing."

Cin lifted her chin, indicating the rest of the room. Charlie eased by them to hit the far side of the room first, the direction in which Matt was still staring towards the blind-covered window. He blinked, drawing her attention to his long eyelashes. Wide forehead, a faint frown dipping between thick, curved brows, high cheekbones above a strong jaw. Plump lips drawn together in a tight line, solid chin. Attractive. "Why you nervous, Matt?"

Rolling his eyes, he shook his head again. "I'm not Moultrie, but I'll let you do the search you're already doing despite the forced entry on the wrong address, unless, of course, my address isn't on the warrant in the first place. If you have a warrant."

Charlie scooted back past them.

"Got all our duckies in a row, Matt," Cin said, pulling the warrants from her back pocket. "Doubt you can read them strung out the way you are."

Pills rattled from the head of the bed. Charlie had already bagged the phone and laptop. He held up a prescription bottle in his gloved hand. "Oxy."

"Jesus Christ," Matt muttered.

"Focus on me, and I'll lay off," Cin said.

He huffed and dropped his gaze.

The sound of Velcro tearing proceeded Charlie's announcement. "FNS nine mil." He dropped the magazine out and racked the slide to remove the chambered bullet.

"Where's Doug Moultrie?" After a moment of silence, Cin continued. "How do you know James Shad?"

"You're in the wrong apartment."

"Come on, Matt, if we're in the wrong place, so be it. You want to answer my questions, prove you're on our side, or you want to spend your night in jail?"

"I've provided picture ID, you haven't found anything to justify arresting me," Matt said, his voice rising with each word until he was shouting. "And you're at the wrong address for whatever it is you're after!"

"ID's clean," Latham said.

Cin stood up, relieving the ache in her thighs. "That bottle labeled correctly, Charlie?"

Rifling through the closet, Charlie didn't turn. "If he's Matthew Loose."

"You on oxy right now, Matt?"

Matt shook his head.

"Verbal answer, Matt, speak up so we can all hear you."

"No, I have not taken any oxy tonight."

"What did you . . ."

"Shit," Charlie said, spinning around. "You blind, man?"

Cin glared at Charlie. "What?"

He waved a hand at the insanely organized, color-coded, and sparsely populated closet. She frowned at it and then glanced around the small room again, thinking about the bare kitchen, the undecorated living room, Matt's thousand-yard stare. Not just a bachelor pad. Latham raised his brows at her, his lips turning down as he bobbed his head in agreement.

Matt's surfer-gelled hair was wrecked, the longer top falling forward over his down-turned face. She nudged him with the toe of her boot. "You're not strung out, are you, Matt."

He shook his head.

"You're blind."

"Only when my eyes are open," he bit out.

The third member of her team, Swinkler, poked his dark head in, a white cane in his hand. "Hey, boss—"

"We know, Swinkler, thanks. Anything else?"

"Naw. It's clean. Bagged a couple of kitchen knives."

"Put everything back exactly as you found it."

He laughed, his cheeks dimpling. "Sure, boss."

"I'm serious," Cin snapped. "Everything back in its place or as close to it as you can remember."

He held up his gloved hands in surrender as he turned away.

"Bag the gun and the phone, Charlie. And whatever ammo he has stashed."

"Will do."

Matt huffed again.

"Not a proper form of communication, Mr. Loose."

He raised his head and let it tilt back, sliding his un-nerving gaze in her direction. "Not against the law for a blind man to own a gun and keep it in his home."

"That concealed carry permit's illegal, though."

"I'm physically able to safely shoot a gun."

Cin lifted a finger. "No, you can't see what's beyond your target. God knows who you could kill."

He made a noise she didn't understand.

"Did you just growl at me? Latham, did he just growl at me?"

Latham had a hand up covering his smile as he shrugged.

"It's not funny," Cin said. "It's verbal assault."

"Cin," Charlie said.

Matt smirked. "Sin?"

"With a 'C', Mr. Loose, short for Lucinda, and you can take up the question of your illegally obtained CWP with a judge. How do you know James Shad?"

"Am I being arrested?"

Latham shook his head at her. God damn Jimmy Shad. He was done as a CI. She leaned in close to speak into his ear. "Concealed carry without a permit is a felony."

"We're standing in his home," Latham said. "And he didn't have it on him. Most we can do is pull his permit and maybe follow up on whoever signed off on it. Put it in the hands of the DA."

"Hello?" Matt said.

Cin wedged a hand through his arm. He startled, shying away from her. "Sorry. Stand up."

Awkwardly, he shuffled around and stood. She worked the key into the cuffs and popped them open. He took a big step to his left to put some space between them before he turned to face them, rubbing his wrists. "Jimmy was in my class last semester."

Considering the location of the apartment and Jimmy's priors, she'd bet that meant Daytona State College. "DSC?"

She handed Latham his cuffs.

"Yeah," Matt said. "Emergency Services. But I also teach Criminal Justice at Bethune."

If Matt checked out, why had Jimmy fingered him? "Nice kid," Cin snarked.

"Give him a punch in the nose from me. I need my gun and I need my CWP."

"Why?" Latham drawled, crossing his arms.

"You try walking down ISB at two a.m. without being able to run or defend yourself."

International Speedway Boulevard was a major, six lane thoroughfare that ran east through Daytona Beach from I-95 to the ocean and west all the way to the city of Deland. Cin said, "They have classes that late?"

Matt rubbed his face with both hands and then ran his fingers through his hair to get it out of his face. "I work at the dog track."

"Ah."

After a long moment, Charlie said, "Okay, I'll pop. What could you possibly do at the track?"

Matt smiled. A thrill ran up Cin's spine as she watched it bloom across his face. She stomped down hard on her immediate attraction. So, he wasn't their guy. Didn't mean he was anyone she wanted to know better.

"I tend bar."

"Seriously, man?" Charlie said. "How do you do that? Don't you have to know what's in the bottles?"

"They're always in the same place."

Cin wanted to ask about people running out on him but chose to stay focused. "You know Doug Moultrie?"

Matt shook his head. "Not a name I know."

"Charlie, check with Swinkler," Cin said. "Let's wrap this up. Thanks for getting us in the door, Latham."

Rolling his hand over, Latham took a little bow. "Too bad Shad's a tool."

"He's not going to like me much after tonight," Cin said.

Charlie held up the gun and two boxes of ammo. "For what it's worth, these are frangible."

Latham grimaced. "Messy."

Cin had to agree. Frangible bullets went in small, but the impact broke the shot into shrapnel that left a big hole on exit.

"Means I don't have to worry about what's beyond my target," Matt said.

"That's true," Charlie said. "He just has to be upfront and personal when he fires."

"I don't care," Cin said, pointing the way out. "Go, Charlie."

"Yes, ma'am."

Matt shifted. "Is my door intact?"

Latham laughed. "Yeah, not so much."

"Wrong address, you gonna help me out?"

"Correct address on the warrant," Latham said. "We aren't responsible, but I'll put a call in to a guy I know. You gotta pay upfront and you can sue Shad for damages as far as I'm concerned."

Matt's face twisted in resignation, but he just flapped a hand in response.

Latham stuck his hand out for Matt to shake before realizing his stupidity and sticking it into his pants pocket. He cleared his throat. "Okay, I'm leaving."

When they were alone, Cin said, "So, Mr. Loose, your response to entry, not going for your gun, what you've had to say indicates you're familiar with law enforcement."

"Five years. NYPD."

"Panic attack?"

"What are you, a therapist?"

"I'm Detective Lucinda Troy, DBPD."

"The guy with the deep voice?"

"Rusty Latham. SWAT team leader. You don't know Doug Moultrie?"

He raised his brows.

"You're good at that. I thought blind people lost the subtler facial expressions."

"Yeah, I took that course, too," he said, rolling his eyes.

Cin opened her mouth on the thought that she found that ability fascinating but managed to bite her tongue. "Doug Moultrie?"

He sighed. "No. Are we done?"

"Want to sit in the living room for the paperwork?"

Matt shifted again and this time Cin saw that he was orienting himself using the foot of the bed. He held out an arm towards the door and said, "I need to put some pants on."

Because she was just that paranoid, she watched while he pulled on worn jeans. He tilted his head in her direction and held his hand out. "Wallet?"

She smacked it into his hand. "After you."

"Actually," he said, lifting his hand toward his face.

"What?"

"I know you're not gonna hand me my cane, but..."

Cin looked down the hall. The SWAT guys had propped the broken front door open. She couldn't see if Swinkler had cleared the living room. A light flashed, which meant he was still documenting. Damn Jimmy Shad. "Just follow me. I'll make sure nothing's in your way."

As she came even with the kitchen entry, she glanced over the island that divided the kitchen from the living room. Latham stood in front of the closed slider to the balcony, and then Charlie stood up from where he'd been crouched below him. A tapping sound rose from the baseboard running between the slider and the island.

Two more strides took her past the little island and its stools. Charlie noticed her, laid a finger on his nose and sniffed. Surprise tightened her chest.

Another stride and she could see Swinkler kneeling on the beige carpet, pieces of the baseboard surrounding him, shining a light down into one of three holes punched through the drywall. She stepped left into the living room, let Matt come even with her on her right, and then shoved him hard at the hallway wall.

Mid-step, he teetered sideways, but then planted his feet. "What the hell!"

Cin lifted her leg to stomp on his bare foot, but he anticipated the action, and instead of moving away like a normal person, he wrapped his arms around her, lifting her off her feet even though she was taller than him. She kicked his shin, which he ignored, but then Charlie pressed the barrel of his Glock against Matt's temple.

"Put her down and step back."

"Do it," Latham ordered from a few feet away.

"What the fuck," Matt spit.

One of Latham's team eased in through the front door, gun first.

"Not asking twice," Charlie barked.

"You just did," Matt said, lowering Cin before letting go of her.

She stumbled and righted herself, spinning away from Latham and his gun drawn at low ready to face Matt, her hand going to her own gun, but not pulling it.

Charlie held his position, keeping the pressure on when Matt stepped back, the barrel of the Glock leaving a red stripe from Matt's temple to just below his eye.

"Face to the wall," Cin said, with as much authority as she could muster.

"Got it all," Swinkler called out.

Reaching his right hand out first to touch the wall, Matt turned to face it. With his gun now aimed at the back of Matt's head, Charlie laid his free hand between Matt's shoulders and pushed him flush to the wall.

Cin tugged her handcuffs off her belt and snapped the cool metal around Matt's left wrist. Reaching under Charlie's arm, she took a firm hold on Matt's right wrist and brought his arm back and up. Although he didn't resist, he fisted both hands hard. His forearms corded with a tension she could feel in the quiver of his back muscles as his breathing hitched. When the second cuff clicked home, he thumped his forehead hard against the drywall, leaving a shallow indentation.

"Hey," Charlie shouted and jerked him back by his shirt.

"Sit him down," she said, not missing the relief on Matt's face as Charlie manhandled him around.

With the wall at his back, Matt sank to the floor on his own.

"What is it?" she asked Swinkler.

"White powder, three Ziplocs, maybe fifty grams each? Three more from the kitchen."

Three hundred grams. Mandatory minimum of seven years and a $100,000 fine. Not as much as Jimmy had led them to believe, but not nothing. Cin exchanged a glance with Latham, who shrugged. Matt Loose had almost fooled them.

"Miranda," Cin said.

Charlie did the honors of reading Matt his rights while Latham stood by, ready to back him up if need be, and Cin inspected Swinkler's find. The bags were all open and caked from moisture. The discarded baseboard lay in three pieces, the edges evenly cut so they could be fitted together. An uneven gap between the subfloor, carpet, and drywall ran the length of the wall.

"Good eyes." She lifted her chin to the holes in the wall. Two on the kitchen side of the slider and one on the other. "Nothing else in the wall? No other weapons?"

"No."

A test tube lay to one side of the open field test kit.

"Not meth?"

"No." Swinkler shook another tube and then opened his hand to reveal the purple color. "Cocaine."

A trail of it powdered the carpet outside the hidey-hole. "Did it spill?"

"It's scattered all over in there, along with a lot of roach poop." He nodded at the bags. "Poop in those, too."

Cin leaned down for a better look at the bags. "They were open? Makes for some nasty stuff up the nose." She glanced over at Matt. His expression could best be described as stone faced with a touch of green. "Did you know you were snorting roach poop, Matt?"

She let his first name pop off her tongue. His stone face soured, telling her he had noticed the shift back to his first name, a common power play move.

"It's boric acid cut with sugar. My sister cut the boards for me."

She looked around. The apartment was older, with wear and tear and stains, but as clean as it could be. No dirty dishes. Nothing on the floor.

"That's what they all say," she said, but crossed the living room and went back past him into the kitchen anyway. Three evidence bags holding one straight-edged knife each sat on the island beside a wooden knife block. The baseboard Swinkler had jimmied off the far wall lay on the tile floor in two neat pieces. To her left, the cabinet door under the empty sink stood open. "Under the sink?"

"One bag, sealed." Swinkler confirmed. "Ease of access. Two hidden behind the baseboard."

Opening cupboards, she found ordered stacks of dishes and glasses, bowls, pans, canned foods with braille labels stuck on them. She ran her fingers over the labels, remembering the label maker she loved to play with when she was little. Behind a narrow, full-length door next to the refrigerator she found all of Matt's dry foods. All of it in Ziplocs.

"I'm blind," she said, "I'm from New York City. I move to Florida and hear all about the palmetto bugs. I'm gonna have a problem thinking about roaches and not being able to see them. What do you think, Charlie?"

He grimaced. "Yeah. Me, too."

"Latham?"

"Gives me the creepy-crawlies just thinking about 'em." He shuddered. "They say for every one you see in your house, there's a hundred more you don't."

"Had one drop on my bed one night," SWAT guy at the door offered. "Freaked me the hell out and I could see it."

"Swinkler?"

The sound of his pen moving on the report stopped. "Boric acid is an insecticide, but you saw the test, Cin."

"Those tests are fuck-all accurate," Matt sighed.

"Gotta agree, Matt. But rules are rules. We have a no-knock warrant for a drug search and six bags of shitty white powder testing as cocaine. Does anyone else live here with you?"

Matt remained silent.

"I'll take that as a no. Custody and control. Sorry, Matt."

Although Matt had visited his NYPD precinct after his accident, booking in at the county jail off International Speedway Boulevard rattled him. The officers spoke too loudly, all the doors on the cells echoed. Having no idea of the layout, he was completely dependent on the random officers moving him from point to point. He found the mix of bleach, Lysol, body odor, perfumes, colognes, old food, and urine overwhelming by the time he sat facing a paramedic.

"Hey, Mr. Loose, it's Tommy Miller. I took your class a couple years ago."

"Pen tapper."

He laughed. "Yeah, that's me. Possession, huh?"

"Boric acid in baggies."

"Shit, man, that sucks. I'm gonna put some ointment and gauze on your wrists, okay? You were a cop, yeah?"

"Yes."

A woman a few feet away started wailing, adding to the general babble.

"They keep you cuffed in the car?"

Matt shook his head. He'd freaked a little when he thought Detective Troy was going to walk him out and down the stairs at his apartment cuffed, but he'd kept his head and used his words like he'd been taught.

"Why are they so abraded then?"

That was not something he was going to tell a former student. "I, uh, panicked a little?"

Tommy's sure fingers rubbed ointment onto each stinging wrist. He rummaged around for a minute before beginning to wind gauze around Matt's right wrist. "I get that. Being blind must suck. So," he said, his voice taking on a more authoritative tone. "Light perception?"

Matt didn't want to answer, but he both knew the kid was just doing his job and that he'd learned how to project that tone from him in class. "Slight."

Tommy cut the gauze and tucked it under the wrapped edge. "How slight? See shadows?"

"No. Direct light is a lighter nothing. If something blocks a direct light, I can usually tell."

"Yeah, that's slight. You don't see black?"

"No colors. Just . . . nothing."

Finishing Matt's left wrist, Tommy fell silent.

Matt discouraged questions about his blindness in class, deflected questions about himself in general. He'd come to Daytona because his sister and nephew were here, and he'd been told he could walk away from his former life. But here it was, tapping him on the fucking shoulder, thanks to Jimmy Shad.

The click of a pen light. "Your pupils dilate normally," Tommy said. "And you use your eyes normally for the most part. I'm not lying though, you got a killer thousand-yard stare, man. Brain injury?"

"Baseball bat."

"Ouch. Got meds you need in the next seventy-two hours?"

"Seventy-two?"

"Just a precaution. Narcotics charges take longer to process, and you may or may not be able to bond out. Meds?"

"I've got Oxycodone for headaches, but don't use it much anymore."

"Noted. If you need that or ibuprofen, speak up. No guarantees you'll get either, though." He leaned into Matt's space and lowered his voice. "Listen, narcotics is a mandatory strip search, but afterwards Sergeant Holland already has a note on here that you're to be held in an isolation cell and accompanied in court rather than in with the crowd. Good luck, man."

He thought the strip search would trigger him, but by the time they got to him, his adrenaline fatigue had muted his reactions. Apparently, someone at the Volusia County Branch Jail thought he'd be here more than a few hours as he was ushered through a shower and a change into jail scrubs and sandals. He was more than ready to take a piss and roll up in the scratchy blanket he'd been issued as the guard described the single person cell and then locked the door behind him. No one appeared to be contained in his immediate area.

But after he was situated, his stomach started growling. It had to be long past whatever breakfast had been scheduled. He shivered. It dawned on him that he'd been cold for a couple of hours now. Among the general din from down the way—voices, footsteps, coughing, laughter, a TV—someone was singing loud and off-key and every few minutes a different irritated voice yelled at him to shut the fuck up. The blanket smelled of chemical cleaner. Matt sighed and rolled over to drop his feet back onto the floor. Fighting to free himself from the blanket, he braced a heel on the edge of the cot and shoved himself back until he hit the cold concrete wall.

His sister hadn't answered his call. Neither did the one-man law office he'd only been to once since he moved to Daytona. He assumed the holding cells had phones in them, but he'd been skipped straight past that stage. Probably thanks to the gift of his blindness, which just kept giving. By now, all his ID had been verified as well, which probably didn't help, since he'd be isolated for his own protection and to keep Volusia County employees from fucking anything up that he might use against them.

He thumped his head back against the wall and shivered again. He had nothing to think about except how the hell a former student had managed to connect him to the name Douglas Moultrie.

"I'm not freeeeeeeee, I'm faaaallling..."

"Shut your face, fuck-up!"

"While I'm frreeeee baaaalllling..."

"Asshole," Matt whispered, on Tom Petty's behalf. No one knew the name Doug Moultrie. No one but him.

"Now meeee baaawwwllling..."

The guy could at least drop the 'g'. But he sang along under his breath because the guy wasn't wrong about how being here felt, and thumping his head every time someone yelled out another insult reminded him there was solid concrete at his back, not the moving wood of a bat swinging at him.

FOUR MISERABLE DAYS LATER, changed and kicked out into the lobby of the jail on payment of his bail, Matt rubbed his wrists.

"Matt," Lily called out.

He stood still, waiting for her to make her way over to him. The bondsman's fee had cost her $30,000. Non-refundable. It was going to take a while for him to free up that kind of money to pay her back.

She arrived in a rush from his left. "Are you okay, Matt?"

"I'm sorry, Lil."

"I put up the house, Matt, and the bank gave me a loan for the fee. I can't believe they'd treat you like this."

"Lily, the only reason I got to bond out at all is because I'm a former cop without a record. They treated me just fine."

She wrapped her right arm around his left and started walking, steering him past small groups of two and three people talking in low tones that echoed off all the tile in the hollow room.

"I talked to Ed," she said, calmer now. "He said as long as you're back to work on Saturday, it's fine."

"Thank you."

"There's one more thing. After the board-up service left, some jerk broke in again before Sebastian got there to meet the handyman. Your stereo, TV, and laptop are gone."

Matt stopped. The cops had what they wanted. Detective Troy had been nice and let him call Sebastian, a fellow professor, to arrange for a new door. Still, if he never heard her voice again, it'd be too soon. So was the break-in a crime of opportunity or an opportunity for whoever got to Jimmy Shad to search his place?

Lily swung around on his arm to face him. "I'm sorry. Didn't you have a gun, too?"

"Cops have it. And the laptop." Not that there was anything on it.

His words had come out too flat. Lily cupped his face in her warm hands. It was a shock, realizing how cold his face was, but the warmth stopped his ricocheting thoughts.

She ran her thumb over his cheek when he leaned into the touch. "They left your speakers."

The speakers were the most expensive item he owned and possibly the most important to him. "I think I can hook them to my phone," he said, quirking his lips up in what he hoped came across as a smile as he took her hands in his and lowered them.

"You have it?"

"Yeah. It's dead, but they gave it back to me just now. Thanks, Lil."

"Girlfriend?" a familiar voice said.

Matt groaned. "Seriously?" He dropped Lily's hands and she turned to stand beside him, her shoulder brushing his.

"Still in the middle of an investigation in which you are implicated as a participant, so it's not unreasonable for me to ask you to talk to us."

"Us?"

"My team."

"And you are," Lily bristled, without any question in her tone.

A rustle. "Detective Lucinda Troy."

"My brother—"

Troy hummed at that.

"—has just been released. Surely you could've spoken to him while he was here or can wait until tomorrow."

"Nope. Need to talk to him now."

The rise and fall of her voice made Matt think she was rocking on her heels.

He had too much to check on. He had to find out if he'd been compromised. "You'll have to arrest me or wait until tomorrow," he said.

Another rustle as Detective Troy moved.

Lily raised her arm, probably trying to block Troy from reaching for him.

Matt stepped back, widening his stance, and braced himself against whatever was coming.

A cool hand took his wrist and Troy's light, earthy scent brushed over him as he allowed her to come around him, taking his arm with her. "Fine," she breathed into his ear.

"Are you sure it's not Sin with an 'S'?" he murmured.

"You can't do this," Lily protested.

"You're being detained," Troy said quietly as she closed a cuff around his wrist. "And it's Detective Troy to you."

"For?" Matt said, as Lily yelled, "You can't do this!"

Troy ignored Lily, even as multiple footsteps pounded across the tile floor towards them, and fastened the second cuff. "Suspicion of conspiracy."

A full chorus of "Sorry, Detective," in various tones, a "Really, Cin?", sweat, and cologne heralded the arrival of jail personnel.

Lily's anger seemed a physical sensation, it was so strong. "She's arresting him!"

"Detaining on possible further charges," Troy corrected.

"Ma'am," one of the male officers said, presumably to Lily.

"It's okay, Lily," Matt said.

"It's really not, Matt." Her voice vibrated with fury and tears.

"It is."

"Ma'am," the officer said again.

"Listen, Lily," Matt said again, worried this situation was about to spiral out of his control.

Troy's grip tightened on his right bicep.

"Please," he said. "It's okay. Drive home. I'll call you to pick me up." He found the cluster around him disorienting and had lost her location in the shuffle. A familiar huff from his left. Lily touched his arm, and he turned his face in her direction. "Please."

"Yeah, okay, little brother."

He could picture the exact glare she would be directing at Troy.

"Step back, ma'am," the same officer requested.

Her hand withdrew and Troy stepped forward, trying to take him with her.

Matt stumbled, sore and stiff after four days in the small, cold cell.

Lily squawked.

A man grabbed his left arm and helped Troy keep him from face planting.

They hustled him onward.

Conversations sprung back up around the room. The vocal officer began giving Lily the detainment spiel. A door swished open and then they were out into the steamy heat of June in Daytona.

"Steps. Four," Troy said.

Matt planted his feet. Nope.

"Jesus, Loose, I'm not going to let you fall."

"You blind?" Matt shot back. He hated the immediate tightness in his chest, the fuzz building in his head.

The man holding his left arm said, "Maybe we should—"

"No," Troy barked at the poor guy and to Matt, "Two steps forward and four steps down. Let's go."

Fuck. She was really going to make him do this in cuffs. He leaned back against their hold and shuffled forward until he felt the top of the steps. Troy sighed but let him feel his way down.

Apparently, Troy's car was parked at the curb. The guy protected his head as they maneuvered him into the back. It smelled of apples and was still cool from Troy's arrival. The door slammed closed. Sweat dripped down into Matt's eyes, making them burn.

"Matt," Troy said from the front seat, though he hadn't been aware of her getting in. The engine was running. "Take a deep breath, you're going to hyperventilate."

"The cuffs—"

"Are staying on," she said.

"Fuck." Straightening up, he took a deep breath, leaning his head back and swallowing down the moment of nausea as she pulled away from the jail.

"What's with the cuffs?" she asked.

Just breathe. Matt pushed his back hard against the seat even though trapping his hands hurt his still tender wrists.

"You were a dangerous guy, Loose. Still are, I'd guess."

Her words dashed over him like ice water. He relaxed into the moment, centering himself without lifting his head. Just breathe.

"Marine. Degree in Criminal Justice," she continued. "Civilian analyst for Naval Intelligence. NYPD Detective-Investigator in the terrorism unit."

The sweat drying on his face itched. She didn't know. He breathed. He lifted his head, but kept his eyes closed and breathed in again through his nose, then let the air flow out his mouth. She didn't know.

"Sounds like you're having a baby back there."

The laugh that bubbled out of him startled both of them and then she was laughing, too.

"What the hell are you doing bartending in Daytona Beach?"

Not investigating terrorism, that was for damn sure. "Maybe the fact that I'm blind escaped your notice?"

The whoosh of cars passing. Tires on pavement. The distant rhythmical pounding of a pile driver that meant they were approaching the intersection of ISB and I-95, which was under construction. Silence from the front seat.

"That means I can't see your response," he added dryly.

"Sorry," she said. "Just thinking about why blindness would stop you from working for NYPD or going back to Naval Intelligence."

An involuntary chuckle escaped him as Matt thought about how rapidly he used to scan the three monitors in his cramped Naval office, comparing what he saw to reams of printed information and photographs as he searched for patterns. He rolled his ankle, dislodging the remembered feel of Lieutenant Coleman's hand on his foot at the hospital.

She'd been sent to reassure him the Navy would find a civilian administrative position for him once he'd recovered. The overwhelming pity and condescending tone echoed by NYPD command made him dead set against trying to return to any of his former positions. And that was *before* he started trying to navigate his new reality, literally, or adjust to being cut off from the easiest ways to communicate with his far-flung network of work contacts, friends, and family.

He'd only been with NYPD through the company—his true

employer, with an official name Detective Troy would never be able to dig up. He'd made the move to New York to be closer to his wife and daughter and go back to the more hands-on field work he enjoyed. After that swing of the bat, the hands-on was out. Done.

The company hadn't even contacted him. Not directly, anyway. They'd probably pulled strings to force Lieutenant Coleman's visit.

Which left pattern spotting. But even given the technical support he'd need to sit all day and compare data as his full-time occupation, the process would be too slow except for background information. Others could do that better. He didn't need to be deadweight when there were things he *could* do, like teach and tend bar.

"Okay," Troy said into his silence. "Maybe that's too personal. Why would you turn away from all your training and start working with a rat bastard like Doug Moultrie?"

Matt rolled his eyes.

"You do that well."

"Shouldn't you be watching the road?"

"How come you can do that?"

"My eyes aren't broken, my brain is." He swayed left as she finally turned off ISB.

"That explains a lot," she said.

What Matt wanted explained was what kind of coincidence would tie some murdering rat bastard with the same name as his deepest cover ID and Jimmy Shad together and lead the cops straight to his door.

His broken brain couldn't fathom the odds.

"Maybe," he said, "you should detain Doug Moultrie instead of me, if what you want are explanations."

"Working on it," she said. "You're going to help me."

"Fat chance of that."

"Better than you think," she shot back.

Matt took a measured breath, determined to keep his mouth closed no matter what she asked next, but Lucinda Troy was done talking, too.

"It's unnerving," Charlie said.

They were standing in the little hall off the bullpen, shoulder to shoulder, arms crossed, outside the observation window of interrogation room three. Matt Loose sat inside, cuffed to the center bar of the table. Legs stretched out in front of him and hands lying palms up, he looked like he was asleep with his eyes open.

Cin shrugged.

Continuing to stare at Matt, Charlie said, "You know he's not Doug Moultrie."

"I know."

But she needed to be sure Jimmy Shad had lied to them. "Jimmy give you any hassle about picking him up?"

"A little. He's still pissed we charged him at all."

They had managed to knock a charge of possession with intent to distribute on Jimmy down to a misdemeanor possession and Cin still wasn't sure that wasn't going to bite them on the ass later. "He sucks as a CI," Cin said as she headed for door number two. "I'm done with him after this."

With one hand on the knob, she leaned over to check on Jimmy's position in the room before opening the door. Knucklehead was sitting with his back to the door. She slammed the door open, making him jump. "Other side, Jimmy."

Charlie followed her in, caught the door on the rebound, and closed it.

Scrambling up, Jimmy turned to face her, a mulish expression on his narrow, angular face.

She swept her arm out in an inviting gesture. "After you."

Grumbling, he hitched his baggie boardies higher up on his slim hips and walked around the table to sit on the opposite side, his flip-flips smacking his heels. Cin noticed the goosebumps spread along his arms and bare chest. "Charlie, did you scoop him up straight off the beach?"

"I did," Charlie said from behind her.

"My board better still be there, man."

Cin turned with her brows raised. Charlie shook his head at her. "I let him give it to a friend and I offered to let him grab a shirt, too."

She turned back to Jimmy.

"I didn't have one with me," Jimmy whined. He folded his arms, hiding the scars of old track marks.

"Let me see," she said.

With a clear reluctance, he lowered his forearms onto the table. No newish puncture marks. And he'd been passing his mandatory drug tests.

"We've got Doug Moultrie next door," she said.

Jimmy winced.

"Want to revise your statement?"

Staring hard at the table, he chewed his lip.

"That description you gave us still stand?"

He glanced up through his lashes. The smattering of freckles over his nose and cheeks seemed darker as he grew paler.

"How do you want to do this, Charlie?" Cin said.

Charlie stepped forward and planted his hands on the table before turning his head to look at her. "We could bring Doug in here, let them talk together."

"Wait, wait," Jimmy stuttered. "I don't want to talk to him. You said, you said I'd be, y'know, like in the shadows, anon . . . anon . . ."

"Anonymous? No, Jimmy, we never said that." It took effort to keep the smile off her face. "We said we'd protect your identity. Charlie, you did that right? Locked up his social security number? Secured his financials?"

"Sure did," Charlie agreed. "Hey, we can take Jimmy to Doug, if he feels safer that way."

"No, uh, no, man. I don't want to talk to him."

"He's gonna want to talk to you, Jimmy," Cin said, nodding gravely. "And we're inclined to let him. It's part of a deal we're making. You're part of that deal."

His eyes widened. "I am?"

Charlie stood up, Jimmy's gaze following him. "We'll drop the possession charges. Your mom will get her bond money back. You don't go away for a year."

"All I gotta do is talk to him?"

Cin nodded. "Yep. We need his supplier's name."

"I don't know his supplier's name!" he cried, raising both his hands. "I told you guys, that's what I told you!" He cradled his head, covering his face.

"We know, but you're going to find out, right now," Charlie said, using his serious, but understanding Dad tone.

He shook his head. "No, no, no."

"Jimmy," Cin said, the voice of reason. "You got us to this point. Doug Moultrie's going down. We know he needs someone to intercept his next shipment. It's already on the way. You're part of his distribution chain. If he thinks you're in and out today, he'll ask you to take care of it or at least take a message to his next in command. Being a CI is like undercover work, yeah?"

He peeked out from between his hands, his gaze flicking between them before he dropped one hand to pick at the table edge, resting his head on the other like it weighed twenty pounds. "What would I have to do?"

Forty minutes later, they had him prepped and wired up on an old unit that seemed more complicated than it was. From his expression, Cin could tell the choice had worked for making Jimmy feel important. Cin and a patrol officer sat with him outside Holding and they watched Charlie walk Matt into an empty cell and release his cuffs. Matt reached out to feel the barred front wall and then followed it over to the side wall and the bench there.

"That him?" Cin asked Jimmy.

Jimmy swallowed before he nodded, his knee bouncing faster than a piston in a Porsche.

"Note. CI answered in affirmative," Cin said for the wire.

"Yeah, that's him," Jimmy said belatedly.

"Okay, let's go."

At the cell, the front desk officer gave his line in a loud voice. "Okay, chill out until the Sargent comes back for you. It's a fine. If you pay it tonight, Jimmy, that's it, you walk. No court."

Jimmy bobbed. Sweat dripped off his hairline.

"Understand?" the officer said as Cin lifted her palm, encouraging Jimmy to speak out loud.

"Oh, um, yeah, yeah, okay." He slipped inside when the officer got the door opened and stood there breathing through his mouth.

The officer locked the door and they retreated. He nodded at her and went back to his front desk duty, while Cin joined Charlie in the bullpen at a spare monitor on a desk tucked into the front corner. A split screen showed two views of the holding cell their boys were sitting in together.

Jimmy was pacing. Matt ignored him. Ten minutes later, Jimmy flopped onto the far end of the bench.

"You okay?" Matt said.

Jimmy tucked a fist into his mouth and bit down.

"There a phone on the wall?" Matt asked.

Closing his eyes, Jimmy nodded.

"I have low vision. Can you tell me if there's a phone on the wall?"

Cin smiled. Matt was smart, not admitting that he was blind. That could be bad in a holding cell. Admitting low vision was a risk, but he probably thought he had the skills to fight his way out of a problem. Jimmy stared up at the camera on the cell's rear wall like he thought they were going to change their minds and come retrieve him.

"Shit," Matt muttered.

Jimmy sucked it up, finally, and slouched sideways on the bench to face Matt. "Sorry, man, yeah, there's a phone."

"Good. You know, you can call someone, collect, if you need to."

"Thanks, man," Jimmy said. "Hey, you want to call somebody?"

"Jimmy Shad? You're Jimmy Shad, right?"

"Fuck, man, I am so sorry." He glanced up at the camera. "Mr. Moultrie."

"Mr. Moultrie?"

"Yeah. I, uh, got picked up on an old speeding ticket," Jimmy said. "I know, I know, but please don't hurt me."

"What are you talking about?" Matt said, confusion clear in his face and tone.

"Aren't you here because I'm here?" Jimmy said.

"What?"

"Oh." Jimmy straightened up, starting to get into the role now. "Don't you, um, don't you have a y'know, a package arriving this week?"

"Fuck, seriously? You're running with this? I guess you *are* the reason I'm here. Why did you give them my address?" Matt said, voice rising as he stood. "And who is Doug Moultrie?"

"Uh, sorry, Mr. Moultrie, what name are you using?" Jimmy lowered his voice. "You can trust me, sir."

"Jimmy, you are digging your own grave here."

Jimmy glanced over his shoulder at the rear camera once more. And then Cin realized he didn't know there was also a camera in the hall at the front of the cell. With the rear camera showing his back, he laid a hand over the mic and said, so low the wire hardly caught it, "I'm sorry, Mr. Loose."

The hall camera clearly showed his lips if anyone wanted to argue the transcript on the wire later. Matt may or may not have heard. He leaned closer and Jimmy scooted over towards him. "I'm sorry, Mr. Loose. I'm kinda in a bind here."

The rear camera caught Matt's frown. Cin could practically see him calculating the situation. "Jimmy—"

"Shhh . . ."

Matt clenched his jaw tight and then whispered, "Why would you do that? Give them my address and somebody else's name?"

"It's not like that, I'm so sorry."

"Then what is it like, Jimmy," Matt ground out.

"They really think you're him, Moultrie. I gave them your description. I panicked, okay? You have to go along with it or I'm dead. I'm gonna die, man, please."

"Why me?"

"You can get out of it, right? You know all the . . .y'know . . .tricks, and besides, you're blind, it's not like they'll lock you up."

Matt barked out a sharp laugh. "It doesn't work like that."

"Please! Mr. Ward killed Chris last month. He'll kill me, too."

"Who's Ward?"

"A badass, that's who. An ex-Army special-ops meth-head freak who is gonna *kill* me if I'm not at the drop on Thursday. I gave the cops a name to keep them busy, a good one, but then they wanted an address, too, and I couldn't do that because—"

"Because why?"

"Just 'cuz. Anyway, that Rodriguez guy from class lives below you, so I knew yours. You can blab on me after Thursday. Please, I just gotta do this one thing and then I'm out. Please, Mr. Loose. Can you please just pretend? Answer Malcolm Ward and tell me to meet him Saturday, please?"

Matt sighed.

"Yes, Mr. Moultrie," Jimmy said in a louder voice. "I can do that for you. Thank you for forgiving me. Who do you want me to meet?"

Silence.

Jimmy grimaced over his shoulder for the camera again, then faced Loose. "Malcolm Ward, yes, sir. On Saturday? At the usual place? Yes, sir."

Matt said, "That do it for you, Detectives?"

"What?" Jimmy said.

Cin slapped Charlie on the shoulder. "Want to do the honors?"

CHAPTER
FOUR

Except for her small directions as she maneuvered Matt through the maze of Daytona Beach Police Headquarters, they didn't speak until Cin had him back out in the late afternoon heat. "Who's Chris?" he said.

"Chris Bolton. Known dealer. Unsolved homicide. The name Malcolm Ward is new to us. Jimmy told us Doug Moultrie had the murder weapon. That *you* had the murder weapon."

"I can just call my sister," Matt said.

"Curb," she said, amazed at how he stepped off in step with her—a total contrast to his shuffling with the cuffs on. "I can take you home."

"You could've just asked me to help."

She hit the locks on her dark blue Impala and opened the passenger door. "Two birds, one stone."

He turned his face towards her and for a moment seemed to be looking right at her. "You really still thought I might be Doug Moultrie."

"After three days of research and background checking every male Moultrie in central Florida without a single viable lead? Yeah, had to make sure."

With one hand on the door, he eased into the car and sat before saying, "I can respect that."

She checked that his hands were inside and shut the door. "Damn straight, you can respect that," she said out loud to herself, already moving around the front of the hood.

"Why does it smell like apples in here?" Matt asked when she got in.

"It's one of those air freshener thingies. It's unreal, isn't it?"

His lips turned down as he nodded. "Yeah. I was kinda hoping it was actual apples. I'm starving." He suddenly smiled, his whole face lighting up. An immediate surge of heat flushed her cheeks and pooled in her belly. "But since you stole me from my sister *and* subjected me to Jimmy's stupidity, you owe me a meal."

She'd been shoving down her inappropriate responses to this guy since she'd seen him cuffed on the floor of his bedroom. But after reading his background check, talking to several of his students and co-workers, and seeing for herself that Jimmy had lied about him, she didn't want to anymore.

"That wasn't"—he shifted in the seat—"a pass, if that's what you're thinking," he said into her too-long moment of silence. "I know I'm still untouchable until that boric acid clears the lab."

It took her a second to focus on his words, the heat fading until she caught up. "Wait. Does that mean you'll be available for touching later?"

Matt's open, unburdened laugh burrowed right into her. She liked it.

"No one wants this, believe me," he sputtered. "I come with too much baggage, but thanks for that. Does an ego good." He chuckled again, the grin brightening his face once more.

She tore her gaze away and started the car. "Druthers?"

"Panera," he said without hesitation. "The one on ISB."

"Done."

It wasn't far. She pulled out of the lot to a left onto Mason and caught the light to turn left again on Williamson. She caught him off guard with the dogleg turn into the strip center next to Panera's, though. His head bounced off the passenger window. "Shit, sorry," she said.

He laughed and rubbed his head and then ran his fingers back through his hair. "You're a hazard to my health."

"I'm really—"

He flapped his hand at her in dismissal. "Can you find a spot out front, on the ISB side?"

Cin shrugged. "Sure."

She parked and opened her door, not sure how to proceed, but he opened his door at the same time. "You can stay here," she said.

"Not a dog," he countered and got out, slamming the door closed. He found the curb and stepped onto the sidewalk, but then waited for her.

"Should I—"

He reached out, fingers bumping on Cin's arm, then clasping her bicep. "Just walk."

He snapped his fingers a few times as she headed for the door and then reached out just as she slowed and opened it for her. "How did—"

"I come here a lot," he said, and then raised his voice. "Hey, Josh."

"Hey, Mr. Loose," one of the three cashiers called from the order counter on their left. Young blond surfer dude. Six-foot, maybe one forty. "You got eyes today!"

They joined the end of the short customer line just inside the door. The woman Josh was waiting on and the two women in line ahead of them glanced back, but the middle-aged man between them continued to stare at the menu on the side wall above the registers. It was an instinctual situational awareness Cin had noticed before, that women, in general, physically acknowledged a change in their surroundings in a way men didn't, even if they were clocking all the details.

When it was their turn, Cin stepped off to move to the counter, but Matt didn't move with her and as she rocked back to his side, the free cashier pointed at the man who came in behind them instead, who hesitated until the cashier said, "Yes, you, come on."

Josh said, "Okay, Mr. Loose," as his remaining customer tucked her receipt away. "The usual?"

"Yes, please," Matt said, taking Cin with him to the counter.

"Ma'am?"

"What's your usual?" she asked Matt.

"Half a turkey bravo, a cup of cheddar broccoli, and a bottle of water," Josh answered.

Matt grinned.

"The same, then. I'm paying."

Josh handled the payment, then said, "Find a table, I'll bring it over."

A five-table cluster of boisterous Lopez Catholic students dominated the back, so she headed for a two-top against the front window. Matt slid his hand down her arm as she slowed, not sure how to help him sit down.

"Just put my hand on the back of the chair and get out of my way," he said. "No offense."

After they were settled, Cin said, "How do you usually find an empty table?"

"I wait by the pick-up counter and then Josh helps me find a table when it's ready."

"And when Josh isn't here?"

"I know his hours."

"Seriously?"

He laughed. "You've seen my resume. I don't let just anyone handle the food I can't see."

Really? His well-stocked pantry came to mind. "You must eat at home a lot."

He tapped the tabletop with restless hands. "Yeah, well. Welcome to my world."

As HE ATE, Matt thought of and discarded a dozen questions to ask her. There was nothing he could ask about her search for Moultrie. Jimmy had said the name was a "good" one, that it would keep the cops busy. And Matt's arrest had certainly kept her busy. But she had no leads on anyone else in Daytona named Doug Moultrie. Had someone fed Jimmy Matt's cover name? He shook his head. What did a "good" name mean to Jimmy? Matt had set up that cover ID himself, years before he went blind. No one else knew the name. No one. Not the company. Not even his ex-wife.

"What are you thinking about?" Troy said.

Anna. Matt swallowed the soup in his mouth. "Jimmy Shad."

He didn't want a simple meal turning into a fact-finding mission for her to further use against him if things went sideways despite the fact that the baggies really did hold boric acid.

And he also didn't want to give the impression that he was hitting on her, so he couldn't ask anything too personal. But he couldn't deny wanting to know more about her. She carried her confidence like a shield and wielded her words, the knowledge that lay behind them, as a sword, favoring short, swift strokes that revealed little. He admired her tactic in placing Jimmy in with him without explanation.

Her spoon clinked on the side of the bowl. "Your sister live near you?"

Based on her voice and height, her litheness of body, he tried to imagine her paused there in front of him—spoon full of her next mouthful, held in the air as he spoke. "I'm sure you already know where she lives."

She blew her breath out in an amused half-chuckle. "Okay, so why aren't you living in Ormond with her?"

"Would you want to live with your sister full-time?" he said, talking around the bite of sandwich he'd just taken. Someone brushed past the table, dragging the scent of coconut lotion and sea air behind them.

She set the spoon back against the bowl. "I don't have a sister." Score one for him. "Maybe?"

"No," he said and then swallowed. "You wouldn't. They're nosy and interfere with living, y'know, your adult life."

"Ahhh," she said. "You're talking about adult activities."

"Well, not so much anymore, but yeah. Sometimes. What I really meant was living your own schedule. Not having your sis in your face if you want a peanut butter sandwich at two in the morning or want to sleep until ten or work on your braille during the season premiere of The Amazing Race."

"The Amazing Race?"

"She was narrating," he said. "And I *really* didn't care."

She caught his hand in hers, which was soft and hot and sent a jolting tingle right through his arm. The classical Muzak and conversations from nearby tables swirled around them, the higher tones pricking at his ears and skin.

"Eating here," she murmured and let go.

He talked with his hands a lot, always had. After he lost his sight, he'd learned to tone it down. It'd been a long time since he'd forgotten to keep his hands quiet with a stranger. Hoping the blush burning his cheeks wasn't too obvious, he picked his sandwich back up.

"You got other siblings?"

"No," he said. "You?"

"A brother."

"Here?"

"No. I grew up in Melbourne. He's still there." A faint trace of melancholy colored her words.

"You miss him."

She cleared her throat. "We don't talk much anymore. He had the greatest laugh ever when he was little."

"You're older?"

"Three years."

"Maybe you can talk to my sister for me, oldest to oldest. Tell her not to worry so much about me."

She patted his arm. "You do realize she just bailed you out of jail, right?"

Score one for her. He rolled his eyes.

"That impresses me so much," she said, laughing. "And you have gorgeous eyes."

His heart stilled for a moment, then started beating harder than it had before. He shook himself. She was just working, trying to make him feel a personal connection. "Do you?" he shot back.

"Do I what?"

He wiped his mouth, wondering if he dared. "Have gorgeous eyes?"

"My eyes are the color of mud flats."

The unexpected response relaxed him, and he sat back against the chair, letting the smile that rose through him curve his lips up. She was good. He liked that. "Somehow I doubt that."

A nearby ringtone started singing about beer for horses and Troy rustled for a moment before it cut off and she said, "Hey." A man's voice on the other end, talking fast. "Shoot me the address. Okay, gotta go."

Her plate slid across the table and then she was standing before Matt understood that last sentence was directed at him. He stuffed the last bite of his sandwich in his mouth and grabbed his bottle of water.

Halfway down ISB on the way to his place, it occurred to him that he didn't have a key for his apartment. "I don't have a key," he said. "My sister was supposed to come get me."

Troy groaned, a sound that got the immediate and unexpected attention of parts south.

Frowning, he held his hand out. "Phone?"

She slapped it into his hand, but the contours were unfamiliar.

"I only know my way around the iPhone," he said. If Siri was on. Or VoiceOver. Fuck. "Or my iPhone, I guess."

After a few minutes of back and forth, his sister's phone rang through on speaker through the car's Bluetooth. And rang. And rang once more before her voicemail answered. "Lily, Detective Troy is dropping me at my place in a few minutes. I'll be outside until you—" A rapid beeping shut him up.

Troy cursed under her breath and then said, "Hello?"

"This is Lily Simon?"

"Lily!" Matt half-shouted, never quite sure where to direct his voice when on speaker in a car. "Detective Troy's dropping me off in a minute. I need a key."

"I was supposed to come get you," she said, her irritation clear.

"Well, it didn't work out that way, just come to my place." Silence. "Seriously, Lil?"

"I have a little emergency here, Matt. It's going to be a while."

"And what, you were gonna let me cool my heels at the station?"

Troy slung him to the right as she turned left.

"I don't know, Matt," Lily snapped. "I thought you'd be longer. I'm on my way to Orlando to get Ethan."

Ethan, his rambunctious, just turned thirteen-year-old nephew, had begged to attend the week-long baseball camp being touted as a college coach showcase at Disney's sports complex. Matt had bitten his tongue hard on that one. "What happened?"

Troy slowed, turning right. Matt braced himself for the speed bump at the entrance to his complex.

"Baseball hit his forearm. The trainer thinks it's broken."

"That could take hours," he blurted, smashing his fingers on the dash as the car bounced and he reached out to steady himself.

"Yes, Matt, I'm aware!" The edge in her voice broke through his own momentary panic over being left on the sidewalk without a cane, phone, or gun.

"I got him," Troy spoke up.

"What?" Matt said as Lily said, "Got who?"

"I'm not going to leave you sitting outside by yourself," Detective Troy elaborated as she pulled into a parking spot.

"I can take care of myself," Matt growled despite the quicksilver of relief wicking through him.

"Just call me at this number when you're on your way back, Ms. Simon, I'll make sure he's safe till then," Troy said, already in reverse, and then driving forward again before she finished.

"I'm sitting right here," Matt protested even as Lily said, "Thank you, Detective," and disconnected. They bounced back over the speed bump.

"Let me out. I'll be fine."

Troy laughed and turned left. "No fucking way will I be responsible for anything happening to a blind, decorated, former law officer because I left him to sit outside his locked apartment in a complex where we make three drug arrests every Friday night."

"Former cop turned college professor out on bond for possession with intent to distribute in a drug riddled community. No one would blame you."

"I need you to write up my paperwork," she said, hitting her blinker and slowing to a halt. "You work more at the Poker Room than DSC and Bethune put together."

"All the more reason to just leave me here." She could drop him at the track, he supposed, but again. No cane. No phone. Sitting in the break room for god knows how long. More time not being able to sort if Jimmy Shad was a message or not. He didn't know, exactly, where Anna and Dakota and the banker were, for their safety. His heart clenched at the thought of his daughter anyway. He fumbled for the door handle.

"We're not there anymore, Mr. Loose."

Matt rubbed his face with both hands. He didn't even know why he was arguing. He didn't want to be left sweating in the heat and nothingness with only a dead phone on him for protection. Though, the fact that he was fine and nothing else had happened when he was most vulnerable had to fall on the "Doug Moultrie's name is an extraordinary coincidence" side of the argument simmering in his back brain.

Troy turned left.

"You're not taking me back to the precinct?"

"I really don't have the time. I gotta get to a scene. You can sit in the car until patrol can pick you up."

CHAPTER
FIVE

T he body dump off West Road was bloody. Cin listened to the rundown of first on scene before ducking under the perimeter tape to take a look for herself. The woman's head and hands were missing, the rest of her spread across several feet by dogs tearing apart the industrial-sized garbage bag she'd been placed in. Their bloody prints covered the ground all around the area. Jeans, a blue silk-type shirt, white fabric that might have been a lab coat. An evening breeze from the west had kicked up, disturbing the cloud of gathered flies.

Dark thunderheads gathered on the horizon, throwing an ominous light over the massive, paved lot for the Cobb movie theaters. The body lay in a patch of woods between the lot and Palm Terrace Elementary. Cin moved upwind and joined Charlie, who had arrived ahead of her.

"The only cuts left were clean," she said. "Right through the bone."

"My guess would be machete."

"It's a thought," she said. And a possible lead, but not where they'd start. With lots of recent press coverage on MS-13 up north, she knew Charlie was already thinking about them. They'd catalogued the presence of Mara Salvatrucha, the gang known as MS-13, in the Daytona area. The Volusia County Sheriff's Office suspected them in the deaths of three unidentified body dumps. DBPD itself had responded a few months ago to the dismemberment murder of one very known drug user who had been spread out on his own lawn, but

Daytona's active MS-13 gang members, called maras, mostly kept a low profile and couldn't be connected to the death.

Aside from two minor drug busts and one count of human trafficking, they hadn't been able to pin down or even ID the majority of the local maras. The gang taskforce was overworked and understaffed. There were *way* more active gangs in the area, and *lots* of machetes in Florida households, so this murder being the work of MS-13 certainly wasn't a given.

As Charlie wrote on his clipboard, Cin re-focused her attention on surveying the scene. The area between West Road and Bill France Boulevard used to be weedy cracked asphalt reserved for parking during NASCAR events at the Speedway. The only business it served was the six-story glass tower of International Speedway Corporation and NASCAR's headquarters, which bordered ISB. To the west, Barnes and Noble, Best Buy, and PetSmart had long been silent witnesses to the criminal dealings that everyone hoped would be curtailed by filling the acreage with business and crowds.

New development on the site over the last few years had surrounded the glass tower with shops and restaurants, a partially built hotel, and a multi-story parking garage. "You got guys canvassing Cobb, Bass Pro, and NASCAR yet?"

"Yeah," Charlie said. "Lots of windows. Someone should've seen something. Asked for security footage at NASCAR and Swinkler's asking the retail guys for theirs before he comes over."

"ID's gonna be tough. Medical, maybe? Halifax Hospital's not far."

"About fifty medical offices between here and there."

Cin grimaced in response and turned her attention away from the two crime scene techs working over the body to watch a third laying out markers next to body fragments in a wide trail leading away from it. "Guessing we're not getting any shoe or vehicle tracks."

Charlie grunted as he continued making notes on a printed grid. "Multiple dogs. Those two guys" —he pointed at two scruffy looking, weathered men, one with a faded backpack, one guarding a shopping cart piled with clothes and blankets—"called it in. Said they ran off four or five. Animal Control's on their way over to see if they can find them nearby. Or trap them when they come back."

Cin's stomach squirmed. Someone at Halifax Humane would be on poop duty later, but why it mattered was beyond her. It wasn't the first time dogs had gotten there first. And once identified, they'd not be eligible for adoption, through no fault of their own.

The third tech waved from where she stood in front of a scraggly clump of bushes edging the tree line, maybe thirty feet from the remains. "I'll go," Cin said.

She skirted the immediate area and made her way to the tech, Katie. As Cin crouched down, Katie held back the low brush to reveal a wet, bloody, dirt covered roll of tooth and claw marked leather. Knotted cords slid through riveted loops held it closed. "I think it's a knife roll," she said. "I've also found two crushed soda cans, several cigarette butts, and a crumpled valet ticket from a Marriot in Orlando."

"I won't assume it's the victim's," Cin said dutifully and without heat. She gloved up, then held the branch back for Katie to finish her photographs before she moved the roll. Cin turned it over for more photos and then plucked at the knots. Several knives sat handle down in a series of pockets along with a couple of narrow spatula-like tools, a honing rod, a stone, a thermometer. No name inside or out.

After Katie recorded the contents, Cin slid the roll into a large evidence bag and then carried it back over to the crime scene unit's truck. She checked the info and statements the responding officer collected and then asked the two men who chased off the dogs to tell her their story again, jotting down her own notes before having them sign off on the officer's paperwork.

Charlie joined her, the long throw of his shadow easing the glare of the setting sun. He thumbed her attention back over his shoulder. "Why you still got Loose with you?"

Matt stood leaning back against her driver's door, hands in his pockets, his hair windblown. "He's locked out."

Charlie gave her the side eye. "Want me to get someone to run him back to HQ?"

"I'm not seeing much else for us until we've secured CCTV, any reports from the canvass, and a prelim from the ME. Tell Swinkler we'll start fresh in the morning."

"Be careful, Cin."

She grinned at his somber expression. "Worried about my heart?"

Charlie snorted. "Worried about his."

"Ouch," she said, smacking his arm. "Besides, I've sworn off all men *and* he's out on bail. So double no."

"My wife and a twenty on the powder being boric acid say different."

"What! Natalie didn't believe my passionate vow?"

He shook his head as he backed away, hands raised. "She'd never reveal the content of your tequila ramblings, boss, I pinky swear and hope to die."

"Tell her I said thanks a lot!"

He turned, spotted Swinkler trudging back across the pavement at the same time she did, and headed his way.

Cin glanced over the scene once more and then strode over to Matt. "You ready?"

"You got an ID?"

"Not yet," she said, becoming aware again of the scent of corrupted flesh carried by the breeze.

He tilted his head back. "A Cobb employee?"

Cin narrowed her eyes. "What makes you think we're at the Speedway?"

"We're not at the Speedway. We're across the street at One Daytona. NASCAR HQ is to your left behind me. Bass Pro is directly behind me. The theaters are to your left behind you."

"How do you know that?"

"I have a pretty good map in my head, and I was paying attention on the ride over. The traffic sounds always tunnel here on my way to class. Not hard to hear the bounce and know I'm on the other side. Plus, there's that annoying electronic yell from the sign at the Speedway. This is a wide-open space, yeah? Body's in front of me, to my left?"

Cin listened for a moment and could hear the faint repeated yell from across the street. She had completely tuned it out. She wasn't about to say so out loud, but she was stunned at his accuracy. He was blind, not brain dead. He'd already proven so, and she needed to stop assuming things about him. She nodded.

"I'll take that silence as a yes," he said, standing up fully and pulling his hands free. "If the theater doesn't make any Indian dishes, you should check with Indian restaurants."

The distressed leather knife roll had left smears of blood on the inside of the plastic evidence bag when she slid it in. "Why?"

He tapped his nose. "Cumin. Coriander. Cinnamon."

She sniffed the ripe smell, trying to avoid a deep breath and shook her head. Death was all she smelled. "Why Indian?"

"Really? You don't eat Indian?"

"Is chicken curry salad Indian?"

"No," he said firmly. "I'm guessing your victim works in the kitchen of an Indian restaurant or one that features Indian dishes. There's only a couple of places here. Maybe an event? Maybe check with DSC. See if their culinary program was doing something yesterday with Indian cuisine."

"Your nose better since you—"

He laughed. "No. I might pay more attention, but I had a good sense of smell before. I can only wish being blind dialed things up."

Cin pulled Charlie up on her phone, hit call, and watched him answer. He and Swinkler both looked her way. As she relayed the request and why, she bumped Matt away from her door. He took the hint, walked briskly around the hood of the Impala, clambered in, and slammed the door before fumbling for the seat belt. She disconnected the call, got in, and started the car. "Too bad we just ate. We could get Indian."

Matt grimaced. "I've been away a couple of years and it's been longer since I smelled anything that bad," he said, pressing a hand down on his belly.

She hit the recirculation button on the AC and turned the fan up. Matt felt for his vent and turned it so that it blew into his face. Cin pulled her damp shirt away from her sun heated skin, letting the cool air blow over her chest. Her bra was soaked already. She sighed. "Summer's really here, I guess."

"I was sweating just standing there. Made me miss my cell."

She laughed. "The jail's an icebox all year. They use all the money they save not heating it during the winter on air conditioning in the summer. I can take you to my place for now. Until your sister gets back."

He chewed on the inside of his lip as he considered her statement. He was so damn attractive. She flushed and looked away, her gaze falling back on Charlie and Swinkler, now standing huddled with the tech who'd found the knife roll.

"I could really use a shower," he said. "A real one."

Putting the ball in her court. Careful, she liked that. She closed her eyes against the imagined sensation of his slow hand along her side. She hadn't been this hot for a complete stranger since she was sixteen. She cleared her throat. "Um, I just washed every towel I own. You're welcome to all four of them. If you want."

"Thank you for the offer," he said, stifling a yawn. "One will do."

Yep. She was being ridiculous.

"YOUR CAR really does smell like apples, but this orange is chemical," Matt said as he stepped into Troy's third story apartment.

"Degreaser. Take your shoes off."

Matt inhaled, allowing the odors to register. One of the first things he'd been taught to do after he was blinded was sort the sensory information he'd become increasingly more aware of over the first several months. Lucinda Troy, the degreaser, cinnamon, coffee, a touch of something he couldn't quite identify. No scents he associated with mold or dirty laundry or food-encrusted dishes.

"No fried food," he said, toeing his sneakers off. He hadn't bothered with socks the night of the raid. "But that peach needs eating."

"No fried foods, and that's fresh peach pie."

"Why degreaser then?"

"I'm soaking front end bolts."

"Bolts? Why?"

He took one more step inside as she crowded in behind him, mumbling as she turned away to close the door.

He cocked his head as she threw the deadbolt. "Did you say 'Civic'?"

She hesitated and then slid the chain as she spoke. "Yes. 2002."

"Oh, my god, you street race. You . . . are a Paul Walker wanna-be."

She brushed by him and kept going. "I am not."

"I bet you got your license right before the first *Fast and Furious* came out."

"You'd make more money as a psychic than a dealer," she said, from elsewhere—a hallway or a kitchen.

Squaring his stance, Matt crossed his arms, determined to wait until she realized she'd stranded him. "You'd be surprised what boric acid brings on the open market."

A moment of silence dropped between them until a carefree and delighted laugh burst from her, sparking a near-painful flare of raw desire in him. Sure, he'd had a couple of encounters early on with curious medical personnel, a nurse late one night and then a med tech during his rehab. But as it became obvious he wouldn't be regaining his sight, he'd lost interest in sex altogether for a while.

When his libido finally made a weak attempt to reassert itself, the loss of visual clues to gauge any possible response to his interest became debilitating. He'd once had a chance meeting with another guy who had experienced the opposite, though, so he knew it was just another thing he needed to learn how to decipher through his other senses. He'd just been too tired and occupied to try anything in company.

Like the thought had reminded his body, exhaustion filled his chest and poured itself into his arms and weakened his legs. He sighed, tilted his head back, and closed his eyes. He should have insisted on the cop shop. He was too tired to map a new room, let alone an apartment. Troy's light tread announced her return before she reached him and laid a warm hand on his forearm.

"Sorry, just wanted to make sure you'd be safe here. How do you—"

"I'm too tired to learn where things are right now, and I won't be here long. Can you just show me to the bathroom?"

"Sure," she said turning and offering him her arm. "Kitchen's directly to your right, there's no wall." Four steps and she turned left one step into a narrower space. He lagged further behind to give her room. Another step as she said "Door." When they were both through, she continued. "Sink straight ahead. To the left of it's the toilet. Shower past the toilet. When you're facing it, the controls are on the right. Do you need me to turn it on?"

Letting go of her arm, he shook his head. "Towel?"

"On the counter by the sink. There's body wash and shampoo and stuff in the shower. Do you want a razor?"

He rubbed at the heavy stubble on his face. Did he want to wage that battle with a manual razor? "Thanks, but I'll wait till I get home."

They stood in silence a moment and then he added, "Okay, I'm good."

"Oh, of course." She edged away. "I, uh, put a fresh tee shirt and a pair of shorts my brother left here on top of the towel. No underwear, though."

"Your brother, huh?"

Her voice smiled as she said, "He came for a race."

He raised his brows.

She laughed. "A NASCAR race," she said and pulled the door shut.

CHAPTER
SIX

M att stepped tentatively out of the bathroom with his tee shirt and the worn jeans he'd put on during the bust tucked under his arm. Soft music issued from the living room, something beachy with steel drums. Troy had something sizzling in a pan on the stove. Butter, onions, celery. Matt wasn't the least bit hungry. Stepping straight forward, he went through the living room doorway and stopped.

"Take two steps forward, there's nothing in your way," Troy called out. "And then three steps sideways to your left." After he did as told, appreciating the thick softness of some rug she'd laid over the apartment's nubby carpet, she said, "Yeah, I'm not very good at this. One more step sideways."

He could tell there was a couch behind him now, but waited for her to tell him anyway before he sunk down and found out she owned the best couch ever. Leather. Soft but not too soft. Deep enough that his full thigh was supported, but it was still easy to get up again. God, he really was an old man.

"I'm throwing a chicken in to roast in case we get hungry, or your sister needs late dinner," she said from much closer than he expected, and he flinched.

"Sorry," she said and then she was leaning over him, tugging at his laundry. "I got this."

He reluctantly let go.

"I'm not killing your puppy," she huffed. "Just going to throw these in the wash."

"I'm not going to be here that long."

"I'll drop them over to you."

Matt gave in and let her take them away. She moved around the apartment and eventually the washer, in a closet next to the front door, started up. He stretched his legs out under what felt like a wood coffee table, dug his bare toes down into the soft rug, and nestled into the couch with his arms crossed. The music shifted to something more somber and dreamy, and the chicken started sending savory tendrils of roasted meat into the living room and then the shower was running.

He shifted at a soft clank, startled that he'd been dozing in a strange place with someone he didn't know. But she was a cop, and he was warm, but not hot, and comfortable for the first time in days and his awareness slowed until he was falling . . . he jerked awake.

No music. A buzzing under Troy's "beer for horses" ringtone. Her voice answering, indistinct. Only half-awake, he could practically sense the shape of her, her forward motion toward him as a gentle ebbing upon his skin, the ambient sound waves parting and sliding off around her.

"Your sister," she said, her voice soft as if aware that he'd been asleep, or nearly so. He lifted his hand. She placed the phone against his palm, their fingers brushing as she ensured he had it before she let go.

"Hey," he said, rubbing at his face and then running his hand back through his unruly hair. "You on your way?"

"We're at Arnold Palmer. Ethan has to have surgery."

Adrenaline dumped ice water into his veins and woke him all the way up. "It's that bad?"

"He broke both the bones in his forearm and one's dislocated from his elbow. They're hoping they won't need to use screws and plates and stuff because he's still got a lot of growing to do, but they said they do need to reset them surgically and repair the dislocation."

"Will he still be able to play ball?"

"Oh, my God, that was all he asked, too! Really?"

Matt blanked for a moment, transported back to his thirteen-year-old self, to the simple joy of straining muscles, bursts of speed creating a breeze against the relentless summer heat, the satisfying crack of a ball against the bat in his hands, sending the vibration straight up his arms to his heart. "Yeah," he said. "Really."

"Yes. Eventually."

"Okay then."

"Okay then. They said he should be released in the morning. Detective Troy said she'll help you figure out tonight."

The familiar burr of irritation that he needed such help heated Matt's chest and tongue, but he didn't let it color his words. "Don't worry about me, Lily. Detective Troy's not as bad as I thought—"

"Hey!" Troy said.

"—she's making chicken. I'm sure I can stay with Sebastian. Can you text her his number?"

"Will do. I'm sorry, Matt."

"We are both well-aware shit happens, Sis. And it always piles up. Sorry I can't be there for you."

"You're always there for me." Other voices started filling the background, a guy, another woman, Ethan's quiet reply. "I'm fine. I better go, they're coming in to prep him."

"Bye, Sis," Matt said. The line closed on her end. Matt held the phone out and Troy took it as it buzzed.

"A number for Sebastian Ramirez."

"Can you call it for me?"

"You could stay here," she offered.

His blood rushed, loud in his ears, a collision of sensations whirling within him, a blur of half-remembered images filled his head. He opened his mouth to pant in a breath, and another, his heart racing, and then her wine-sweet breath was on his face, his lips, the heat of her body right there in front of him.

"Okay," he breathed. His hands settled on her hips without thought as he stretched up and met her open mouth. Leaning back without letting go, he pulled her down.

She settled on top of him like a body part he'd been missing, her long, hot thighs bracketing his, her tongue sliding along his to flick the roof of his mouth in a tingling rush. Matt wrapped his arms around her, and she dropped that crucial inch, crashing into him. He gasped and wrenched his mouth away to bury his face in the heated scent of her neck. She curled around him, then tilted her head back to let him taste her skin.

Trailing kisses along her collarbone, he held her there against him with one arm, while the other rose along her back. He cupped her head, burying his fingers in the wild damp hair she had pulled up in a loose pile. The texture stilled his hand and sent a wild wish that he could see her skin right through him. "Tell me," he muttered, immediately sorry that she stiffened, knowing exactly what he was asking, but not quite sorry enough to beat back the bitter knowledge that he'd never know the exact shade.

"A lot darker than your pale ass."

She tilted her hips and he groaned, having to rest his forehead on her chest. She straightened, the slow rub across him making him ache as she brushed his face with her breasts. No bra. She'd either wanted this or realized she could sit across from him, and he'd never know. His dick grew impossibly harder. He shifted, that delicious pressure so good.

"That gonna be a problem for you, Loose?"

God, no, Detective Troy. He didn't say it, though. Instead, he opened his mouth over one nipple to send his breath through the thin cloth of her tee shirt. Her nipple pebbled and he sucked it in.

Everything exploded then.

She rocked back, their hands tangling at the hem of her shirt to shove it up. Her mouth found his again as soon as the shirt cleared her face. Matt jerked it down over her hair with one hand and dropped it while the other found her right breast, his thumb brushing over the nipple hard. She whined into his mouth and then encouraged him downward until he was licking and sucking and nipping at each handful of breast in turn.

When he could take no more, he stood up with her in his arms, turned with her legs wrapped around his waist, and set her down there on the skin-warmed couch. This he could do without sight, though he wanted to see her spread out there before him. Matt dropped to his knees on the soft rug and skimmed his fingers down over her torso to hook the narrow band of her thong underwear. He pulled them down her smooth thighs, over her crooked knees, along her silky shins to fling them to one side.

He ran his hands up her rounded calves, along the back of her taut thighs. She dropped them open and the rich, natural scent of her filled his nose, drawing him in. She jumped and squeaked when he went unerringly for her center, closing those wonderful thighs on his head. He drew back slightly, and she opened them again. Wrapping an arm under and around each one, he tugged her closer so he could kneel more comfortably before he pressed one hand flat on her lower belly to keep her still.

She twisted against his hold, feet sliding on the leather, but her fingers danced over his scalp, and when Matt lowered his head again to nuzzle her, she opened herself all the way again and let him possess this part of her.

HE DIDN'T RUSH like most men did, to fill her, to take his own pleasure as she came down from hers. Cin reached down to stroke his face as he traced the lines of her belly, his eyes on her, but unseeing. His thick blond hair stood up in wild clumps and fell over his forehead and curled over the shorter hair over and behind his ears.

She shivered, pressing her thighs together, wanting his mouth back on her again already. She couldn't remember a time when she ever felt so raw, so tender, so needy all at once. This wasn't her usual MO.

"So," she said. "Tell me why magnificent you is so untouchable."

He shook his head a little, his lips and chin drawing tight before he spoke. "There were a couple of encounters, early on, not like this. Medical people. Just a few minutes of curiosity on their parts, a quick release of tension for me."

"That happens?"

"It did to me."

"You've been blind . . . "

"For close to three years."

"And you're how old?"

He chuckled, a deep pleasing sound. "Thirty-five. Which you already know."

"I'm thirty-two, but you already guessed that somehow."

He lifted his gentle hand from her stomach and tapped his ear. "I listen when people talk."

"That's a good skill to have, Mr. Navy Spy guy."

Something, some emotion so fleeting she couldn't decipher it, crossed his face. "I was never a Navy spy."

Cin almost believed him, but then he moved his hand from her belly to her swollen clit with a little circular rub that had her hips thrusting up into it and her hands clutching at his biceps. He surged up over her, letting her feel his patience snap, his desire for her, through the layers of clothes he still wore, and she wrapped her hand around the back of his neck to bring him home into a breath-stealing kiss.

They skinned him of his shirt. She scrabbled at his waistband, her fingers and all the rest of her suddenly aware once again of how hard he was everywhere, totally ripped. She was getting nowhere until Matt's hand joined hers to shove the shorts away before he kicked them the rest of the way off. Dropping his shoulder, he rolled across her onto the couch, wrapping his arms around her, somehow taking her with him so that she ended up on top, their legs entwined.

Cin bit her lip against the delicious shift of him, bare skin, hard body, sliding against hers, fever-hot, his mouth demanding her attention, capturing hers until she thought she'd die from want. Relishing the feel of him beneath her, she sat up slow, ran her hands down the planes of his chest to the wings of his hips, until she closed her fingers around the hottest part of him.

"You have a beautiful cock," she breathed.

"Cock?" he huffed.

She didn't want to wait or tease or delay—she couldn't. "Wait."

He lifted his hands off her.

"Just, condom." She got up and retrieved the box from the nightstand in her bedroom and shook the last one out. It'd been months since she'd been with anyone, and she'd never remembered to pick up more.

He'd sat up, flagging a bit.

"I've only got the one," she said.

"We'll take this slow then."

"In that case," she said, slowly straddling him. "Do you mind if I—"

He shook his head, already recovering as she tore the wrapper. She took her time, enjoying the catch of his breath, the stroke of his hands over her shoulders and breasts. Finished, she cozied herself up against him, shivering at the touch of the condom's coolness before his heat overwhelmed it. He pulled her down to kiss her, the kindling spark between them blazing up again and torching the idea of slow.

Cin lifted herself and took him all at once, both of them gasping at the hot, shocking thrill of it. When she moved to rise again, Matt's callous-roughened fingers closed on her lower back, his thumbs pressing into the hollow above her pelvis, hard enough she knew there'd be fingertip bruises left behind. He held her firm and rolled his hips up in a way that made her head swim. Closing her eyes, she let her head tip back as he repeated the motion, lighting everything up inside her. She rocked into it as he continued, discovering there was riding a man the way she'd always thought she was, and then there was this, riding his motion and muscle while need built and built and built, their bodies seeking the breaking point.

But then he stopped, releasing her, and for a moment she froze, stunned, before the need overflowed and she rose, the pull of him inside her exquisite before she braced herself on his shoulders and let him take them there on the repeated power snap of his hard, fast hips, until she was coming and coming and coming.

After they'd caught their breaths and disposed of the condom and stretched out together on the couch, Cin's stomach growled. Matt laughed. She liked the rumble of it beneath her ear as she lay half-on and half-off him. He lifted the tendrils of her curly hair trailing down over his ribs and tucked them back behind her ear as she rubbed her hand over the wiry hairs on his chest and then circled his closest available nipple with one finger, bringing it to attention.

"What?" he finally said into the lengthening silence filled with the evening noises of the complex, water running, the occasional drift of indistinct voices, the constant summertime cicada buzz and frog song that she only heard anymore at times like these, when everything inside her had been tempered and calmed, at least for a few minutes.

She propped her chin on one hand and studied the delicate skin of his closed eyes, the shadows of his long, thick lashes on the rise of his faintly freckled cheeks, his full, kiss-swollen lips, the thick blonde stubble ranging over a jaw that matched the rest of him. Solid. Hard. "You've ruined me."

One corner of his mouth twitched up. He traced circles over the curves of her back and butt with one hand, the other tucked behind his head. "I have?"

"I'm normally easily satisfied, but you and your sexual ways already have me wishing I had another condom so we could try the slow thing again."

"We did screw that up," he said, scrunching his face up as he shook with silent laughter. "Pun intended."

After a moment, he said, "Are you on—"

"Yeah," she said. "I am."

Now he grinned, his eyes opening to let her see the brilliant blue of them, the darker flecks of gray. "No one has ever declared I had sexual ways before. I haven't had actual sex in four years."

"How can that be? How are you unattached at thirty-five?" She sat up, swinging her legs down, bare feet hitting the floor, even though he groaned in protest and tried to stop her before sighing and letting her go. He sat up, too, so their thighs were pressed together. His feet were so white next to hers, and wide, his toes blunt. Hers were narrow, her toes long. They were the same length. "That was—"

She didn't know what that was. She wasn't one to forget herself like that, get overwhelmed, forget everything that made this such a very bad idea and still want more. Because she did, she wanted more of that. Of him.

"That wasn't one-off sex," she said, still staring at their feet. "Sorry if you weren't aware. But you are one hot lay and you're gorgeous on top of it and I like the way you think." She looked at him. "I'm going to tell everyone you followed me home and I'm—"

Elbows on his knees, Matt scruffed both hands back through his hair, but then turned his head towards her. She remembered the way he'd tapped his ear and said he listened when people talked. He was listening to her, and she was being crazy. Ridiculous. She'd hardly ever had more than a one-off. Even the two guys she had months-long relationships with were one-offs she could have walked away from anytime.

"You're what," Matt murmured. Like he cared about what she was saying. Like he wasn't gonna get up and walk away. Of course, he couldn't just get up and walk away, so it didn't mean much if he didn't.

"I was going to say I'm keeping you. But then I realized it wouldn't mean much unless you want to stay."

He reached out across his body, a motion her body read before her brain got too involved and she was already moving by the time his arms wrapped around her, their mouths finding their way together again, until Cin found herself crawling onto his lap and then he was shoving the coffee table away, candles and magazines sliding off it as it tipped over and her back hit the soft oriental rug beneath it.

THEY SAT on her bed and ate the chicken with their fingers, tearing it straight off the bones.

"Want a grape?"

He opened his mouth in response, his soft lips closing on the tips of her fingers when she placed the grape on his tongue. He rolled it in his mouth before he bit down on it, and it was damn near the sexiest thing Cin had ever seen.

"So," he said, "beyond birth control, should I be worried we failed at proper protection?"

She closed her eyes for a moment against the remembered sensation of his skin sliding on hers. "Cheese?" she said, plucking a cheddar cube from the picnic spread out between them.

Again, he opened his mouth and let her feed him while she wondered if she should tell him. No sense in hiding it, though, except to worry him. "I've never had sex without one before," she admitted.

His slow spreading grin told her all she needed to know. "Don't go getting a big head," she said.

"I'm honored," he said. "Was I worth it?"

"I'll let you know when I decide. Grape?"

When they had stripped the chicken and polished off the grapes and cheese with most of a bottle of red wine, she set the plates aside and retrieved the peach pie. Ignoring the fork she'd stuck in it, Matt dipped a finger into the middle and proceeded to lick it off. "This? Is great pie."

"My grandmother thanks you. Can I have some?"

He tilted his head, obviously considering his response.

"Please?"

He scooped two fingers in and offered them to her, tense as a cat stalking a bird. She took his hand in hers and licked at the peach filling, sweet with heavy syrup, under the rich, deep tones of cinnamon, before she closed her mouth over both fingers and took her time sucking them clean. Then very slowly, with repeated swirls of her tongue, she drew back again.

Closing his hand on hers, he fell backwards on the bed, taking her down with him, nearly upending the pie. "God, I'm an old man. You're killing me."

"Really want to die?" she said. "Hot water, tall, beautiful Black girl, lots of wet skin and lather?"

"Hell, yes," he crowed.

They cleared the picnic, crowded into the shower together, and about a minute after she went down on him, he lifted her, put her back to the wall and changed her perspective on the whole universe. He had every bit of the bull strength she had imagined. And none of the guile. He stood her on her shaky legs afterward, keeping a steady hand on her although he couldn't possibly know how weak he'd made her. They rinsed again and she shut the water off.

Cupping her face, Matt kissed her deeply before sluicing the water from her body and hair with deft, caressing strokes. They dried off and he collapsed on her bed while she switched his clothes to the dryer and threw all four of her towels in the wash. He was asleep, belly down, one of her pillows crushed up under his head, by the time she returned.

She'd fucked up big time, no doubt about it, bringing him here under the circumstances. But the powder secreted behind his baseboards would prove to be boric acid. She knew that now. And she'd be holding on to him with both hands for as long as she could, she knew that, too. He never stirred as she curled up against his warm back and drew the sheet up over them both.

Minutes later her ringtone sung out. Cin fumbled for it, realized it wasn't on the bed where she normally left it, and groaned. She shoved Matt's heavy arm off her to his incoherent protest and staggered up in the early light. A car door slammed outside, and an engine cranked up. Matt rolled over. She stumbled into the living room and dug into the couch just as the phone stopped ringing. "Damn."

She finally located it and jerked it free. The time said she'd slept five hours. Perez, a homicide detective who worked late shift. She rang him back. "It's Troy, what's up?"

"Givens said you'd want to know he has an ID on your girl from last night."

"It couldn't wait till I got there?"

"Francis Duncan. Twenty-four. Sous chef at India Star down on Beach Street. And Jimmy Shad's girlfriend."

"Shit."

"Yeah. And guess who I got an hour ago?"

Only one guess with that lead-in. "Jimmy Shad."

"Jimmy Shad," he agreed. "Want to come look before the M.E. moves him?"

"Yeah. Give me the address."

CHAPTER
SEVEN

Matt bit into the hot, soft doughnut he held. He was starving and with Jimmy Shad dead, he had no idea how long it would be before he ate again. Yeasty sweetness exploded across his tongue, and he hummed in pleasure.

In the driver's seat of the parked car, Troy laughed. "The expression on your face is priceless. When was the last time you had a fresh doughnut?"

"New York." A second bite finished off the doughnut.

"Obviously that wasn't a Krispy Kreme."

"*Au contraire*!" he said and then took a careful sip of his hot coffee before continuing. "Penn Station. Hot and now."

Dakota had been seven, protesting she wanted chocolate iced until he stuffed a bite into her open mouth.

"But you've never had one here?" Cin asked. "That's as wrong as the fact you're single."

"I haven't had one since I moved here," he corrected her as he set the hot coffee between his knees and then fished around again in the bag she had plopped into his lap. "But I used to visit, so yeah, I've been here."

"So you just don't eat doughnuts much?" she said, her words muffled by doughnut.

There was a slight breeze wafting through their open windows, stirring up a damp river smell, the ever-present exhaust of ISB, and a sweet, grape-y scent. "Jelly? Is that what you're eating?"

Paper crinkled. "Yeah. The only real doughnut."

He held up his second choice, a Boston Crème. "You're actually a teenager, right? Jelly doughnuts and fast cars. I'm dating a teen."

She audibly gulped her coffee, god only knows how since his was still too hot for more than sipping. "Dating? Is that what you call it?" He could hear the laugh buried in her words.

He could be crass since "fucking" immediately rose on his tongue, but what they'd done was something else altogether. In some cultures, he felt sure, they'd be married or as good as because of what they'd done. He'd never had such an encompassing experience or lost himself so totally in sensation that there'd been whole stretches of time that he'd forgotten everything about himself, even his blindness, which took up most of his thoughts these days if he were being honest.

"Hey," she said, "I didn't—"

"Sorry, sorry," he said, waving his untouched doughnut in the air. "I get lost in my head sometimes."

"We shouldn't—"

"Stop." He wished he knew where she was looking— at him, out the windshield? Her tension pressed into his skin like a physical force. "Don't you dare say we shouldn't have. I've never . . . there's never been anything, ever, anyone, I should've had more."

When she remained silent and tense, he became aware of his hand on his thigh, still holding his Boston Crème. He lifted it and took a huge bite. His eyes closed as flavor spread across his tongue.

She laughed, the sound bursting out of her, making him jump, which made her laugh harder. He resisted the impulse to laugh with her, concentrating on chewing and swallowing without choking instead. "That's the sweetest thing anyone's ever said to me," she gasped. "But that doughnut must be some stiff competition." And then she was laughing all over again.

"Your cream's better."

She whooped and laughed harder while he finished his doughnut and then licked his fingers. She caught her breath and closed her hand on his. He let her take his hand, shivering at the first caress of her breath before her hot mouth closed on his thumb, the sensation going straight to his groin. When she moved to his index finger, his entire body responded and somehow his fingers were tangled in her hair and his tongue taking possession of her mouth.

The cup he had tucked between his legs gave, hot coffee spilling onto his thigh. He yelped and fumbled for it, her hands tangling with his before she managed to move it, slapping a handful of napkins down at the same time. He took over blotting, cursing under his breath, while she dissolved into laughter again.

"There you go," she said. "Fuck really is a great word."

"Fuck," he repeated, louder and with great emphasis.

"Fuck," she yelled, the word bouncing off the roof of the car. "Oh, whoops, sorry, ma'am," she said and then laughed harder.

"Oh, shit," he said, unable to stop the giggles from taking him over at the sudden image of a woman holding a goggle-eyed child's hand as they walked by.

"Sorry, sorry," she called, shoving his coffee cup back into his hand. She started the car, rolling the windows up right away. "Oh, my God."

Matt braced himself against the motion of the car as she backed out from their spot. He remembered the tight parking at this Krispy Kreme. The doughnuts were worth the maneuvering and near mortal danger required to get back out onto either ISB or Nova Road. From the feel of it, she was headed north on Nova.

BEACHSIDE, Cin leaned forward at every small intersection to find the street names on signs that were aging, not fully trusting her GPS. Beside her, Matt balanced his nearly-empty coffee cup on his thigh with his left hand and, in reaction to a blaring horn as she cut the light close crossing over Beach Street onto Main Street Bridge, still gripped the oh-shit handle above his head with his right.

Grover Court was filled with emergency vehicles. Uniformed officers stood in clumps on the lawn of a house cordoned off by crime scene tape. Neighbors and press had congregated a few hundred feet away, spilling out onto the street.

"Big scene," Cin said. "Way too many cops, a fire truck, an ambulance."

She crept by them. Someone slapped the trunk as she passed and Matt finally let go of the handle. Two officers blocked the street ahead. She rolled down her window and held out her badge as one of them lifted his hand to stop her. He glanced at it and waved her by. She pulled up behind a cruiser parked in the street next to the engine truck and rolled all the windows down before she killed the engine. "You're staying here," she said. "Inside the car, okay?"

"Woof," Matt said without turning his head, looking for all the world like he was surveying the scene.

"I'll keep it short."

Cin threaded her way between the responders and the curbside vehicles. Two of the cars in the upper part of the drive belonged with the house in some way. The Jeep Wrangler had three beach-towel festooned surf boards of varying lengths hanging out of the rear. Like everyone else, she walked across the weedy grass in the front yard to the little, green-painted concrete pad and single step up to the house. On the threshold of the open front door, the cloying scent of blood already in her nose, Cin glanced back at her car. Matt was already standing outside of it, leaning back against the driver's door with his hands in his jean pockets.

She shook her head and brushed past the uniform who said, "Ma'am," with a tip of his head. Two technicians in CSI polos were focusing their efforts along the edges of the tiled front room, where Jimmy Shad lay on his back in congealed blood wearing nothing but boardies and the zip ties cinching his swollen wrists and ankles. Bruises littered his ribs and thighs.

Rarely had Cin known a victim in life. She'd heard over and over how death diminished but hadn't seen the truth of it until now. Jimmy without his fluster and bluster seemed much smaller than he had appeared just yesterday. Below his paper-white freckled face, dried blood descended from the slice through his throat. It covered his chest. His cloudy eyes stared up at the slowly revolving ceiling fan.

One of the county's death investigators stood over him, scribbling on a form at least two-thirds down in the stack on his clipboard.

"No iPad, Emilio?"

"Naw, IT's holding it ransom, I think."

The Volusia County Medical Examiner's office was woefully understaffed and while everyone pulled eighteen-hour days and did a brilliant job, there was no keeping up with the surge of fentanyl overdoses. They struggled to house an average of twenty-five bodies a day in a cooler built for twenty and issue thousands of death reports in a time period that didn't hinder families and courts. They prioritized known homicides, though, so both Jimmy and his girlfriend would move to the front of the line.

If the same suspect, namely the heavy Jimmy had mentioned in the cell, Malcolm Ward, had taken out both Jimmy and his girlfriend, his MO was unpredictable. On the other hand, maybe two different hired hands had been dispatched to do the dirty. Jimmy hadn't mentioned an AWOL girlfriend yesterday.

Cin tugged her cell phone from her back pocket and hit the speed dial for Charlie. He picked up but didn't speak. "Charlie?"

Rustling ensued before he said, "I'm up, what?"

Cin glanced at her watch. Quarter to seven. But first week out of school equaled night-owl kids, so she'd woken him. "That woman last night was Jimmy Shad's girlfriend and now I'm standing over Jimmy Shad himself. Dead—" She glanced up at Emilio.

He narrowed his eyes at her and shook his head.

"Come on, Emilio," she said. Without putting hands on Jimmy, she could only assume the blood pooled in his body was fixed in place and couldn't tell if he was in rigor at all. "Before or after midnight?"

"We're thinking eight to ten hours," Detective Perez said from behind her. She half-turned as he stepped up beside her. He jerked a thumb up towards the interior of the house. "Neighbor kid who called it in says he saw Shad at nine last night. Found the body this morning cause Shad said he'd take him out for early waves. We're already knocking on doors."

"Nothing changed after you left," Charlie said into Cin's ear. "Jimmy was scared about Ward, but he knew he needed to stay quiet, and had the plan memorized."

The plan had been for Jimmy to live his normal routine for less than forty-eight hours before making the scheduled pick-up, meeting Charlie and Cin, and then dropping the drugs as Malcolm Ward had requested, in a towel bin at a hotel on the beach.

A simple transport. That's all Jimmy had to do. Which meant his death was either unrelated, Ward found out Jimmy had been picked up twice in the past week and was off-the-scale paranoid, or DBPD had a leak. Maybe all three. Maybe none. Why go after the girl?

"Let's dig into the girlfriend this morning," she said. "I'll exchange info on Shad with Perez here and ask him to keep us informed." Perez was nodding as she spoke. "I gotta drop Loose off and then I'll be in."

"Jesus, you've still got Loose? Seriously?" Charlie said.

"I'll tell Natalie all the details later and you can pretend you aren't eavesdropping."

"Just—"

A serious tone had crept into that single word, not the lighthearted sign-off she had expected before their day and the next few weeks inevitably dove into the heaving darkness this case seemed destined to become. "What?"

"Nothing. I just got a bad feeling."

"I do, too, but it's centered on Malcolm Ward, not Loose. I'm keeping him."

"TMI," Charlie muttered as Perez said, "Who's Ward? And who the hell is Loose?"

She disconnected and while Emilio set about arranging Jimmy's transport to the morgue, filled Perez in regarding Jimmy Shad and Malcolm Ward. "Loose is just an ex-cop I'm dating."

Perez would, no doubt, learn all about Matt Loose once he got back to the precinct. Cops were worse than teenagers about gossip. All who and why and what happened then.

"Hey," Emilio said as he came back in with his gurney. "Give me a hand? I gotta check his back before we lift."

Cin gloved up and they tilted Jimmy over on his side. Oh, yeah. Full rigor mortis so he was dead before midnight. Circular burns covered his shoulders and mid-back. His neck made a squishing noise and the cut gaped open, his rigid head flopping over to the side a long moment later. "Damn, he's nearly decapitated," she said.

"Are we sure he didn't piss off MS-13?" Perez said.

"Don't even joke about that," Cin said.

Perez and Emilio got to work documenting the apparent cigarette burns Jimmy had been subjected to before he died on their separate paperwork. Esteemed CSI department head Miller arrived with the team's only forensic vacuum in hand. Greetings wafted up before the three CSI's already in the house drifted over to Miller for an informal meeting in front of the dirty living room window.

"Were the drapes open when you came in?" Cin asked Perez.

"Yep. Only lights on in the house were in the kitchen. He was interrupted making a sandwich."

"Okay," Emilio said. "Let him down."

Cin stood, noticing the vehicles beyond the window as the techs broke up and spread out again. Matt was still leaning against her car, patient as the sphinx. A bubble of joy rose in her chest at the unexpected thought. Her mother had said that of her dad one time, when they'd been out shopping and glimpsed him at the fountain in the mall, handing penny after penny to her hyperactive three-year old brother.

Miller strode over, drawing her attention back to the matter at hand. "Hey, Cin. Emilio, got whatever help you needed?"

"Yes, sir."

"Good. Perez?"

"Yes, sir."

Miller was older, imposing, and direct. He'd been in his position years before Cin joined the force. Hell, before most of the current crop of detectives had joined. "Ready to move?"

Together, they all lifted Jimmy Shad with care and placed him on an opened body bag laid out on the gurney. Emilio zipped it up. Cin and Perez tugged their gloves off. Miller cast a look over the room as he said, "I'll get to this today. Maybe late before I have an initial report."

Perez nodded at him. "Thank you, sir."

Emilio tugged on the foot of the gurney to roll it to the open front door. Cin, Miller, and Perez followed. The uniform at the door grabbed it, helping Emilio lift it over the threshold and then out over the step.

Cin turned to Miller. "Wa—"

CHAPTER
EIGHT

A wake?
      Not awake.
      Dreaming.
Hands on her arms, in her hair.
Cin can't open her eyes.
But she sees.
I'm not me.

Silence.
   Antiseptic.
   Bitter burn of heavy-duty citrus cleaner in Matt's nose.
   On his tongue.
   Hard mattress.
   Hospital. He should open his eyes.
   Or not. His lids were heavy. Weighted down.
   Silence.
   The back of his head ached.
   Spicy musk. Hair trailing over his face, his collarbone.
   Matt lifted his right arm.
   A slight, familiar pull below his elbow. His clumsy, thick fingers

brushed the dangling hair up and, after opening his eyes, over Troy's ear. "You're beautiful," he muttered.

"That gonna be a problem for you, Loose?"

God, her bee-stung lips. Her nose. Her wide cheekbones. Her eyes were dark and bright. Not the color of mud flats at all.

"My only problem with you, Detective Troy, is that my friends are never going to understand what Ms. Tall Black Beautiful sees in me, Mr. Short White Guy."

"You underestimate your physical looks, Loose."

He shrugged. "So you're not just in this for my charm?"

She chuckled. "And you're overestimating your charm."

"Did a runaway firetruck hit me?"

"Some asshole slit Jimmy Shad's throat and slid a bomb inside him."

And yeah. Okay. They'd been at Jimmy Shad's house. He'd been leaning on Troy's car, listening to the activity around him.

"But—you're okay?"

"You're looking at me, aren't you?"

His stomach noticed the motion first.

He grabbed at the edges of the moving bed beneath him, meeting nothing.

The walls and Troy herself rose away from him faster and faster.

Plummeting up.

He flailed, hands grasping, heart racing. Right before he hit the ground, Matt startled awake. Every muscle in his body contracted to launch him upright into blind nothingness. A burst of cool air hit him. Cool hands on his arm, his chest. Distorted sound batted at his ears. He lifted both hands to them, again aware of the familiar pull below his elbow—tape—an intravenous line.

More distortion, too loud.

The cool hand on his bicep slid up and patted his shoulder. Motion under his back, wheels unsteady. A gurney. He fumbled and grabbed a slender forearm, aware of a thunderous rush of white noise and the rise of his chest and how the two must go together. He leaned over, retching.

More hands. Sharp scent of plastic under his nose. Tugging at the tape. Rush of warmth up his arm, into his chest where it bloomed like a mushroom cloud and he panicked, kicking out and rolling, meeting metal rails, hands on his hands, his arms, his chest. Bona fide darkness closed in on him as he flushed hot, and his muscles melted, and the black behind his lids swallowed him whole.

When he next woke, it was to an annoying, muffled beeping and the stroke of fingers through his hair. An irritating pressure rode the bridge of his nose and cheeks. He groaned, the sound too loud and harsh. Trying to relieve the pressure, he found padded gauze over his face, rolled right around his head, covering his eyes.

He laughed and then cringed at the noise. "I'm blind already," he said, but it came out all wrong and hurt his throat.

A straw at his lips, through his lips.

A voice.

He sucked and cool water slid into his mouth, soothed his throat, until the straw was taken away. Thirsty, he reached out for it. A hand took his. His sister? "Lily?"

Something being said to him. Lifting his other hand, he meant to wedge a thumb under the bandage over his eyes, but she blocked him.

The annoying beep increased.

He fought harder to get at the bandage, get it off, now.

She was saying something, but he needed the bandages off to hear her.

What was she saying?

He couldn't hear her.

More voices, stronger hands.

The hated warmth and then the blessed dark.

CIN WATCHES LOOSE SLEEP.

They've bandaged his eyes.

He shifts when she climbs onto the hospital bed with him, but it makes no difference.

She sees the way their bodies overlap. His shoulder inside hers. His hip taking up space inside her belly as she lies curled against him.

No.

Curled up inside him.

She wraps her hand over the thumping muscle of his heart.

And wonders at the beat of it against her palm.

"Hey, Loose," Troy said. "Wake up."

He rolled over onto his back, happy to feel her stretched out hot beside him. He wrapped his arm around her, and she nestled in, her head on his chest. He brushed her hair away from his face and then anchored it with his cheek. She traced random patterns on the sheet spread over his belly with her long fingers.

Nude, blunt nails.

It was dark out, but the hospital room lay bathed in dim light. Lily slept in a brown pleather recliner, her mouth hanging open.

"I wonder where Ethan is," he said.

"Sleeping over at his best friend's house. Your sister called your ex."

Anna? "That's . . . unexpected." Especially since the number he gave his sister was to a company line. "Did she answer?"

"Yes."

He'd thought, at best, given his circumstances, any call to it would be sent to voicemail for later review.

Into his thoughtful silence, she said, "Lily was afraid for you."

"What about you?"

"I'm here, aren't I?" She tilted her face up and he kissed her. Only kissing her was to lose himself in her once more, until he forgot the room and the annoying beep and his sister and then everything as he slid back down into exhausted darkness with the taste of her lips on his tongue.

"Matt," someone said, a woman, only it was muffled and strange. Matt wanted to rub at the pressure on the bridge of his nose, but his hands were trapped. "Matt. If you can understand me, squeeze my fingers."

The weight of fingers crossing both his palms.

"Matt? If you can—"

Matt squeezed the fingers.

"Can you tell me your name and birthdate?"

He answered, the sound of his own voice as strange and muted as the woman's.

"You're going to be fine, Matt," she said, letting go of his hands. "With time, we're hoping your hearing will be fully restored. You also suffered a mild concussion. On top of your previous damage, you may have headaches for a while, but you got lucky. Your eyes aren't seriously damaged, but after flushing them, we felt that a couple of days of rest along with some IV antibiotics for your skin lacerations wouldn't hurt."

It was hard to follow her words over the faint, annoying, background beep. Heart monitor. "My eyes."

"Yes, they may feel irritated or burn slightly. That will pass."

"Am I—" But that was stupid. Of course, he was still blind. And yet, he knew he'd seen his sister earlier. Hadn't he? "Am I still blind?"

"Yes, Mr. Loose."

"But I saw my sister," Matt said, sweeping his hand to the right. "Sleeping there, in that chair, the recliner. Where's—" The name "Troy" stuck on his tongue. She'd been here, waiting for him. She'd met his sister, for real, as a woman, not a detective. She'd said she was keeping him. "Lucinda?"

"A dream, perhaps," the woman said. "Who is Lucinda?"

"Who are you?"

"I'm Dr. Linda Gardener. I'm your neurologist and part of your treatment team. Let's get another CT, today, okay? If everything looks good, we'll think about discharge tomorrow."

"You'll stay with me for a few days, Matt," Lily said from his left side.

Like the doctor, her words were distant and indistinct. It took a moment for his brain to register them. He hadn't understood the level of his anxiety until she spoke and the tension in his chest broke. "Lily!"

She captured his raised hand and held it tight.

"I saw you," he said. "Sleeping."

"You were dreaming, Matt," she said.

"I don't dream. Not—I don't see in my dreams anymore, Lily. I haven't in months now."

"The brain is an amazing and not fully understood organ, Mr. Loose," Dr. Gardener interjected.

"Where's Cin?" he asked again. She'd just been here.

A moment passed. Matt knew this moment, the one in which sighted people exchanged looks they thought he was unaware of. His stomach looped. "She was here. Lucinda? Detective Troy. I saw her. Where is she?"

"Matt," Lily said, her voice reluctant, his name heavy with regret, despite the strangeness of their sound. *I regret to inform you*, that tone said, and he shook his head, but shaking it hurt. He couldn't stop. The annoying faraway beeping stopped though, and he took a deep breath.

Lily squeezed his hand tighter, her other hand on his shoulder. Another hand on the other side. Dr. Gardener's, he presumed. Matt stilled his head, pressed it back into the thin hospital pillow and forced himself to take another breath. His eyes burned like hell with the welling tears.

"Detective Troy didn't make it," Lily said. "Seven people died. Five were injured. You're lucky to be here. You were far enough away."

"But facing forward," Troy said. "That's why your eyes got burned."

"Cin."

"Is gone, Matt," Lily said, her voice stretching, loud one second, hardly there the next.

"Kinda," Troy said, and laughed, the sound pure, crisp with amusement. "And I like the way you say Cin."

Matt nodded and kept his mouth shut and loosened his grip on Lily's hand. After a few minutes, they let him be. After a few more, someone came in and the beeping, muted, started up again. Matt lay still and listened. Lucinda Troy's scent lingered in the air, but there was nothing to hear.

CHAPTER
NINE

Where is her body? Cin's definitely not inside it.

But she's here, so she's not blown to smithereens.

But where is *here*, exactly?

Matt talks to her when she talks to him.

She can be here, in the moment, with him.

Or she can be *there*, dreaming of a river, and still aware of him.

If she's here, she can talk to him when he talks to her.

If she's *there*, he can't hear her.

Sometimes, it seems, she's nowhere.

But that's just sleep.

Isn't it?

LYING on the couch in the dark of Lily's living room, Matt watched Ethan breathe. Seven people had died, and he hadn't. He was watching Ethan breathe. Light from the TV flickered off the boy's face, the beige walls. On screen, a pack of twenty-somethings roamed through a gray city, talking at each other in words Matt couldn't understand. He'd noticed in these dreams that his vision of the "real" world was spotty at the edges. Occasionally objects he knew were there weren't until he thought of them.

The blue glass vase, for instance, usually on the floor speaker next to the TV, had been missing until just now, but the misshapen multi-colored pottery dish Ethan had made at school when he was seven never wavered. It might have been bolted in place, it was such a fixture in his view.

He'd thought that maybe it was only his brain giving him what he mostly remembered or could intuit, like what an average hospital room looked like or the well-known image of his sleeping sister. Maybe the warmth of Cin beside him was sense memory from that only night they'd had. But then he'd been at his audiology appointment, something he'd never experienced before, with people he'd never seen. And while he was sitting there, Cin breathed into his ear, a sound like a chuckle of delight, and he had closed his eyes at the intense pleasure that hit him.

When he opened them, the room lay before him. A diagram of the ear, the see-through window of an enclosed booth, varying sizes of brightly colored headphones hanging from hooks on the wall. A pencil of a man, all height and sharp edges, walked into the room. Dark upright hair and a southern twang. He'd stuck his hand out, forgetting Matt was blind, and Matt had forgotten, too, until their hands met. On contact, the room plunged into the nothing that was Matt's normal visual existence, the nothing he couldn't articulate about because he was blind in his brain, not his eyes.

So now he lay still, arm wrapped over Cin as she lay stretched out on Lily's couch with her back to his front, and watched Ethan sleep. He wore a baseball jersey and athletic shorts. Half on his back, good arm thrown out across the greige carpet, bare legs curled up awkwardly, his torso twisted away from his broken arm in its bright blue cast, propped on a gold pillow.

He was that old cliché, coltish. Long legs, short torso. His shoulders were wider than the last time Matt had seen him, his muscle not as ropy looking as it felt under Matt's hand when Ethan walked with him. His dark hair was summertime long, curling down onto the pale nape of his neck.

He looked like his dad, a Navy pilot Matt had brought home on leave and Lily had stolen. Not that Pete had been a pilot back then. He'd just been a guy whose parents had been off on a cruise, leaving him at loose ends. When Ethan was three, Pete disappeared on a support run over the Indian Ocean. Plane and crew. Just gone. Lily hoped for a while, but then resigned herself to his loss. Although she was trying, she was having a hard time understanding the depth of Matt's grief over Cin, someone he'd only known for what amounted to a day.

Since he couldn't describe what was happening to him, the madness of Cin's on-again off-again presence, the visions he was experiencing . . . they had to be visions, right? He could see even when he covered his eyes. Brain researchers said all those strangers in dreams aren't imagined, they're memories of the people encountered in everyday life, even though they aren't consciously registered at the time. Is that how he saw the audiologist? Had his brain just attached a convenient memory of a stranger seen in passing years ago?

"Stop thinking so hard," Cin said. "I can practically hear your thoughts."

"Can you hear my thoughts?" Because if she could, there was no hiding his secrets from her.

"No, I can't," she said, that new, ever-present amusement coloring her tone. "My own thoughts are more than enough for me, though I'm wondering what you're hiding now."

"You don't find this weird?"

She sat up and turned to look down at him with a frown. "This is not only weird, it's fucking weird, but it's better than nothing. I said I was going to hold on to you with both hands and obviously the universe was listening." A considering expression crossed her features. "Or this is a case of be careful what you wish for right before you die."

"Are you dead?"

"Fuck if I know."

Matt studied her. Large dark brown eyes. Depthless eyes. Defined cheekbones. A serious mouth, her full lips pressed tight as she watched him back. "Fuck if I care," Matt said and kissed her.

Coming up for air, he must have woken up. He didn't know anymore. He was blind and still warm from being pressed up against Cin, but she was gone. Matt felt for the quilt folded at the end of the couch and draped it over Ethan on the floor, who didn't stir. Lily had gone to bed some time before. Fingering the remote, he turned off the

TV, made sure he had his bearings, and traipsed to the hall bathroom, centered between Ethan's room and the guest room.

A few minutes later as he turned back the covers on his bed, Cin slid her hand up his arm. The vision was like sliding into syrup. It gradually became his until he could see his fingers trail the length of her neck, follow the line of her shoulder, trace the dark circular rise of one areola. He leaned forward to suckle her nipple. Her fingers slid into his hair. His hands found the muscle of her sides, her back, her thighs.

SHE'S LIVING INSIDE HIM.

Is that possible?

She sees everything, though.

Even when he doesn't.

Even though he can't.

So, she's living outside him.

Maybe.

She absorbs everything. His touch travels her skin, all of it, outside and in.

Every ridge on his every fingertip. Every ghosted breath. Every sigh and whisper of her name.

Oh, God.

Everything.

Every.

Thing.

IT WAS slow and hard and silent and when she finally, finally unraveled under him, Matt came undone. And when she faded away, lost to his touch, he finally cried.

L ily shoved what Matt knew to be the milk carton across the counter island that divided the kitchen from the living room. The house was small and old and beachside, requiring more maintenance than he thought was reasonable, but Lily was a teacher and had Pete's dependent compensation and insurance. She made do.

"Ten o'clock," she said as he walked by, meaning the location of the milk in front of his usual seat, which is how almost every morning he'd spent here started since he'd moved from New York. Matt brushed his hand across Ethan's back and the boy grunted a good morning.

Matt sat and poured cereal into his bowl. Lily had shopped yesterday. Did he dare ask? "Rice Krispies?"

"Special K," Lily said. "Sorry."

They ate in silence, the TV blathering and distorted in the background. A freaking bomb. He would recover his hearing, but seven people were dead. Cin was dead, despite the fact he could feel the echo of her skin sliding over his last night. Somebody out there was very good at making bombs.

After the clatter of a dish in the sink, Lily said, "We're going to the library this morning, if you want to go with."

Someone out there wanted bombs made. And used. Because there was no doubt that bomb was meant to take out first responders—the timing, the cluster of professionals in the doorway, the size of the charge, the proximity to the walls which created that much more shrapnel than exploding it in the open living room—he couldn't let go of wondering if it had been triggered by someone watching. Then there was still the question of Jimmy Shad connecting him to the name Doug Moultrie. Matt had no resources and only one other name besides his own to connect to Shad. But it would be a start. "I want to go home. Can you drop me?"

She sighed.

"It's Saturday, yeah?"

"Yeah, but I called Ed from the hospital. You don't have to go in. Call him when you're ready."

Matt wanted to do more than call him. He needed a conversation with him. Ed was one of the few people he knew who was helpful without treating him any different than anyone else. "My rent won't pay itself, Sis. I gotta work."

"Can I go with you?" Ethan said.

"Not today," Matt said as Lily said, "No. Go get dressed."

Mumbling to himself, which Lily let go, Ethan left. Lily cleared his bowl and glass and then took Matt's bowl when he set his spoon back down in it although he wasn't finished. "Seriously, Lil?"

"Is your phone charged?"

"Yeah."

"Okay, then."

"Okay, then."

LILY HAD CLEANED his place and bought him fresh groceries. Matt unpacked and stored the small duffel she had brought to the hospital and then wandered through the apartment touching surfaces. Ran his hands over the new front door and locks, the balcony sliders and their locks, the window in his bedroom and its lock. Riffled through his clothes. Reassured himself his back-up hard drive remained in the tool chest on the floor of his closet.

When he'd talked to Sebastian Ramirez earlier, having to turn the volume all the way up on his phone, Sebastian agreed to help him replace his laptop at Best Buy on Monday. Matt had been promised a summer session B class to teach, but Sebastian told him not to hold his breath since the cops had been around not once, but twice already. Admin was unhappy that Matt had been named in the Daytona News-Journal as a DSC adjunct professor connected to the murder of law enforcement personnel while out on bail for possession.

He sighed and rubbed his eyes in an attempt to relieve the constant dry itch. Just a little. He wanted to crank some tunes up. Maybe. But everything still sounded wrong, and his ears didn't need the trauma of anything loud. His neighbors would be happier if he didn't, too. He showered, half hoping Cin would join him, half wondering what it would mean if she did.

She didn't.

After dressing in a black button down and black slacks, he pulled his employee badge on its lanyard off his clothes tree and placed it over his neck. Someone pounded on the door. Matt heaved in a breath and blew it out. Cops all knocked the same way. It wasn't taught. It must be genetic. He did it, too.

The dark glasses he was required to wear for the next few weeks lay on his nightstand. He scooped them up and put them on. Unfolding the cane he'd laid out on his bed, he unnecessarily swung it down the hall, tapping the walls on either side, relishing the solid feel of it in his hand after days of absence.

He paused, his hand over the deadbolt, to call out, ask who was knocking, when his vision cleared. His head spun, brain on visual overload. He flattened his hand against the coolness of the metal door. Even as he watched a brown-haired man—Caucasian, five-ten— raise a firm fist to the door, his apartment door, Matt felt the vibration of the knock under his hand. It made no sense.

"Charlie," Cin said from nowhere and everywhere at once. "Hey, Charlie."

"Cin," Matt croaked and sagged when nothingness returned. He wiped his clammy forehead on his shirt sleeve, then threw the locks and opened the door.

"Mr. Loose," Charlie said. "Detective Charlie Stance. I worked with Detective Troy."

"I remember," Matt said.

"Are you on your way out?"

He wanted to say yes. Damn his loyalty and curiosity and drive to solve a puzzle regardless of the consequences. The only reason he had dressed for work was to start his search for Malcolm Ward the only way he knew how, and he couldn't hide that motivation from himself with Charlie standing in his doorway.

He stepped back and swung his arm wide in invitation.

They didn't sit.

Charlie stood in the living room while Matt simply leaned back against the closed door. "Is this an official visit? Finally?" Matt asked.

Charlie hesitated, and then cleared his throat. "You were pretty far down our list of priorities."

"Being blind and all," Matt said.

"Cin always did have a penchant for self-deprecation. She never dated a dumb man."

The words pinched Matt's heart and filled his mouth with the taste of doughnut. His measured breath probably gave him away, but he could hear the pain in Charlie's voice, so did it really matter? "You'll have to speak up," he said, tapping on one ear.

"I knew. That she took you home. That you were there that morning because she . . ."

Matt let the silence stretch. He directed his gaze downward. Although it didn't really matter, it made the sighted more comfortable. It was polite in mixed company, or so he'd been taught.

"Are your eyes okay?"

Matt raised his brows.

"I knew they'd been damaged. And you're wearing glasses."

Ah. Redirected gaze unneeded. He'd forgotten. He reached up and took them off. "They'll be fine. Just need these in daylight for a while." Aside from the mild thermal burn and possible blast wave effects, the ophthalmologist had been appalled Matt was living in Florida without wearing shades. Whatever.

"Did you notice anything unusual, Mr. Loose?"

Matt closed his eyes, thinking back. Exhaust and cut grass and body odor under deodorant from the firemen. A tinkle like wind-chimes

from the house behind him. A rustle from the palms above. A mix of
voices, snippets of conversation, salt on the mild breeze. The
temperature had dropped when clouds covered the sun. He
remembered thinking rain was on its way. A man in boots had walked
close by to get to the engine truck.

MATT'S THINKING and Cin can *feel* his thoughts.

She's blind.

Wind chimes tinkle somewhere out in front of her. Boots clunk by
on the pavement.

Sweat rolls down her spine, as she stands out there in the street.

BEHIND MATT'S EYELIDS, the street unfurled in full color vision,
right in front of him. The heat from the asphalt warmed his feet and
radiated onto his arms and face. He watched Cin turn in Jimmy Shad's
doorway and then he was looking out on himself, leaning back against a
standard issue dark Impala, his hands in his pockets.

Opening his eyes, Matt pressed his shoulders back against the
apartment door and breathed through his nose. It made no difference to
what he was seeing. He still stood in Jimmy's doorway, surveying the
cul-de-sac, although he could feel his own apartment around him. He
remained aware of Charlie there in front of him.

The view changed again.

Matt suddenly understood he was seeing through Cin's eyes, her
memory.

She scanned the cul-de-sac, the cluster of firemen, the neighbors and
reporters standing on the lawns, a little ash-haired girl straddling a pastel
blue bicycle and staring at a man sitting on the curb a few feet away
from her. The man lifted his head to meet Cin's gaze.

Wide.

Wide face with a nose so crooked Matt could see it across the
distance between them. Wide shoulders and arms. His knees, wide. His

calves bulged. He wore shorts and beach sandals. His fingers were interlaced, his arms wrapped around his splayed knees.

Matt knew him. Or thought he did. The angle of his jaw, the fierce, hooded eyes, reminded him of someone. In memory, a lowered head near his, the murmur of a voice in his ear. But Matt couldn't grasp it and then the man looked away, and the resemblance slipped away. He let it go as Cin turned, the scene sliding past, to look at the cop on the step outside the front door.

Young guy, patrolman. He reached out and grabbed the front of the gurney holding Jimmy Shad's body to help yank it over the threshold.

Matt's belly flipped again as he was dropped, falling back into his own limited world of nothing to see, the apartment door hard against his back.

"Are you okay, Mr. Loose?" Charlie said.

"There was a man," Matt said, feeling his way into the lie. "Cin noticed him on the way in. Big guy, crooked nose. Sandals. Sitting on the curb a couple of houses down from where we parked. She noticed him enough to mention him while she was describing the scene to me." He tapped his cane on the floor like he was thinking. "Because there was a girl on a bike watching him instead of the scene. That's why Cin mentioned him. Otherwise, no."

"Thank you. We've pulled all the private security videos on the street, but there were only two that showed a view of the crowd. I'll look for him."

The moment stretched once more.

"Was there anything else, Detective?"

"The Chief. I, uh, I don't know what he thinks you'd do, being, y'know."

"Charlie," Matt said a moment after Charlie fell silent again. "Can I call you Charlie? I'm blind. I know I'm blind. You don't have to be so careful."

"Okay," Charlie said, and Matt heard him swallow. He almost felt sorry for him. Almost. "He doesn't want you trying to pull anything, those are his words, or solicit any help to investigate on your own. We've got this. We'll find out who killed our people."

Matt shrugged. "What am I going to do about it?"

"Exactly. Just so we're clear."

"Is there a date for the funerals yet?"

"For the police memorial open to the public? No."

"For Cin."

"No. That'll be private." A stab of fury rent Matt's guts. He held the acidic words that formed on the back of his tongue, but it must've been evident because Charlie added a belated "Sorry."

Matt nodded instead of speaking.

"Look, can I drop you? At the Kennel Club?"

Matt nodded again before he straightened to let them out.

He had to give Charlie kudos for not offering to help him as he followed Charlie to his car. The ride was quiet except for Matt's directions on where to drop him outside the club. He stood beside the building and listened to the distorted sound of Charlie driving away.

The door to the employee entrance beeped beside him. Unlike the street Cin died on in little bitty pieces, the Kennel Club was covered in cameras, inside and out. He swung around and grabbed the handle and jerked it open. Ed's cologne was overpowering as he walked down the hall towards Matt.

"Hey, Mattie! You're three hours early for your shift. You running from your sister? She's been calling me all week. Think she's changed her mind about me."

"I'd bet my life she hasn't."

"Heard you almost lost that life," Ed boomed, clapping a hand on Matt's shoulder. "But it's only the fifth or sixth outta nine, right? You got a couple to spare."

It was more like his eighth or ninth, but that was classified. He had no qualms about burning what he had left. He started down the hall, Ed falling into step with him. "So, Ed, you know a guy named Malcolm Ward?"

"I don't know Malcolm Ward, but I know a guy who knows a gal and she's quite a woman if you know what I mean," Ed said. He held the door at the end of the hall while Matt went through it. Matt rolled his eyes. "I can guess."

"You do that really well."

"So I've been told." At about the right place, Matt swung his cane a couple of inches further and tapped the wooden frame of Ed's office door. He stopped. "Your guy?"

"Johnny Smith," he said, brushing by Matt to enter the small office first.

"Ed."

"Seriously. Johnny Smith." He tapped his hand on the spare wooden chair as he whooshed past. "Tire guy."

Matt resisted asking. Lifted his brows instead, with a slight shake of his head as Ed dropped with a grunt into his wheezy leather swivel chair.

"Y'know. He brokers spare tires. That's how he knows Jane."

Matt slid his fingers over the back of the chair Ed had marked for him. "I guess I've been out too long," he said, sitting down. He snapped the top link of his cane down so it wasn't sticking up in front of his face. "What the hell are you talking about?"

"Sex. No strings."

"He's a pimp."

"It's different. This is classy shit. High end. The women are Maseratis, Ferraris. Jane? She's a Bugatti."

"Jane," Matt repeated, suppressing his amusement. Ed could be sensitive. "I gotta talk to Johnny Smith to get to Jane..."

"Jones," Cin whispered in his ear as Ed said, "Johnson."

The chortle rose from his chest unbidden. Matt rested his forehead on the back of his hands, stacked on the top of his cane. He laughed silently, his shoulders jerking as he tried to grab a breath. An odd choking sound issued from Ed's desk and Matt lifted his head, sobering, before he deciphered Ed's strangled wheeze as laughter, which set him off all over again.

"Yeah, yeah," Ed finally said.

Matt heaved in a deep breath and thumbed the tears from his eyes, nodding. He had needed that.

"Anyway," Ed said. "I can set you up with Johnny. He likes the Waffle House. What else you need?"

Time to recover some of his previous life. Going with Sebastian to Best Buy would net him an everyday laptop, but he wanted something else for a secure stash he was already building in his head. Ed had a guy on retainer who kept all his computer systems running. No reason not to ask. "A new, ruggedized MacBook with the latest in voice recognition, voice over, and speech installed and the best IP scrambler on the open market. And Tor."

"Do you need, I don't know. A braille keyboard or something?"

"I suck at braille, Ed. Ever eat tuna when you were expecting deviled ham?"

"What's deviled ham?"

Matt smirked. "Never mind. Regular keyboard's fine. I type okay. As long as I don't over focus, I should be good."

"It's gonna cost a bit."

"I got money, Ed. I just been saving it. How long?"

"Got you covered," he said, his chair protesting as he shifted. "I'll make a couple calls. You'll have it yesterday. Won't even have to ask me for it that way." He snorted at his own joke.

Matt tapped the floor with his cane. "Can I start early today? I'll stay to the end of my shift. I just can't—I need to be moving." And I need to make rent, he didn't add. That money he was dipping into was for his little girl, not living expenses.

"Lisa'll be happy to sub out early, Mattie. Go ahead."

***

HE FROZE on the edge of the carpet that marked the long wall of the Poker Room. The noise was louder than he remembered, and his ears rang with the echo of a hundred different conversations. He became conscious of the dark glasses sitting on the bridge of his nose, the pull of his shirt across his chest, the distance of the tip of his cane from himself and how even now people were walking around it, leaving him an island. He didn't want to be an island. Except he kind of did. It was safer to be an island. Once he walked out onto the floor, his back would be exposed. The back of his head would be exposed.

Matt's knees folded and his pants soaked up cold blood puddled on a concrete floor.

His cold blood.

And Sam's, too.

His partner Sam lay on his side in front of him, one eye staring at him, the other bulging out of the broken bones of his face and head.

Matt shook.

"Hey, buddy, back it up here," an unfamiliar voice said.

A radio was playing. Into the Night. He knew this.

Something hard at his back. A wall. A huge, solid hand on his chest. Matt tilted his head back, cool relief wicking through his veins, aware of the sweat on his skin, trickling down his temple. The murmur of a thousand voices. The Poker Room.

"Mattie," a man said.

Sam was still there, lying in front of him. He could still see him, close enough to touch. His knees remained wet and cold from the blood he'd been kneeling in, but he could hear the riffle of cards, the clink of glass. "It's too late, isn't it?" he whispered.

"Too late for what, bud?"

"To save—" But what did he mean? To save Sam? Sam was dead.

There'd been a girl there, too, wasn't there? A woman. Tall and lithe. Smiling at him.

The lights cut out, leaving him in utter nothingness.

Matt swung his arm out, slamming it into a solid mass of man and grabbed a fistful of shirt.

"Yeah," the man said.

Ed. Eddie. That was his name. Ed stepped in closer, an anchor, as Matt sagged.

"Nothing to see, move along," someone said.

The sound rose all at once, voices, the murmur of music, a loud slap, a brief cheer from the far side of the room, rising and falling in a moment. A wave of sound he knew. A pattern he recognized. Dark, sharp scent of the man still shielding him.

Sam was gone. Had been gone for years now.

It wasn't dark, he was blind.

Cin was dead. Only...Matt opened his eyes.

She held his face between her hands, staring intently at him.

SAM.

It's like Matt's memories are her own.

Sam's head broke open.

Right before Matt's head broke open and the lights went out forever.

Cin's palms still register the coolness of Matt's fresh-shaven cheeks. Her fingers cup his ears, brush the softness of his close-cropped hair. But she's standing in the hallway of Matt's stark apartment, his cuffed hands under hers.

Charlie's crowding her. SWAT's murmured conversations drift in from outside. Swinkler's in the living room. She's looking past Matt's shoulder at the indentation in the drywall from his forehead.

"Hey," Charlie shouts in her ear, grabbing the back of Matt's shirt to yank him away from the wall.

Cin steps back.

Charlie manhandles Matt around and follows him down as he sinks to the floor with the wall to his back.

Marine. Degree in Criminal Justice. Civilian analyst for Naval Intelligence. NYPD Detective-Investigator in the terrorism unit.

Father.

I was so blind, but now I see.

In the Poker Room, Cin sinks down with him, her hands on his face, Eddie's living force bristling, hot and fierce, at her back, until Matt's butt hits the floor.

I'm here, Matt.

I'm here.

I'm here.

MATT HELD Cin's gaze a moment longer and then his blind nothingness flooded over her and washed her away. There was only Ed's hands on Matt's shoulders, Ed's minty breath and sharp cologne in Matt's nose, the noise of the Poker Room spread out in front of him, and the wall at his back. He swallowed his grief and said, "Okay, Eddie. Okay."

He still had his cane gripped hard in one hand. He forced his other fist open and patted Ed's back. Cold sweat dripped down his sides, ran over his ribs to pool at his waistband.

"Too soon, Mattie," Ed said. "Jessica can run you home."

"I don't—"

"Let me re-phrase. You're going home right now, or you're fired."

"Help me up."

Ed grabbed Matt's upper arm in one meaty hand and then caught him with the other when Matt stood up too fast. Matt swayed into him, a faint reminder of the vertigo he'd experienced when first blinded passing over him, there and gone. He sucked in a deep breath and found his balance.

Ed clapped his shoulders with both hands, as if testing Matt's steadiness, before he released him and called Jessica over.

AT HOME, Matt threw the newly installed double deadbolts on the door one after the other. Jess, he knew, stood on the other side of it, thinking he wouldn't know that she was hesitating to leave him. It took thirty long seconds more before he heard the click of her stiletto heels tapping away.

He walked through the apartment, running his hands along his path, over his things. Checking. Making sure it was all as he'd left it, but then just pacing, stalking his known space like a caged bear, unable to settle on a single thought. There's Sam, glancing over at him under a streetlight. Then Sam's broken head. Then Cin, laughing in the car, a bite of doughnut on her tongue, although he never saw that. He never saw that. Then Ethan, sleeping on the floor at his feet, his blue cast laid out like a prize on the gold pillow. Which reminds him of Sam's glance under the golden light, the bulge of his bloodshot eye. Cin's hands on his face, the flash of doughnut on her tongue, her warmth along his side. Ethan, sleeping. Over and over.

At some point, sweat drying on his skin, he became aware of sitting on the carpet in his bedroom, bed at his back, as the light rose around him. It was shabby, his apartment. The stained carpet he knew was clean. The painted frame surrounding his closet, latte-colored with age. The water-marked window, clouded with dust from the parking lot below. Bland beige comforter over pseudo-burgundy sheets. He stood and stripped, inspected his skin, what he could see of it. Gave his soft dick a tug and rolled his balls in his fingers as he watched them shift.

In the bathroom's silver-spotted mirror, he traced the pink scar that ran from behind his right ear onto his neck and almost to his collarbone. Ran both hands back through his hair. It was longer on top than it felt, his eyes bluer than he remembered.

"Matt," Cin said as she leaned into his back and he almost—almost —closed his eyes as he reached back to touch her, pull her naked body tight against him. She dropped kisses along his neck, onto the tops of his shoulders. "I'm so sorry, Matt."

He turned then, letting her slide into his arms. "For what?"

"For not understanding. For Sam. For ragging on you while you were panicking."

He ran his hands up her back, absorbing the fact that she knew Sam's name, that she had really been there at the Poker Room. "You haven't seen me panic yet, Cin." His fingers found the back of her head, burrowing up under her hair along the smooth unbroken curve of her head as he kissed her.

He wanted more. Intending to surprise her, he sank to his knees. The cold bathroom tile greeted them. A rushing swell of emotion caught him unawares—a deep and profound sadness—coursing below the aching pang of the grief he knew so well. It flooded his throat, and he choked on the sudden sob that broke from him.

He stiffened and tried to turn away, to stand, to stop, but she closed her strong arms around him. She held his head to her belly, one hand splayed on his back, his hands clutching her thighs. She shushed him, saying something he couldn't understand. He gave up and wrapped his arms around her waist, forehead against her, his throat burning, gasping as he fought to regain his control. Embarrassed and comforted at the same time, his dick limp, he still ached for her. Hitching in a ragged breath, some knot he didn't know he carried let go in his chest. Matt's next breath filled parts of his lungs that hadn't seen air in ages, forcing out another choked sob when it hit bottom.

"Hey," Cin said. "It's okay. Hey, now. Go ahead, I don't care."

God only knows why, but he relaxed then, turned his head, and pressed the side of his face against her, let the hot tears come, which eased his breath.

She stroked his head and neck and back, humming a hushed singsong until he heaved in another deeper breath and eased his hold on her as the terrible feeling, the sadness, the . . . sorrow . . . calmed.

"I was there, with you, for a moment," she said. "I know what happened to Sam. I know what happened to you."

He inhaled deep again, letting the moment be. This was different than the sharp, familiar, pang of grief, a far deeper current than the steady ache of sadness. He turned that word that had come to him over again. Ran the shadows of the thoughts he refused to grasp over its edges. Sorrow. A few more tears dropped hot and fast down his drying cheeks as he tried not to think anything at all. "Are you real?"

Cin's arms closed tighter around him. "Are you?"

She drew him up and kissed him.

The heat that never seemed to leave them flared.

They made their slow and stumbling way down the hall to light his bed on fire.

THE KNOCK on the door at one a.m. dropped him back into blindness and Cin into nothing but the brush of cool air along his side as he startled, rising halfway from the bed. He thumped back onto the mattress and rumpled sheets and rubbed his face with both hands.

The knock came again. Sharp, rapid.

"Coming," he yelled. "Blind man waking," he muttered to himself.

Cin's laugh filled his ear. "You call that sleeping?"

Jerking on the briefs he'd dropped by the bed earlier, Matt huffed, unable to pull any words off his tongue. He wasn't awake, was he? When she showed up? Was he? He snatched up his black slacks but didn't bother with a shirt.

Taking his cane with him, which felt a little better than proceeding without anything in his hands, he went to the door just as whoever it was knocked again. "Who is it?"

"It's Jessica."

And he could believe that. He knew her voice, but he doubted her hands were capable of that knock. "Who's with you?"

"How'd he know?" a guy said. A tenor. Matt could read all sorts of things into his tone, but he'd learned better than to judge a voice by its sound.

"I told you so," Jessica said, smug. If she were that confident in the guy's presence, she probably felt safe with him. Probably. "This is Spider, Mr. Loose." Jessica was Ed's youngest front office gofer at twenty-two, Southern, and raised polite. The most casual she'd gotten with him was Mr. Matt. In front of company, she'd reverted. "We brought you your computer."

He unlocked the door and opened it like a shield, but when it wasn't shoved back, he stepped aside. They brought summer-night Daytona in with them, exhaust and hibiscus and tanning lotion and salt and coffee. And weed. "You got a blunt on you, Spider?"

"Uh," Spider said. "No, sir."

Matt made a gimme-motion with his right hand, closing the door with his left. Spider placed the joint in the center of his palm. Matt closed his fist around it. A fattie. He slid it in his pocket. "Add it to my costs."

Jessica giggled. "I told you he was all right."

"What you got for me?" Matt asked.

"Exactly what you asked for, sir," Spider said.

Fifteen minutes later, Matt was showing them back out the door, Spider having agreed to pick up Matt's cash payment from Ed the next night.

CIN'S FOLLOWING the click of Jessica's knock-off Manolo's before she notices she's shifted into some new space between here and *there*. It's weird, but intriguing. She's not, after all, in lock step with Matt. Because she can, she drifts along down the stairs in Jessica's wake.

Spider opens the driver's door to Jessica's little Acura SUV for her and Jessica tilts her head to receive his peck on her cheek. He closes it, watches her back out, and only heads to his crotch rocket Honda after she's pulled out onto the road headed to ISB.

He settles himself on the bike and then takes a long considering look upstairs, at Matt's white apartment door.

Cin's vision doubles.

Shaking her head does nothing.

Then the doubles of Spider elongate and morph. When her vision clears, she's seeing everything from a higher perspective.

Much higher.

She can see both inside and out.

Spider's silent introspection of Matt's door, pale fingers wrapped around the handlebars of his bike—

—and Matt's blank eyes, looking right through the useless-to-him screen throwing ghost light over him. Between bursts of its flat, computerized voice, his deft fingers move rapidly over the MacBook's keys.

There's the dark crown of Spider's head, the gleam of the bike waiting beneath him, a blue pickup to his left, a battered white former cop car on his right, and, at the same time, as exposed as if she were peering into a dollhouse, Matt's dark living room, the glow of his blonde hair, the flash of his hands.

Spider kicks his knee up and then down and the roar of his bike shatters the early Sunday morning quiet, the sound spiraling past Cin into the scudding storm clouds high above. Matt pauses, listening, she thinks— maybe focused on the sound of the engine in the parking lot below—before his fingers move on.

Cin's detective gut kicks in. She decides to follow Spider, but nothing happens. She's still watching Spider leave and Matt listen. She's thinking 'follow' so hard that she's halfway to nowhere before she registers the tug of the distance between Spider and Matt. She leans into it and snaps back down to the rush of blacktop. White lines flicker by. The thrum of Spider's bike tows her into the dark.

THE COMPUTER SPOKE with a pleasant mid-tone woman's voice. While Matt had some practice with voice-over and the frame by frame, html tag to alt text tag method of browsing for the vision impaired, he hadn't bothered to access his old online accounts since Sam died. It would be painfully slow to do it this way. The enterprising Spider had also brought him a new, wireless, unobtrusive Jawbone type earpiece that contained an ultra-sensitive mic and was worth every extra dollar Spider wanted for it. After pairing it to both the laptop and his phone, he ran himself back through the keyboard shortcuts Spider had taught him. Then he double-checked the IP scrambler and checked his regular email accounts, which had received little but junk mail in the past few days.

A motorcycle started up in the lot, not the one he heard as a weekday six a.m. alarm belonging to the guy with the growly voice, but not unusual on the weekend despite the hour. A note from Daytona State informed him he was under investigatory advisement, whatever that meant. Bethune-Cookman had sent only a request that he contact his supervisor when he was able to do so. He wasn't expecting a class with them until the fall semester. He fired up Tor. After he confirmed his Vidalia control panel had opened, Matt sat back to think.

The fattie lay in his pocket under his open hand. He stretched his legs out and retrieved it. "What do you think, Cin? Should I light it up?"

Nothing.

It'd be nice to see what he was doing online. Easier.

"Cin?"

Was she a "just say no to drugs" girl, or just not here? A certain spark of pride questioned if he had worn her out. Another piece of him immediately questioned his sanity. He lurched up and found the Bic lighter Lily insisted on buying with his first load of groceries when he moved in. He'd never used it. It's not like he needed candles when the power went out. After a couple of false starts while standing in the kitchen, he got the flame going.

He sucked in deep on the joint, held his breath, and then released an explosive cough. The second hit went better. He retrieved a sandwich plate while he was up, returned to the new laptop, and set the joint on the plate next to it. This was going to take a while.

From Vidalia, he checked his dark web anon emails and deleted everything that had piled up in the past two years without trying to listen to any of it. Then he installed I2P. The websites he needed were still accessible. Two of his old intel logins failed, but the third got him into the active forum he was hoping for and the fourth into the database he wanted. Two hours and most of the joint later, he'd parsed the set-up and then mapped and memorized the sites.

He straightened up, took a last hit, stubbed the joint out, and went to work on learning everything he could about underground Daytona, local law enforcement, and Malcolm Ward.

CHAPTER
TWELVE

Malcolm Ward was a ghost online. A mention here, a threat there. A Daytona bogeyman. If Ed's spare tire, Jane Johnson, knew him, she'd be Matt's only solid lead. Underground Daytona wasn't buried very deep and didn't consist of much variety. Meth, heroin, oxy, weed, all the usual poppers and dots, everyone boasting of the purity of their product while cutting it with detergent, caffeine, creatinine, or increasingly, fentanyl. Years before, the area between Madison and Mason Avenues had been targeted by the DOJ's Weed and Seed program, but drug and gang activity persisted and spread north into Holly Hill. Beachside, the Boardwalk was the place to buy whatever you wanted.

Daytona prostitutes made either an abysmal living or the kind that kept them in all the drugs they wanted and let their kids attend private school besides. Local law enforcement did a heavy clean-up of the streetwalkers and their johns before big events like the Daytona 500 and Bike Week.

At five, when car doors slamming and an early morning still-drunken argument broke through his thoughts, Matt got up and made coffee. He slapped together a peanut butter sandwich and ate it standing at the kitchen counter.

The small arms market was just that, small. He suspected the car scene was larger than he could dig up. Mostly cash trading hands on untagged vehicles. The street racers had a coded Twitter account. He found it and moved on, leaving exploration of it until later. Cin would have said if she knew of Ward from that playground. There was an interesting roving sex club. High dollar membership, one night every couple of months, a different location every time. Girls acting as sushi boards and hired sex performers for the voyeurs in the crowd, private orgy rooms for the hands-on members.

Matt stretched after all the Sunday morning noises had come and gone and the stupor of ten a.m. hit the apartment complex. The road noise was a constant hum and a weed-eater whined around the next building over, but the kids were either gone to Sunday School, off to the beach, or had retreated to the air-conditioning after their first bursts of morning energy. The basketballs and skateboards wouldn't come out until late in the afternoon, when everyone could anticipate a slight breeze and lots more shade between the buildings.

He rinsed off under a cool shower and then changed his sheets. The bed creaked as he lay down. He couldn't stop thinking about the stained carpet, the dingy paint now that he knew what the bedroom looked like. The drone of the TV in the apartment above him lulled him to sleep.

WHEN CIN IS HERE AGAIN, she knows only that time has passed.

She's still with Spider, who is still with Jessica.

He wakes and slides out of her pink and white bed.

It's habitual. This is nothing new. He showers and lets himself out of the apartment Jessica obviously shares with an absent roommate. Cin hesitates as the door snugs shut, pulled back to the bedroom by the soft buzz of a cell phone.

"Yeah," Jessica murmurs and with no sense of movement, Cin is hovering above her. "Sure, Ed, I can do that . . . okay . . . bye." She fumbles the phone back onto her white princess nightstand and rolls over onto her back, stretching.

A blink and Cin is looking up at the ceiling, drowning at the shock of sinking into Jessica.

She's thinking about Matt, standing shirtless and barefoot, holding his door open for her as she waltzes in with her keys in her hand and a sense of purpose burning in her head. What the fuck?

Cin flails up and out of her.

Jessica grins and sits up.

Cin tries to enter her again, on purpose. But the moment is gone.

She wills herself back to Matt but can't rise higher than Jessica's ceiling. Jess swings her feet out of bed.

"Matt, Matt, Matt," Cin says out loud. Or thinks she does. "Matt," she says again, but she can't tell. What if she can't get back to him? She's a nothing, right? A what, a ghost? A spirit? Can't she just think herself to wherever the fuck she wants to go? What about home?

Cin closes her eyes and pictures her own bedroom, so different from this one—dark where this is bright, minimal where this is cluttered—furniture and posters and scarves are tied everywhere—but she can't hold the image in her head.

Jessica flounces off to the bathroom.

Cin follows, trying to shoot herself through the front door to go home. Instead, she careens off it, into the basic, carefully neutral living room. She spins and doubles back, zipping down the hall through Jessica's open bedroom door faster than she intended, and ricochets off the cobweb hiding in the far back corner of her bedroom ceiling, bounces again off the front door. She spreads her arms and legs and fetches up again in the high corner. She peers through the crisscross of the dusty web. The walls are too white, the rooms too small, the air too thin.

She fills her head with the cool, roundness of wet grapes between her fingertips, Matt's soft firm lips brushing over them. But there's only concrete and grass and heat and blood misting out into the hot air and then she's misting out with it, she's nothing but mist, blood mist all that's left of her, breathless, dead, trapped, trapped, trapped . . .

Warm, warm, water pouring over her.

Her arms lift without thought, body turning, swiping the suds off. Anticipation. Anxiety. Forty minutes to dress and eat, fifteen to Matt's. Twenty-five or thirty to the Waffle House out by Destination Daytona.

She's inside Jessica.

"Who are you meeting," she says out loud, just like when she's with Matt.

But nothing happens, Jessica just goes on thinking her own thoughts. It's like another inner voice. Cin tries to turn those thoughts away from the feel of Spider's hand running down her side and orange juice and if her mom will need money to make her rent this month and how much does her little brother eat anyway, but they just roll on.

Stilling her own panicked thoughts, Cin soaks in the physical, the heat of the water and the strawberry scent of Jessica's conditioner and the slide of her hands over her skin and down the length of her long, smooth hair and the flash of her white skin, so different from Cin's own in innumerable exasperating everyday ways.

Yet Jess is not so different from her.

Not here inside.

We are woman.

And when at length she turns the water off, Jessica's thoughts turn back to Matt.

Cin closes her eyes and leans into the sound of his name as it forms, lets it wrap around her, like he wraps around her . . .

And there he is, grumbly-growling at the beep-beep-beep of his phone as he pours coffee into a mug. He takes a long drink and then thumbs the phone. An electronic woman with a British accent says, "Ed at Card Room, received on Sunday at one-oh-nine p.m." She pauses, then continues reading. "Hey, blind boy. Johnny at 2:30. Jessica's picking you up."

"I think Jessica might actually try picking you up," Cin says. She'll be disappointed that he's already dressed in worn jeans and a faded blue polo.

A slow smile spreads across his face and he relaxes all over. Cin can see it and feel it inside her all at the same time. "Jealous?" he asks.

Cin phases out of him and slides her arms around his neck.

He sets his phone on the counter and wraps that arm around her waist while still coveting his coffee. "Where have you been?"

"Apparently, besides here and *there*, I can follow other people." She quails, thinking about being inside Jessica.

"Hey, what's that face?"

Cin shakes her head. "It took me awhile to get back to you. I was . . ."

He waits a moment for Cin to find her words, but she can't.

"So, death doesn't make life any easier," he says into her ear. "You were scared."

He gets it. Cin hugs him hard. "Yes, I was scared."

Matt turns them so he can put his coffee down and then hugs her back. "What do you mean by *there*?"

"*There* isn't here, but I'm at peace *there*, warm and safe and . . . I don't really remember my time there. It's kind of like sleeping, but I'm awake. And I come right back to you from *there*, with just a thought. Only I didn't this time."

His hands come up to steady the back of her head as he draws back just far enough to kiss her like the world is ending. When they come up for air, he searches her eyes. "I'm sorry you were scared."

Cin loves his eyes. She loves the scruff of his beard and his kiss-reddened lips. She reaches out and runs her thumb over his lower lip.

"Hey," he says, drawing her gaze back to his. "Don't leave me again, okay?"

And then he worships her. Right there in his kitchen.

On Jessica's elbow, Matt walked through the Waffle House door with confidence and right into a sensory wall of baking waffles, chicory coffee, the clank of silverware, onions, bacon frying, yelling staff, the sweetness of syrup, overhead music, and the rush of a hundred conversations at once.

"Welcome to Waffle House," a mismatched duet of voices called out above the rest before it all rushed back in again.

His feet stuck.

The door brushed past his shoulder and clunked shut behind him. The AC vent above dropped frigid air on him, a shock from the blazing heat outside.

Jessica took a step back to him and pitched her voice low, for his ears only. "You okay, Mr. Loose?"

How many times had he been asked that in the last two years alone? "Yeah. Just need to acclimate."

He shut out the music and furthest away sounds, concentrating on what lay directly in front of him and to his sides. Forks and knifes hitting plates. A woman talking with a child. Someone thumping a foot against a booth. Three men talking golf. He squeezed Jessica's elbow and followed her lead as she threaded adroitly through the crowded space.

The kitchen lay to their right. Nearly every stool, booth, and table held a diner. Past the kitchen, the restaurant opened up to the right. More people. But Jessica steered them left.

"Mr. Smith?" she said.

"Yeah, sweetie, you Ed's girl?"

"Jessica, yes, sir. This is Matt Loose."

Smith's voice was neither deep nor high. There was no smoker's rasp or other distinguishing feature. He remained sitting in front of and a couple of feet to Matt's left. He said nothing following Jessica's introduction of him.

"Back corner booth, Jess?" Matt asked.

"Got it in one, Mr. Loose."

"And I got your back," Cin whispered.

But not his sight at the moment.

Matt let go of Jessica's arm. "Thank you. I've got it from here."

"Okay, Mr. Loose," she said. "Should I wait in the car?"

"Yes, please."

She retreated. He brushed the edge of the table with the back of his hand and slid into the booth, setting his folded cane on the bench beside him.

"Must be a bitch," Johnny Smith said.

"Naw, she's a good girl," Matt said, and Smith laughed. An average, nothing-to-notice-here chuckle. "I've adapted," he said, addressing Smith's actual meaning.

"What can I do you for, Mr. Loose?"

"Ed thought maybe you or one of your acquaintances could introduce me to Malcolm Ward."

Smith settled back into the booth and after a moment, a light clunk in front of Matt indicated the setting down of what Matt presumed to be a coffee mug. Smith pushed his plate away to Matt's left. "I wish I knew him," Smith said. "That way I'd know when I needed to be heading the other way."

"So you know of him."

"Yeah. I've heard the name." Reservation leaked through every word.

Matt waited, hoping Smith wasn't as cagey as he seemed. Someone was walking fast towards their booth and Matt braced himself against a possible assault.

"Coffee?" a harried male voice asked from right beside him.

"Uh, sure," Matt said. "Leaded."

"Anything else?" the waiter said.

"No."

"Why you asking?" Smith said.

Hitting Matt up when he was still off-balance from the interruption was a good tactic. Matt nodded, unable to squash the smile that turned the corner of his lip up. "Nice timing."

He could practically hear Smith's shrug. "Good to know you're teaching baby cops and lawyers from a position of experience."

Smith had taken the time to look Matt up. He had skills controlling a meet. Whether that meant anything, Matt couldn't tell. Professional career criminals of a certain ilk could be hard to distinguish from long-time federal agents.

In a sudden flurry of movement, Smith leaned forward. Matt straightened, his back hitting the booth. "Lean in," Smith said.

Wary, Matt did as asked.

"Look, Malcom Ward is—I don't know who he is. That's not his name, I know that much. It's not even the name he does business under, if you know what I mean. You could be Malcom Ward for all I know. Daytona's a backwater. But every major deal? Every minor screw-up? It's Malcolm Ward's name on everyone's lips. You were there, right? At Shad's house? Your name was in the paper."

"Yeah."

"Shad had a big mouth. Dropped Ward's name to the cops. Now they're everywhere, asking around like they haven't ever heard it before." Smith talked with his hand, air brushing Matt's face, his tone scoffing. "I'll never believe that."

"Glad they think we're better than we are," Cin breathed in Matt's ear.

"Shad," Smith continued, with emphasis, "said the wrong thing at the wrong time, someplace where someone who *does* know the person behind the name heard him. I ain't making that mistake. Because I got nothing. Nada."

Matt waited for Smith to sit back, maybe get up and leave. But he didn't.

He lifted his right brow.

"What I got," Smith finally said, "is a problem that needs solving."

"Can I solve it?"

"Don't know."

A family rounded the corner into the aisle beside Matt, and trooped past, dragging dog and a floral perfume and dirty diaper with them. Matt checked in with all his senses, clocking the close by, what he could identify. The shuffle of diners coming and going. The animated conversation about a high school soccer schedule in the booth right behind them. The relative quiet of their corner bubble. Smith remained close, their heads nearly meeting in the center of the table.

"What do I get if I solve it?" Matt asked.

"That's up to Maria."

Maria. Ed had implied Jane Johnson could get him to Ward. And that Smith could get him to Jane. Who the frig was Maria? "Does Maria know Malcolm Ward?"

"I just told you. No one knows anything about Malcom Ward. Malcom Ward doesn't exist."

Hearing the quick step coming this time, Matt straightened and turned just as the waiter set his coffee down. "Thank you."

"Yep," he said without fully stopping.

Locating the cup with the back of his hand, Matt slid it over and cupped both hands around it. Smith wasn't going to hand him Jane Johnson. Not today anyway. "You want to tell me what Maria needs?"

"A resourceful guy with contacts."

"That's not you, Johnny?"

"There's the cop I know you are. No, Mattie," Smith said, amused now, emphasizing Matt's name, Ed's influence. "I ain't Maria's guy on this one."

Matt sipped his coffee.

Smith shifted and then slid something across the table and tapped it. "Maria's address. Say four? I'll call her."

CHAPTER
THIRTEEN

Maria lived beachside on the Halifax River.

"Holy cow," Jessica breathed as she slowed her car to a crawl on John Anderson drive in Ormond before turning right into what Matt assumed was a driveway.

"It's fancy," Cin said.

Matt flapped his hand at the breathy intonation that apparently meant she was elsewhere or nowhere or maybe just in his head.

"Tell me," he said.

"It's—fancy," Jessica said.

For a fervent moment, Matt wished more than anything he wasn't blind. Was the phrasing coincidence? He wanted to hiss at Cin, ask if she was influencing. Could she influence? Was she talking in other people's ears?

"No," Cin said. "I can feel what you're thinking. That doesn't work."

He opened his mouth to ask again—

"No, I can't read your thoughts. Hers, however—"

If she knew it didn't work, then she had tried. Both to influence others and to read his thoughts. And Jessica's. He opened his hand instead of speaking aloud, lifting it as he did and closed his hand in a fist.

Cin laughed, an amazing sound. "Okay, I'll be quiet."

"Describe the house," he said to Jessica.

"Spanish style. Arches and stucco. Red tile roof. It's got to be four or five thousand square feet. Circular flag-stone drive. Old-fashioned wrought-iron double gate to an enclosed courtyard where I'm guessing the front door must be."

"What do you mean by old-fashioned?"

"Ornate. Los of twists and curlicues."

"Where'd you go to school?"

"DSC. I have a degree in hospitality."

Matt suppressed his surprise, hoping it didn't show on his face.

She opened her door. "Ed hired me straight out of school. I'm going to run the Poker Room someday while he lounges in Key West."

"I believe you," Matt said, opening his own door.

The sidewalk curved through the yard, the size of the house evident from the way it blocked the faint sounds of the river and any breeze off the water. Hibiscus and citrus and salt tinged the still air.

"There's an intercom," Jess said, leaning forward and away from him to trigger a soft electronic buzz.

A bird trilled behind them, up high. Matt counted out seven seconds.

"Yes?" a woman said through the speaker.

"Johnny Smith sent us to speak with Ms. Maria."

"Us?"

"Matt Loose, I'm just his driver."

The gates swung open with a low electric whirr.

They walked into the courtyard. Matt lifted his head, trying not to snuffle like a hound. "Are there lemon trees here?"

"There are. Two on each side of the courtyard. The lemons are huge! And so are the doors. Very European. Like wooden slab dining tables turned vertical. Wrought iron handles and hinges."

The right-side door opened just as Matt swept his cane and hit a barrier. Cool air and the scent of chocolate chip cookies rushed out to greet them. "I'm Susan," a young-sounding woman said, her tone effusive. "Maria will be down in a minute. Oh! Do you need help?"

"No," Matt said as Jessica said, "Two steps, threshold."

"Well, come on in," Susan said, stepping back to let them by. "You can take him right through to the back there, honey, to the outside couch, and then join me in the kitchen. I'm making cookies."

Matt bit his tongue. He hated when people talked like he was deaf as well as blind. The room in front of him was massive and open. A breeze teased his face and arms. While he wanted to just ask Jessica where the couch was located and find it himself, it was more trouble than it was worth. Pick your fights, right? And Jess was an excellent guide.

The tile floor echoed with Jessica's heels as she led him through the room and outside onto a shaded lanai. The river had a different feel to it than anywhere else he'd been in Daytona. The water lapped at the retaining wall that lay past what must be a shallow yard below him. "There's a pool down some steps less than ten feet from here, so don't get too adventurous just because of her," Jess said, patting the back of the couch.

"I didn't think you knew me that well."

"I've seen you in the kennels when you think no one's watching."

He liked being down among the greyhounds. They were large and solid, but calm. Affectionate, even. And their handlers didn't spook at him wandering into the middle of their strings. Not one of them had ever so much as acknowledged his blindness beyond an occasional hip-check to move him out of their way or put a dog into the path of his hand.

"They call you '*Suertudo*', y'know."

He didn't and Spanish wasn't his strong suit, but he still felt like he should know that one.

"Lucky One," she said, apparently reading confusion into his frown. "I'm going to where the cookies are now. Good luck with Maria."

She made a quick exit before he could marshal his thoughts enough to reply.

Lucky One? Him? He'd had nothing but bad luck ever since Anna's —ever since Anna left him. It did explain a lot though, about how he was accepted in the kennel, the dogs put under his hands before they went out onto the track.

The woman was halfway through the great room before Matt heard her. Lush was the word that came immediately to his mind as her grassy springtime scent hit his nose. He rose, holding out his right hand, folded cane in his left. Both her soft, warm hands grasped his in a firm hold. "Mr. Loose, I'm Maria."

"How can I help you, Maria?"

"Sit, please." Her voice was deep, measured, with a slight southern accent that placed her hometown further north than Daytona Beach. She sat down across from him before continuing. "Johnny says you're a cop."

"A former New York Police Department detective. I no longer work in law enforcement."

"My David is seventeen. He has some information, about kids who are being hurt." The evident strain in her quiet words had him sitting forward, aware again of the new dullness of his hearing. "My work makes it difficult to approach the police, especially under these circumstances."

The river lapped against its boundaries, or perhaps that was the pool. Laughter drifted out from inside the house. A door slammed.

"What circumstances might that be?" Matt asked, breaking the silence between them.

"It's the campus resource officer at David's school," Maria said, her tone wary, feeling him out. "He's soliciting services from kids in exchange for drugs."

Matt sighed. The thin blue line was often a thick gray one, but it could still be crossed. He knew three officers were arrested every day nationwide, most were men, and many of their crimes involved sex, but there was still the desire to deny, to believe no cop would commit crimes against the people they were sworn to protect. He chose his own words with care. "Even an anonymous call would be investigated under that claim."

"Several of those calls have been made. He's been spoken to by his department, according to the gossip on campus, but convinced everyone that the kids are trying to get him dismissed because several drug busts have resulted in expulsions. David refused him and now he's in juvenile detention for smoking weed in the boy's room, but he swears he's never smoked at all, let alone pot."

Matt held up his hand. "Hold up. There's more to that story."

Her heel bounced with a staccato beat. "Okay. He stole a car last year. He was mad and took a client's car for a joyride. It all blew over."

"Except he had a delinquency petition drawn in family court."

"The point is," she said emphatically, her voice louder and closer, her feet silent. "He doesn't smoke weed or do any other kind of drug and the car was just a teenage thing. He's got a four point oh GPA and he's taking more AP courses this coming year."

"Did they do a drug test?"

"Yes, but it's not come back yet."

"Charlie," Cin said.

Matt flapped a hand at her voice, like he was waving a gnat away. There was a growing scent of damp in the freshening breeze. The usual summer afternoon downpour on its way. "I have no pull with law enforcement here," he said. "But I know a couple of people. I'll take it to them. Tell them a friend is verifying there's a problem. Can I ask you about someone you might know?"

Silence.

"I can't . . . can you answer out loud?"

"Oh! Of course," Maria said. "I'm sorry. Yes, who are you thinking of?"

"Do you know a Jane Johnson, who also works for Johnny?"

"Yes," she said, but there was something in her tone—

"Matt," Cin said, like he wouldn't notice it.

"Yeah," he said in reply to her and then, "Are you Jane Johnson?"

Maria laughed then, a light, girlish sound, carefree. "No, I'm not, but yes, I know her. And if you can help me," she said, laying her hand upon his forearm, "I'll certainly introduce you to her."

He was sure her negotiation skills held her in good stead against the demands of her high-income clients. Only intelligent, empowered women made it this level of the game. In normal life, he'd never have learned of her, let alone made it through the front door. Sometimes he longed for that quiet, normal life he'd never led, wished he'd walked right past the Marine Corps recruiting office instead of turning in. He'd been the same age as David.

"Is he safe?" he asked. "Right now? David?"

"Yes," Maria said, more relaxed with him now. "He's a smart kid.

He's not sensitive or a prima donna. He'll come out of detention on a clean drug test with a story to tell and probably a cause to pursue."

"It can be—"

"He knows how to use his fists, Mr. Loose, although his timing suffers. He never knows when to pick his fight," she said with amused fondness before it hardened. "But this resource officer, he is not a good man. And most of the kids he's preying on are not David."

"I'll do what I can," Matt promised.

"WHERE NEXT," Jess said once they were settled, dripping, back in her little car.

Rainwater ran off Matt's hair into his right eye. He took his stupid glasses off, swiped it away, and finger-combed his hair straight back. "What kind of car is this?"

"An old Acura MDX."

The Acura SUV hatchback. No wonder it seemed so long inside. He tried to think of where to stash the glasses, but he'd not brought the messenger bag he carried to school, and he refused to tuck one stem down in the vee of his polo to display them on his chest. He stuck them back on his face. "When do you need to be at the club?"

"Ed said I'm yours for as long as you need me."

"Charlie," Cin said.

Matt tilted his head, considering. They were close to A1A. He wanted to follow up his only knowledge of the name Doug Moultrie, but he needed to do that alone. Cin sighed, a breath on his neck. His skin prickled with goosebumps as the hairs all stood up. She chuckled.

"That just sounded wrong, didn't it," Jess said, starting the car. Matt had to shake himself to recall her comment, *I'm yours for as long as you need me.*

He smiled, turning his head so she would see it.

She slapped his arm. "Where?"

"Daytona Police. The building on Williamson."

"You're not going to report Johnny and Maria, are you?"

"No. But I gotta go there to help Maria, which is what Johnny asked me to do."

Wiper motor whining, the car lurched around in a tight left turn and then eventually back and forth in a multi-point turn. Matt reached out and braced himself on the dash, but then Jessica revved the little engine, and they were shooting back down John Anderson Drive towards the Granada Bridge to the mainland.

Until Cin, he'd not ridden much in cars while blind except his sister's. He mostly kept his eyes shut in cars, to stave off the anxiety of flying forward through the dark. With Cin, he'd thought nothing about it. The difference, the safety, he'd felt with her, was only now obvious to him. He found himself wanting to open his eyes, to check where they were, watch for other cars careening into their path.

Maybe it was Jessica's age. Or the pounding rain.

"It must be hard," she said into the silence between them; the silence he expected to be broken at any second with squealing tires and the crunch of metal.

What twenty-something didn't automatically put on the radio? Not that he wanted the radio on, because then he couldn't hear the road noises. "What must be hard?"

"Riding in the car blind," she said, like she could read his thoughts even if Cin couldn't. "You know how sometimes you get drowsy in the car and then the driver hits the brakes, and your eyes fly open to see what's happening? Even when it's nothing really, it takes a few minutes to relax again. I'd just always want to know. What's about to happen."

"You get used to it," Matt lied.

Fifteen minutes later, at the Williamson Road DBPD headquarters, Jess hesitated before shutting the Acura off. "Should I wait here, or—"

Jess was definitely more than met the eye and smarter than he'd given her credit for. Given that Ed, generous as he was, did nothing without a reason that would benefit himself, and that Matt had no idea yet what that benefit might be, he should probably not involve her.

On the other hand, Ed had no reason to think Matt would do anything other than leave Jess waiting while he talked to Johnny. And no idea where that conversation might lead, so the benefit he'd be claiming would most likely be directly related to tying Matt down to some future favor. Matt couldn't immediately think of any possible use a blind ex-cop with no local contacts would be to Ed, though. He didn't even know why Ed hired him in the first place beyond good PR. A disabled veteran on display.

"Have you ever been here before?" he finally said.

"Nope," Jess said after a long moment that told him she had probably shaken her head or whatever and then caught herself. Or that she was fibbing. It was hard to tell. His own slight delay in response triggered a nervous giggle from her. "I really haven't. I forgot to use my words and for some reason, I almost want to hyperventilate even though I've done nothing wrong and there's no reason not to go in with you."

"Ah. Super-Responsible Citizen Complex."

"What?"

"Something my ex-wife used to say. Most everyone gets nervous walking into a police station unless they're there to report a crime, and then they're just angry."

"You grow up being told to find an officer if you're in trouble, but just standing next to a cop in a store or something makes me feel like I'm in trouble and makes me all anxious and itchy."

He grinned. "So you don't want to go in?"

"No," she said, finally turning off the engine. "I do. I need to get over it."

"You don't seem nervous around me."

"One, I've known you for over a year now. And two, you aren't a cop."

Ouch. "So right you are. Ready?"

The rain had shut off as suddenly as it began. There was nothing else like the smell of Florida asphalt steaming following an afternoon rainfall. As they entered the double glass doors, a sigh brushed across his eardrums. Jess jostled against him as she avoided someone emanating strong BO who swept by them.

A few steps through the open lobby brought them to the reception counter. Jess's step faltered. Her free hand came up and landed on top of his where he grasped her elbow. Her fingers were cold on his. "It's fine," he said. "Just talking to a friend."

An alto who should've been on radio asked how he could help

them. Matt opened his mouth and realized he didn't remember Charlie's last name. "I'm looking for Charlie. Lucinda Troy was a friend of mine."

"Your name?"

"Matt."

"You got a last name, Matt?"

How observant would the guy be? Would he recognize Matt's name from the media coverage? Would an average cop have seen a report with his name on it? "Loose."

Jess's hand tightened on his. The alto tapped on his keyboard. "Sorry, he's off-duty. Check back tomorrow around two."

The outside door opened. Multiple voices and footsteps entered on a rush of hot air. "He's at his desk," Cin said within the midst of the noise.

"He said he'd be here," Matt told the alto. "Can you check?"

"You talked to him?"

Two people broke off and approached them.

"I did," he lied. Seemed to be a trend today.

"Hey, rookie," the alto said in a louder voice aimed away from Matt. "Call back and see if Charlie Stance is around." Talking to the new arrivals, he seamlessly continued, "Can I help you, ladies?"

Jess stepped to the side away from where Matt knew the door into the rest of the building lay. He resisted and pulled her close, taking her with him the other direction, but only a couple of steps, as the women started describing some encounter they'd had with an ex-boyfriend.

The door beside them opened. "Come on back," a woman said. She must've been talking to them because Jess made a move. Matt gave way, letting her lead through the doorway and down a hall filled with ambient noise and voices coming from various rooms. It'd been hard, learning to let someone guide him. He still hated it.

Walking on his known routes, along ISB, at the colleges, along the strips where he shopped, and using an app that gave him a volunteer if he got turned around or needed help with a label, Matt had achieved a freeing level of independence he'd never thought possible when he'd first been blinded. But it was still easier to have a guide when he was away from his regular routine. And as much as he hated it, he had to admit being out of his routine reminded him what a rut he'd fallen into. Cin had woken him up in more ways than one.

They turned right into a larger space. "Loose," a familiar voice called out over the low mutter of voices.

Matt closed his fingers on Jess's arm, and she stopped, letting Charlie come to them. She was smart, this girl.

"What the fuck, Loose?"

"Can we speak in private?"

"Interrogation rooms are right behind you."

Charlie brushed past them with a firm step. Down the hall, he closed the door to the room as Matt sat in the chair Jess indicated for him. The deep quiet after the cacophony of overlapping voices was a relief.

"Who are you?" Charlie asked, still standing by the door.

"Uh, Jessica Meyer? I work at the Daytona Beach Kennel Club and Poker Room?"

"Are you sure?" Charlie said, his tone dry.

Jess shifted on her seat beside him, her clothes rustling. In a stronger voice, she said, "Yes. I work with Mr. Loose whenever he needs help in the Poker Room. Sometimes I drive him home."

"Yeah," Charlie said, sourness leaking from the single word. "You want her to stay, Matt?"

Back to "Matt" for his name, but not in a good way. Smoothing the frown from his face, mind made up, Matt said, "Yes, she stays. Jessica works for me and she's privy to any conversation I have with you."

Jessica kept her mouth shut, reinforcing his confidence in her.

"So, Jessica, you're aware Matt here is out on bail for drug possession? That my team detained him last week for questioning in a drug trafficking case? That my partner, our team lead, was blown up in the same case and killed while Matt was present because for some reason my partner thought it was a good idea to befriend him?"

"I'm not—we're not . . ." Jessica said, her hand wafting air against Matt's cheek.

Some look or gesture, a visual cue, must have passed between them. This was a different man than the one who had addressed him with deference on Saturday afternoon. "What's changed, Charlie?"

"Excuse me?"

"Yesterday you were civil, when we spoke."

"I'm off-duty, Matt," he bit out. "But you're telling the clerk that we had an appointment, which we don't. Nice bluff. I've spent hours and hours going through security footage looking for the guy you mentioned. The one with the crooked nose. I'm tired. I'm broken-hearted over a friend, which is obviously not a problem for you, having only known her a day. You can only be here because you're trying to involve yourself when we both know you know nothing. Or nothing useful, anyway."

Okay, Matt understood this anger born from grief. It was the same anger burning in his gut right now. A scary rage when released. One he'd become friends with over the years. The monster under his bed. "Charlie," he said.

"Don't say you know," Charlie yelled. A bang that made Jess jump. Fist hitting door, Matt guessed, since drywall would've absorbed the punch a little. A deep breath before Charlie continued in a more controlled and quieter voice. "You don't know."

"I do know, Charlie. I watched my partner's eyes as an asshole swung a bat at his head and caved it in. His blood and brains and skull fragments were still on it when it hit me." Matt resisted raising his left hand to the unevenness of his skull across the occipital-parietal suture. The scar tissue there radiated a tingling, itchy heat across his scalp if rubbed. An older grief dug a claw into the deepest part of him and tried to pull itself up. He ignored it, focusing instead on Charlie's ragged breath as he sought control. Charlie'd be embarrassed now that he'd dropped his shield of professionalism in front of them. "Look, we caught you unprepared. I'm the guy, that guy, that your friend took home even though she shouldn't have. And then she died. And the last thing you got to talk to her about was a case."

"Oh," Jessica said.

"She asked if I was worried about her heart," Charlie said. "I told her I was worried about yours."

"With good reason," Matt said. "She's worth your loyalty."

"Was. Now it's *was*."

Cin's hand settled on the back of Matt's neck. Possessive. Solid.

And then gone.

Matt nodded.

Charlie cleared his throat. "So give it to me. Why are you here?"

"Maybe I remembered something that might help."

"You'd have called."

"Why'd you say you know Mr. Loose knows nothing," Jessica blurted, "when he must know something if he's actually involved in drug trafficking?"

Matt didn't stop the smile that rose through him.

"The powder we arrested him for is boric acid. With his help, we cleared him on the trafficking case."

When Jessica didn't say anything else, Matt figured she'd nodded and said, "I actually came to ask you to look at someone for a friend."

"I don't owe you any favors, Matt. And if you hadn't noticed, I'm a little bit angry with you."

"I didn't kill her, Charlie."

"I know. Doesn't matter. If you weren't with her, she'd have been in and out and gone by the time they loaded Shad."

"You've determined she wasn't the target?"

"Just tell me what you need, Matt."

"It's for me," Jess said.

Matt wished for the billionth time he could see.

"I have a family friend," she continued, "whose son is in juvie because of a bad cop."

"That's—"

"A true statement," Jessica said. "The school resource officer at Seabreeze is a perverted creep and has been for years. He started half-way through the year when I was a senior. Back then he was just a lurker, but now he's a leech."

"I'm sure—"

"He's been reported. He's been investigated. He's still there. He arrested David and filed a false report when David pushed back."

"I can look into it, but if he's been investigated, there's not much I can do."

"I'll wear a wire."

Charlie laughed. "You're jumping the gun a bit. This guy ever do anything to you?"

"No."

"You know anyone beside David that he's messed with?"

Matt sighed into the resulting silence.

Charlie came to the table and set something down. "Give me both their names. I'll look into it. Jessica, right?" Jessica pulled the pad to her and started to write. Charlie tapped the table in front of Matt. "I'm glad you didn't come here looking to crash the case, Matt. No offense, I know you were a cop, but no one wants you thinking you can help."

"Did you mean it?" Jessica said as soon as they were back in the stifling hot car, and she had started it up.

"How'd you know all that about David?"

"You met with Johnny. You took me inside one of his houses. If you were buying in, you'd have left me outside, I'm pretty sure."

"Wait. Back up. *One* of his houses?"

"He's got six," she said.

Matt felt out the AC vent and adjusted it so that more of the cold air was hitting him. "Buying in?"

"His women are exclusive. Six clients a year. Payment upfront for scheduled access. Emergencies extra."

"Emergencies? Sexual emergencies?"

"It's not all sexual."

Matt waved a hand in front of him. "Of course not, what was I thinking?"

"Where are we going?"

"Back to my place."

"So, did you mean it?"

Bracing himself as she backed out of the spot, he asked again, "How'd you know all that about David?"

"You met with Johnny," she said again. "You took me inside. After you asked for that laptop with those specifications? I figure you're trying to find out who killed those cops. The paper made it sound like you were a suspect."

"DSC heard that loud and clear, too."

"I pumped Susan for info. I thought maybe I could help."

"You,"—he tamped down his amusement—"pumped cookie-baking Susan for info."

"Yeah. And now that I know you were, uh, involved with one of the officers—"

"She's a detective. Lucinda Troy," he said, remembering the chemical cleaner smell of the bedroom carpet stuck in his nose, the heaviness in his chest, her bluntness regarding his panic attack right before she introduced herself to him.

"Was," Jessica said absently. She slowed down almost to a stop before accelerating again.

AFTER HE SEES Jessica and Matt out, Charlie goes straight to the restroom. He splashes cold water on his face, but then braces his hands on the counter and lets the water run down his temples and drip from his nose and chin. Cin places her hand on his back, but it sinks into him, and she jerks it back. She doesn't want to be inside Charlie. There's a noise in the hall and Charlie shakes himself, reaches for paper towels and dries his face, lobbing the crumpled paper into the trash by the time the door swings open and two patrol officers Cin knows come in.

On the way to his desk, Charlie fishes out the notepad. He has David's sheet up on his monitor in seconds. Cin sees Maria had been truthful. A stolen car arrest, remanded to his mom. And then a possession arrest at school by Officer Karl Thompson. Tapping Thompson's name in, Charlie's privy to the man's vitals and stats. He's an average officer with an average career. He's been working as the resource officer at Seabreeze for about five years, which matched with what Jessica said.

After entering his personal code, giving him a higher security level, Charlie finds the investigation, run by Detective Green in District one, a man Cin only knows from occasional department-wide meetings. It was a straight-forward look-see following a parent complaint. Three kids gave statements and were dismissed as troublemakers looking to stop a good cop from doing his job.

Charlie sighs and shuts down his computer. Grabbing his keys from the top of his desk, he calls out a general good-bye to the room. Several voices rise above the general din in answer. Cin rises with them, lets herself be tugged along in Charlie's wake.

Time seems to speed up when she lets go a little like this. And she knows Charlie. This'll be quite the ride if she can catch it. But in the rush of her speed drag down Williamson Boulevard as Charlie lead foots his accelerator to blow off steam, she lets go too much and swirls into the *there*, spinning . . .

MATT CLOSED his door and waited for the sound of Jessica's Acura. When she finally pulled away, he leaned his forehead against the door in what was becoming a familiar ritual. Even with the short nap, he was tired after the all-nighter and being out in the world in a way he wasn't much anymore.

A warmth spread across his back. Gripping his cane tighter, he waited for the intruder to close the space between them. The warmth gained weight in a slow, confusing build. Bands of it cradled his hips. The hairs on the back of his neck and along his arms rose. He lowered a hand to caress Cin's arm, as solid now as in life, her weight now pressing him closer to the cooler door.

No light came up to relieve his nothingness. Maybe that was all he was going to get. Those glimpses of his sister, of Ethan, of Cin, of himself. An ache tightened his chest. Cin's hands moved up, unerring. Warmth against the hurt. She held him there, trapped between her hands and her impossible being.

Vertigo slammed into him.

Head spinning, his belly tried to bolt.

The useless slide of his fingers clutching at the flat door made it worse. His pulse thumped in his ears before the hissing vacuum of an air lock filled them. Something yanked at him, at Cin. His polo split at the vee in the collar under Cin's grasping hands. Matt staggered back a step. Another mighty yank and she was gone, taking his shirt with her.

He fell backward into her absence.

A lifetime after the thunk of his head hitting the floor, Matt became aware of his own harsh pants for air. Propping himself up on one elbow, he leaned over and puked up the bile in his empty belly. He lay back down and breathed.

Something lay trapped beneath his thigh.

Jerking it free, he discovered the remains of his shirt.

Cold, heart beating way too fast, he fingered the edges of the ripped fabric.

C in tries to hold onto Matt. Her fingers scream and then there's nothing in them. For an instant, she thinks he's in the *there* with her, but then he's gone. And then she's...

...in the here.

A blonde woman is standing beside a plain steel exam table in what looks like a lab.

There are eight of the tables in the room, in two rows.

In the center of the woman's table is a cardboard cold box. Ziploc evidence bags are piled on either side of it. She reads something on the clipboard in her left hand, her right hand hovering over the bags before she plucks one up and compares the label on it to whatever's clipped to her board.

The bag contains small pieces of meat. Cin drifts closer. Two fingers. Medium black skin. No polish. Blunt. The woman places the bag of fingers into the box. Choosing another, she goes through the process again. There's a bag with part of a scalp and hair in it. Another with a fragment of a large bone, maybe part of a thigh or an upper arm.

Both feet are intact, one includes the ankle below the ragged flesh where it parted from the leg. The woman turns that bag as she lowers it into the box, to make it fit. The ankle lies exposed on its side. A terrible faintness consumes Cin on sight of the seagull tattoo that glides just above the bone, one wing dipping over the rounded front of the bone.

This is what's left of her.

MATT SWUNG his legs off the bed and sat up, still feeling the stretch of the polo across his chest. The grating rip of the fabric again filled his ears, and the eerie static hiss that was Cin being torn away from him. His questing fingers found the square clock box on his nightstand. It was only two in the morning, but he was done sleeping.

He pulled on sweats and his favorite NYPD tee, marked with a double stripe of fabric tape. His sneakers lived in the front right corner of the closet. His confiscated gun crossed his mind. He'd taken comfort in the familiar routine of strapping his holster on, the added weight that meant protection if he needed it. But it's not like he depended on it so much that he'd lock himself inside just because he didn't have it.

Letting himself out, Matt walked down the outside stairs with a hand on the rail and his cane tip sweeping the stair below to make sure nothing had been left on it. Towards the bottom, a soft heaviness blocked the swing of the cane's tip and a rumbled, questioning vocalization rose as his cane shifted. He reached down, hand open, and the big neighborhood cat arched its back into his palm with a scratchy growl of a purr. Hard muscles, short coat, ragged ear.

Matt slid his hand along its back and up the long tail with its crooked tip as the cat stood with its front paws next to his shoes and rubbed its head against his ankles. "Okay, babe," he said, scratching its backbone one more time before he straightened. He nudged it away with his foot and took the last two steps to the parking lot.

Three blocks took Matt down to ISB. Turning left, he walked about two miles, passing the echo of the mall, the flat sound between the speedway with its inane recorded greeting and One Daytona, the softer hush of Daytona State on the left, before he crossed a final intersection. Traffic was light, only an occasional car whooshed past. No pedestrians this time of the morning.

Lifting his hand, he waited for the way the clack of his cane changed at the Plexiglas tri-wall shelter of the bus stop. He let his fingers trail along the backside of the shelter. A car passed by on ISB. Veering left, he reached out with his left hand and snapped his fingers, listening for the deeper sound of the entrance alcove in the shallow wall of the store front he wanted. When Matt heard it, he knew the rubber mat laid out front would be a couple steps away. The cane tip found it.

He hovered before the door, listening to see if anyone was nearby. Certain he was alone, he dug the key from his pocket and let himself into Hagler Gym. Inside the family-owned boxing club, he locked the door and went straight to the warm-up area. He pulled a jump rope from the hooks on the wall and set to work.

A COUPLE OF HOURS LATER, Matt filched a bottle of water from the gym fridge and sat on the floor near the heavy bags, cane folded beside him, sweaty back to the wall while he drank it. A scratching at the door caught his attention just before the deadbolt flipped. A second later, someone entered with a soft curse, the rustling of plastic, and a thud. The hum of overhead lights sang from the ceiling above Matt's head.

"Fuck," Randy half-yelled. "You fucking scared me! Turn on a god-damned light when you come in."

Matt shrugged and finished his water.

Randy stomped to his office and back to the door a couple of times before he headed Matt's way. Stopping in front of him, he said, "You've had a rough one. Saw it in the papers."

Matt nodded.

Something soft hit his chest. His hand followed on auto and closed around fabric. Not a towel.

"Dry shirt. Bring it back clean."

"You know a Malcolm Ward, Randy?"

"Naw, don't know that name. Want me to ask around?"

"Quietly. Yeah. He's a drug dealer."

"You know our boxers aren't allowed anywhere near drugs or they're out."

"I know. That doesn't stop them from hearing things."

"True dat."

AT HOME, showered and dressed, and with still no sign of Cin, Matt ran through his emails. He checked the dark-web sites where he'd left a couple of covert messages for any word of Malcolm Ward or details on the Daytona drug route stops. His screen reader tripped up several times as he clicked through, impatient to get to anything useful. No messages.

He hesitated, his fingers hovering over the keyboard. His thoughts had been whirling for hours, seeking and rejecting keywords that might help him figure out if he was crazy or Cin truly existed. He'd stuffed his torn polo in the kitchen trash last night, but the brush of the textured fabric remained on his fingertips. Just thinking about it filled his ears again with the static hiss.

"Poltergeist," the screen reader said on the first line of the Google search page. Matt cringed inside. It read through the list as he hit return, return, return. Movie. Movie. Movie. He added the word "definition" and discovered Cin was definitely not a poltergeist. He moved on, eventually losing himself in the dense world of the paranormal internet until a fierce rapping on the door pulled his head up.

"Matt," Sebastian Ramirez called through the door before knocking hard again.

Was it that late already? Matt fingered the time on his Bradley watch. Sebastian was late, actually. "Coming," he yelled. He keyed out of the window he was in, slapped the laptop closed, and then slid it under the couch. Not ideal, but it would have to do.

He opened the door to Sebastian's fabric-softener and coffee scent.

The man filled the doorway like a concrete wall. "I've only got ninety minutes."

"Let me grab my stuff," Matt said, stepping off but leaving the door open. "I know what I want so that's plenty of time," he continued, retrieving his wallet and key from the kitchen drawer. He grabbed his folded cane off the counter and snapped it out to full length.

CIN'S somewhere between here and *there*, aware of her body bits burning in the crematorium, but also watching Matt finger the touchscreen of a souped-up iPad in Best Buy. The young salesclerk already has a MacBook in her arms. Matt's friend is hovering nearby.

"Is that really all that's left of her?"

Archer. Her brother's voice is a magnet. With no sensation of transition, Cin's standing right in front of him.

He's wrecked.

Somehow, she's missed everything that led to now. She missed that he was here already. Her chest aches with the need to touch him, hold him, hug him.

Charlie nods.

They're sitting in an office. The open notebook on Archer's lap is a picture book of urns. If Cin could slap it closed, she would. Her little brother shouldn't be here dealing with her death. He should be surfing or joy riding in the Civic, since it's his now. He doesn't need to mourn another Troy family death. They're cursed with death. No one's lived past fifty in the last hundred years. Neither of them have kids yet. Now she never will. None of the first cousins have any yet, either. Archer's got some fast living to do.

She pushes at Archer's chest, to get him up out of that chair, but she can't feel him, and he can't feel her, despite her hand sinking into him. Charlie frowns and looks around, though. Cin steps over to him. His head tilts back, like his gaze is traveling up her body, but he keeps going until his head's all the way back. He sighs at the ceiling, his gaze darting as if he's searching for something.

"You okay, man?" Archer mutters.

"Yeah. Just tired. There's been a few moments when I swear I can feel her, y'know? Like she's right next to me." Charlie lowers his head to glance over at Archer. "But then I remember she's gone."

"I started to text her this morning," Archer tells him. "Let her know I was coming to Daytona. Then I remembered why I was coming."

A short, plump white man in a dark suit and bright yellow cravat, reeking of Axe, bustles into the office. He puts an Amex gold card, a paper receipt with Loman's Funeral Home in large script at the top, and a fancy black pen on the desk in front of Archer before he goes around the desk to his swivel chair.

Cin eyes the gold card and yes, it has Archer's name on it.

Well, right on, little brother. That accounting degree is starting to pay off.

Archer picks up the pen.

A clicking sound fills her ears, fills her whole head.

When Cin shakes it, she loses the world.

And there is only nothing.

A century has passed.

Or maybe only seconds.

Warmth floods her.

She opens her eyes, only then knowing they were closed.

A dark-haired woman is sitting on a worn-out hardwood floor next to a ragged blue couch in a living room that seems awfully familiar.

She's holding a lighter in her hand, re-striking the flame, over and over.

"Friday," a man's voice calls out from behind Cin.

It's Jimmy Shad, in his kitchen. A countertop island separates the rooms. Over by the sink, he's slicing up something that looks like raw tuna on a round wooden cutting board. A whole mango, what smells like diced onions, and various bottles of condiments fill his workspace. It seems a little sophisticated for Cin's take on Jimmy as a person, but poke is a no-cook meal and he was dating a chef, so okay.

She turns her attention back to the couch and squints a little. Maybe the woman's the movie theater murder victim, but not having lived long enough to see a true photo of her, Cin can't tell.

Wait. She's undead . . . so why aren't they? Cin glances at Jimmy's front door. No way it survived the blast, yet there it is, intact.

Click. Click. Click.

"It's all set up," Jimmy says.

Click. Cli—ck.

A man's hand, scribbling an illegible signature across a digital checkout screen.

Matt's hand.

Click.

"Thank you, Mr. Loose," an older woman says, holding out Matt's Visa card.

Click.

Matt turns his hand palm up and after a split second of hesitation, the woman gets it and places the card in his hand.

Click.

Cin lifts her head and meets the gaze of the man with the crooked nose. He's standing back by the impulse buys, clicking through the colors of a four-color ballpoint pen while he waits for his turn at the register.

He sees her.

BLINDING bright light speared through the nothing of his vision, shattering it. Matt crunched his eyes shut, raising his hand to block it.

"Matt?" Sebastian said, his hand landing on Matt's shoulder. "You okay?"

"Yeah," Matt choked out. "Migraine."

Sebastian patted his shoulder in sympathy.

"My girlfriend gets those," the cashier said. Matt squinted at her as his vision came into focus. Brunette with streaks of gray. Mid-forties. Large dark brown eyes. Heart-shaped face. Best Buy cashier set-up exactly as he remembered it.

"To the right," Cin said, a mere echo in his head, but there. The anxiety he'd barely been aware of, that he had pushed into the background of his day, eased, the vague ache in his chest giving way.

Pressing his raised hand to his forehead, he turned his head to the right, as if in pain. He'd had plenty of practice. An impatient looking woman in a power suit and flats, a ream of paper and fresh ink cartridges in her hand.

"The man with the crooked nose," Cin said.

Matt shook his head.

Sebastian tugged him gently to the side, trying to get his feet moving. "Let's get you home, Matt."

Matt nodded. He stuffed his credit card into his pocket.

"He's right there," Cin insisted.

"Receipt's in the bag," the cashier said at the same time.

Sebastian reached past him to grab the laptop off the counter. "Come on, chief."

Matt reached out, let Sebastian place himself under his hand. About the same age as Matt, Sebastian was softer and thinner than Matt had imagined him. He had a slightly long, genuinely kind face, thin, firm lips, and a nose that was neither sharp nor doughy. Deep wrinkles followed his clean-shaven jawline and crinkled around his dark eyes. He reminded Matt of the men he'd met on a mission in Barcelona one sweltering afternoon.

Heat radiated off the black pavement of the Best Buy parking lot in shimmering waves. The strip center was huge, U-shaped. Big box stores. Michaels. Bed, Bath and Beyond. Dick's. Two women in shorts talked while their kids ran around them in circles, singing some song Matt couldn't decipher while he was busy seeing everything. Cars rolling down the aisles. Shoppers pushing carts. The high blue sky, streaked with jet trails. The green, green palms at the ends of the rows of parked cars. So many different colors of parked cars.

"Door," Sebastian said. Red four-door. Kia.

Matt automatically brushed his hand out back-first, down Sebastian's extended arm to the door handle. Only two years and already his blindness had changed his every habit. "Got it," he said.

A great guide, Sebastian continued on around the car without hesitation. Matt took the moment to savor the sky, the light.

"Matt," Cin said. "He's followed us. He's out by the entrance."

Sebastian's driver-side door opened. Matt tugged on the handle to the passenger door, sliding his gaze back to the store as he cracked the door open. A mother with her toddler on her hip walked out onto the sidewalk and stopped, looking at her phone.

"Close your eyes, Matt," Cin breathed.

Sebastian slammed his door.

The crooked nose man stood near the mother. He turned and ambled off in the direction of Bed, Bath, and Beyond. Matt opened his eyes to nothingness. The car started. A drop of sweat rolled down his temple. Irritated by all of it, he swiped it away. "I hate this, Cin," he muttered.

"You gettin' in?" Sebastian yelled too loud over the purr of the engine.

Matt jerked the door all the way open, and shuffle stepped over until he felt the edge of the frame against his calf before he lifted his leg to seat himself, raising a hand to the upper frame to keep from hitting his head. Being blind required so much energy. Several steps for every easy one he used to take. Cin was only reminding him of everything he'd lost.

And what was he supposed to do now? It's not like he could call Charlie and tell him he saw the crooked nose man at Best Buy, could they please request the security footage. And it could be entirely coincidental. After all, he, himself, had been both at the blast and here today.

"Where to," Sebastian said, pulling out of his parking spot. "Home or Urgent Care?"

Urgent Care? Oh, yeah. Migraine.

"You're sweating," Sebastian added.

"I'll be fine. Home's fine," he said.

And Cin was fine, or at least present, when he thought she was gone for good. He needed to be home where he could talk to her, see her, touch her.

———

CIN RISES to that in-between place on purpose, so she can watch both the crooked nose man and Matt, but the wind gusts. She spins, light-headed, and whatever she is now spreads—like a sheet on a clothesline, mayo on dry bread, oil in water. She tatters and tears and then shatters—

—into a billion points of light.

———

AT THE APARTMENT a few minutes later, Sebastian got out and then came around the car to give Matt the bag with the laptop in it and orient him in the right direction. "Looks like you have a visitor. There's a gorgeous blond headed our way with a determined stride."

Knowing Sebastian, Matt debated asking if it was a man or woman, but then Jessica said, "Hey, Mr. Loose."

He squared himself to her voice and footsteps. "Jess."

"I've got info on our case."

"Our case?"

"The Seabreeze resource officer."

"That's—"

"Our lead on clearing your name."

"Clearing your name?" Sebastian said.

"I'm not a suspect, Jessica, except in the eyes of Daytona State's admins."

"Then your duty as an experienced officer of the law."

"I'm not a cop anymore."

"Then as a private citizen with knowledge of a crime being committed."

Sebastian coughed out a laugh. "She's got you there, Matt."

Dropping his chin to his chest, Matt sighed.

"Detective Troy's killer, maybe," Jessica said, going for his solar plexus.

"I wish I could stay," Sebastian said. "Now I want to know what the hell y'all are talking about."

"Y'all?" Jessica said.

"My dad was from Tennessee," Sebastian said.

That explained so much about Sebastian that Matt had wondered about over the past two years. Why hadn't he asked? How much did he know about anyone he worked with? He knew Ed pretty well, but nothing personal. His favorite drink, what the women he hit on smelled and sounded like. Randy at the gym had kids. He searched his brain for any idea how many beyond several. He'd been so caught up in his own sorry self that he'd let others befriend him, rather than forging actual friendships. Is that what Jess was doing?

"You okay here?" Sebastian asked. "I gotta go."

"Yeah. Thanks, Sebby," Matt said, "for everything."

Matt and Jessica stood in silence for a few minutes, listening to

Sebastian shut his door and start the engine. Lifting the bag with the laptop, Matt sketched a wave in the direction of Sebastian's car as he pulled out.

"Seeing things fills up your head, doesn't it?" Jessica said.

"What?"

"Seeing things. It fills the time. I closed my eyes while he was leaving, and it seemed to take forever."

"What are you doing here?"

"I told you. I got something for the case."

Matt's cane swept the bottom step before he even realized they were walking. She had a way of making him forget the minutia of his blindness. "We don't have a case," he said, even as he started up the stairs with her in tow.

"Ed said I'm with you for as long as need be, and you said I was working for you."

He leaned his cane into the crook of his elbow and fished his keys from his front pants pocket. "I didn't—"

"I have the supplier."

The key scraped across the lock, missing it. "You what?"

To her credit, Jessica didn't try and take the key from him the way Lily would have, just leaned a little closer to him, spoke a little quieter. "I have the guy Officer Thompson gets his drugs from."

The knob turned and they both entered. Matt shut the door and locked it, waiting to feel Cin, to hear her snark about Jessica coming up with him. The refrigerator kicked on with a low buzzing hum. Cold air from the vent above the door dried the sweat on his neck and back, making it prickle. Pushing away from the door, Matt strode into the kitchen to place the laptop on the counter before he folded his cane. "This guy is willing to talk to the cops?"

"No. But he told Spider that Thompson's a perv, plus he's in the way. He doesn't like middlemen."

"And Spider knows this guy . . . how?"

"He attends church with Spider's mom. Spider built him a computer."

The sheer banality of most drug dealers' lives still astounded Matt. He rubbed his temple, feeling the headache he'd been pretending to have crouching there waiting to materialize. "So this guy would prefer to sell direct to the students Thompson is coercing."

"Oh. I guess?"

A sudden thought sent a bit of useless adrenaline shooting into his blood stream. "You didn't talk to this guy, did you?"

"No. Spider went to Seabreeze, too, a couple years ahead of me. I asked if he'd heard about Thompson, and he told me about this guy."

Matt's heart rate dropped after he heard "no". In a calmer voice, because he really did want to know, he said, "What do you propose we do with this information?"

"Tell that officer we talked to. Charlie?"

Matt expected Cin to pipe up, but she was still silent. There was a certain sense of hollowness that he only now recognized as maybe not emotion, but the lack of her. He'd felt it before, hadn't he? "We could make an anonymous call, maybe get someone else moving on it."

"Strength in numbers?"

"That's a good way to put it. What's the drug dealer's name?"

It's the scent of chicken that pulls Cin back together. Figures. Archer has plunked shredded chicken along with diced celery and onions into a roiling broth in her stock pot. Now he's ripping pieces from the biscuit dough he's rolled out on her kitchen counter and dropping them one by one into the broth.

Chicken and dumplings.

The dough is one they learned to make from scratch at their Mami's elbow from the time they were old enough to stand on the stool in her kitchen. Archer's humming tunelessly, something he's done forever. Even when he has a tune in his head, Cin would defy anyone to recognize it. He's totally tone deaf.

Her apartment is spotless. The orange and red blanket she inherited from Mami is folded on the couch. But the candles and magazines and all the other detritus of her life are gone. She wonders what he did with the tie rods for the Civic. In the bedroom, there are boxes stacked against the wall on the far side of the unmade bed. He's packed her clothes and books and knick-knacks away.

Cin runs her hand over the tape closing the top boxes. She's not sad, exactly. Maybe nostalgic. She thinks she's taking this un-death thing pretty well. Is this what's meant by eternal life? Where are the angels? She looks up. Nothing but ceiling. The same one she's studied for the past three years. She shakes her head. What is she thinking? That they've been waiting for her to notice them?

Archer's phone rings. He answers it absently. Cin drifts back in time to hear him say, "Ten-thirty. Tomoka. Yeah. Yeah, I got it."

He drops the last of the dough in the pot, gives it a stir with the long wooden spoon. Mami always cooked with wooden utensils, so Cin does, too. She doesn't know why, exactly, Mami used wood. Maybe it was all she could afford. Archer spills salt into his hand and rubs both hands together to transfer it into the pot. Spinning on his heel, he opens the fridge and pulls out an open bottle of red. He swipes at his eyes with his wrist and it's only then that Cin sees the tears tracking down his cheeks.

Pulling the cork, he raises it to the empty living room. "To you, Cin," he says and drinks straight from the bottle.

JESSICA SLAPPED her hand down on Matt's thigh and squeezed. Matt stilled his bouncing knee. How was this his life? How had a twenty-two-year-old-barely-a-woman talked him into staking out the supposed favored location of a small-time drug dealer to catch a cop? Cops bought illegal drugs all the time. They're only human after all. And they needed to sleep. Or stay awake. Or chill. Just like anyone else.

"There he is," Jess hissed.

"We're in the car, with the windows up, you can talk normally," Matt said, even though he wanted to say, "This is stupid."

And it was. During the day, they had left separate anonymous tips with DBPD at two different departments. He'd called Charlie, although it went straight to voicemail. Matt knew patience wasn't just a virtue in police work, it was required.

But by early evening, Cin was still both dead and AWOL. He wasn't any closer to Malcom Ward. And he'd had enough of picking through the audio minefield of the internet as a blind person. "Call Spider," he had said to Jessica. And now here they were—in the middle of the weed and seed area between Mason and North Street watching a guy named Centro conduct his business from a residential yard. Well, Jess was anyway. It wasn't quite nine, and a few minutes before, she'd reported the streetlights were just coming on. How dark were the yards past the pools of light now?

"Are you sure?" he said.

"Short, crew cut, pink high-tops, colored ink on both arms."

Spider had said Centro always wore pink high-tops. You'd think a drug dealer would want to be a little more low-key, but it's not like a defense lawyer couldn't shred any conviction hanging on pink high-tops, so it probably didn't matter. All that mattered was if he was actually holding drugs when arrested or could be proven part of a distribution ring, and Centro had never been convicted on possession or conspiracy. Petty theft, a couple of stolen rides, never drugs.

"We could spend every night for a month watching Centro," Jessica said. "Maybe we should be watching Thompson."

"One, we don't have the manpower. Two, parking for hours outside the school or near his house is going to get us noticed. And three, following anyone, let alone a paranoid cop, on the way to a drug drop is a lot harder than you probably think it is."

"And you don't think Centro's going to notice us? It could be days before Thompson shows up."

"Exactly," Matt said and opened his door.

"Where are you going?" Jessica said, alarm raising the pitch of her voice.

"Across the street, turn right, and how far down?"

"No, Mr. Loose—"

"How far?"

Her door opened.

"No," Matt barked. "Close your door and lock it. When I wave, come get me. How far?"

"Matt—"

He shut his door, trailed the back of his hand along the hood and around the front of the car. Cars meandered past in both directions. Houses lined the two-lane road. Centro and all the neighbors were no doubt already very aware of their presence.

The motor of the Acura's window purred, and Jessica's voice drifted out to him. "Fifty yards, I think."

He nodded. No cars. He crossed the street, turned right, and walked confidently, sweeping his cane in front of him, counting off fifty confident steps while trying to remain aware of his surroundings. The street itself was quiet, though the sound of cars on the larger roads around the neighborhood filtered through, along with random bits of conversation and music, the wind stirring around corners, through whatever passed as landscaping here, sweat and pits and fish and smoke off dirty grills and exhaust, always, here in central Daytona.

"Yo, man, you blind?" Young male. Too young for Centro.

"Looking for Centro," Matt said in passing.

"I know him," the boy said, and stifled a laugh.

Matt paused without turning. "Spider says I need to know him, too."

"You know Spider?" a man said from behind him, in the same vicinity as the boy.

"Yeah."

A car slowed as it approached them on Matt's right, headed towards Jessica.

"What he tell you?" the man said, sounding bored.

After it passed Matt, the car stopped. He turned to face the boy and man, as well as the back of the car. Light footsteps crossed in front of him. A low murmur of voices at the car and then it pulled away again.

Raising his voice a little, Matt said, "Kool-Aid sucks."

Laughter. Then the man said, "Kool-Aid does suck, man. What can I do you for? Painkillers? Weed? I got amp joints if you want both. Look like you need both."

"You Centro?"

"Probably, man, probably," the man said.

"I want to broker a deal."

"Broker? Big talk from some blind old cop."

"I'm not a cop," Matt said.

"You is so," the boy said, followed by "Ow! What you do that for?"

"You *are* so," probably Centro said. "Only he hain't, now, is he? Use the li'l bit of common sense the good Lord gave you. What kinda deal?"

Matt assumed the question was aimed at him. "The kind that stops Officer Thompson from buying anywhere in Daytona."

Another car approached, bass thumping.

"That all, man?" Centro said, pushing the sarcasm out thick enough for Matt to touch.

"Maybe the kind of deal that sees his job compromised," Matt said.

The car rolled on by.

"Why I want to do that?"

"To cut out the middleman."

"Shit, man, those kids not coming down here and why I go there? Get myself all arrested like."

Matt turned his head, listening to the canned laughter of a TV sitcom coming from the nearest house. Water running as someone washed up in the kitchen. This little street was a world away from the homes on John Anderson, but at the heart, they were the same. Meals, bodily pleasures, tit for tat. He couldn't ask about Malcolm Ward until Centro trusted him. "What do you need? If I can facilitate it, you take care of Thompson for me."

"My choice how I do that?"

"As long as no kids, animals, or innocents are harmed."

"I want my truck back."

The boy whoop whooped. "Ow," he said.

Matt rolled his eyes. "Who took it?"

"I TOOK IT, CIN," Archer says. "Too hard to pass up. Sold out, just like that." He tries to snap his fingers, but the wine has overwhelmed the chicken and dumplings in his system.

Cin's still not sure why he thinks he sold out. Yes, he wanted to work for himself, but working for a corporation isn't exactly a sin. Money is money. If someone's willing to give him a fat salary and benefits, why should he care? The money would give him a chance to enjoy his no doubt short Troy life and maybe put some aside so his future kids could skip the struggle and go straight past go. Maybe skipping the public servant role so many of the Troys had chosen would break the family curse and Archer would live to be ninety. That'd be something.

Cin leans into him, but he can't feel her the way Matt does. She's careful not to sink inside him, that'd be . . . yeah. No.

He staggers up.

Looks at his watch.

Nine-thirty, she sees.

"Coffee. Yep. Need coffee before I can drive."

Drive? No. No, no, nonono . . .

Cin stands right in front of him. "Turn, turn, turn," she shouts, knowing he can't hear her. She points. "The bed is that way."

Archer walks right into her.

Cin gets dragged along the tracks of his coffee thought train. He's smelling the coffee house he worked at during his summers in Melbourne, seeing the way the beans gleamed and fell against each other as he turned them in the roaster, his hands on the crank; and then she's looking at herself, there in his memory, mouth open wide as they laugh while Cin drives them down the beach, the wind whipping the tears from their eyes, followed by overwhelming sadness as he thinks of the Civic sitting pristine and shiny in her snug warehouse space down the street.

Cin gets a foot out and Archer leaves her standing in the hallway as he carries on into the kitchen.

The Civic. Ten-thirty. Tomoka Farms Road.

No, no, nononono . . .

"They're open twenty-four hours," Jessica said while she and Matt sat in her car in the parking lot of the Volusia Mall.

"Call them, see if Papa's around." Because if Matt was going to negotiate for the return of Centro's truck, he wasn't going to waste his breath on anyone who couldn't sign off on the deal.

Papa himself answered the phone. He didn't ask why Jessica needed to see him. But then young women calling during the night probably wasn't an unusual occurrence for a bail bondsman. Jessica was silent after she disconnected.

"What are you doing?" Matt asked.

"Grinning," Jessica said.

"Why?"

"So far this is way more interesting than a Monday night at the club."

"Let's try to keep it interesting and not dangerous," Matt said.

"Not dangerous, check," Jess said as she started the Acura back up. "I've never met a bail bondsman before."

"Really? With Spider around?"

"We're not . . . "

Apparently, his skeptical eyebrow lift still worked. She made a right onto ISB. The bail bondsman was out by the jail, several miles west of town. Being in the car was annoying on this road Matt knew so well on foot. He couldn't hear the way the sounds changed to judge where they were and, thoughts tumbling, he lost track of the intersections after the first green light. He did notice when they crossed under I-95. Which reminded him . . . "Why don't you listen to the radio?"

"Oh! Do you want it on?"

"No, I just want to know why you don't."

The hesitation was ever so brief. "No reason," she said.

And then Taylor Swift singing about the slam of screen doors drowned out the quiet engine and the hum of tires on pavement and the swoosh of passing cars and Matt had to work twice as hard to hear the sound of an impending crash.

<hr />

CIN'S CIVIC is red and while the best parts of her are hidden inside, she looks good under the stark bright light of the storage bay. She has a couple of gravel dings, but the paint that's left on her is shiny from Cin's efforts at buffing it. Archer inspects it from several different angles in the space that's just big enough for the car, Cin's portable lift, her workbench, and the twin full-size Craftsman toolboxes she uses. Used.

The combination of coffee and rising adrenaline has made Archer visually sober, but Cin knows whether he's capable of the reaction times he'll need to race her prize possession is anybody's guess. He spins Cin's keyring on his finger and squats to check the left front tire. Cin squats beside him, and he stiffens.

"Cin?" he says.

"Right here, baby brother."

He shakes his head. Lifting his hand to the back of his neck, he sighs, and then roughly slides it forward over the top of his head as he stands. "Fucking listen to me."

He spins away, throws her everyday keys onto the workbench, and snatches the Civic's key from the top of the toolbox next to it. Stalking around the car, he slams himself inside and cranks the engine up. Cin thinks he's going to screech out the second it roars into life, but he doesn't.

He takes a deep breath and lets the throaty growl run, warming the engine up, listening to the beauty of the note. As he pulls out of the tight space, Cin lets the music of the exhaust wash over her. It bounces off the walls. Damn, she's smooth. *I do good work.*

Archer stops and gets out to close and padlock the garage door.

Cin slips inside the Civic with him when he climbs back in.

She has no volume.

She can settle on his lap or beside him or in the back corner of the rear window without his notice.

Maybe she really is a ghost. What does that make Matt?

JESSICA'S VOICE wavered when she announced they'd arrived. A fact Matt had already deduced when she parked the car.

"Is this Super-Responsible Citizen Complex rearing its head again?" he said.

Her easy laugh made him smile. It was so girlish compared to the professional Card Room demeanor he was used to from her. Had he ever heard her laugh for real before yesterday? He couldn't remember and he was pretty sure he'd have remembered this particular laugh.

A woman's voice greeted them at the door. The building had an old musty smell covered by the fake flowery scent of an air freshener. A fan chugged away next to the door, but no air was moving.

"I'm Jessica. We're here to see Papa?" Jessica said.

Not fan. Dehumidifier.

Someone coughed at waist level. Seated along the front wall to Matt's left.

"Have a seat," the woman said.

"Thank you," Jessica said, but remained where they'd stopped a step from the door. Sensible. Matt relaxed, simply absorbing the atmosphere, the warmth of Jessica's skin against his palm, the way the hollow spot inside himself remained. Cin was still gone. Although she'd not been torn from him again, the loss was the same.

Had Cin followed the crooked nose man? Why had Matt not been able to see him until he closed his eyes? The memory of the vase in Lily's family room came to him again. A puzzle he had nearly dismissed at the time as just part of his new...what? Brain injury? Mental illness? That vase hadn't been there until he remembered it. But he didn't know the crooked nose man. So how accurate were the visuals Cin had showed him? Was it all just in his head?

A door opened, the whole room's attention shifting physically. "Robert," an effusive, warm, genderless voice said. "It's so good to see you."

Robert, presumably, stood from his chair by the wall and shuffled across the thin carpet.

A different door opened. "Jessica?" a deep-voiced man said. Ageless. "I'm Papa. Come on back."

Papa said nothing as they settled into chairs in his small office. Cigarette smoke, the air freshener, stale cologne, and, inexplicably, butterscotch. Papa closed the door and walked past them to sit behind his desk. "Detainee's name?"

"We're here on behalf of Gavin Smock," Jessica said.

"Centro? Has he been arrested?" The disbelief in Papa's tone spoke volumes about Centro's wiliness as a dealer.

"No, he'd like his truck back," Matt said. They had agreed in the car that he'd carry the conversation from here.

Papa threw something down on his desk. Matt's brain gave him an image of his NYPD Captain throwing his pen down, his face twisting at Matt's new proposal of some outlandish Navy-Intel-learned foolishness. "That fool knows he's not getting that truck back," Papa said. "He should've made sure his uncle showed up in court."

"He feels pretty sure you still have it."

"I do. It's a nice truck. I decided to keep it myself."

Matt tapped his folded cane on his knee. Should he make the same suggestion he'd made to Centro? Centro said Papa had refused him. "He wants to buy it back."

"Usually on the table until I sell what I've earned. Most bonds do their job, the detainees make their appearance," he said. "I don't actually end up with things like trucks or boats or houses very often."

Matt held his tongue. Jessica kept her mouth shut as well.

Papa sighed. "Centro owed on that truck, still. The title had a lien I paid off. It worked the same way it would have if I sold it on to anybody else. It's not personal."

Jessica shifted in her seat. Matt thought she'd break and say something, but she didn't.

Papa's chair squeaked, but he didn't stand.

Matt tilted his head in a considering pose and held it for a second before he spoke. "He'll pay you full value. Highest Kelley Blue Book plus ten percent for the trouble."

"It's a nice truck," Papa repeated.

"What else do you need to make it happen," Jessica said.

Matt closed his eyes. This was starting to feel like a never-ending series of devil's deals. All he wanted to know was how he could find Malcolm Ward. "You ever heard of Malcolm Ward?"

Papa stopped breathing. Until that moment, Matt hadn't registered the heavy rasp of his breath, but the room felt stuffed with cotton in its absence. "Malcolm Ward?"

"Yeah. Malcom Ward."

"You have him sweating, Mr. Loose," Jessica said with more cold in her voice than Matt had thought her capable of. Icicles. Glaciers.

"You sayin' Malcolm Ward got a hand in this deal?"

"Yes," Jessica said before Matt could speak.

A drawer in the desk slid open and then snicked close. Papa stood up and left by a back door, which had Matt recalculating his take on the room.

"Jess—"

"You ever see a Black man go pale, Mr. Loose?" Jessica said in a low voice.

"I need to know—"

Papa's returning footsteps, quick on the hard floor of the back hallway, shut Matt up.

"Got the title right here," Papa said as he entered.

His chair rolled back and groaned when he dropped back into it. Papers rustled. A loud click that must be a ballpoint.

"I don't—" think you understand, Matt tried to say, but now the distinct tread of high heels in the hallway stopped him again.

"Here you go, Papa," the warm voice from the reception area said.

"Here you go," Papa said, standing again. "The title signed over to Centro and a bill of sale for the DMV."

"That's not—" Matt said, at the same Jessica stood, her hand swinging back to hit his arm as she said, "Thank you. We'll take this back to Mr. Smock. Mr. Ward is certain to appreciate your cooperation. Mr. Loose, I have the paperwork in hand, shall we go?"

He could stop this charade right now, but should he? If he did, no doubt striking a deal with Papa would be ten times harder. If it stood, he wouldn't be stuck trying to make another bargain for God only knows what, but if Malcolm Ward heard about it...ah. He stood. "Thank you, uh, Papa, and you, too," he said, nodding to include the warm voice who had remained in the room. "I'll tell Centro he owes you what we discussed. He'll bring it when he comes to pick up the tuck."

"Thank you, sir," Papa said.

Matt took Jessica's elbow. They made their way out of the building, crossed the lot, and got into the car in silence. Matt waited until Jessica had made the left-hand turn across four lanes of traffic onto eastbound ISB to speak. "What happened to interesting, not dangerous?"

"You didn't tell me you were looking for Malcom Ward."

"Do you know Malcolm Ward?"

"No. But I'm thinking Ed does, which means you're on the hook to him for putting you onto Johnny Smith. Johnny Smith obviously didn't tell you and he sent you to Maria. Maria sent you to the police to complain about Thompson. They aren't going to do anything, so I gave you Centro. Centro won't cross Thompson up for Maria unless you get his truck back. Papa loves the truck. You should've seen his face. He wasn't going to give it up without extracting a favor until you mentioned Malcolm Ward's name. How many hands were you going to play, favor to favor, before anyone connected you to Ward?"

"You're angry."

"No shit, Sherlock."

Matt raised his open hands up in the air. "Why?"

"The way I've heard it, there is no Malcolm Ward."

"I want the person behind the name."

"Malcolm Ward isn't just one person."

Matt's brain blanked.

"Malcolm Ward is a bunch of people."

"My point," Matt finally managed, "stands. You just rang the dinner bell."

"You don't get to Malcolm Ward," Jessica said, hitting the accelerator hard. "Malcolm Ward gets to you."

ARCHER WEAVES on purpose on the dark two-lane from the warehouse, feeling out the Civic's steering and tire grip. Once out on Bellevue, he guns the engine and lets her out a little as he passes the airport and Speedway. He turns south on Williamson. Wider along this portion, it invites speeding, and Archer greets it with enthusiasm. He's a controlled risk taker.

But there's a dark edginess to him that Cin has never seen before. She doesn't like it. Brooding in the passenger seat, she tries to put her finger on what's so different about him, but that only makes her even more aware that her own difference in being is no longer something she can pretend to ignore.

It's odd not having any physicality. She's nothing but a point of view. In her head, she's sitting sideways with her leg tucked under her, but there's no sensation of it. No aches, no pressure, nothing brushing her skin, no itches or tickles or anything to shift to get more comfortable. All she is at the moment is . . . sight. Not with eyes, though, because she doesn't need to blink now, does she? This is the most aware she's been that she's existing without the boundaries of her body since she woke up this way. She's not drifting or watching or reacting, she's observing.

Archer is driving with focused purpose. He's hunched forward. His left hand is white-knuckled on the steering wheel at twelve o'clock and his right has a death-grip on the leather knob of her after-market shifter. He's a better driver than the last time she was his passenger, which, thinking back, was a long time ago. She always drove when they were together. There are shadows under his eyes and a new definition to his jaw, like he clenches it a lot these days. The changes in him are more than just learning she's bit the dust. Still, Cin wishes he knew she was right there beside him.

Past the Pavilion, a big outdoor mall in Port Orange, he slings the car in a hard right-hand turn onto four-lane Taylor Road. Cin watches the pavement disappear under the hood. He swerves around a Ford pick-up truck. But once they hit the place where Taylor narrows to two-lanes, he straightens himself up, drawing his shoulders back and down. He slows down to something that won't get him packed straight into a patrol car if he gets busted.

It's early in the evening for street racing, but Cin figures he'll head right at the upcoming light on Tomoka Farms Road, aiming at lovely, lonely Shunz Road near the landfill to burn off his angst against whoever he's meeting. Early means no spectators. Time to talk and drive and practice. It draws less attention, gives you a longer time to do your thing before the cops cruise out to check the hotspots.

Instead, he takes them left, the Civic's headlights spearing southbound through horse country. The first stretch has pockets of subdivisions, but the houses are mostly hidden behind the wooded roadside. Following an SUV loaded with kids, they pass Silver Sands Bridle Club on the left and a couple of miles later, the go-cart dirt track on the right before crossing Pioneer Trail at the Cabbage Patch, a biker bar technically in Samsula. The SUV slows to a crawl and then turns left onto a dirt drive.

Archer lays the accelerator down and they leave the parade of four or five cars Archer is now leading far behind. There are no streetlights out here. Cin scans the shoulder for deer eyes for a few minutes before she remembers there's nothing she can do to warn Archer if she sees any. After they cross Highway 44, they're left on what's now State Road 415 all by themselves, headed into the no man's land between New Smyrna Beach and Deltona.

They go five miles before Archer slows down, looking along the left-hand side. He brakes hard after passing two tall oaks standing guard on a white pipe gate. He performs a mild reverse drop to get off the road as headlights appear behind them. He throws the Civic into park and opens his door but leaves the engine running. A later-model GTE pulls in behind the Civic.

The driver, white, male, dark beard, maybe six foot two and broad in a white tee shirt and blue jeans, meets Archer between the two cars. "Archer," he says, engulfing him in a fierce hug. "I'm sorry to hear about your sister."

Archer hugs him back and then pats the man on the back with both hands and they separate. The man holds a key out. "You know where, right?"

Archer nods.

The man slaps his shoulder, gets back into his GTE, and leaves in the direction he came from. Not even aware of having followed Archer out to the end of the drive, Cin memorizes the license plate. Archer waits until the GTE's taillights disappear around the curve in the road before he moves. He doesn't unlock the gate with the key, though. Instead, he slides into the Civic and backs onto the road. Cin curls up again in the passenger seat, and they keep heading south at a slower pace than before.

"Where we going, little brother?" The sound of her own voice makes Cin feel more there, even if he can't hear her.

Eventually he turns left onto a paved road, somewhere close to Lake Ashby. She's never been down this particular road before. There's a variety of houses set on large, heavily wooded lots. Nothing organized. A small barn here and there. The Civic's lights reflect off the eyes of two horses grazing next to a three-board fence where Archer doglegs right onto a dirt road.

They bump along over washboard ruts and patches of softer sand for maybe a half-mile before he leans forward, watching the right-hand side of the road. A knee-high white painted post marks a driveway consisting of two ruts with scraggly weeds growing between them. It leads to a conventional beige-colored brick ranch. There's a security light on a pole burning in the yard. No lights on inside.

Archer turns the engine off but makes no move to get out of the car. He stares at the house through the windshield. Cin knows this look. It's his I'm-scared-but-I'm-going-to-do-it-anyway face. He hits the steering wheel with the palms of both hands and throws his door open. The crumbling concrete pavers that form a sort of sidewalk to the front door crunch under his Allen Edmonds.

The house smells moldy and damp inside. Archer's footsteps clack across the chipped and scuffed tile floor. It's been a while since anyone has lived here, but there's furniture in the great room and the kitchen off to the right has a blender and coffeemaker and all the other accoutrements of daily living. There's a crusty knife lying next to the sink and a dishtowel crumpled on the counter.

Archer goes left down a short hall to the first bedroom on the right. Carpeted, double bed, Star Wars posters, a dresser with a dinosaur lamp. The closet is one of those where the two doors slide open from either side. He slides the far door open, throws a striped blanket out into the room, and then drops to his knees to scrabble at the carpet. Cin stands between his calves to see what he's doing. He tugs the corner of the carpet up from against the side wall and then folds it back on itself, revealing the tile floor underneath. Fingering some sort of catch that clicks when he triggers it, he frees a tile and sets it atop the folded carpet.

The hidden cubby swallows his arm past his elbow. He pulls out a plastic wrapped white brick. Cin's vision blitzes. She swings her fists out to pound his back, but they just sink into him. He twists to place the brick off to one side behind him and reaches for another.

Cin falls into him.

Panic.

Her breath hitches in Archer's chest. She feels the bead of sweat that slides down his temple. His jumble of thoughts are too tangled to sort. A blue and white boat at a dock, the cool stem of a martini glass in her hand, a sharp thrill of pleasure as a hand slides over her bare back, flashes of tanned skin, blue eyes, blonde highlights, now a surfboard under her feet, leaning into the crush of the wave, bone-deep need, sand grinding into her knees, skin sliding over wet skin—

Cin jerks back, phases out, spinning, hits the wall, rebounds.

Heat rushes up, steam enveloping her.

Arms catch her under the onslaught of hot water.

THE HOT SLIDE of slick skin on his was Matt's only warning before heated flesh hit his chest, his thighs. Even as he closed his arms in grapple mode, he stepped back in the shower, trying to balance, registering only "female" before they were falling.

By the time his shoulder hit the side of the tub, he understood, was already wrapping his arms tighter around Cin, keeping his body between her and the hard porcelain as he landed. His head snapped back, but her arms broke loose from around his neck, bouncing open just enough for her forearms to protect him from yet another concussion.

"Oh, God, oh, God," Cin cried out, looking down at him, their legs bent and tangled. "Are you okay?"

Matt took stock, but the only thing that hurt was his heart. "I was so worried for you, that maybe you were gone altogether."

She buried her face in his neck and he moved one hand up to press her head closer to him. Hot water spilled over them. Whole droplets of water caught in her wild hair. Steam rose to fog the high, dark window above. Rivulets ran down the old green tile from the leak below the shower head. The streaming water broke in bright flashes of light over her firm, naked body.

His left shin was pressed hard against the end of the tub, his foot turned at an awkward angle. He shifted and they untangled themselves in a slow-motion slide of skin that did nothing to quell his body's growing reaction to her despite—

Despite what? These even stranger circumstances?

The fact that she couldn't possibly be here? Like this?

Cin rose until she was straddling him, breaking him from his thoughts.

He watched her studying him, her firm hands traveling over his biceps and caressing his collarbone. With his feet planted flat in the tub, Matt's bent legs supported her as the water hit her back and shoulders, cascading off her hair to run over and between her breasts, pearling on her nipples.

If she wasn't real, Matt didn't know what was anymore.

He smoothed his hands up the long runway of her thighs.

She finally met his gaze.

"Not that I'm complaining," he said, "but you don't usually show up nude. Are you—?" But she wasn't all right, he already knew that.

"Oh, God," she whispered. "I need you."

He took that as permission to let go, give in to his own need for her. He slid a hand between them.

She spread her fingers wide on his chest, flexing them when his thumb brushed her swollen clit, circled it. She leaned forward, reaching down with one hand until her fingers closed on him. He groaned, his hips lifting, his head pressing back, his eyes closing to a comforting true darkness before she drove down on him and they both gasped.

She circled her hips...and an involuntary groan of pleasure escaped him. Opening his eyes to meet her heated gaze, he grasped her hips and held her there a long moment before she lifted to let him take the lead. Eyes locked, they set up a bruising rhythm that had her clenching around him in minutes, her fingers clamped around his wrists. Her back arched.

Tilting her head back, she raised her face to the heavens, her wet hair swinging. "Matt," she shouted. "Matt!"

He stopped.

Body drawn taut above him, Cin shuddered, hanging on the very edge. Matt's heart pounded, near breaking, with the unbearable suddenness of her, his raw desperation for her, the hard, hot sway of her under his hands. She took a gulping breath.

"Cin," he whispered.

His blood surged. He closed his fingers hard around her waist, held her down tight against the driving piston of his hips, no space between them, until she cried out with wave after wave of orgasmic pleasure, and he let go of all control to find his own release with an uncontained shout.

She fell forward, tucking her head under his chin. He tucked his nose into her hair and breathed in deep, inhaling her scent. Rocking against her, Matt brought her down as easy as he could. Her heart beat against his chest, making him aware of his own pulse beating in his throat.

The water was cooling.

"My legs may never be the same again," he said.

She pulled away enough to turn her head and kiss him thoroughly.

Once they were dried off, they crawled into Matt's bed and lay side-by-side under the ceiling fan. After a while, Cin rolled over, lifting her hand to prop her head up. When Matt glanced over, she had somehow acquired a black tank and loose black boxers. He reached over and fingered the cotton strap crossing her shoulder. She shrugged.

"Do I need clothes for this conversation?" he asked.

She traced circles along his belly, eyes downcast. "It's my brother."

"I'll take that as a yes," he said and got up.

He pulled on sweats and an old Navy tee and lay back down facing her.

CHAPTER
SEVENTEEN

M att sat on the couch with a cup of coffee warming his hands and lap. The normal before dawn weekday morning sounds drifted from all around him. TVs, singing pipes, an occasional raised voice, door slams, the idling of engines as his neighbors waited to pull out onto Fentress. It occurred to him that his hearing was normal, or near enough.

He thought of his sneakers waiting for him, the jump ropes at the gym. The heavy bag. The not-quite-satisfying feel of beating the shit out of something that doesn't hit back. In the dream that woke him, he'd been running into a gentle breeze on a deserted beach, just the right amount of crisp in the air, calves starting to burn, long, easy stride. That perfect combination of factors when you have some time to think you could run forever and be happy. But then he'd seen something offshore, a roiling of the water, a glimpse of hair, of sleek skin, silver glint of the sun. He'd stopped, raising his hand to block the sun, seen the bat coming at him too late, and woken gasping and drenched to blindness and an empty bed.

The TV shut off in the apartment next to him. The door slammed. The usual heavy tread past his own door. Now was when the morning zinging around Matt's bubble of stillness would begin to taper off until the next rush at eight. His cell phone buzzed on the coffee table. He didn't need to listen to Lily's text to know what it would say. Something along the lines of not appreciating radio silence and would he still be getting Ethan after baseball practice tonight.

After months of dreams in which he only drifted through an endless abyss listening to sounds he couldn't quite identify, he didn't even care that this dream ended with the bat coming at him. He really missed full-out running. And baseball. God, to swing a bat at a ball again, the stretch of his shoulders, twist of his hips. His brain gave him the sound of the bat connecting with bone instead of ball.

He raised his cup and sipped, forcing himself to think instead about the pounding of his cleats across hard-packed clay down the baseline, the way that sounded, the drop of his hip, the press into the slide, the judder of his upper foot across the hard ground, the flex of his ankle, and the punch of the base when he hit home under the tag. The coffee ran down his throat like Cin's warm hand down his neck and spread its fingers into his cold chest.

He didn't know what he'd thought, but confirming Cin's brother's name was Archer and that her private service, no details, was being handled by Lohman Funeral Home by a simple check of her obituary had left him chilled. He was either psychic now or she was somehow actually existing beyond the grave.

Had he been assuming he'd had a psychotic break, one he could live with? Guessed it was Charlie at the door that first day home? Tore his own shirt in some black-out moment of grief? Imagined the crooked nose man that Charlie hadn't found on the security tapes? Was knowing things he couldn't have possibly known better? Had she told him Archer's name and he just didn't remember? Had Charlie mentioned Lohman's?

Unless he called her, it'd be hours before Jessica showed up to ferry him to Centro's to deliver the bill of sale Papa had given them. Matt would hold the title, though, until Centro completed his task of dragging Officer Thompson down where he belonged. There was a lot of gray in police work, even with minors, but Thompson hadn't merely crossed the line, he'd obliterated it. Matt wouldn't regret siccing Centro on him. The phone buzzed again. He ignored it. Lily would insist he see someone. Try to shut him down.

He could call Jess. Ask her to drive him out to the address at Lake Ashby. See what there was to see. And if it matched everything Cin had told him? He shuddered. He couldn't do that to Jessica. One, who knew what Archer was mixed up in? Maybe someone taking advantage of his trip to Daytona. Maybe something worse. Two, he didn't want to tell her about Cin. She'd tell Ed, who'd tell Lily. And three, asking more favors of her would keep her in on his pursuit of Malcolm Ward and he wanted her out of all that, especially if what she said about Malcom Ward not being just one person was true.

He took another long drink of his coffee, pushing down the thought of adding a bit of whiskey warmth to it. Cin said the name Malcolm Ward had been totally unknown, not even a whisper around the department, before Jimmy Shad spilled. If bail bondsman Papa was any indication, though, Ward had to have brushed up against law enforcement to have made such an impression on the sucker fish. Cin had a hard time believing the name wasn't floating around in jailhouse conversation often enough to catch a guard's ear and Matt agreed with her.

Unless Malcolm Ward was new in town. In which case, they again agreed, the idea of Malcolm Ward as a "bunch" of people, a gang, was patently false advertising. Someone, a special-ops meth-head freak, according to Jimmy, came in hard and fast and put a scare in everyone.

And getting ahold of a bomb within hours of Jimmy Shad uttering the name in a holding cell was also hard and fast work. And maybe misleading. Jimmy's girlfriend had been killed hours, maybe even a full day before Jimmy blabbed. But pursuing Ward for whatever answers he could get was still Matt's only lead to the person responsible for Cin's death. And following up on Cin's revelations about her brother the only way of discovering if he was truly haunted or suffering from psychosis.

Fuck.

Fingering his watch, Matt decided a quarter till seven was too early to call Jess considering how late they'd been out. A second later, he leaned forward anyway and scooped the phone up.

Jess answered on the first ring. "Hey, boss!" she said, sounding wide awake.

His planned *I'm sorry I woke you* morphed into *I'm not your boss* into *I need a ride . . .*

"Matt?"

He shook himself. "What you doing?"

"Winding down."

She couldn't have been home before midnight, let alone in bed. Would she have what, gone on a run already? To work out? "What?"

"I just got home from work."

His mind blanked.

After a moment, she said, "Ed called and said he didn't mean it."

"Mean what?"

"That I was yours as long as you needed. If I want to get paid, I need to come in. And so do you. He said he likes to say the right thing, but doing the right thing is a different thing altogether."

A huff of breath escaped him. Lily said he was a huff-dragon, but he wasn't usually so aware of it as at that moment. "I—" he said and got stuck again. "Are you drunk?"

"Only buzzed. It helps me sleep during the day," she said in a more serious tone. "I won't get drunk. Not when I know Malcom Ward might show up anytime."

He took a deep breath in through his nose. Letting it seep out between his pursed lips, he was faintly surprised when the remaining iciness in his chest unfurled and melted at the thought that because she was buzzed, he wouldn't have to ride out to the house this morning. Was he that afraid of knowing?

"Did something happen already?" Jessica said into his silence. "Do you need me?"

In his mood, the way she said *do you need me,* like she really needed him to say yes, broke his heart a little. It was getting a real workout these days. "No," he said instead, finally processing her declaration. "If Malcolm Ward's coming, it's my name he's got. They've got. Whatever. I just wanted to tell you to go back to work. I don't want you anywhere close to this."

"Someone killed your girlfriend, Mr. Loose. And I thought—I don't know what I thought when I thought I could help, but that cop,

Charlie, he pissed me off when he said no one wanted your help. And not because you can't help, but because you're blind. They don't know who you are."

His heart bumped hard, which was dumb, all things considered, but he was having a rough morning. "And you do?"

"I'm still invisible at the club. I hear things. Ed's *thorough* in his hiring process, and Spider and I, y'know. Spider sometimes tells me things."

"You didn't answer the question," he pointed out.

"You were some kinda hotshot detective in New York. And before that you worked Naval Intelligence. You were a Marine. That has to mean something, doesn't it? That you still have a lot of skills even though you're blind?"

That was more than he thought Ed would know, let alone a club staffer. Or Spider. But okay. He could deal. "Keep that last to yourself, will you?" he said. "I don't want anyone to know I'm blind."

"Ha-ha," she said. "Now, what do you need? Because no matter how many skills you have, you *are* blind, and you do need help and since I pulled the trigger on Malcolm Ward, I'm going to help you."

He sighed. "It doesn't have anything to do with what we're doing."

"Shoot, Mr. Loose."

"You know, I don't mind when you call me Matt."

"It just feels right, or it doesn't, Matt," she said, drawing out his name. "Now quit stalling and tell me."

"A friend wanted me to check out a house near Lake Ashby."

"For you?"

"I really only need a drive-by and you're good with description, so—"

"I can totally do that right this sec. What's the address? And where's Lake Ashby?"

"I looked that part up. New Smyrna Beach, but we don't have to go right now."

"Drive by, right? I can do that online."

Matt let his tired head fall back on the couch. Google Earth or even Zillow. Realtor.com. Apps so visual, he hadn't even thought of them.

He gave her the address and within seconds, she had the house pulled up.

It matched, right down to the crumbling pavers.

"What do you think? Is it for rent or something?"

"How far away is it from civilization?" he asked just to say something until his guts thawed out.

She hummed while she looked. "Nearest grocery store is Sav-a-Lot. Almost ten miles."

"Ten miles!"

She laughed. "Anything else?"

Matt said his thank-yous and let Jess go to bed and sat there blankly until his stomach growled. Shoving himself up off the couch, he made himself some eggs and choked them down. The touch on his nape as he rinsed his plate startled him. "Say something first," he snapped.

Someone pounded on his door. He jumped, his heart leaping, and dropped the plate in the sink. A glass under it burst. "Fuck!"

Storming to the door, he started to wrench it open before he thought of Malcolm Ward, before he thought of being blind, before he thought anything at all. Berating himself, he jerked his hand off the third bolt and laid it flat on the door's cool surface. "Who's there?"

"Charlie Stance."

He should've known. A cop was the last person he needed in his face right now.

He opened the door and stepped back in invitation. Charlie took it, bringing a whiff of leather and Rem gun oil in with him. Matt swung the door shut and turned on his heel, going back into the kitchen to clean up his mess.

"Stop," Charlie barked.

Matt froze.

"There's a piece of glass on the floor, six inches northeast of your toes."

Matt grinned. Seriously? "Northeast?" he mocked.

"I've been looking at maps all morning. Sue me."

"It's like seven-thirty, how long you been up?"

"I don't know. Want me to get that off the floor?"

"Please. Coffee?"

When Charlie gave the all-clear, Matt waved him off, telling him to grab a stool at the counter, and went about setting the sink to rights and making the coffee. Once it was brewing, he leaned on the countertop. "Last time I saw you, you were pretty pissed."

"Yeah. Sorry about that. Cin never crossed that line before, taking a suspect home. Shit, bringing you to a crime scene, and then bringing you to another the next day? She wasn't—"

Matt couldn't tell if he was searching for what he wanted to say or had stopped himself from saying something he shouldn't. "She wasn't what?"

Charlie took a quick breath, a sniff. "She wasn't like that. She was, but she wasn't. Not in that situation. Bars, parties, sure, of course, but not from work—you were different. I don't know why."

Matt shrugged, a movement he'd practiced over and over, with Ethan critiquing every lift of his shoulders, until he'd re-learned casual rather than calculated. It was all in the facial expression.

"I don't know why," Cin whispered, the words trailing from one ear and behind him to the other, "either."

"I'm trustworthy," Matt said in answer to them both, voice firm, maybe a little too loud, but fuck it. "I'm loyal. And I don't pick people up at bars and parties and such. Cin was the first woman I slept with in four years. And the first person I spent a whole night with since I was divorced six years ago. I have a very bad tendency to fall hard and fast when I fall, and I admit it," —he stood up straight and held his arms out wide— "I fell. For the second time in my life, I fell." Heart aching, he let go of his self-consciousness, so she would know. "Right there in her living room." Lowering his arms, he pressed his fists into the countertop to anchor himself. "Howl to the moon, kill anyone who got in my way, mate for life hard. For Lucinda Troy. Black?"

Silence. Charlie wasn't even breathing.

"Want your coffee black?" Matt said in the same intense tone he'd ended on.

"Black. Yeah," Charlie finally said.

Matt spun away and then slammed the cabinet door a little too hard getting the mugs down. He took a deep breath and slowed himself down before he ended up burning himself or spilling the coffee. When he placed Charlie's mug in front of him, Charlie said, "I'm sorry."

Cin pressed her hand to Matt's heart.

Matt placed his hand over hers, pressing the fading remnant of her touch into his skin. He sipped his coffee. Burned his tongue. Of course. Because today was turning into a winner. "So why were you looking at maps?"

C harlie blew on his coffee.

Stalling while he decided whether or not to trust Matt before answering, Matt guessed. But Charlie hadn't come by just to say hello, and he'd gotten personal, so there must be some reason Matt and the maps Charlie had been studying were connected by an early morning visit. Charlie wanted something from him.

"We've been correlating the cell phone data for Jimmy Shad, his girlfriend, Lucinda, the death investigator, and our forensics head, Miller." Carefully worded trust then, rather than asking Matt where he was on some random day and what he might've known when. "We're looking at contacts, texts, GPS, notes, matching them with anything we think might be relevant off their work and personal computers."

"You're trying to narrow down the target."

"Yeah. Shad was already dead. So was the bomb a warning to cops from this Malcolm Ward, who none of us had heard of until Shad prompted us to poll our CIs? Or was it meant for a specific target?"

"You're assuming Cin or Miller."

"Yeah. Either past history or something specifically related to Shad."

"Or related to the investigation into his girlfriend's murder, as a distraction, since Cin and Miller were both involved there, too, right? What about the death investigator? Was he working the girlfriend's case, too?"

Charlie made a non-committal noise deep in his throat and then gulped coffee to cover it.

"Why not Detective Perez?"

"What do you know about Perez?" Charlie said, suspicion creeping into his tone.

"Only what was in the paper. So why couldn't he have been the target?"

"No reason, really, there's just better ones to go after Cin or Miller."

"But they're leading to dead ends, or you wouldn't be here."

"Bingo," Cin whispered, and Matt really wanted to tell her to stop doing that, to just speak up since no one else could hear her. He jotted the request on his mental notebook for later and swept his hand through the air in response instead. "Gnat," he said.

"They're annoying," Charlie agreed.

"So?"

Silence. A thumping started from the far end of the outside hallway coming towards them and resolved into a thunder of footsteps when they passed his door before a chorus of laughter and a young boy yelling, "I beat you, Jamal, I beat you," as they clattered down the stairs, the others throwing garbled insults at each other.

"Charlie," Matt said. "I can't see you if you forgot. Silence is annoying to a blind man. Can you please just get to the reason that you're here? Because I know it wasn't to apologize."

"Shad's girlfriend and Cin both had calls from the same burner phone in the days before they died."

The reasonable assumption would be Jimmy Shad as the caller, but Charlie was here so . . . "Not Shad's?"

"It pinged seven different towers in the two days after Shad died. All local. No data after the time Shad's drug drop was supposed to have occurred."

"Coincidence?"

"Could be."

Could be coincidence. Could still be Shad's phone if someone took it from him before or after he died. Could be someone else altogether. "Days before they died? This person call Cin before Shad spilled about Malcolm Ward?"

"Yeah. After your arrest, but before we jerked him off the beach to talk to you."

Still could've been Shad's. Matt sipped his coffee. He, himself, had been in jail, his apartment already searched, which removed him from suspicion. "What does this have to do with me?"

"The last number it called was a pre-paid registered to your girl. The conversation lasted a full twenty-one minutes."

"My girl?"

"Jessica Meyers."

"I told you before, she's not my girl."

"You said she works for you."

Matt dropped his chin on his chest on a big exhale, suddenly remembering her question when they got back into the car at the station, *"Did you mean it?"* The question he'd ignored because of course he didn't mean it. He'd only said it to put Charlie at ease and keep Jessica in the room as a witness. But between last night, their plans for this afternoon, and the call he'd made to her this morning, he'd practically cemented the idea. "Yeah. Okay."

"So what do you know about her?"

She worked for a man with a lot of connections. She knew how a certain Daytona pimp operated. And, for cash, her boyfriend was happy to set up both legal and illegal operators with military-grade computers and software they didn't want advertised. "What makes you think you can trust me?"

"You told me not five minutes ago that you're trustworthy."

"You did," Cin said, sounding almost normal.

Matt lifted his head so Charlie wouldn't miss his purposeful eye roll.

"Look, we made a mistake," Charlie said. "Give me a break here. It was boric acid. You have a resume from hell. Cin was good at reading people, and she took you home. I know you're one of the good guys. I can't help being pissed at you over Cin, I just am. You know what the last thing she said to me was?" Without waiting for Matt to answer, Charlie plowed on. "'I'm keeping him.' That's what she said. My wife said I should stop being such an ass to you, that considering who you are, you might be an asset, so I'm giving that a go. Before I go round this girl up to ask her what she knows, what can you tell me?"

"What's the pre-pay number registered to her?"

Charlie read it off.

Matt punched through his contacts on his cell and let the voice over on Jessica's contact information confirm it was different from Charlie's number.

"That's a pain in the ass," Charlie said.

"The voiceover or the different number?"

"Both."

"Tell me about it." Matt sipped his coffee, trying to decide what to share. "Jessica works as a floater for administration at the club. She's quick and she listens. She knows a lot about both sides, the greyhound track, and the Poker Room."

"How clean is the club, really?"

"Not once have I overheard a drug deal or talk of one while working there. Ed runs a clean operation. Patrons are like customers anywhere. They could be anybody. Sometimes they do things you'd rather they didn't. If you're asking if Malcolm Ward frequents the club, not that I know of. If you're asking if Jessica is connected to Malcolm Ward, I'd have to say no. Not unless she's a high-clearance operative with a lot of training in deception, and I kind of doubt that."

"What makes you think I'm asking about Malcolm Ward?"

"Seriously?"

"What's Jessica do for you?"

"If we're slammed or have a private party where they've shifted all the tables and added a bar set-up, she acts as my assistant. We also have a private arrangement that allows me a little more personal freedom. She mostly drives me here and there when the bus is too inconvenient, or I need something from someplace I don't normally go."

"Like a known prostitute's house?"

Matt took another sip of coffee and waited.

"There's nothing solid on Officer Thompson," Charlie said. "Her kid'll be out next week. Nothing I can do."

"I saw the report he pulled up," Cin offered in that hushed elsewhere voice that made all the hairs in Matt's ears rise up. Was she drifting away on him? "No witnesses. All hearsay."

Charlie cleared his throat. "Has she offered you drugs?"

The prostitute? "No, Maria has not offered me drugs," he said, only half-focused as he tested that feeing in his chest he was beginning to think of as a bond to Cin. Still there.

"Jessica Meyers," Charlie said, in an exasperated tone that snapped Matt's attention back to him. "Has she offered you drugs?"

"No," Matt said, even as he thought about the remainder of the fattie hidden in his safe along with the military-grade laptop. Spider had, but Spider wasn't Jess, was he?

"You know any of Jessica's friends?"

"Only the ones at the club. They seem clean enough."

"Clean enough?"

"Yeah," Matt said and took his cup to the sink. "Clean enough."

"You going to object when I bring Jess in?"

Matt shrugged in a very deliberate way. Not calculated.

"You leaving the question of Malcom Ward alone?"

"Yes," Matt lied because, unlike Jessica, he *had* been a high-level operative with a lot of training behind him and lied very well, thank you very much. He opened his hand palm-up on the counter. "You done with your coffee?"

"I don't believe you," Charlie said, placing the mug on Matt's palm.

Closing his other hand over it, Matt turned away to wash up. "I did the same looking you did and came up empty, now I'm leaving it to you. But since you're here, my money's on Ward for that explosion, or you'd be off bothering someone else."

"And you don't think Jessica is mixed up with Ward or had any hand in Cin's murder."

If Charlie knew Ward was a group and not a "him", he wasn't letting Matt in on it. "No," Matt said. "Call it my gut, but no." That didn't mean she wasn't unknowingly connected though. "Was there only one call from that number to hers?"

"Yes."

"Ask her, then. Maybe it'll stand out to her. Ask her why she even has a pre-paid."

"I will," Charlie said.

Matt shut the faucet off and stuck Charlie's mug next to his on a folded dishtowel to dry. Charlie took his cue and stood up, patting his pockets from the sound of it. They met at the front door and Matt grabbed the edge as Charlie swung it open and stepped out into the breezeway. "You find the crooked nose man?"

"No," Charlie said. "Did you know Doug Moultrie's a real person dealing beachside?"

Matt forced an easy laugh. What were the chances that there would actually be someone besides himself named Doug Moultrie in Daytona Beach *and* connected to Jimmy Shad? "You gotta be kidding me."

"Nope. No pictures of him, but a beach-rat CI confirmed it."

To deflect, Matt said, "Will you tell me what Jess says to you?"

"Maybe." Charlie moved off, two steps down the stairs before he spoke again. "Hey, we're scattering Cin's ashes tomorrow night at Tom Renick Park in Ormond. Seven. We're paddling out, but . . ."

"I'll be there," Matt said. "Thanks for telling me."

As soon as the door was locked back up, he said, "Cin?"

"I'm here," she said, still breathy.

"Can you, you know, be here?"

She didn't answer and didn't touch him until he was back in the kitchen, swiping his phone from the counter. The slide of her hand on his.

CIN CAN'T FORCE the change although she's not inside him. Part of her is watching Charlie leave. She's beginning to think she's affected by people's thoughts of her and how focused they are at any given moment. But that doesn't explain how she saw Jimmy Shad. She has no idea what that was. Was she asleep? Can she dream?

She has no great desire to be physical right now. She's languid, more and more in-between. Shouldn't she be raring to hunt down this new clue? But it seems hopeless.

"It's not hopeless," Matt says, scrolling back down his contacts, the phone's annoying voiceover keeping track for him.

Did she say that out loud?

Charlie is talking to Swinkler while he sits in his car in the parking lot, giving him Jessica's address so they can meet there to detain her.

"Charlie's going now," Cin says. "To get Jessica."

Matt hits call. Jessica doesn't answer on the first or second or fourth ring. Long enough for Cin to wonder why Matt doesn't use Siri. Jessica's voicemail kicks in. Matt ends the call and calls back. No answer. Cin thinks hard of Jessica's apartment, of being inside her. Something tugs at her. Dread swirls her guts. Can it work this way around? Cin's scared, but then she does it anyway, lets go, thinking hard on Jessica, her hands sluicing water from skin that's not hers, turning her face up to the hot water. She spreads out, lets the insistent tug take her, too late recognizing that it's been pulling at her for hours.

Light blinds her as she's pulled apart.

"Yeah," Jessica croaked into the receiver on the third call, her voice muzzy and thick.

"That cop is on his way to pick you up," Matt said. "Get out right now. Call me when you're in your car."

"What?"

Using the voice of command that used to be such a part of him, Matt said, "Move! Now!"

A fumbling of fabric and the call cut off.

He stalked into the living room, aware of the bruising grip he had on the phone and the hollow spot in his chest that was Cin's sudden absence, and paced, waiting for Jessica's return call.

Heat spills through Cin.

Click.

Now Jimmy Shad is layering sliced avocado onto slices of toast. He's in his own, undamaged kitchen, the living room where she'd stood over his dead body just beyond.

The woman on his blue couch with a metal lighter in her hand rolls the striker. A small flame leaps up. She claps the cover closed. Click. Flips it open again.

"I'll protect you," Jimmy says.

Flame rises from the lighter.

Click goes the cover on the lighter.

The sound rings through Cin's head, almost painful.

"How are you gonna do that, Jimmy?" the woman says. "Chris is dead. And now Doug—"

"It'll work, Francis," Jimmy says, squeezing lime over the toast.

Francis Duncan, Jimmy's girlfriend. Torn to pieces in the field near the Cobb theater. Someone coughs behind Cin. She spins in that swimming through air way that seems familiar from some place deep inside her and yet not.

Click.

The crooked nose man lifts his chin at her in greeting.

The click that comes next is distorted.

The crooked nose man wavers in place.

Darkness crowds into Cin's peripheral vision.

Is she fainting?

She falls into the sudden swirl of everything and her vision greys out.

The next click is crisp.

The crooked nose man slides the nose of another bullet into the magazine in his hand. He's sitting on the edge of a queen bed.

Click.

"That's a lot of bullets," her brother says.

Hands in the pockets of his gray slacks, Archer's leaning against the white frame of an open bathroom door at the back of an older, very plain motel room. A double. Facing him, the crooked nose man is sitting on the bed closest to the front of the room, his back to the closed curtains of a large picture window. "I like to be prepared," the man says without looking up.

"Hey," she says.

They both ignore her.

Archer seems comfortable enough with the man. Not nervous, anyway. Cin goes to walk between them, but the air is thick.

This isn't real time. This is past time. Like Jimmy Shad and his ahi poke and avocado toast.

What the fuck?

"What is he like, the Zeta?" Archer says.

"Just a guy who likes cars. I suggest you stick to the paperwork and don't ask any personal questions."

Archer nods. "I didn't expect to be handling sales paperwork for a drug dealer."

Cin's non-existent stomach drops.

The crooked nose man's face tightens, but he says, "Gang lords need cars, too."

He slides another bullet in the magazine.

Cin's nothing, and nowhere, before she can hear the next click.

"TALL GIRL COMIN' in, blonde," Randy said. "Oop, she's seen you and is comin' this way."

The boxing gym's parking lot would conceal Jessica's car for a while, just until Matt could speak to her, find out first what was going on. He was sitting beside Randy on one of the four chairs lined up against the wall outside Randy's office. The whap of jump ropes hitting the thin mats of the warm-up area and the steady thud of someone working a heavy bag filled the gym and concealed Jessica's approach until the last few feet. He stood to meet her waft of ginger and vanilla scent, an improvement on the gym's usual body odor, cheap cologne, and chalk.

"What's going on?" she said.

"This is Randy," Matt said. "Randy, Jessica."

"Hi," Randy said as Jessica said, "Okay."

"Is your phone still on?" Matt asked Jessica, knowing that if Charlie called her, she'd have to lie to him.

Bad enough that she had apparently already been compromised before he dragged her into this mess. No need to make it worse. And what he was asking wouldn't hurt in case Charlie tried to get a court order to track her down. Dead officers had a way of speeding everything up.

"Of course, why?"

"Turn it off."

"Why?"

"Jessica, please, just turn it off."

"Okay, okay," she said, her voice fading a bit as she rooted around in her purse.

"Is that a pre-paid phone?"

"No."

"Do you own a pre-paid or have you ever had a contract with a pre-pay company? Cingular or something?"

"No, why?"

"Did you know Lucinda Troy?"

"The cop you . . . no. I didn't know her."

"What about Jimmy Shad or Francis Duncan?"

"The guy who . . . no. I didn't know him. And I don't know anyone named Francis. I don't understand."

"An unregistered pre-paid called Francis Duncan, who was Shad's girlfriend, and Cin in the days before they were killed and then a pre-paid registered to you a couple of days afterward."

"Are you asking if I used a burner to call myself on a phone I don't own?"

A laugh burst from Randy. "No, he's asking if you know a killer," he blurted.

"How am I supposed to know that?"

"We gotta get out of here," Matt said, fingering his watch. "I'll explain, but not here. We good, Randy?"

"Yeah, man. All good here. I'll let you know if anything pops."

"Be careful."

"Always."

Jessica followed Matt to the glass doors at the front of the gym before she slid past him, jabbing her elbow into his side in offering. He took her arm. After parking her car in a larger lot further down ISB, Matt let his Daytona Votran app talk them to the bus stop, knowing they'd be cutting it close.

"Bus," Jessica said and hurried them a bit. After they were seated midway down the aisle, she leaned closer to him. "Where are we going?"

"Beachside," Matt said and shut up again. His thoughts kept tumbling over themselves. Jimmy Shad and Cin's brother and Malcolm Ward and Papa's reaction to that name, and Johnny Smith's nondescript voice saying, *"What I've got is a problem needs solving."* And Jessica's on its heels, *"Malcolm Ward is a bunch of people."* Round and round. His gut wanted to fit it all together, but logically, it was three separate things.

Just because Jimmy had tangled with Malcolm Ward didn't mean Archer was—there were lots of dealers in the world and Archer lived in Melbourne, anyway. And, yeah, what Matt wanted from Johnny Smith's mysterious call girl, Jane Johnson, was the head honcho behind the name Malcolm Ward, but getting Officer Thompson canned was only a means to that end and didn't mean Thompson or for that matter, his dealer Centro, were connected to Malcolm Ward themselves.

But Jessica.

Jessica, who had been sent to him by Ed, who himself claimed no knowledge of Malcolm Ward, now had two strikes against her. She'd been the only one willing to say anything at all about Malcolm Ward, which made her either too innocent for her own good or more knowledgeable than anyone else.

And someone who had called two people immediately connected to Jimmy Shad before all three were killed, called a phone registered to her, a coincidence that stunk like fish guts rotting in the sun. Then again, if he was condemning by association, he actually knew Jimmy and Cin and Jessica personally, so did he also know the caller? Was that person a murderer?

The bus driver's intercom broke Matt's zone with the announcement that they were nearing the transfer station. On some level he trusted Jessica because he'd never zoned-out on the bus before. But what the hell? What was she mixed up in? "You ever been on the city bus before?" he asked her as the doors opened and they stood.

"No. Are we transferring? What do I look for?"

"Just follow me."

It felt good, being somewhere he could guide Jessica for once. On the number one, he concentrated on his surroundings—listened to the conversations around him, picked out every scent he could identify, held onto the slick vinyl of the seat back in front of him as the thumb on his other hand slid over a nub on his cane handle over and over again.

Matt's phone started buzzing just as the bus dipped, airbrakes hissing, and slowed at Bellair Plaza. He and Jessica stood without speaking. Swinging his cane, Matt made his way off the bus. He walked south a few steps, listening to the small group of exiting passengers flow around him and away.

The doors closed.

"Why are we here?" Jessica said from his right, a step behind him.

The bus roared off in a wash of hot exhaust that overwhelmed the sticky salt air.

"I need to see a man about a horse," Matt said as he inserted an earbud from the pair looped over his neck and checked his phone. Charlie had left a voicemail, asking him to call in an overly polite voice.

"What?" Jessica said.

It was hot. Matt jerked the earbud free and let it drop on his chest. Now he wished he'd bothered to pair the new jawbone Spider had brought him that was sitting in his safe. His shirt was already damp, and he wished he had shorts on rather than jeans. It was three short blocks south on A1A to Lily's street, where there wasn't a sidewalk or any shade to be had on the two long blocks west to Lily's house, which sat dead center on the barrier island between the beach and the river.

He hesitated, thinking about everything Cin had told him, thinking about Charlie's determination.

"Which way?" Jessica asked.

It would be a risk, especially now, but he was at a dead end, and he couldn't let Charlie blunder in blind. Suppressing the rise of a smile at that twisted thought, he said, "The ocean. I want you to tell me what you see. Can we cross?"

They waited for one car to pull out of the plaza before Jessica said, "Go."

"I need coffee," she said, complaining for the first time since he'd woken her, although she came along as he started walking to the next intersection. "I don't understand why I can't just tell the cops I don't know anything. I don't."

"Are we alone?"

"Yeah. No one else sweating out here but us."

"You can tell them that. You will, when we let Charlie catch up. I just needed to know first."

"Know what?"

"If you've been lying to me."

She stopped. The pavement radiated heat. Cars rushed by. Matt swiped at the annoying trickle of sweat from his temple as he kept walking.

The volume of her voice built as she caught up again. "What would I have lied about?"

"How much you know about Malcolm Ward."

"The only thing I know is that Mr. Ward knows a lot of people."

"Then why does everyone claim to not know Mr. Ward?" Matt said, putting verbal air quotes on "Mister".

"Have you ever seen the movie *Fight Club*?"

Matt rolled his eyes before he could stop himself.

"You should put your glasses on, it's bright out here," she said. "What's the first rule of Fight Club?"

"No one talks about Fight Club. Only they all do."

"Only to each other. Malcom Ward only talks to Malcolm Ward. All the rest is rumor."

"So either you're a member of fight club or—"

"I'm a young, blonde, white girl working a service industry job. I hear things because people assume I'm planning my next manicure or deciding if I should buy the red dress or the blue. And yeah, I'm not a philosopher, but I am ambitious. When I said I'd be running the Kennel Club one day, I meant it. So I listen."

"And by 'people', you mean Ed?"

The cars were slowing, an engine idled ahead of him. He swept his cane and hit the bottom of the pole at the crosswalk.

"Ed's smart," Jessica said. "He sees things. He knows what I'm capable of, he relies on me, so, no, I don't mean Ed. I mean customers and those boys in the kennel who think I don't speak Spanish."

Matt had negotiated this intersection across A1A a thousand times when he'd lived with Lily. He reached out and smacked the indicator button, then turned on his heel into the lank ocean breeze drifting across four lanes of traffic.

"The dealers yapping in the break room, the other students when I was at DSC, my mom's friends," Jess continued to rant, putting an interesting tone of disgust on "friends". "The people that show up to the clubs I go to and the employees working them—"

"Spider and his clients?"

Her energy flagged, an anchor that tugged him around in a quarter turn to face her. Sweat rolled down his back. A car slowed and turned right, its driver no doubt taking a good look at blind guy and blondie stalled on the sidewalk.

After a beat, she said, "Yeah, maybe. We can walk."

He raised his right arm, blocking her. A car rolled through the crosswalk, making a California right turn.

"Asshole," Jessica yelled after it, then in the next breath said, "How'd you know?"

"I was listening," Matt said.

They walked across the road, motors growling on either side, waves of heat buffeting them, a man saying, "Walk, Katie," as a giggle erupted ahead of them.

"Is he blind, Daddy?" a little girl said.

Someone, maybe "Daddy," hushed her.

"I am," Matt said as they passed.

"See, Daddy," the girl squealed, her voice now behind Matt. "He is blind! Why doesn't he have a dog?"

"Why *don't* you have a dog," Jessica asked.

"Spider?" Matt said, staying on track.

"He's not a bad guy."

He steered her right, finding the curb of the smaller street, a beach access, in front of him, sounding clear of immediate cars. He stepped out into the road. "But he's not picky about who he works for, is he?"

Nothing.

They crossed and continued south.

"How well do you know him, Jess?"

"You mean, would he buy a pre-paid and register it to me?"

They passed the odd-sounding downward tunnel into the underground parking of the Aliki Forum. Voices from inside carried out onto the street.

"Exactly."

"Couldn't anybody?"

"The likelihood of it would be pretty small, in my opinion."

"You can be very dry when you try."

"Jess."

"Yes, okay? He'd be capable of that. But he's not a bad guy."

"Is he a part of fight club?"

"No." She took a deep breath. "I don't know. I don't think so."

"Then how, exactly, do you know anything about Malcolm Ward except rumor?"

She touched his arm, and they stopped. A car crossed in front of them and turned out onto A1A. Parking lot. Condos and time-shares lined this stretch of A1A.

"Maybe it was a wrong number."

"The call to your phone? No. It lasted twenty minutes. It wasn't a wrong number."

"Okay," she said, and he matched her stride as she took off again.

Matt listened to the sultry roll of small breakers from the beach across the vacant lot they were passing. The hot, still air lay heavy on his skin.

"There's a group that comes into the club every month," she said. "To bet on horse racing. Mostly guys, a few girls. A few months ago, we were short servers, so I was helping Melissa until someone could come in. One of the girls was pretty toasty early on. Another girl took her to the restroom, and I followed them after a few minutes to make sure they weren't going to lay a line out in the open or anything. They, um, they were in a stall together. Together together. And while she was, uh, prepping Toasty, the second girl said something like, 'you don't get blasted with Malcolm Ward, no matter who it is' which sounded weird and then she laid out exactly what was expected of Toasty and made sure she, um, knew the ins and outs of her . . . duty."

"See? Talking about fight club where anyone could walk in."

"I crept in. They didn't know I was there. They were, uh, done talking by the time someone else walked in and I turned the water on. That woman banged on their door on the way by and then started singing real loud so she wouldn't have to listen to them getting it on and then a bunch of poker players came in all at once and I left."

"And?"

"And then I listened for the name and when I didn't hear it again, I talked to Ed, who played dumb, and eventually I asked Spider if he had ever heard of Malcolm Ward, and he laid a hand over my mouth and said he'd tell me what he knew later, but all he ever said was that the less I knew the better and that was all he actually knew about them."

"Them."

"Yeah. Them."

"The Island Crown is right in front of us, yeah?"

"Yeah."

"We're going in," he told her.

He walked like he belonged, sweeping Jessica with him through the tiled lobby and past the waterfall.

On the fourth floor, Unit 402 faced the street. Jessica knocked and a few minutes, knocked again.

"Can I help you," a woman's strident voice called out from near the elevator, and Matt startled, turning hard to face the threat, reining himself back even as it happened.

"I'm sorry," the woman said.

He held up a hand and waved her apology off.

"That's my unit you're knocking at."

"Thank you," Matt said. "We must've gotten the number wrong."

"Maybe I can help. Who are you looking for?"

"My friend Doug. Doug Moultrie?"

CHAPTER
TWENTY

"Who's Doug Moultrie?" Jessica asked as they made their way back down to A1A.

"Someone I'm hoping knows Malcolm Ward." Because chances were, drug-dealing Doug Moultrie had somehow stolen a false identity Matt set up years ago. And connected the name to Matt through Jimmy Shad. While he'd found out in the field that the saying "truth is stranger than fiction" was a saying for a reason, it still seemed unlikely that Jimmy Shad would tag him with that name without a better reason than he thought his blind professor would skate on a murder charge and he happened to know his address. It was too big for coincidence. Maybe he needed to be grateful Jimmy hadn't also parked the murder weapon with him. It would've been easy to do.

"If you really want to meet Malcom Ward, we should take that bill of sale to Centro now and tell him how we got it. Between Papa and Centro, all we'll have to do is sit in front of your apartment until Ward comes for you."

"Everyone's afraid of Ward," Matt said, letting his irritation show. "If no one speaks the big bad's name out loud, waiting for them to show up could take weeks. I want to get to the guy in charge, and there must be one, before they come looking for me." He sliced his hand through the air. "Scratch that. I don't even care if I get to him. I just want to know if he killed Cin, or if he knows who did."

"Cin's short for Lucinda?"

"Spelled with a 'C', not an 'S'."

"Only a guy would think otherwise," Jessica said, in a tone that said "duh".

Good to know she could act her age.

"Where are we going now?" she said.

"To get you some coffee at the boardwalk."

"That's oddly specific. You like the boardwalk?"

"I like the grill there," he said as they pushed through the condo building's front door to the shady portico in front. He'd expected that after he'd been injured, he'd lose the condo, but it'd been the only direct lead he had. Now he had to go with his indirect resources and ask for help from his ex-employer to find Moultrie, as much as he hated doing it.

"Let's wait here," Jessica said, side-stepping away from the door. "I'll get us an Uber."

"I don't trust them."

"That's because you're old and blind," she said absently.

"Watch it, blondie," Matt said, but followed her a few yards down the sidewalk.

After a bit of silence, Jessica said, "Okay. Three minutes away. How about this? The sooner we get that bill of sale to Centro, the sooner he'll get started on tarring and feathering Officer Thompson and the sooner Maria will give you the big bad."

Tarring and feathering? God help him. "One, that house wasn't Centro's and that address on the bill of sale isn't Centro's either, I guarantee it. We'll wait and see Centro at our meeting this afternoon. Two, Maria isn't going to divulge anything she might know about Malcolm Ward. She only promised me a contact who does know someone involved with Ward. If Ward's a group, not a person, I have no idea what that means now. Or how long it'll take."

Jessica took a noisy breath.

Someone opened the door behind them and walked by fast with a short, "Hey," thrown in their direction.

"Jogger," Jessica said. "I thought Maria was a sure thing."

"No such thing, babe."

"Babe?"

"Just a figure of speech." He folded his cane. "Do you remember what you overheard, specifically, about the rules of fight club?"

"Not really. They were kinda general, what you'd expect from any kind of gang or whatever in Daytona. The women are mostly afterthoughts, only there because the guys pay their rent or buy their drugs. Keep your lips zipped unless there's body parts involved. Don't get involved in business. Don't talk to the cops."

"But getting blasted is a no with Malcolm Ward."

"In public, anyway."

Matt nodded. He needed a foothold, some info that would get him more info until he could trigger an avalanche. This was the most frustrating point of any investigation. He had a few odd-shaped puzzle pieces that refused to fit together. And God only knew if they all belonged to the same puzzle.

"Our car," Jessica said, leaning away from him, probably to wave at the driver.

The ride down A1A was short. The driver dropped them on Main Street as close to the boardwalk as he could get. "More construction," Jessica said. "Half the city's under construction right now."

Sweating, they loitered surfside near the Mardi Gras Arcade for a few minutes until the place opened, literally. There were no front walls, the whole arcade lay open to the beach once the employees rolled the garage doors up. They placed their orders at the grill a few minutes before nine and then sat on bar stools at the long counter, listening to the sounds of the boardwalk coming to life. Matt sat sideways, trying not to let the half-sensed movement of the morning walkers at his back bother him.

After the coffee arrived and Jessica had, apparently, somehow negotiated a bit of it without burning her tongue, she groaned in pleasure. "How did I live without coffee in college?"

Amusement caught Matt by surprise. He'd smiled more in the past two and half weeks than in the last two years together. "Late to the party?"

"I was. I've missed coffee my entire life and didn't know it." She leaned closer to him and lowered her voice. "Should I call Spider and ask?"

About the pre-paid phone, she didn't have to say. She could. No way Charlie would be worried yet about finding her, though he was probably already on his way to the club to see if she was there. "Would you be able to tell if he lied to you about it?"

"I don't know anymore, but I do know Spider wouldn't kill anyone. He's just a techie. He's good at it. Maybe he bought the phone for someone else, a client."

"And his clients might kill someone?"

"That's not what I said," she hissed before straightening up in her seat.

"I suspect he doesn't discriminate in his choice of client as long as money's involved," Matt said, aware he was forcing her to lean in again to hear him. "He'd definitely be aware that phone could be traced back to you. At the very least, that puts you in an awkward situation should his client ever be investigated. At worst, you could be in danger from someone looking to eliminate connections to themselves."

"Am I in danger?"

"Only if whoever used that phone actually has anything to do with Cin's—" His throat closed up. He swallowed, but it didn't help.

"Yeah, okay," she said, her voice drawing away again. "Food."

"Pancakes," the man who'd taken their order said and set Jessica's plate down seconds before Matt's. "And scrambled eggs, home fries, whole wheat toast. Anything else I can do you for?"

"Yeah." Matt fingered the edge of his warmed plate. "Tom working today?"

"I'm Tom."

"I'm a bass player, heard there's a place on Noble and you're the guy can get me a gig there."

"You know Henry?" Tom said, suspicion creeping into his tone, but lucky for Matt, this was the right Tom and if the pass phrase wasn't current, at least Tom still knew the reply.

"Adams? He's an old friend. Saw him last Tuesday."

"Hey, can I get more coffee here?" A raised Jersey voice said from a few stools down.

"Yeah, man," Tom said and left to get the coffee.

"You play bass?" Jessica said.

"I do," Matt lied. "Where are my home fries?"

"On the right," she said. "At three o'clock if that actually helps."

"It does. Eggs?"

"Nine, toast twelve. Butter in a little dish in front of your right hand."

"It's a private club," Tom said as he arrived back in front of Matt. "By invitation only."

"My favorite kind. The patrons always tip in Jacksons."

"Give me your number and I'll text you the info."

Matt rattled off his cell number. "They call me Slider at the clubs."

"Is that true about the tips?" Jessica said when Tom walked off again.

"Sometimes," Matt said and stuffed a torn off piece of toast in his mouth. The company was at least going to find out he was still breathing, if they cared. Whether they would help him or not, he didn't know.

"I should learn to play an instrument. Why Slider?"

He'd earned that codename for sliding into base too hot more than once, but almost always pulling off the win. That last time, which landed him here in Daytona relying on his sister, not so much. Matt shrugged. How did one explain slippery as hell in bass player terms?

He worked through his breakfast for a few minutes, voices and music and the persistent rhythms of the electronic games of the arcade swirling around their little bubble of silence. Eating wasn't the pleasure it had been before unless he was somewhere quiet and relaxed enough to savor the flavors and smells and textures. That thought took him right back to Cin feeding him cold chicken and grapes.

Matt set his fork down and pushed his plate a couple of inches away in favor of wrapping both hands around his coffee.

Jessica said, "So how do we go about finding Doug Moultrie?"

"He'll be around."

"Maybe he moved."

"Jimmy Shad mentioned him. He's still around."

"And if he's not?"

"I'm going to have to start shouting."

Jessica gasped dramatically. "Shout 'Fire' in a crowded theater? What happened to interesting, not dangerous?"

"You ran that rule over with a tank last night and that call to your non-existent phone shot what was left point-blank with a double-barrel shotgun this morning," he said with a wave of his left hand.

She caught it in the air. "I'm scared," she said in a totally different tone.

He squeezed her hand. "You should be," he said.

CIN BECOMES aware of a rising light.

It's like she's rising with it.

But it takes her a hot minute to make sense of what she's seeing.

It's her apartment from the ceiling.

She's looking down on Archer, who's stretched out on the couch staring up at her. An open laptop sits on his chest. His chest rises and then slowly falls. He blinks and then his gaze wanders the ceiling.

Cin's comfortable. Weightless. She just exists in the moment with him for a while.

Eventually he sits up. Catching the laptop in one hand, he sets it on the coffee table and then scratches his hands through his buzz-cut hair.

She wonders what he did with the drugs.

He reaches out and traces his finger over the laptop's track pad to wake the screen. In the photo open on it, his arm is thrown over the shoulder of a handsome white man. They both like blonds apparently because there's no mistaking this man is Archer's. He's the same one she'd seen inside Archer's head when she fell into him. The overwhelming passion she'd felt had been for him. Tall, freckles, sloping shoulders to powerful arms, very GQ with a surfer core. In tee shirts, jeans with belts, dress shoes and dark sunglasses, they're styling at a marina in front of a spotless electric blue corvette.

Well, baby brother, you could've told me.

He drags the photo onto his desktop, and then scrolls through his photo roll. He pulls up one of him and Cin together on the beach and drags it over, too, before exiting out of his photos. He enlarges both photos and situates them side-by-side. "Carlos, this is my sis Lucinda. Cin, this is Carlos," he mutters. "Y'all better not be meeting anytime soon, but Cin, if it's a thing, if you can, could you watch out for him? Just until I can get him back. Keep him safe."

Shit. How many times had she put her grandmother in this very position? Had Mami heard her? Was she still here somewhere? Then again, it's not like Cin's seeing other ghosts like her everywhere, just the crooked nose man and she's not sure that's what he is. So maybe there really is still a heaven with angels and her family watching out for them and she just hasn't gotten there yet.

Archer's phone is next to the laptop. When he picks it up, Cin thinks about sitting next to him and then she is. She feels more like herself than when she's swimming through air. The movement focuses her. What does Archer mean, until he can get Carlos back?

He checks his texts and then his recent calls and then his voicemail before he clunks the phone back down. "Shit," he says, and curls his arms over his head. "Shit. Shit."

Cin places a hand on his back. It sinks.

Tilting over until he's lying on his side on the couch, Archer pulls his legs up so that he's a little ball of misery. She's not going to get any answers by asking questions. And there's no guarantee she'll get any answers by doing the only thing she can.

She does it anyway.

He's thinking about her, wondering what to wear to the beach for the funeral, then wondering when the call will come, what if he gets stopped for speeding or something and the drugs are found, what if they want him to come when he's supposed to be at the beach, fuck that, Carlos is alive and Cin is dead, how can she be dead, how can she, but how can she not, the Troys are cursed after all, and if they have kids, they can be Carlos's kids, he doesn't care if it's him, doesn't want it to be him unless he can forbid them to be brave and heroic.

They'd need to be selfish cowards like him who believe in superstition and curses and think of themselves first, only that didn't work out, did it, because here he is, working for a damn drug cartel LLC that holds a Florida business permit and pays corporate taxes and gives its employees 401Ks and family leave and all their temp agency secretaries fucking flowers on their birthdays.

And he knew it when he signed, he fucking knew it, that the job was too good to be true, but he closed his eyes and signed anyway because he fucking wanted what they could give him and that was to build a life no Troy had ever even imagined. But now look where that had gotten him. He was only a fucking accountant and he had tried to fix it all, but now he had a shit-ton of powder to move because Cin had found out and Cin was his sister and how fucking stupid of Jimmy Shad, anyway. . .

The phone rings and Cin reaches out for it, Archer's heart leaping in her chest, only to crush itself against her ribs when he sees that it's Reardon. The flash of an image—the bearded man who met Archer at the pipe gate on Tomoka Farms Road—lets Cin draw herself back just enough to regain her own perspective.

"Yeah," Archer says, and his shudder, his fear, ripples through her.

"Archer," Reardon says, bright and carefree. "How'd you do, son?"

The pain of his knee on the hard wood of the closet, the rough bulge of the folded carpet under his shin, the cool of the plastic wrapped bundles, the quiet rush of the Civic along the dark road, following the headlights like they might lead him back to the place he was before he met Carlos. Before he met Reardon. "I did what you told me to do."

Reardon laughs. A cold trickle of raw adrenaline spreads into a flood and loosens Archer's bowels. "Good."

A knot of snakes writhe in his belly. The sheer weight of the drug bricks in the back of the Civic pull on him, tugging at him like a rip tide, bloody shirt in his hand, bright flash, bright flash, bright flash, round and round his head. "I picked up the load. I'm ready to deliver. I just—is Carlos okay?"

"Carlos is fine. Carlos is kicking back with a martini right this minute."

Archer knows this isn't true, so Cin knows it, too. The last time he saw Carlos, he was lying on a grungy gray carpet, gagged, his cheek bruised, his shoulder bloody, his hands and feet hogtied together. The swell of Archer's terrified grief becomes the distinct motion of an ocean swell, disorienting Cin. The rip tide tugs and tugs and she doesn't know it's not Archer—

—until she's torn free, into searing pain, a boom in her ears, and a bright flash, bright flash, bright flash round and round as Archer, her apartment ceiling, the roof of her building, the streets of her home rush away from her and the clouds above them obscure her vision and Cin's torn apart by a vicious wind.

SWEEPING his cane in front of him, Matt walked north on the boardwalk beside Jessica until he heard the familiar sounds of a volleyball game in progress. He meandered to the railing fronting the beach and propped himself on folded arms, facing the salty breeze.

"So, are we just going to watch the ocean? It seems like we should be doing something."

"You ever read the Spenser books?"

"No."

"Spenser's a detective. He drinks a lot of coffee and stares out a lot of windows at the women walking by. That's pretty much the largest part of real-life detecting. Setting things in motion and then waiting to see if leads drop out. Rinse and repeat."

"Do you miss watching women go by?"

The noise that came out of his mouth was less laugh than groan. "You ask me things no one else does."

"So?"

"Yeah. I miss it."

His phone vibrated. He lifted his dangling right earbud in time to hear his phone inform him Lily was calling. He took the call.

"Matt?" Lily said before he could say anything. "Matt? Hello?"

"Yeah, Lily. Here."

"Some cop just called me. Wanted to know where he could find you."

"Charlie Stance."

"That's the one."

"He asked me a bunch of questions. None of them seemed like anything I shouldn't tell him, so I answered them."

"That's good."

"Where are you?"

"I'm buying socks."

"Oh," she said, sounding faintly surprised. "Why are they asking more questions?"

"Lily. It's what cops do. They'll keep asking questions until somebody knows something, anything, about the explosion. Then they'll ask more."

"Okay then."

It was their touch phrase for reassurance that everything was five by five. It felt like lying when he replied, "Okay, then."

"Can you get Ethan later? He has to be at practice even though he can't play."

"Yeah, I'll be there."

They rang off. A couple in an intense conversation passed behind Matt and Jessica before Jessica said, "Socks?"

"My sister."

His phone vibrated. "Unknown calling," it told him. He answered but didn't speak.

"This call is regarding your recent purchase. We have six units with eighty components for you. The Oleander. Your receipt for three-hundred and forty-three dollars will be emailed to you. If you have further need of us, we can be reached at our on-call number, which you have. Thank you." The caller hung up without waiting for a reply.

The depth of his relief that the company would hear him out surprised him. Matt pulled the phone from his pocket and tapped out the start of the address hidden in the message into his GPS app before it gave him the rest. It wasn't an address he knew. It wasn't far. Someone would meet them there.

They could walk down through the shops at Ocean Walk and then cross into the Hilton to catch a cab to another address nearby. Jessica could be his eyes. He could try to get them a little margin, though once they arrived, the safe house would be blown since he had no way of being sure he wasn't followed.

The only reason the company had given it to him was because they'd lost contact and figured if he was asking, there was a problem they were unaware of. They were also unaware he'd set up a false identity in Daytona, but he'd cross that bridge only if forced to do so.

"What's up, Mr. Loose?"

He turned his head and raised an eyebrow at her. "Time to walk. Feel free to shop a bit."

"I have a feeling I'm going down a rabbit hole with you."

"Too late now. At least know it isn't your fault. We're going to meet someone. Play along."

They wandered down and in and out of the few stores. The summer crowd was starting to emerge from sleeping in after late nights. Kids ran circles in the coquina rock band shell, their laughs carrying out across the open plaza in front of it. A guitar player busking for lunch earned a dollar from Jessica.

Picking up their pace, they headed to the Hilton, where they took an elevator to the fourth floor, crossed the entire length of the floor through the corridor across the hotel, walked up two flights, Matt listening for footsteps, for all the good that would do him, and then rode back down and headed to the front, where they took the first taxi on the line.

They rode over to the law office Matt had pulled up on GPS on North Peninsula and then walked a circuitous route to what Jessica reported as a rundown building on Oleander. The movement wasn't much for shaking off a tail from the arcade or a casually posted observer who might've taken an interest if Matt had been recognized, but it would have to do. They used the inside staircase to climb up to the third-floor apartment. Whoever the company had meeting them at the apartment would be watching for them and there was likely someone else outside.

Jessica knocked twice before the door swung open.

"Matt, Jessica," a familiar voice said, "come on in."

Confused, Matt frowned as he swept his cane ahead of him and stepped into the apartment ahead of Jessica. The cold air hit the sweat on his skin like a dump of ice water. The rattle of a window air conditioner. The apartment stunk. "What's with the smell?"

"Spoiled food," the man said.

Spoiled food his ass. Wait—"Sebastian?" Matt said, just as Jessica said, "Oh, we met in Matt's parking lot."

"You're clean," Sebastian said. "I doubt anyone caught onto you."

"What's with the cloak and dagger?" Jessica asked.

"It's obvious the occupant hadn't planned to be away this long."

"What occupant?" Matt asked.

"Doug Moultrie."

"You're friends with Doug, too?" Jessica said.

"What do you know about Doug?" Sebastian said, his voice sharp in a way Matt had never heard him use before.

"Just that Mr. Loose is looking for him," Jessica shot back. "What's going on?"

"It's complicated," Matt said as Sebastian said, "Why'd you bring her?"

"I can't believe this," Matt said, raising his voice, the slow burn of his anger flaring up in his chest. "You stupid fucking shits."

"Close the door, Jessica," Sebastian barked.

"Where the fuck is Doug Moultrie?" Matt said as the door thumped shut behind him.

C in's standing in fog over the body of the crooked nose man. There's a hole in his forehead, ringed in black. The crooked nose man himself is standing on the other side of his body. Movement on the edges of her vision has her turning her head, but the scene is changing too fast for her to follow.

White shiplap walls appear out of the fog. Light brown hardwoods and blood form under the body and their feet. A blur of shadows in motion resolves into Jimmy Shad and Archer beside her staring wide-eyed at the bearded guy from the gate on Tomoka Farms Road, Reardon. The room rocks. They're on a boat. When she glances down, the body is no longer the crooked nose man.

Now it's Carlos. And he's still breathing. Cin crouches down beside him and reaches out to feel the pulse in his neck before she processes the molasses thick air of memory rather than real time. Her fingers pass right through him.

Jimmy fades away until he's disappeared totally. Archer and Reardon are swaying as the ship, yacht, whatever, rides the current. There's a gun in Reardon's hand.

At the station, in the holding cell, Matt had asked, *"Who's Ward?"* and Jimmy answered, *"An ex-Army special-ops meth-head freak who is gonna kill me if I'm not at the drop on Thursday."*

Is Reardon the special-ops meth-head freak? Cin's gut says no, but meth-heads and special-ops both come in a lot of different packages. The crooked nose man, steroid-cut and with a military edge fits the bill better.

A room layers into being around Archer and Rearden and the prostrate Carlos. A table and a couch now. Windows onto a deck, and outside them, the lower part of a shiny railing outside. The day is brilliant. There are voices above, the combined sounds make her think "party". It's inconceivable that no one has heard the commotion that must've proceeded this event, that no one will come down the open hatch behind Reardon and see what Cin's seeing.

Just the recognition of her circumstance changes how she physically feels it. She rises and falls with the sway of the boat. The crooked nose man is watching only her, ignoring the men staring at each other over Carlos. Sunlight is dropping through the room in a bright stream. Shadows cross it as people walk past above. A woman laughs, and then there's a more general wave of mirth passing over their heads.

A second Archer comes down into the room through the hatch, a big grin on his face, another Carlos clattering down behind him. Of everything Cin's experienced so far, this may be the most surreal. Is it memory overlapping memory? And they aren't her memories, so how the hell? The version of Archer standing beside her remains. His mouth moves, but no sound comes out.

Jimmy Shad thumps down the stairs. "No, seriously," he says to the second Archer and conscious Carlos. "I want to come with you. I want to race."

"What are you going to race," Carlos scoffs. "Your Wrangler?"

Jimmy walks through the crooked nose man and then Carlos's body and the whole standoff separates into long white wisps that flitter away. "I just want to ride along with you. I could do that, right?"

"Archer here has a lifetime ticket as my second," Carlos says. "You'll have to work it out with him."

The smile that spreads across Archer's face at those words is painful to see. He never dated while Cin still lived at home. He's never been in love before as far as she knows. It strikes her now how much she doesn't know about her own baby brother. How does he know these people? How did he know Jimmy Shad?

Jimmy passes by her. She turns to see where he's going. Behind her now is a wide bar, trays of hors d'oeuvres spread out upon it, beyond which is a spacious galley kitchen. Two chefs move confidently around the kitchen. One of them is Jimmy's girlfriend, Francis Duncan, who'd she'd last seen in life torn to pieces out in the field near the Cobb theater, and—in what? A memory of the past?—flicking a lighter at Jimmy's house.

Jimmy stuffs a cheese biscuit in his mouth and leans back against the bar. "How'd you two meet anyway?"

"At a race in Daytona," Carlos says. "Archer's sister is badass."

Cin freezes.

"She's a cop, y'know," Jimmy says.

Carlos shrugs. His gaze slides sideways, runs the length of Archer's body and wanders back up. "He's worth it."

"Does Reardon know?"

"Yeah. Reardon knows," Reardon says, emerging from what must be the head. "Archer knows how to keep his mouth shut, don't you, Archer?"

Archer nods, his smile gone.

"Do you, Jimmy?" Reardon asks.

The light fades and spirals into darkness.

Cin spins away with it into nowhere.

THE SILENCE that fell in the apartment lasted long enough for Matt's stomach to notice a more familiar stench, although it wasn't strong. "Sebastian," he said again. "Where's Moultrie?"

"Can we have a moment, Jessica?" Sebastian said in warning, which meant he understood Matt's question, but still wanted to save this situation with Jessica.

Fuck that. She needed to understand exactly what rabbit hole she'd fallen down.

"Sebastian," Matt said and then clenched his jaw shut to regain his control before saying more. He could individually strangle everyone at the company involved in this stupid, stupid decision. What the fuck. "She's in now. Where the fuck is Moultrie?"

"Bedroom," Sabastian said on a sigh.

"Jessica, you can stay here or come."

"Matthew," Sebastian said, like this was just another philosophical argument in the faculty lounge at DSC.

"Doug's dead," Matt said to Jessica. "If you're gonna be dramatic, stay here, because we've only got a couple of minutes."

"Oh. Um, I'll come. There's a short hall. To your left. The bedroom and bath are down there."

One step away from the front door had his cane marking the hallway wall. A couple of steps down on his right, the first open door yielded a damp smell, though he couldn't pick out anything individual over the thread of I-think-the-dog-rolled-in-something-dead tainting the air. The click of his cane on the doorframe echoed right back at him, indicating the space was small and mostly bare. Bath. He kept walking.

Two more steps and the tip of his cane hit the closed bedroom door directly in front of him. Closing the distance, he reached out, grabbed the knob, and swung the door open in one motion, sweeping his cane through as he walked in. The smell was stronger here, actually rank with corruption.

"Oh," Jessica said again from behind him.

Matt stopped. "Tell me."

Jessica swallowed a couple of times, no doubt saliva filling her mouth as her stomach rolled. He remembered the first time he saw a body in situ with a clarity that all the other times started to lack as he progressed in his career. His own stomach was a little queasy. He'd been out long enough to get used to his life away from the game. And his sense of smell was more developed.

"He's, uh. All I can see are his feet." She thumped Matt in the back, getting by him. He wouldn't have asked her to go for a better look, but if she volunteered, he wasn't going to stop her.

"Oh," she said yet again, from his right this time. She was silent long enough that he opened his mouth to call out to Sebastian, but then she said, in a shaky voice, "He's very dead. Like there's mold or something on him, but, um, he's been shot? I think. In the forehead. There's blood under his head and shoulders. A lot of blood, but it's, um, thick, with a skin on top, like pudding."

God, he liked this woman.

"What does he look like?"

"Sad."

He almost, almost, laughed.

"No," he said. "I mean race, height, build."

"Don't you know him?"

"No, I don't. I know of him."

"White," Sebastian said from the entrance to the hall. "Six-foot. Wide. Broad shouldered. Heavily muscled. Dark brown hair, dark brown eyes. Thirty-six. Hodad."

That was one Matt had never heard before. "Hodad?"

"Yeah. A beach rat. Doesn't...didn't...surf. Sold a little to keep appearances up."

Jessica remained silent, which made Matt once again grateful that Ed had chosen her to help him when he first hired on rather than one of the many other not-so-swift choices he could've made. But then she said, "There's no blood on his face."

Now that Matt had seen him through Cin's eyes, he could imagine Sebastian shrugging. Jessica wouldn't have said it without a reason, though, so he'd bite. "Why should there be blood on his face?"

"Because someone broke his nose, and it hasn't been re-set."

"It's been like that for years," Sebastian said.

Shit. The crooked nose man. Like Matt had summoned her, that peculiar hollow spot in his chest filled and even though she didn't touch him, he knew Cin was there. "You called it in?" he asked Sebastian.

"A co-worker's going to call in a wellness check."

"Wipe off this handle, Jessica," Matt said, taking charge without thinking about it until he heard himself. "Are there security cameras here?"

"Disabled on my way in," Sebastian said.

"Curious neighbors?"

"Not in this building. Anyone who ends up here keeps their blinders on." Sebastian was moving already, headed back down the hall as he added a muffled "No offense. That's why we picked it."

Matt turned on his heel to follow, trusting Jessica to do as he asked, hoping Cin stayed with him until he could talk to her. "You're driving, Sebby," he said, just in case the man, or the company, thought they could ditch him.

ONCE THEY WERE on the move again, Jessica leaned forward in between the front seats of Sebastian's Kia and said, "So what are you guys? Who are you guys?"

"I'm just me. Same me I was yesterday. This guy"—Matt threw his hands up in the air and clocked his right on the passenger window—"ow, works for my old employer." He shook his fingers out. "And no, I didn't know that before now. What the fuck are you doing, Sebastian? Did you know I was former company?"

"Yes, of course," Sebastian said in his normal measured way, like they were passing the afternoon in a café, a bottle of wine between them. "But I was already here before you came, teaching, recruiting, collecting."

"It's Daytona," Matt said, in a disbelieving way. But he was already recalling all the info he'd dug up. With the rise in heroin and opioid addiction, both drug-related and violent crime rates in Daytona had climbed. At least fifty named gangs operated in the area. Crips. Bloods. Bikers like the Outlaws had existed here for years.

"Exactly. It's not flashy." He made a slow stop and then put his blinker on, driving the way he talked.

Matt approved. There were questions he wanted to ask, but didn't, with Jess between them.

"Recruiting?" Jessica said.

"I work for a private security company," Sebastian said easily. "We collect information and recruit people to help us do that."

"What kind of information?"

"The law enforcement kind," he said, easing the car back into motion and turning left.

Cin's hand settled on the back of Matt's neck as the familiar rhythm of the Seabreeze Bridge passed beneath the car's tires. "You need to go to my place," she said, her voice low. "Archer's involved in this."

"In what?" Matt said.

Sebastian cleared his throat. "Um, in . . . what do you mean?" as Cin said, "The crooked nose man."

Matt dipped his chin in a brief nod to acknowledge Cin. To Sebastian, he said, "What account are you working?"

"Terrorism."

Everything in Matt stopped for just a second. It was not the answer he'd anticipated.

"Wait," Jess said, "What?"

What had he done? Why had Sebastian even answered if that was the case? Letting Jessica in on the fact that he'd worked intelligence was one thing, getting her involved in a murder case, using her as a guide and for ancillary info on a drug ring like Malcolm Ward appeared to be, maybe dangling her for bait at some point . . . Matt closed his eyes. This was his fucking fault. Sebastian had taken his lead and for whatever reason, trusted his judgment. Shit.

"Moultrie was recruiting Malcolm Ward insiders," Sebastian said. "Jimmy Shad was on his radar. And yes, we're aware that DBPD is asking around now about Malcolm Ward as part of their investigation into their officers' murders." He braked hard at the end of the bridge. "More like crashing around," he added in a hard tone under his breath and then turned left again.

Beach Street. They'd be passing by the old storefronts on the right, now housing a drag show, Indian and Thai restaurants, a jewelry store, a magic shop, a chocolate factory, a pub. On the left would be the hurricane-destroyed City Island Library and next to it, Jackie Robinson ballfield, where he and Ethan spent many, many hours last summer while Matt was still living at Lily's and adjusting to his new normal. God, what he wouldn't give to be at a baseball game right now instead of here, ruining Jessica's life and feeling trapped in his own.

"Matt," Cin said, her tone urgent.

Sebastian spoke up again. "We're trying to establish if Malcolm Ward is related to or using local maras for extortion, trafficking, hits, whatever they need."

"Maras as in MS-13?" Jessica said. "I know some. Are you guys like, Blackwater employees?"

Matt sighed and pinched the bridge of his nose between his thumb and forefinger against the headache blooming behind his eyes. "Of course, you know MS-13 gang members. And no, Blackwater's dead."

Sebastian slowed down and stopped.

"Matt," Cin said again, louder. "Ask him to turn right."

Matt let go of his nose and waved his right hand. "We're going the wrong way."

"How do you know where we are?" Sebastian said, his tone harder than seemed warranted.

"I'm blind, not geographically challenged," Matt snapped. "Turn right."

The blinker flipped on and after a car pulled past them, Sebastian edged the car right and then turned right. "Where we going?"

Cin recited her address, Matt repeating it out loud.

After they were turned around, Sebastian said, "Why?"

"Lucinda Troy's brother might be useful to us."

"We heard you had a fling with her."

"You did? Did you hear I was arrested? Why'd you let me sit in jail for four days?"

"I'm just a college professor," Sebastian said. Jessica snorted, which Matt was grateful for, but Sebastian continued as if he hadn't heard. "You don't know Archer Troy. How would you know he can help?"

"He works for a drug dealer."

"He works for RWS Motors. Did Detective Troy tell you he works for a drug dealer?"

Shit.

"Did you know Detective Troy before your arrest? Was Detective Troy involved with running drugs?"

"He's in interrogation mode," Cin said.

She was right. The smart thing to do would be to shut up. But then Cin's reputation would get dragged under. "No."

"Shut up, Matt," Cin said.

Sebastian said, "Come on, Matt. Where else could you have gotten that information from?"

"Just drive, Sebastian," Matt said. "Let me think."

"About how to cover yourself?"

From the sound of it, Jess slapped Sebastian's arm with the back of her hand before she settled back into the rear seat.

"Archer knew the crooked nose man," Cin said into the silence. "They were in a hotel room together. I don't know why, but Sebastian might?"

Matt swayed into Sebastian's next turn, reaching again for the dash. Fucking Sebastian. No wonder he spit out the fact Archer worked for RWS Motors so fast. Doug Moultrie knew Archer.

"At some point, earlier?" Cin continued. "Or maybe later? There was a party, on a yacht. Archer, his boyfriend Carlos, Jimmy Shad, and another guy, Reardon, were all there. Jimmy told them I was a cop, trying to put Archer on the spot, maybe. But Carlos and Reardon already knew. Reardon asked Jimmy if he knew how to keep his mouth shut."

And they both knew the end to that story. No, he didn't.

"Carlos knew me," she said. "From street racing. I didn't recognize him, though. Reardon was the bearded man Archer met out on Tomoka Farms Road, the one who sent him to the house at Lake Ashby."

"Who's—" Matt pressed his lips together. Damn not being able to ask Cin questions. Who the fuck was Carlos? But If Archer and Jimmy knew each other and they also both knew bearded-guy Reardon and fucking Doug Moultrie, and Reardon sent Archer on a drug pick-up after Jimmy died and therefore missed his pick-up, Malcolm Ward was sure to be a factor. Right? Either that, or Daytona was lousy with drug caches the same guys all knew about.

Cin laid her hands on both Matt's shoulders, as if she were sitting right behind him. "Are you listening? Archer has the drugs stashed in the Civic. I think he knows—"

Matt's chest tore itself in half. Folding over, a groan ripped up his throat, pouring out his open mouth. He clutched at his chest, smacking his cheek bone with the folded walking stick in his hand.

The car swerved.

Sebastian's right hand landed on Matt's bicep, squeezing hard. "Hang on," he yelled.

The sharp pain vanished.

The car slammed to a stop.

"Matt!" Jessica's voice was too loud. "Matt!"

"Call nine-one-one," Sebastian told her.

Matt sucked in a deep breath, his lungs whooping like he'd had the wind knocked out of him. "No," he huffed.

"What do you mean, no?" Sebastian demanded. "What the hell was that? Are you having a heart attack?"

"No," Matt said, sitting up. "It's fine."

"That was not fine, Mr. Loose," Jess said, still hovering over him.

The only thing that wasn't fine was that Cin got ripped away before she finished telling him what Archer knew. Not just ripped away this time, torn from him, like someone had reached in and ripped his heart from his chest.

Which brought him back to wondering if he was just mental, but Lake Ashby was real. Archer was real. He had no reason to doubt her. "It was just a muscle spasm," he lied. "I have bruising from the blast wave. Let's go, come on."

"You're a liar," Sebastian said, but he was pulling the car back out into traffic by the time he finished speaking.

Jessica remained crammed up between them.

Matt would swear on his pledge as an officer of the law that he could feel the twenty-pound weight of her glare. He rubbed his chest, not knowing if the ache settling in was real or imagined.

A WOMAN IN JEANS, a white tee shirt, and gloves is pouring a gray powder from a zip-lock bag into a brushed silver vase. The vase is standing alone on a marble counter topping an island in a room of cabinets and shelves that is definitely not a kitchen, although there is a deep farmhouse sink. More urns fill the shelves. On the long counter along the wall, there's a neat stack of collapsed cardboard boxes and a large cube of small plastic drawers, each with a different size or shape metal name plate affixed to it. Next to the cube is an engraving machine.

"Well, Lucinda Isabella Troy, I hope this urn suits you. You won't be in it long, or you'd still be in the bag," the woman says. "I read about you, y'know, in the paper. Online, too. I wondered if you'd be coming my way. You sound like someone I'd have liked to know. Maybe we crossed paths somewhere along the way. At Publix, or Planet Fitness, or I don't know, the Ocean Deck, maybe."

No one's thinking harder about her than this woman right now?

There's a chuckle behind her.

Cin whips around.

Daddy shakes his head, that familiar wry lift of his lips lighting her up.

She rushes to him, lifting her arms, but the feel is that of two clouds meeting in the sky, merging. An indescribable feeing of comfort and contentment and depthless knowing suffuses every molecule of her. Every single one. She's limitless, infinite, Here and Now and All.

Cin has a choice here.

She Knows. Everything.

She feels the last of herself falling into the urn.

She is Knowing and she's also ash particles falling through the light above, landing on a bed of herself.

"I hope they find whoever did this to you," the woman says, and Cin is her in that moment. "Whoever did this to all of you, before someone else dies."

Cin makes her choice.

CHAPTER
TWENTY-TWO

At Cin's condo, Sebastian threw the car into park with a clunk and turned the engine off. "How are we playing this?"

Matt wanted to say, *we're* not, but he just shook his head instead. "I don't know. By feel, I guess."

They tramped upstairs to the right number. On instinct, Matt swung his right arm up and blocked the lift of Sebastian's to knock. "You knock, Jess."

She knocked twice with no answer.

"Tell him you're a friend."

"Are you there, Archer?" Jessica called through the door. "I'm a friend of your sister's." Matt tipped his chin at the door, and she knocked again. "Archer?"

A scrabbling as Archer slid the chain and then the deadbolt clicked, and he opened the door. Matt could feel him like a block of energy in the doorway. He was tall like his sister.

"Hi, Archer," Jessica said, putting on her Poker Room voice. "We're friends of your sister's."

"Cop friends?" he rumbled.

She laughed. "No, we're so not cops."

"He is," Archer said.

"He's an ex-cop," Jessica said. "His name's Matt. I'm Jessica. This is

Sebastian, he's a professor at DSC. Look, Matt knew your sister better than we did. They were seeing each other before . . . before."

The mass that was Archer moved back, the door opening further. Jessica stepped in. Matt lifted his cane just to feel the door frame. Past Archer, he swung it a bit wider, got his bearings in the short hall and then slid the cane up in his hand, bringing it in close to him as he followed Jessica into the living room, Sebastian on his heels. The scent of the candle on the coffee table assaulted him. Cin's long neck, the heat of her breast cupped in his hand, the cool leather of the couch on the backs of his hands as he lay her down on it, her soft pant of breath as she arched against his tongue.

He started at the suddenness of an actual hand closing on his forearm.

"You okay, Matt?" Jessica said.

He swallowed the remembered taste of her, willed his ache for her to calm the fuck down, and nodded. "Yeah, sorry."

"I keep thinking I can feel her here," Archer said. "Like I'll be in the kitchen, and I can feel her walk in from the bedroom, but I turn around and remember she's gone."

"We thought maybe we could help," Sebastian said. "But it looks like you're almost done packing her things."

"Yeah. I have to go straight back to work after the service tomorrow."

"You're an accountant," Matt said.

"Yeah," Archer said, his voice betraying him with a wobble. "Been in corporate for close to a year now, RWS Motors."

"RWS? I love that place," Sebastian enthused, moving towards the little balcony area as he spoke. "You're in Melbourne, right? Ever been to the showroom in Miami?"

Matt knew nothing about RWS Motors. He couldn't remember if he'd ever heard the name before Sebastian mentioned it in the car.

"When I interviewed. I'm sorry," Archer said, his voice shaking now. "I'm waiting on a conference call."

Matt wished Cin were here to guide him, but she wasn't, and he was done with charades. "We know you're in trouble, Archer." He wished like hell he could see Archer's face, gauge his reaction. Sound was getting him nothing except Jessica's held breath and the click of the blinds as Sebastian fingered them, no doubt checking their surroundings. "Cin knew you were in trouble."

Archer was moving then, away from the entry by the kitchen and into the living room proper. Matt held his ground, but Archer only dropped onto the couch, his breath whooshing out of him.

"She knew about Carlos," Matt added. "She knew about Malcom Ward."

"She knew about Carlos?" Archer whispered, sounding destroyed.

Matt wanted to keep him off-guard, hoping he'd over-share before his brain kicked back into gear. "You aren't surprised she knew about Malcolm Ward?"

"Jimmy told her," he said. Bitter words, louder than before.

"Is that what got her killed?" Matt said. "That Jimmy talked about them to the cops?"

Archer said nothing.

Matt didn't want to distract him by giving him his oft-repeated refrain that blind men couldn't see a silent answer. Taking a guess, Matt said, "Reardon did it?"

"Reardon? No. He's just—he's not Daytona. I don't know who did it."

"He ordered it be done?"

Silence.

"No, he's shaking his head no," Jessica said.

"Sorry," Archer said. "How do you know Reardon? Who are you guys?"

They were losing their advantage. "We know you met him out on Tomoka Farms Road. We know you went to the house at Lake Ashby. We know you have Malcolm Ward's drugs hidden in Cin's Civic."

The blinds rattled.

"You can't know that," he breathed. "How could you know that?"

"You've been under surveillance," Sebastian said into the gap, his voice tight. Matt was just glad he was backing him up instead of echoing Archer.

"Why?" Archer said, standing up, verging on panic. "Why would you do that? Who are you again? I thought you said you weren't cops."

"We're private security, under contract to law enforcement," Jessica said before Sebastian could. Her instincts were good. She knew enough about current events to realize Sebastian was a contractor, despite Matt's deflection on Blackwater. Coming from her, the lie reinforced the idea they were united in purpose and fact. "Some of us have more info than others. Keeps us all safe."

Damn. She was wasted in hospitality.

"You're Cin's brother," Sebastian said, like he'd known her, walking as he spoke to stand shoulder to shoulder with Matt. It was a good answer, but the urge to hit him still filled Matt's fist and mind. "We were watching out for you."

"I didn't know, you know, about this, this drug thing." Agitated, Archer brushed past Matt.

Matt leaned a little, pressing his shoulder to Sebastian's. Sebastian took the hint and remained where he was, letting Archer pass by them. Jessica was still between Archer and the door. Matt hoped he just needed to pace his anxiety out.

"Malcolm Ward," Archer spit. "I was so excited to work for RWS. The money was good. I should've known it was too good to be true."

It was a wild guess, but . . . "Carlos brought you in?"

"No. He was hired a few months after me. He sells their racing line."

"He isn't involved with Malcolm Ward?"

"No," Archer said.

The word hung in the air, short and sharp.

And then Archer drew in a long breath. "Shit," he said, the word riding his exhalation. "He is, isn't he?"

"So, Carlos *is* involved with Malcolm Ward?" Matt said.

"Maybe?" Archer hedged. "I don't know."

"You said no. What made you change your mind?"

"A couple of weeks ago, we were on my supervisor's boat, for a small corporate party, buyers coming in the next day for more of the same. Jimmy was there. I'd never met him before. He was on the boat and said he knew my sister was a cop and did Reardon know. And then Reardon came out of the bathroom and said I knew how to keep my mouth shut, did Jimmy?

"I didn't understand why he said that, or why it mattered Cin was a cop. All that mattered to me was that Carlos thought she was cool. We started talking about other things, and, I don't know, I just didn't think about it again. But Carlos comes to Daytona a lot. He knew Cin from racing here. And Reardon said this is Malcolm Ward's territory." Archer took in a deep breath and sighed, his resignation clear. "I was just trying to fix it."

"Fix what?" Sebastian said.

"Carlos. Last week I found out he was downloading financials off my computer. I—God, I didn't know what to think. I reported an unknown hack. IT looked at it and then had me meet with an internet security consultant. Some whiz kid here in Daytona. Reardon came to the meeting as back-up, someone who could protect RWS's interests and meet with law enforcement if the kid could trace the hack."

Shit. Was the kid Spider? Did Spider know Reardon, too? And work directly with RWS Motors? No, that was a fucking leap. A door slammed in the apartment beside Cin's. Matt startled hard, and in the next instance, a woman shouted at someone. The TV shut off. The sudden silence was unnerving, but Archer didn't seem to notice. He just kept talking.

"No one knew Carlos and I were together. He wasn't ready to tell anyone. I didn't think they would figure out who got in, but Carlos used his security code to . . . he screwed up. Reardon sent a team to get him. They shot him. They shot Carlos right in front of me. I said I'd do anything. They could fire Carlos, but I'd do anything for that to be the end of it."

"And?" Sebastian prompted when it seemed like Archer might not say anything more.

"Carlos was supposed to make a Daytona run, pick up a delivery from Jimmy. From Malcolm Ward. But after Jimmy died and Carlos . . . fucked up, Reardon said I had to get the drugs, if I wanted Carlos back. If Carlos was moving drugs, he had to be involved with this Ward guy, right?"

Classic. Reardon wanted to bring Archer into the drug mule fold, probably with Carlos onboard, looping both of them harder into the life, but still wanted him in the dark on the nitty-gritty details.

"Carlos isn't with Malcolm Ward," Sebastian said.

Suspicion rising on a not-fully formed thought, Matt lifted his head. "He isn't?" Archer asked. "How do you know?"

"He's with us."

Voice low and strained, Jessica said, "How many freaking people do we know who are with you?" Heavy, ironic air quotes on "with". Matt could kiss her. His own brain was giving him nothing.

"Need to know," Sebastian said.

So there were more. "Fuck you, Sebastian," Matt said, the words climbing out of his tight throat. "I need to know."

He ducked his head down, having to work to put a damper on everything he wanted to say. He wanted to storm out, be the old Matt, the one who did his best work alone and pissed. The one who wasn't dependent on sharing his every move and other people's eyes to get anything freaking done.

His cell vibrated in his pocket.

Case in point. He couldn't even simply check the display. His earbuds were lying on his chest. Matt ignored it. "Archer, do you know Doug Moultrie?"

"He's shaking his head," Jessica said.

Why would he lie? And should Matt call him out on it? "I gotta make a call," Matt said instead. "I'm going to go outside. Sebastian, come with."

Sebastian grunted in reply and brushed by.

As Matt passed her, Jess laid a hand on his arm. "This is, I don't know, crazy," she stage-whispered.

Archer giggled, a slightly unhinged giggle. "It most certainly is."

"Look," Matt said to both of them. "We're going to solve this and get you both out of trouble. Neither of you is here by your own fault."

"Jimmy fucked up and got my sister killed," Archer said. "Reardon has Carlos. If he's really some sort of undercover cop, RWS or Malcolm Ward or who the fuck ever are going kill him, too."

"I can't guarantee they won't, but if Carlos is with us, he's well-trained. And well-trained people will go get him. Hold tight."

Sebastian had left the door open. Matt pulled it shut. "Car?"

"Yeah."

They traipsed down and climbed into the front seats and shut their doors. Sebastian turned the engine on and cranked the air up on high. "Archer thinks we know what's going on," he said. "For the record, you were talking about Sean Reardon, correct?"

"Tall, stocky, full beard?"

"He's RWS's head of security."

Matt's phone vibrated again. He ignored it. There were too many questions he needed answered and not enough time. "Did you know Jimmy Shad gave the locals the name Doug Moultrie with my address and description?"

"No. Explains why hits on Moultrie's social media were up."

"Did you know I set up that cover four years ago and never used it?"

"Fuck," Sebastian said, drawing the word out. "Someone must've been saving time. A cover that deep takes a lot of effort and Moultrie was a fairly rapid insertion."

Matt's estimation of Sebastian eked up a notch. He'd known the crooked nose agent calling himself Moultrie. In the apartment, he'd said Moultrie's nose had been like that forever. In most of the teams, no one knew each other's birth names, instead referring to one another by nicknames or false names so old, not even admin knew their birth names anymore. But to so easily speak about someone you knew by one name by using, without the slightest hesitation, their most recently adopted cover name took experience.

"Do you know why Moultrie was on scene at Jimmy Shad's house when it blew?" A car started up somewhere behind them and pulled out. It needed tuning in a bad way. When the sound faded, Matt said, "Sebastian."

"Just thinking. I wasn't aware Moultrie was there. I've, uh, reviewed the collected video. He's not on it. I'm sure one of us would have noticed if he were there."

Fuck, he'd forgotten. Charlie had told him that as well. Still . . . "There was a girl on a bike."

"Her, I remember. She was alone. She dropped her bike and bolted after the explosion. Why did you think Moultrie was there? How did you know about—"

"Was Jimmy one of ours?" Matt said, letting his anger color his commanding tone.

"No. He was a nobody. Surfed. Couple of possession charges. Got involved with Malcolm Ward through a friend of his, we think. Chris Bolton. Bolton was killed in May, about three weeks before Jimmy. Moultrie had them both on his contacts list."

The Chris that Jimmy had mentioned in the holding cell. Killed by Malcom Ward, a badass ex-special-ops meth-head freak who was going to kill him, too, if he didn't make the drop and deliver the drugs to Malcolm Ward a few days later. "How'd Jimmy know Moultrie and I were connected?"

Another long moment passed before Sebastian said, "He didn't. He couldn't have. Malcom Ward scared him, we know that. Maybe he thought he'd throw Moultrie at the cops to get himself out of it, but then panicked. You had him as a student. We checked."

"He said he chose me because he thought I'd know how to get out of the charges," Matt said. "Get someone digging, though. It doesn't sit well with me."

"He was just a stupid kid, Matt. Got himself in too deep."

"Explain why you're here working terrorism."

"NASCAR. It makes a good target. It's highly visible. In the US, it's second only to football for TV viewership. It's televised to a hundred different countries. Its fans are generally patriotic, Christian, affluent, and white."

"And how does that tie into Malcolm Ward?"

"We don't know. It's just that everywhere we poked, we found Malcolm Ward. I punted to our drug unit, but you know how it goes."

When he didn't say anymore, Matt unclenched his teeth and said, "We both know I know how it goes. Drugs and terrorism go hand in hand. The company isn't sending more teams down when there's already people here. Brief me."

"It's complicated."

Matt kept his mouth shut.

Sebastian sighed and gave in. "It took months to link Ward to RWS Motors, which is a Salvadoran corporation that specializes in high-end yachts and cars. They have wealthy clients and global operations, but they don't advertise. Strictly word of mouth. They have showrooms in New York, LA, and Miami. A lot of cash goes through the corporation, which makes it good for laundering, but no one knew they were doing it until now.

"From all appearances, RWS corporate has managed to limit the internal structure of the drug operation to a very small group, but we don't know all the players yet. They stay out of the bigger drug markets, Miami, Orlando, Tampa, Jacksonville, but have active distribution going in a string of smaller to mid-sized towns along both Florida coasts. Even there, the structure appears tightly controlled. We don't know much yet, but Carlos learned there's one lieutenant per area distributor with a handful of dealers. He also discovered all the RWS distributors hire MS-13 cliques for their dirty work, which means MS-13 is more widespread in Florida than the Feds think they are. And implies an RWS alliance with MS-13 at a higher level than the local distributers."

"Drugs and terror," Matt muttered. "Malcolm Ward?"

"RWS's Daytona distributor. There's less than twenty dealers directly associated with Malcolm Ward on the street team in Daytona, maybe forty total across Volusia County and south Flagler. We sent up another flare and the company's drug unit finally put Moultrie on the beach here in Daytona. They put someone in Port Charlotte, too, because there's a strong MS-13 presence in that area, but she's only been there a month. I think there's someone in Miami, but I don't know that officially.

"The terror unit wants to know who RWS's biggest clients are and where the laundered cash is going. We maneuvered Carlos into racing sales at RWS Melbourne because that's where the accounting division is headquartered, and our investigation had already identified Archer Troy as a good target. Here in Daytona, Moultrie managed a shallow infiltration of Malcolm Ward through dealer Chris Bolton, who introduced him to Sean Reardon."

"RWS's head of security."

"Correct. Then Reardon started asking Moultrie in on security work for RWS."

Matt's phone buzzed again.

Sebastian stopped. "Somebody really wants to talk to you."

"I really want you to keep talking."

A tapping answered him. Sebastian's wedding ring against the steering wheel, Matt was almost certain.

"Okay," Sebastian said when he had gathered his thoughts. "Carlos checked in with us on schedule. He cultivated a relationship with Archer Troy by using our knowledge of Detective Troy's penchant for street racing and he took RWS financials off Archer's work computer. The analysts are working them. He said he thought he'd be meeting Malcolm Ward's top guy ten days ago offshore. They were coming into Ponce Inlet for a day of fishing with the brokers selling cars and boats to RWS, followed by an invitation-only soiree for central Florida RWS clients, and then an off-shore meeting with the drug lieutenants and top dealers for Volusia, Flagler, and Broward counties. If he's been compromised, we haven't heard about it yet."

"Did Moultrie miss check-in?"

"We're in deep here. He only checks in monthly. The Malcolm Ward dealers were starting to warm up to him watching their backs during drug deals because Reardon trusted him, assigning him meet and greet duty with RWS clients in the area. He logged a higher-up in Los Zetas on vacation, the wife of a general in Barrio 18, a couple of royals from the Emirates, and an Afghan opium exporter suspected of supporting whatever jihadists are in power at any given time."

Mexican drug cartel Los Zetas. Trans-national street gangs MS-13 and Barrio 18. Middle East heavies, maybe. Matt laid his head back. All he wanted was two heads on a plate. The bomb-builder's and whoever ordered it detonated. How did he go about separating what he wanted from this entanglement with his old job that he didn't want and matters way more complicated than he could handle right now?

"All I want to know," he said, failing to keep his frustration from bleeding through, "is who ordered up that bomb. Where do I have to go to wring his neck? Melbourne?"

"Melbourne?" Sebastian said.

Matt lifted his head. That simmering ball of red-hot fury lodged under his ribcage since he woke up to a world where Cin only existed for him was begging to light off. He stomped on it. Breathed out slow. "RWS owns Malcolm Ward. Melbourne is where RWS is headquartered, right?" he said, hearing the vicious tone that laced the words together but unable to stop himself. "Don't tell me El Salvador."

"Oh," Sebastian said. "Oh."

"Oh?" A car pulled into the space next to them and the engine died. "Can you see my cane, Sebastian?" Matt said, and if his voice shook, at least he hadn't come off his seat yet.

"Yes, Matthew, I can see your cane."

"Then you can see the white knuckles on my hand that means I am trying very hard right now not to hit you."

"I didn't realize why you were asking Archer if Reardon ordered a hit. RWS doesn't own or run Malcolm Ward per se. Their drug operation is a lot like MS-13's. The distribution lieutenants oversee independent cliques. Malcolm Ward is just one clique. RWS would simply cut them off if there was trouble with law enforcement. Reardon has no authority with them at all. If—and that's still an if, Matt—if Ward was responsible for that bomb, Ward's lieutenant ordered it."

"Sebby," Matt ground out. "Where is Ward's lieutenant headquartered?"

"Right here in Daytona."

The tension in Matt's muscle ran out like the tide. "Who is he?"

"I have no idea."

C in forgets most of the Knowing before she remembers she's forgotten something.

What she does remember is crashing into her daddy and all the love he holds for her. And how to move through the currents of time. As she thinks about them, they push back against her, giving her elusive quicksilver flashes of knowledge without context.

She's swimming through the thick dawn fog that rises from Daytona's yards and beaches on those days when the wild, mysterious She that is Florida asserts herself. This fog is deep, dark like the shadows under the oldest oaks, but also as bright as the reflection of a full moon on sand. It's drawing itself from the coquina rock below.

Daytona's specters rise with it.

Cin kicks. Stroking forward into an eddy of fog, she pulls her arm down and through a Florida cracker on a white, misshapen horse, his whip hand trailing, the lash curling back into the years long past.

A native Timucua woman with her dark hair piled high on her head, her shoulders bare, smiles at Cin, lifting a child high into a swirl, and swinging it away, laughter trailing from it in blue curves.

A soldier and another and another. A whole platoon of tired men surrounds her. The last raises his rifle, the movement a ripple that has them scattering in all directions, their faces long and tattered.

There's a boy with a pinwheel streaming a rainbow of colors that kaleidoscope over her.

The colors shatter into raindrops falling on another native, a man standing on the bank of the Halifax River. He's not Timucua. He's young, but there's moss growing on his shoulders and his feet are roots extending too far down into the past to see the tips. The brush of the current on her skin gives her the quicksilver knowing that he's the oldest of Daytona's ghosts, so old the name of his people has been lost thousands of years downstream. He turns his head to consider her passing.

His lips move soundlessly, but Cin has no trouble understanding him. "Purpose," he says. "Swimmers must have purpose."

Cin thinks of Matt and then she's dropping through the fog, fading from the inside out and then filling back up from the outside in. It's like being turned inside out but it doesn't hurt. Her senses come online like they're being dialed up on a stereo. It's a slower process than her drops into being have been up until this point.

She's first aware of a gentle, steady rain on a tin roof overhead. Then there's Matt, sitting alone on a lower bunk in a small eight bunk barrack, a packed duffle bag beside him. Cin was hoping to have found him in the now, but he's younger. His hair is military cut, shorn on the sides, short on top. On him, it looks unruly. Elbows on his knees, he's staring down at the dog tag strung on the lace of his left boot.

Cin sits down beside him. He doesn't notice. She looks down, too.

It's weird how physical she feels even though she knows she's not really here with him. Her heart pounds in her ears and she has to tell herself to slow her breath. The name Loftin is visible on the dog tag, and a blood type, O+. The rest is hidden by his laces.

Another Marine pulls the barracks door open and sticks his head in, his ball cap dripping water. "Transport's here, Mark."

She's both surprised and not that his name isn't Matt Loose.

He stands and shoulders his bag, looks around at the spartan quarters. Cin follows him out. He carries himself differently than he does as a blind man. His shoulders seem squarer. His feet more sure of what will meet them.

The raindrops soak him as he trots through an alley of barracks identical to his and then veers diagonally across an open muddy field to a troop transport truck with an open back and canvas top. Cin has no idea where it is they are. He tosses his duffel up to a waiting Marine and then scrambles up and inside.

In seconds, the truck is pulling away.

She rolls his name over her tongue.

Mark.

It doesn't fit him.

And that doesn't matter.

There are more pressing matters.

She closes her eyes and thinks of the crooked nose man, of the bullet hole in his head, of the sway of a boat, and then she's fading again.

WHOEVER HAD BEEN TRYING to reach Matt had given up. He lifted his ear bud and thumbed through his prompts until his phone told him he'd missed four calls from Ed at Daytona Kennel Club and Poker Room and had no voicemails. Fine by him. He jerked the earbud loose and let it fall.

"Why do you insist on going through all that rather than using Siri?" Sebastian said, his annoyance clear. "It's ridiculous."

"I hate Siri, that's why."

"That's it? You hate Siri?"

No, he hated having to ask out loud for help from a programmed assistant and anyone standing near him knowing what he was asking about and knowing how many damn times he had to ask when she didn't understand him. "Yep."

Back upstairs, Matt didn't even let the door close before he said, "Doug Moultrie. Did you know him before the motel room?"

"He's in the bathroom," Jessica said.

"Where are you getting your info from, Matt?" Sebastian demanded.

The toilet flushed.

So much for a hard-hitting entrance. Matt's phone vibrated. He sighed and answered it this time, hyper-aware of Sebastian and Jessica's focus on him. "Loose."

"Cops are looking for Jessica," Ed said, "Why is that?"

"Someone who called two other people before they were murdered called a disposable phone registered to Jessica and talked for twenty minutes."

"So, if she knows someone who's killing people, don't you think it's in her best interest to let the cops catch up to her?"

"Yeah. We're going to do that later. You know a Sean Reardon?"

"No."

"You know Doug Moultrie?"

"He's on our watch list."

"Why?"

"Because of the people he associates with."

"Who are?"

"Other people on our watch list."

And that would be Ed shutting him down.

"Look, Loose," Ed said, and that stung. Ed hadn't used his last name since his initial interview two years ago. "I may not throw Jessica many bones, but I know what I got in her. Don't get her killed because of this Malcolm Ward shit you got going on. They ain't my cup of tea, but I only thought you'd get far enough to get laid and forget your troubles for a bit, which was *my* mission sending you to Johnny. Now I'm hearing you've been kicking Mr. Ward's nest. Don't be surprised if you get stung."

"What do you know, Ed? You know who the big boss is?"

"Nobody fucking knows that, Loose. Every member is Malcolm Ward to outsiders. Give it up."

Matt shook his head. "I'll send Jessica to the cops."

"You do that," he said and hung up.

Matt checked the call was disconnected and punched down through his contacts list.

"Am I fired?" Jessica said, as Sebastian said, "Did he tell you?"

"No, says he doesn't know. And no, Jess," he said, while he used both thumbs to write a text, only half-listening to the voice-over feeding him letters. "But you'll be resigning soon to go work for him," he said, nodding his chin in the direction he thought Sebastian was standing.

Having come out and stalled in the hall between the bath and bedroom, Archer said, "What's going—"

Matt held up a finger, gratified when Archer immediately shut up and let him finish his text. He hit send. "The man you met in a hotel room was Doug Moultrie. What were you doing with him?"

"I don't know—"

"Tall, crooked nose."

"Oh. Doug," Archer said, drawing the name out.

"Hotel." Sebastian said, before Matt could. "Why were you there?"

"We were sharing a room. I was doing the financing for a very large purchase by a member of Los Zetas. Doug was security, he was one of the drivers. We had a block of rooms off I-4 in Orlando. When the client was ready to take the meeting, Doug drove me over to Disney."

"The Zeta," Sebastian said in disbelief as Jessica said, "Disney?"

Matt cut his hand through the air to shush them. "Do you know Moultrie well?"

"No. He's just security."

"How'd you know the client was a Zeta?"

"Carlos told me before I left. He knows the guy who made the sale in Miami. The client was on a Florida vacation with his family. I didn't say anything, though. I mean, yeah, word gets around the staff about some of RWS's bigger clients, but we have confidentiality agreements. It's not like . . . I didn't know, you know, before I started working there, that RWS had anything to do with drugs. I didn't know they handled drugs until Reardon grabbed Carlos. Everything I've done and seen in accounting is legal. It's not like RWS launders drug money or anything. I verified the accounts. The client made a deposit, but I set up a payment plan for the rest of the purchase. Except for the part about him being a drug dealer, it's all legal."

"We don't care about the accounting part," Matt said, although he wanted to tell Archer that money laundering was the only reason why RWS Motors was in business and catering to a Zeta. If Carlos and Doug Moultrie and Archer all knew about the Zeta, clientele weren't a corporate secret. The hotel meeting itself, then, meant nothing. It was just another security detail. But Reardon spent enough time with distributor Malcom Ward to recognize Moultrie's competence. As head of security, though, what role did Reardon, an insider with a foot in both the drug operation of RWS and the motor sales, play with Malcolm Ward? Liaison? Regional director? Messenger boy? Why the head of security? Why not one of his team?

"Then what—" Archer's confusion was clear.

"It's a puzzle," Jessica said, her voice lighting up in excitement, "of who knew what and when and if or why it relates to what we really want to know, which is who set off a bomb that killed your sister and why."

Someone made a strangled kind of coughing sound. Archer, Matt thought, but couldn't be sure until Jessica said, "I'm sorry, Archer. I didn't mean to sound so . . . I'm sorry."

"This," Archer choked out. He inhaled a hitched breath, a wounded noise slipping out before he continued. "She died because of me? Because of the Zeta? I did this?"

No, Reardon did this. Matt closed his eyes, trying to grab at what his brain was tossing up. Did Reardon step on Malcolm Ward's turf, take out one of their own, no matter how peripheral? Or two, if he did Chris Bolton three weeks before Jimmy's jail cell blabbing.

That made no sense.

The distributors operated independently. An operation as large as RWS wouldn't care about a single shipment or whether one of Malcolm Ward's own talked to the cops. And Reardon wouldn't be head of security if he were stupid enough to micro-manage a single distributor. He'd simply tell them to clean up their own mess.

"No," Sebastian said firmly. "That's just information that may or may not mean anything in the long run."

Information. High-level contacts with big players in the drug trade. Zetas. Arabs. Afghanis. Did Reardon piss off Malcolm Ward's lieutenant by elevating Doug Moultrie, a newcomer to Malcolm Ward, into the larger dealings of RWS in a very short time?

"Reardon was here," Matt said. "In Daytona. He met Archer just a few miles from the drug stash. Why Reardon? He's RWS Security. Malcolm Ward runs the Daytona territory. Jimmy Shad ratted out Malcolm Ward, not RWS. Why would RWS step in? Why would Ward let them when they have other people who could have recovered the drugs?"

Silence.

"Archer," Jessica said. "Out loud."

"Oh. God, sorry. I don't know. I don't know anything except yes, Reardon is head of security for RWS. I don't know how all the drug stuff works."

He fell silent again.

"Maybe," Jessica said. "Because Malcolm Ward drew attention to themselves with the bombing?"

Matt tapped his cane on the floor. That was a very good thought.

If Matt himself went with Archer to whatever deal Reardon was dictating for Carlos's release, what were the chances he could get Reardon talking? A blind man wouldn't present much of a threat to a guy in Reardon's position. And Matt didn't care about the rest. He just wanted whoever ordered the bomb and eventually the bomb-maker. If RWS had an issue with Malcolm Ward having chosen to make such an over-the-top statement, would Reardon care if a blind man knew who'd made that decision?

Invisible Moultrie-In-The-Middle had been on scene at the bombing. What Matt really needed was Moultrie to start talking to Cin. Or maybe he could just shoot Reardon in the face for the hell of it and ask Carlos, who was supposed to have met Ward's lieutenant offshore. "The meeting on the boat was for buyers. Carlos is a salesman, but why were you there, Archer?"

"They needed a rep from accounting because deals frequently occur at those kinds of things. I've been to a few of them. And Carlos deals directly with a lot of the Central Florida buyers, so for once" —his breath hitched—"we could go together."

"Did Carlos meet with any Daytona locals while you were there?"

"Buyers, yeah, a couple."

"You know who?"

"Like names? No."

"Was Moultrie there?"

"No."

But Jimmy had been. "Why was Jimmy Shad there?"

"Carlos said Jimmy wasn't supposed to be there, but no one wanted to cause a scene in front of the buyers. He came with one of the dinner chefs or something."

Francis Duncan. Jimmy's girlfriend. The dead chef. Matt rubbed his face with one hand, ran his fingers back through his hair. He didn't want to think anymore. He needed to do.

Apropos of nothing, Archer said, "I've never even smoked pot."

Matt could use a toke on the fattie in his safe about now. Spider had to know more about Malcolm Ward than Jess thought he did. As Ed's go-to and the way he put together exactly what Matt needed with little instruction on short notice, he had to be supplying IT to everyone who was anyone in Daytona and Matt would bet he was Reardon's whiz kid.

His phone buzzed.

He pressed one earbud in and thumbed the switch on the cord. "Loose."

"I know she's with you, Loose," Charlie said. "What are you trying to hide?"

"Who? Jessica? I was texting to see if you still had her. She's not picking up her calls and we have an appointment this afternoon."

"Oh," Charlie said.

"Look, maybe she's with Spider."

"Spider? The computer geek?"

"You know him?"

"If it's the same guy. Blonde? A little bit stud, a little bit nerd?"

"Asking the wrong guy, Charlie."

"Oh. Sorry. Mid-to late twenties? Contracts with half the city to untangle what the corporate IT guys fuck up?"

"Jessica dates"—*dating? Is that what you call it, Loose?* —"this guy named Spider. Ed at the Kennel Club can tell you if her Spider is your Spider."

"Ed's not too happy with me at the moment."

"I can imagine," Matt said. "Never wake the man between eight a.m. and noon. It's the only sleep he gets, I think."

"I'll ask him."

"If you find her, remind her I need her this afternoon."

"Not your damn messenger, Loose," he said, and hung up.

"Holy shit, Mr. Loose," Jessica said. "I bought it, and I'm standing right here next to you."

"Turn your phone on, Jess. I need to talk to Spider, hopefully before Archer gets the call he's waiting on."

"Too late," Sebastian said, from further across the room than Matt thought he had been. "Looks like we have company."

CHAPTER
TWENTY-FOUR

C in's standing in deep sand. The sun is early-morning bright, low in the east. Curious, she lifts her arm. She casts no shadow. The middling surf rolls in its comforting eternal rhythm, retreating with a hiss. A couple of kids run in and out of the waterline, playing tag with the ocean while their mom sits on the sand. Cin turns her face up to let the morning breeze kiss her skin but can't feel it. This isn't something she thought she'd miss. Until she became ashes pouring into an urn, she'd been caught up in a strange acceptance of her circumstances. For the first time, she mourns her life.

She takes a deep breath of ocean air, surprised she can taste the salt on it, before she lowers her chin and scans the beach. This is where she landed when she tried focusing on Matt and Jimmy Shad. If she'd expected anything, it was a classroom, not this. A surfer is riding into shore. Two or three others are bobbing on the water as the set starts coming in. Shading her eyes, she studies the rider.

It's Jimmy Shad.

The shore is a shallow shelf here. Slogging through twenty yards of less than knee-deep water at the end of his run, Jimmy tosses a shaka over his shoulder to his friends and keeps walking through the dry sand. He glances around, looking for someone. Cin turns when he passes her and follows him to the seawall. He plants his board upright and snatches up his towel from atop his backpack to dry his face and hair.

She tries not to sigh with impatience but fails. Should she try to refocus?

"Hey, Jimmy," a gravely baritone says.

They both spin on their heels. It's the crooked nose man. Evidently besides his badly set nose, his throat is damaged.

"You see Chris today?"

"Meeting him in a few, dude."

"I gotta message for him."

"I'll tell him."

"I need to deliver it. It's from Reardon."

"That guy from Miami?"

Crooked Nose shakes his head. "He's from Palm Bay."

Jimmy shrugs and loops the towel over his neck. "Whatever. He's not from here."

"No, but Mr. Ward would still appreciate your help."

Eyes widening and nostrils flaring, Jimmy says, "He's not with Malcolm Ward."

"He is. Did you think Mr. Ward would limit himself to Daytona?"

Jimmy searches the view around him like he'll find an answer hanging in the air. "I guess not. Didn't know you were mixed up with . . . Mr. Ward."

"You don't like Mr. Ward?"

Holding his hands up, Jimmy says, "Peace, dude. I leave the dealing to Chris. You got business with him, that's aight."

He gathers his stuff, and they kick sand up behind them as they trudge along. Beyond them, all Cin sees is spectral fog. The sand shifts around Cin's feet, but it's not hot and there's no effort needed to move through it. After everything she's experienced, it still strikes her as odd.

A closed beach access takes shape ahead and a small grassy park with a pavilion appears uphill from it. Now she recognizes the Granada approach in Ormond Beach. The fog drifts away until she's simply seeing the world as it has always looked to her.

They walk up the pavement past the empty attendant's booth. Crooked Nose parks himself on top of a picnic table under the pavilion while Jimmy rinses himself and his board off in the public shower.

There's an older couple at another table. Cin looks past them to

Granada Boulevard, the eastern end of State Road 40. Matt and Ethan are crossing A1A from the shopping center. Ethan is talking with earnest enthusiasm and Matt has his face turned down to the sweep of his cane, listening intently.

They've almost passed the pavilion when Matt says something, and Crooked Nose's head snaps up.

"Hey, Mr. Loose," Jimmy shouts. "Jimmy Shad. You're styling those boardies, Teach."

"Test tonight, Jimmy," Matt says without slowing down, Ethan eyeing Jimmy up.

"Got it covered, Mr. Loose."

Matt casts a shaka over his shoulder. Ethan launches back into whatever they were talking about before Jimmy interrupted.

Jimmy tugs on a tee shirt without drying off and slips into his flip-flops. "Let's go, man," he says to Crooked Nose, who, like Cin, is still watching Matt and Ethan go down the ramp and across the sand toward the water. "You know him?"

Cin can see he does, but he says, "No. Never saw him before," and falls in beside Jimmy.

She tries to follow but can't. Every step she takes is right back into the place she is. There's pressure on her right wrist. She can't lift her arm. The pressure wraps itself around Cin's wrist in a familiar way. Fingers. A hand.

She freezes.

There's nothing in front of her but the park, A1A beyond, Jimmy and Crooked Nose walking away from her.

Someone invisible tugs on her wrist, trying to pull her sideways. Cin pulls back, but she's anchored to the memory. She changes directions, leaning forward to straight-arm her assailant, but nothing solid meets her and then the color bleeds out of the world like it's a fading polaroid.

The green grass goes greyish-green, and the men become ghosts and the roadway is just a slash of gray with streaks of light moving over it.

The veil.

The hold on Cin's wrist tightens and releases and then tugs on her again.

She squints in what seems the right direction, but there's nothing to see.

Among all the others babbling on the sand, the cadence of Matt's voice carries from the foggy swath that she knows is the ocean.

If Cin yells, he won't hear her, not from here in the veil. And not from there in the past before he even knew her.

Besides, what could really hurt her in the veil when she's dead already?

Cin lets it draw her away.

One step. Two. The veil gives easily around her. Maybe she's getting the hang of this.

As each finger of the—what? Spirit? It must be, right?—tugging at her presses into her skin, that disconcerting feeling of fading passes through her as she crosses over.

A CELL PHONE RANG.

"Who is it?" Matt said.

"Reardon," Archer said.

"On the phone or in the car?"

"On the phone, Matt," Sebastian said. "I got eyes on a known local Mara in the car and another man."

"Reardon," Archer said, in a tone that Matt recognized as him answering the call.

Archer listened to whatever Reardon had to say, the tension in the room palpable. Car doors slammed outside.

"Mile Marker 228. Yes," Archer said. He blew out a noisy breath. "It was his phone, but some other guy had it, said Reardon was tied up. I'm supposed to leave now and call him from—"

"He say anything about an escort?"

"That's a no, Matt," Sebastian said, apparently translating Archer's answer.

"Let's just see then," Matt said, "if they're here for us or we're just being paranoid now."

The maras were talking as they came down the hall, a low murmur with no distinct words. One of them knocked on the door.

"Jessica," Matt said. "Take a seat on the couch."

"We're just friends of your sister, Archer, got it?" Sebastian said. "Answer the door."

Matt stepped back further into the living room. Aware of the kitchen's corner wall, he turned a little, placing his left shoulder near it so that he wouldn't be immediately visible to the newcomers. Archer passed in front of him and called out, "Who is it?"

"Friends of your sister," one of the maras said. "We've brought you something."

Archer hesitated, probably looking to Sebastian for guidance. He flipped the deadbolt over and swung the door open.

"We see you have company," the one who had spoken through the door said as he entered. He paused in front of Matt, then moved past, his friend close behind, carrying the damp odor of the Halifax River in with them, stale cigarette smoke, and faint sweat. "Hi, miss, I'm sorry to bother you. You, too, sirs. We're sorry for your loss. Lucinda was a wonderful woman, was she not?"

Archer stopped in the short hall, standing to Matt's left.

"She was," Sebastian said.

The space felt tight with six adults filling it.

"You're Ethan's uncle," another voice said. "The cop."

"Former," Matt said automatically. Ethan wasn't supposed to talk about that, but part-time professor didn't have the same ring to a young boy.

"I seen you," the first one said. "You bartend at the track."

A major disadvantage to being blind. No longer being familiar with the faces of people around you in the routine course of your days, taking note of you without ever speaking. He held out his arms. "Not much work for a blind cop," he said, keeping his tone mild. "How do you two know Cin?"

"Oh, you know, here and there. Track days."

"They know she was into street-racing," Archer said, "if that's what you mean."

"Oh," the first one continued. "Then, yeah, that's where we know her from. You're Archer, right? Her brother? She talked about you a lot."

"How'd you know her . . . Matt?" the other said. "Your name's Matt, right?"

"That's right. Which is your kid?"

"Rodrigo. The shortstop."

"You know Reardon?" the first one said.

"No, I don't," Matt said.

"Can I talk to you in private, Archer?" he said. "Reardon wanted me to pass something along."

"Uh, sure, outside?"

Not the smartest choice.

"I'm leaving anyway," Sebastian said. "I'll go out with you."

"No, man," the first mara said. "We just want a moment."

Matt spread his open hands. "Then stay, talk to Archer. We'll go."

"No, man, we're good," the same mara said, and patted Matt's shoulder as he strode back past him.

The front door opened as Rodrigo's dad shuffled by with a muttered, "Good to see 'ya, man."

Archer eased by. "It's fine. I'll be right back."

The front door shut behind them. "Crap," Sebastian said for all of them, his voice traveling back to his post at the window.

Nothing to be done about it. Sebastian could make calls if he needed to. "Did you recognize them, Jess?" Matt said. "You got your phone dialed up for Spider yet?"

She stood and spoke as she came over to him. "No, the ones I know look like gangbangers, all tatted up. Here," she said, touching his hand. "Phone."

"The tatted ones are MS-13's public face, the talkers," Sebastian said. "The taller guy is Israel Portillo. US citizen. Army Ranger, honorable discharge. Raised inside. He's new generation enforcer. They get their training from Uncle Sam and then take their place within the organization."

Matt listened to Spider's phone ring.

"They go from the military to selling drugs?" Jessica said.

Sebastian's voice was muffled, turned away from them at the

window. "Drugs are the least of MS-13's business. The military guys don't sell or steal. They enforce respect and loyalty, step in when things go south. They don't advertise themselves. They're the reason the local cliques don't just eat themselves."

"Yeah," Spider said into Matt's ear.

"It's Matt Loose, Spider."

"Is Jess okay?"

"She's right here. Listen, what will you tell me about Malcolm Ward?"

"Malcolm Ward?"

"You gave Jess Centro's name, Spider. I know you know most of the players in this town, if not the county. And beyond."

"Don't know what you're talking about, Mr. Loose."

"Jessica does."

That shut him up for a second.

"Come on, Spider."

"It's not my business what Jess does or doesn't know. My business is to not know anything."

"I'm going to make a few statements. You can correct me if I'm wrong."

More silence.

"Malcom Ward is an independent group but affiliated with the drug arm of RWS Motors." When Spider remained silent, Matt went on. "Malcolm Ward contracts with MS-13 for some of their dirty work. You contract with Malcolm Ward. And MS-13. You know who's in charge."

"Damn it. They're headed to the car," Sebastian said.

"You registered a pre-paid phone in Jessica's name," Matt continued, "that she was unaware of."

"No, I didn't," Spider said, for the first time.

"A man named Jimmy Shad called her on it after calling several people who died before he did. That painted a big target on her back for the cops, but she has no links to these people. You do."

"They're opening the trunk," Sebastian said.

"I didn't register the phone," Spider said. "I'm the tech geek. Why would I do that to her?"

Matt had been wondering that same thing. "It was a threat, wasn't it? Malcolm Ward's bid to keep you quiet. At any time, the big boss could implicate Jessica in any crime they committed. And the threat worked, until you fucked up and they pulled the trigger, so to speak."

"Okay," Sebastian breathed.

"That's weird," Jessica said from over by Sebastian.

Matt redoubled his attempt to ignore them since Sebastian would do whatever needed doing. He swung the folded cane in his hand to give himself the doorways and retreated into the bedroom as he listened to Spider's return to silence. Spider fucked up and Malcolm Ward, with malice aforethought, kept their threat to what? Implicate Jessica, maybe bring Spider down by association during the investigation? No. They had proved they'd kill an innocent if they paid MS-13 to kill Jimmy's girlfriend as Charlie and Cin had first suspected. Any good defense lawyer would get the calls from the pre-paid as evidence Jessica conspired to commit murder dismissed before the prosecutors could even open their mouths. Why would Malcolm Ward threaten Spider and not just kill him?

Because a spider with a different leg in every hole in town had to be a threat, dead or alive. They didn't mind batting it around to make sure it knew who it belonged to but pissing it off too much or killing it was a line they wouldn't cross. "You fucked up, but they can't piss you off too much," Matt said, testing that theory, keeping his voice low, "by straight-up killing her, or getting you arrested, because you've got knowledge. For them to actually follow through by pointing a finger at Jess, and for something this big, they think you compromised them in some huge way. They've been exposed. Cops died. What exactly did you do to them, Spider? Was Reardon involved?"

Silence answered him. A frisson of surprise raised the hairs on his arms. "Just how bad did you fuck up?"

"I didn't fuck up. And I'm beyond pissed," Spider said, and hung up.

Matt yanked his earbud out. Well, maybe Spider hadn't fucked up, but Matt had by not just letting DBPD do their thing without him, and he needed to make this situation work for him. Pocketing his phone, he strode back out to the living room. He needed to ensure Sebastian didn't shut him out before he spoke face to face with Reardon. "What's weird?" he said, louder and harder than he intended. "The maras aren't driving away with him in the trunk, yet?"

"They're leaving and it looks like Archer's coming back up," Sebastian said.

"That's weird," Matt agreed.

"What did Spider say?" Jess asked.

"It wasn't him."

"Do you believe him?"

"Yeah."

They stood waiting for Archer. Matt rubbed his thumb over one of the sectional seams on his cane. Some sort of shoot-em-up TV show full of shouts and screeching tires blared from next door, turned on sometime in the past little while. Matt became aware again, among the various odors staining the air with everyone's movement in and out, of the sweet, subtle scent of Cin's coffee table candle. He rubbed at the hollow soreness of his chest. Where was she?

The door opened and Archer swept in, swinging the door shut again in the same motion. It slammed home in the frame as Archer stopped beside him but said nothing.

"What was in the trunk?" Sebastian asked, conversationally.

"Reardon."

Matt barked out an unexpected laugh. "Is that what the guy who called meant by tied up?"

"He's dead."

What the ever-loving fuck.

CHAPTER
TWENTY-FIVE

The crooked nose man shows Cin his face for just an instant before he swirls into the gray fog of time, still holding her wrist, but there's no sensation of touch in the veil. Still, they flow along together, or the visions they pass do, Cin can't really tell. Among the wisps and swirls and fully formed specters, a woman in a full ball gown appears ahead of them.

The dress gains color and volume as she nears. Only the dress. It's the deep blue of a Florida sky right before the last of the light dies on night's doorstep. Without expression, she turns her gray head to watch Cin and the crooked nose man pass.

And then there comes a feeling of entry, being swallowed in dense mist, and Crooked Nose lets go of Cin's wrist. Her heart flutters, her belly turning, but before she can panic, she finds she Knows what to do. She concentrates on Here. Now.

The gray veil falls away and Cin's looking at herself.

She's sitting at the back of the Daytona Taproom on beachside, with Charlie and his wife, Natalie. It's late. They're having chocolate shakes after beers and burgers. Cin remembers this night from a few weeks ago. The sweetness of the cold shake floods her mouth and she closes her eyes at the intense sensation. When she opens them again a second later, she's looking right at Charlie. He's looking back, his eyes and the slow smile that quirks his lips full of fond affection. She's inside her body, and, wildly, for just a moment, she wonders if she's alive again.

Then Natalie says something, drawing Charlie's attention, and then they are all getting up and going out into the warm late May night. They go their way and Cin goes hers. She walks along Seabreeze Boulevard towards the ocean, just like she did that night. After crossing A1A, she threads her way through the late-night tourists still wandering along the Boardwalk to the beach itself. After stripping off her work boots and socks, she carries them in one hand down to the water line and walks north, reveling in the coarseness of the sand on her soles, the slight cool of the sea breeze over her skin.

It's a gorgeous night under a new moon. Its light tips the barely rising curls of the calm wavelets that stretch forever into the dark. The beach is quiet, the only sounds the voices and music drifting from the Hilton. The only other walkers on the sand besides herself are staying high on the beach. Cin's well past Ocean Walk and the band shell before she sees two men coming her way, directly in her path.

They wear nice shirts and slacks with the cuffs rolled up. Having left their shoes somewhere on the beach, they're barefoot. They're engaged in intense discussion. The Hispanic man is talking the most, one hand in his pocket and the other waving in front of him. The other man, Caucasian, dark hair, has his head down, listening and nodding. He glances up as Cin nears them. It's Reardon.

In real life, Cin did what women are trained to do and gave way, skirting around them on the dry sand without thought. This time she stops. Her body doesn't. She watches herself walk on, ducking her head, and giving way. Both the men fall silent, turning their heads to watch her. They exchange a look, and the Hispanic man shakes his hand like he's touched something hot.

"Damn hot," Reardon mutters, low enough that Cin never heard him that night.

She Knows she can re-enter the veil to follow their time trail, but the Knowing doesn't give her the "how" to do that. She holds her breath and lets Reardon walk right through her. There's a moment of dark gray shadow, like driving under an overpass on a sunny day and then Cin's back on the beach and Reardon is behind her. Well, that didn't work.

His companion begins to talk again. "The third cache will be in place next week with a very grateful holder."

Cin releases her breath in a rush. All sensation has walked away with her body.

She follows them, just an observant ghost drifting in their wake. Nothing to see here.

"You're moving fast," Reardon says.

"I have fifteen cache holders across central Florida," the Hispanic man continues. "We will be in place before they know we're here, undercut their prices, and disrupt their operations within days. They can keep Miami."

"And what do you need from me?"

The man, Cin thinks he's Mexican, stops, turning to face Reardon. "I need you to move that cache when I ask you to. Two weeks maybe. No more. I need you to ensure we have Daytona locked down. Controlling the I-95 and I-4 corridors is vital to holding our territory once we take over."

"I can deal with Malcolm Ward."

The man slashes a hand through the air. "No deals. I only want the maras."

"Getting the maras to switch teams is going to be tough," Reardon says. "They like the fact that RWS is Salvadoran —"

RWS? Like where Archer works?

"Then they will like the money and power the Zetas offer them," the man says. "They will have more to send home than their current agreements can give them, just like our mara brothers in Honduras and San Salvador."

Zetas. In Daytona.

"The X3s—"

"Are already here. They're waiting for my word to take control if the maras decline your invitation."

The Sureños, or X3s, like MS-13, have made a name for themselves as enforcers. They maintain loyalties to Mexican concerns, primarily the Gulf Cartel, and when imprisoned, the Mexican Mafia. MS-13, in theory, pledges allegiance to homies in El Salvador, Guatemala,

Honduras, but are most loyal to themselves, in it for short term gain and the adrenaline rush of criminal violence.

In the U.S., members of both gangs have a disconnect from their ethnic origins and, as Americans, military training provided by good 'ol Uncle Sam. Like the more public maras of MS-13, the most visible X3s are the least informed, most violent, and most likely to end up in prison. The rest are committed, trained, and scary. You might know them for years as a neighbor or social contact without knowing about their gang affiliation.

"Yes, sir," Reardon says, gesturing back the way they'd come. "We should start back."

They about-face. Cin ducks out of their way this time.

Reardon says, "I'll make it happen, sir."

"Yes," the man says. If the X3s are waiting on word from him, he must be a Zeta. Arguably the most dangerous Mexican cartel, they do it all, drugs, sex trafficking, gun running. Gaining a foothold in central Florida would put them in direct opposition to the Sinaloa Cartel, which currently dominates the territory. A bloodbath in the making. Cin thought the Zetas were in disorganized decline with the loss to law enforcement of nearly all their founding leadership, but this man appears confident in every way. "Yes, you will."

When did that other conversation take place on the beach, Jimmy Shad and Crooked Nose about giving Chris Bolton a message from Reardon? Before Bolton died. And she came walking here on the beach about a week before his murder. Jimmy said Bolton had been killed by Malcolm Ward, an ex-special forces meth-head freak. Had Reardon flipped Bolton into working whatever conspiracy he had going on here? Did Malcolm Ward find out?

Oh, God. Archer.

What time is it?

The fog inside Cin rises fast, like her pulse, her heart rate leaping.

How much current time has spun away from her while she's been wandering in the past?

Hours? Weeks?

Is she too late?

"I HAVE TO GO," Archer said, without moving.

"But Reardon's dead," Jessica said.

Sebastian crossed the room, saying, "Carlos has changed hands."

"Yeah," Archer said, his resignation clear.

"To Malcom Ward," Jessica said, catching on fast. "Or maybe just the maras?"

"I have to go," Archer said again, but this time he lurched into motion.

Matt threw his left arm out straight and closing his hand, caught Archer's bicep before he could get away. "No," he said. His words again came out harsher than he meant but hearing himself strengthened Matt's resolve that much more. "No. We have something they want. If they knew where it was, they'd have taken it."

"What, the drugs?" Archer said.

"Yes."

"Okay, Mr. Loose," Jessica said. She'd crowded in closer to them, so they were all huddled in the entry hall. "That's what Archer's doing. Trading the drugs for Carlos."

"Sebby," Matt said, hanging onto Archer, making it harder for him to try and ditch them. "You got support on this task?"

"Not officially. And we're need to know. No local law enforcement back-up."

"Unofficially?"

"We get a location, I can get a team."

Until they got a location on Carlos, then, they needed to play offense. "They won't kill him," Matt lied, because if the maras had him, they'd do it just to make a point, and if it were Malcolm Ward, they'd use the maras to make a point.

Except.

Except Malcolm Ward had managed to stay under the radar until Jimmy Shad, presumably, pissed them off. And Archer was an unknown to them. Ward, as a whole, was cautious, as proven by having a plan to keep even a smartass like Spider under their thumb. "They know if they kill Carlos, they won't get their drugs."

An icy-hot phantom hand slap hit his chest and sunk deep inside, making him gasp.

"Not Malcolm Ward's drugs," Cin said, her sharp, near panicky words hurting his right ear drum. "Zetas."

Matt's fingers dug harder into Archer's bicep. Archer shoved him back. Using both hands, Matt shoved Archer back in turn and then stepped right into his space. "They won't kill him. We *will* get a location."

Archer pushed him back again and this time Matt let him.

Distraught, stifling his sobs, Archer retreated to the kitchen.

Conscious of Cin at his back, Matt said, "What time is it, Jess?"

"One-thirty."

"Sebby, I need you to stay with him. Find someplace else to be. Coach him. When they call because he hasn't shown, Archer needs to insist on proof of life. And if you really do have somebody else on the ground here, you need to get them out there to watch that mile marker. See who shows, if anyone."

"I'll map it. I can't imagine it's not just a checkpoint. If it's clear," he said, admitting there was someone else in the know, someone on speed dial who could act fast, "he can call at the time he should be there, say he's there, see what they say next. If there's someone there, we'll wait for them to call, get proof of life."

It was a risk, but not unreasonable. Matt nodded. He raised his voice. "Did the maras know you were supposed to be transporting the drugs, Archer?"

Cin laid a hand on his shoulder. "MS-13?"

"Yeah," Archer said from the kitchen. The kitchen floor, it seemed.

"Time limit?"

"No. But I told them five minutes to get rid of you. Ten minutes to get on the road."

"They won't be lingering with a body in the trunk in June," Sebastian said.

"Eww," Jessica said.

Sebastian snorted, a soft amused sound. "I'll call DBPD with an anonymous tip."

"Cin's keys, Archer," Matt said. "Jess, you're driving.

C in's car was stored south of ISB, down Clyde Morris near the airport. They took Sebastian's car, in case Archer's was known to whoever was expecting him. Cin was quiet on the ride over. Without a word, she had let Archer give them directions and Jessica follow them. At the entrance to the storage units, Jessica rolled down the window and entered the code Archer had given her.

"There's parking to the left," Cin said. "If you're taking mine."

Sebastian's car was less conspicuous, but they'd have more control over the situation by having the drugs at hand, especially if time was short or the company didn't come through for Sebastian. And if they did, despite Matt's skepticism, did he want the company looking over his shoulder by tracking Sebastian's car?

"Is there parking?" Matt said out loud. "We're going to leave this car here."

"Gotcha," Jessica said.

They climbed out.

He let Jessica take the lead, keeping pace with her by feel and sound, swinging his cane. When he opened his free hand in invitation, Cin entwined her fingers with his. It felt physical, except that when he fisted his hand, he could also feel the close of his fingers against each other.

He thought about Spider as they walked, wishing he could ask for Cin's help in hashing out whether Spider was even worth his worry except in relation to Jessica. Spider knew Reardon. He knew Carlos. Since Ed knew Moultrie, maybe Spider did, too. But Spider knew a lot of people. Then again, Spider had done something, with Reardon, to piss Malcolm Ward off.

Did it have anything to do with the bomb, though? With killing cops? Matt's brain kept circling back to the thought that here was another local that Reardon was throwing into the bigger pool of RWS Motors. Maybe Malcolm Ward was simply hanging Jessica over Spider's head to keep him on their team. Still, Spider had to know who was running fucking Ward.

A plane roared from their left, rising into the air and directly over their heads. Cars went by them in a constant stream on Clyde Morris to his right, confusing Matt's ears. There was someone shouting. And then a number of voices yelling in cadence. Matt stopped to listen. "Who's shouting?"

"ROTC," Cin and Jessica said at the same time.

"Embry Riddle," Jessica clarified. "They run all over the place down here. The unit's right here, another twenty feet."

Jessica fiddled with the keys before she slid the rattling overhead door up. Light came up with it and it took a second for Matt's brain to process the shape of the car crouching inside. Jess flipped the fluorescent lights on to reveal the front of the gleaming patchwork-red street racer, sporting an air-scooping menace of a front spoiler. The car exuded an undeniable allure.

The palms of Matt's hands itched, wanting the steering wheel beneath them.

"Holy cow," Jessica said, her gaze roaming the lines of the car. Her blonde hair hung loose, tucked behind her small ear, pierced not only through the lobe, but with several hoops encircling the rim, as well. "Wish you could see this car, Mr. Loose."

He turned his head slightly to look up at Cin beside him. Schooling his tone in hopes that the awe he was bottling up didn't show, he said, "She's gorgeous?"

Jessica laughed. "Well, she's a bit mismatched. The hood's a different red than the quarter panels, which are different than the doors, and the front spoiler is black, but yeah. The light's bouncing off her and she could make even a Prius-driving environmentalist rethink their choices in life, if only for a moment."

Letting go of Cin's hand, Matt walked into the unit as he folded his cane. He ran his right hand over the slope of the spoiler to the hood and then along the passenger side curve of the front panel, Cin trailing him. Smooth as glass. There was enough room to open the door without hitting the work bench and toolbox along the wall, but Matt just stepped back. Careful not to look right at Jessica, he said, "Why don't you start her up and pull out before I get in?"

"Do you want me to check the back?"

No, he wanted to. But he couldn't, could he? "Yeah."

She swung the hatch back up and leaned inside. "Hang on. The spare's sitting on top with a blanket over it. Holy shit."

"What?"

"It's a lot of drugs," Cin said.

"The spare's on top of a bunch of white bricks, like the ones you see in the movies."

As much as he wanted to join her, Matt made himself stay where he was, but chanced leaning a bit to watch her. Cin ventured closer. Jessica shoved the tire up on edge and pried at something underneath it. "Yep," she called out. "The tire well is full, too."

"Put everything back the way it was and wipe your prints from the handle. We get stopped, you're just the driver, got it?"

She was already in motion before he finished. She slammed the hatchback closed and pulled the bottom of her shirt up to wipe her prints. "Got it," she said with a determined nonchalance.

Her confidence in him was a bit scary.

She shot a tight-lipped smile at him and went to the driver's door. Her mouth widened into a true smile as she slid into the car. She had a raised-on-a-beach, polished surfer-girl vibe going. It made her approachable, but still let her blend in. Good not just for hospitality, but for the work he was sure Sebastian would recruit her for when their current crises passed.

"Tell me," he said to Cin, when Jessica slammed her door shut, already reaching for the seatbelt.

"Reardon and a Zeta met maybe three weeks ago on the beach here.

The Zeta laid out his plan to take over the drug trade across central Florida, whatever portion Reardon controls now. I think the cache that Archer picked up belongs to the Zetas. They talked about RWS, where Archer works."

"RWS is a front. Reardon works for them. So does Malcolm Ward," Matt told her. The Civic's engine roared into life and then settled into a pleasant growl of an idle. It sounded more like a muscle car than any Honda he had ever heard. Cin frowned but let him continue. "Their drug operations are limited to Florida, but I think laundering is their main income and it's large, international. Archer oversaw a recent fleet purchase by a Zeta higher-up. Doug Moultrie acted as his driver cum bodyguard in that deal."

"Doug Moultrie?"

"Yeah, the guy you keep seeing?"

"The crooked nose man is Doug Moultrie?"

"Yeah. He got in with Reardon through Malcolm Ward." The trapped exhaust reeked. Matt reached out and banged on the roof twice. Moment of truth if Jessica couldn't drive stick. She gunned the engine once and then shifted into first and eased out without a lurch.

"Why did Jimmy say you were—"

"I don't know," Matt said, wishing he had time to really talk to her. How *did* Jimmy link him to Doug Moultrie? "You saw him before you died, right, at Jimmy's?"

She nodded, but looked unsure.

He thought of the blue vase in Lily's living room. Maybe Moultrie was like that vase, an afterthought, inserted into the scene after Cin died. And damn if Matt's heart didn't still jump at that thought even though he was looking right at her. He cleared his throat. "Reardon's dead, too. Two maras showed up at your apartment. They had his body in their trunk. And they have Carlos now. They want the drugs. They may or may not know that Carlos is on our side. He's been undercover."

Her surprise showed in the lift of her brows, but she didn't waste time on it. "MS-13 has a deal with RWS. Reardon was supposed to ask them to work with the Zetas instead."

"Guess they turned him down," he said, tilting his head at the idling car. Cin took the hint, following him back out into the bright sun. "The maras deal isn't with RWS, it's with Malcolm Ward."

"So, are they horning in on the Zeta take-over of RWS territory by taking the drugs for themselves, or are they taking the drugs to give to Malcolm Ward?"

The sunlight dimmed, almost instantly making the warm breeze feel cooler. Clouds were starting to gather, building towards Daytona's standard afternoon shower. The maras weren't exactly known for being organized. It depended on who was nominally in charge of the local clique. Matt shrugged. "That's the question of the day. If I can get to whoever's in charge of Malcolm Ward, maybe I can hit two birds with one stone."

The Civic's driver side door opened, and Jessica's head popped up over the roof of the car, her gaze meeting his. He held it, hoping she wouldn't see him seeing her. "You should be wearing your sunglasses, Mr. Loose," she said, disappearing again. "Let's go."

"Can you stay?" he said, going to the passenger door.

Jessica's door thunked shut again.

"I could, but I can do more now, I think," Cin said. "I'm learning. I think I can, I don't know, navigate? I think I can navigate to where I want to go? I can try to find out how we got here."

Here. This place where she was dead, and he was dragging an innocent surfer-girl into danger. "Okay," he said, pulling up the handle, but not opening the door just yet. He hated this. He hated this need he had to be near her, but still couldn't shut his mouth on it. "Come back, okay? Come back to me."

She nodded, lifting both hands to his face, and kissed him. "Still not letting go," she murmured against his lips. And then she was gone, taking her sight with her.

"Where to, boss?" Jessica said after he'd maneuvered himself into the passenger seat and shut the door.

He pulled the seat belt down and fumbled for the catch, blinder, it seemed, after being able to see for a few minutes. She didn't offer help, thank God. It finally clicked home. He pulled on the too-tight strap across his chest and let it go again. "Wherever it is we found Centro last night." Had it only been last night?

"You got it," she said.

Listening to the deep rumble of the engine through the pipes, he tried to just ride along, letting his body absorb the motion, suddenly aware how comfortable he'd been to let Sebastian drive. Was it because he knew Sebastian on a gut-level, despite the revelation he didn't know much about him at all? That Jessica was a woman? But he'd been more comfortable with Cin than with his own sister. Was it automatic cop trust? Jessica's relative youth?

"It's okay," Jessica said. "I've driven stick before. I won't stall us in an intersection or anything."

Matt took his hand off the dash. "It's a stick shift?"

"Smooth, boss."

"What's with calling me boss?"

"Just reminding you in case I don't have a job after tonight. Or we get arrested."

"Smooth."

She lapsed into silence.

Matt wondered if she had smiled his way again. It must die hard, the automatic body language, even knowing he couldn't see it. Did everyone he knew go right on sending him signals he never responded to? He had just assumed that people stopped doing that once they'd been around him for a bit. On the other hand, he'd worked hard with Ethan to ensure he had the right expression on his face as needed, so maybe it shouldn't come as a surprise that people still reacted to him the way they always had.

He thought of everything and nothing all at once, concentrating on the sounds of the cars surrounding them, the pleasing bass of the Civic's exhaust, the vibration of the powerful engine as they idled at lights.

They hadn't gone far when Jessica said, "Here we go." She turned left, a big looping arc, and then made another a minute later. "Oh."

"What?"

"The truck's already here."

That was just information. Not good or bad. Matt was supposed to deliver the title and bill of sale to Centro. Centro was supposed to pay what he owed to Papa when he picked up the truck. A bump in the order of go didn't mean trouble. He'd already decided not to hold the title since who knew how this day would end. "Doesn't change the game plan," Matt said.

"We have a game plan?"

"I have a game plan," Matt clarified. "Your role is to stay in the car."

"And?"

"That's it. Call Sebastian if I'm not back in ten minutes."

"Not the cops?"

"Not the cops."

He scrolled up Sebastian's number, pulled his earbud jack out, and let his phone read it to her before he shoved the jack back in. "You see Centro?"

"No."

"Okay, where's the truck? Exactly?"

CIN'S STANDING on the sand again, but the sun is setting over the ocean instead of rising. It's a beach somewhere on the Pacific. A call and response fills the air. She turns to her right. There's a two-by-two column of fine young things in military tees, camos, and boots trotting along the surf-line. The guy running in the back yells something unintelligible and the line splits. The surf-side line pivots and splashes into the water. The men sand-side spin the opposite direction and pelt hell-bent-for-leather across the wide beach in an increasingly ragged line.

In the water, the men are swimming now, stroking hard, and ducking beneath the waves as they roll in, one after another in the medium surf. On the sand, the men in the lead have dropped to their knees and started digging. In less than a minute, they're all digging except the two furthest down the beach from her. They're casting about, searching for something. One of them breaks towards her at a dead run and then the other. They run along the line of digging men.

In the water, half the men seem to have disappeared. Cin watches for a long moment. Heads pop up above the surface for quick breaths. The officer who initiated the exercise is standing opposite her, hands on his hips. Cin hears the motor at the last second and leaps towards the ocean in reaction. A Jeep containing three older men trundles past her, yards away from her over-the-top reaction considering she's just a . . . whatever she is, not a memory, because they're the memory, right?

But whose? Matt's? She wasn't aiming for him.

The two runners, the closest men to her now, shout at each other, pointing, and then they're also digging, the sand spraying up behind them like they're Great Danes after the world's best bone. Along the digging line, first one man and then another and then a clump of them leap to their feet and run back towards the surf, each carrying a small, plastic bag. Two of the swimmers are now staggering ashore, streaming water, and clutching heavy-looking canvas bags in both hands. The men pair off just above the shoreline, ripping into the bags. Cin walks closer to see what it is they're doing.

They're assembling some sort of weapon, like a rifle, but not. A deep thump booms across the beach and a smoke grenade explodes over the water. Another thump and then another and two more grenades are spilling violet smoke into the sky. The thumps layer over one another in succession, violet smoke now forming a screen that dims the day. Silence falls before one final thump.

Along with everyone standing on the beach, Cin turns her head to locate the last two-man team to launch. While the digger is still staring up at the sky, the wet swimmer drops the rifle-like launcher in the sand like it's burned him, draws his right arm back, and punches the digger square in the face, following through with the full strength of his body as the digger falls away from him. The next pair of men closest to them surge forward and grab each of his arms, dragging him backwards as he screams his fury.

The digger is silent, sprawled face-down in the sand, his body twisted. One hand on his bloody face, he flattens the other on the sand and levers himself up. Blood gushes from his broken nose over his lips and his chin onto the sand. He shakes his head. Red splatters onto the chest and shoulders of his beige shirt. A medic appears at his side, but Cin can't tear her gaze away as the digger looks up, right at her.

It's Doug Moultrie.

WITHIN FEET of reaching the truck, Centro's voice rang out from further away and above Matt. "What the hell you do?"

"I got your truck back." He slid the folded paperwork from his back jeans pocket and held it out. "Your bill of sale and title so you can register it. Delivery wasn't included."

Centro whisked the papers from Matt's fingers. "Well, it here. You think Papa wanting it on his property anymore?"

"You going to tell me who's in charge of Malcolm Ward now?"

"I don't know, and I don't wanta know."

"You going to hold up your end of our bargain?"

"Going down as we speak."

"Thank you."

"Don't thank me. Don't mention my name to nobody. Don't come back. If Mr. Ward shows up, I'm tellin' him everything I know about you."

"And what do you know?"

"That you blind. That that blond girl work for you. That you a former cop wantin' a beat down on a cop and I obliged."

"As one does."

"As one does, that's right. Not my fault some blind man stupid enough to mention Mr. Ward to satisfy his end of the bargain. We done now."

"All right. We're done now."

Centro didn't leave though, just continued to stand there in front of Matt. Nothing moved on the street. No kids played. Thunder grumbled in the distance. Blocks away, traffic whooshed along on Mason Avenue. Centro snorted and crinkled the papers in his hand. "You something else," he said. "Go on now."

Matt turned himself about and swept his cane out to mark the curb before he strode off, the skin of his back crawling until he reached the far side of the street and the passenger door of the Civic. He took a careful breath and tried to quell his rising anxiety, the remembered breath of air that brushed the back of his neck, his scalp, before the baseball bat landed.

DEEP in yet another alcove of the veil, concentrating on Doug Moultrie once more, Cin thinks *now*. She opens her eyes just in time to see the bat swing.

It breaks the back of Matt's skull with an audible crack.

She flinches back.

Why is she here?

She doesn't want to see this.

On his knees, hands zip-tied behind him, Matt's eyes roll up in his head and he face-plants onto the shoulder of his partner, who is lying on his belly, the side of his head caved in, blood spread out in a pool around him.

Three white men stand over them.

The maniac with the bloody bat lowers it and spits on Matt for good measure. "Should've learned your lesson when your girl bit it, asshole," he says in a heavy Spanish accent.

The guy to his right, a lanky man who looks like the boy next door in his thirties, crouches down beside Matt. "He's still breathing."

"Keep your hands off," Bat Boy says. "If she dies, he dies. Maybe he'll live and we can do this all over again."

Motion beyond the three men draws Cin's eye up. Doug Moultrie is walking by, just beyond the veil. For the first time, she notices that there's nothing here, just these guys, Matt, and his dead partner, the smooth, stained concrete of a warehouse floor. No building, nothing above or around them.

Moultrie turns his head to look at her. The bullet hole in his forehead is visible, powder burns spreading out from it like a fat black spider. His killer had stood as close to him as Bat Boy stood to Matt. He glances down at Matt's still body, the blood weeping across his scalp, dripping onto Sam, running onto the floor, but keeps walking.

The lanky man stands and brushes nothing off the thighs of his pants.

With each sweep of his hands, the scene fades a little more until Cin's back in the ether, standing on the river.

Something glitters on the bank.

Compelled, she crouches down and scrabbles in the wispy white mud that both wafts away and clings. The river tumbles and froths less than a foot away. The water leaps in the shapes of the drowned, an arm, a horn, a dog's head as it paddles frantically and endlessly, eternally swept downstream even as some other version of its yellow Labrador self struggles onto the bank, whining, while Cin continues to chase the glitter deeper into the mud.

The dog shakes puppies off its skin and they run yipping into the veil.

It, he, decides to dig beside her. The glittery thing slides and slides, down and down.

The dog leaps in after it and then Cin's falling after the dog.

She falls and falls and falls.

It's only when she closes her eyes against the rush of nothing towards her that she finds there's ground beneath her palms. Grass.

Green and brown grass in a tiny, urban yard.

Sparkles fill the air, water droplets arcing away from the rat-a-tat-tat of a tension sprinkler.

CHAPTER
TWENTY-SEVEN

"We can't pick up a kid in a car full of drugs," Jessica said, her tone incredulous. "Can't someone else get him?"

"Between me and Ethan, Lily's missed too much work. I need to get him home safe and tell Lily I fucked up by getting involved in person."

Jessica slowed the car and angled it to the right.

"What are you doing?"

The Civic rocked to a halt. "Pulling over!" she said in exasperation. "We should've left this in storage and taken Sebastian's car."

"We don't know if we'd have time to get back to it. The situation's too fluid."

"Then we especially don't need a kid in the car. What if we don't have time to take him home?"

Matt waved a hand. "These things always take time. They have to get proof of life and try to get a location. So yes, while I didn't want the drugs sitting in storage in case we have to move fast, there'll be plenty of time to get Ethan locked down."

"What if we get stopped?"

"It's a calculated risk. Don't speed."

"The maras recognized you. They know they can find you at the ballfield."

The ballfield was very public. Lots of people knew him. It'd be busy.

The maras had been neutral towards him at Cin's apartment. If word had gotten to Mr. Ward that Matt was looking for him, he either hadn't told his pit bulls yet or the maras had a different agenda with the Zetas. "They weren't interested in me, which means they don't know anything yet. Let's hope it stays that way."

They drove a meandering route, headed generally in the direction of the Ormond Beach ball fields off US 1, rather than bee-lining directly for them. Every now and then, Matt reminded Jessica to check her mirrors for familiar vehicles, anyone trailing them too long. There was nothing to do now but wait.

Wait to hear from Charlie once whatever Centro set up hit the fan and Thompson went down, because Charlie would certainly think of the last two people in his office bitching about Thompson first. Wait for news to break of a corpse in a trunk being found on an anonymous tip and the fallout of public awareness that MS-13 had been active in Daytona for God—and law enforcement and the criminal element and any real reporter with an ear to the ground—only knows how long. Wait for Sebastian to call with details of the trade for Carlos. Wait for the inevitable contact from whichever of Matt's higher-ups at the company was still in play, though whether that would be by phone or in the flesh and when that might happen wasn't something Matt would try to predict. Wait for Ethan's practice to end so that Matt could pick him up, get him home, confess to Lily. Wait until he could get back to hunting down the Mister in Mr. Ward.

If it turned out Mr. Ward wasn't the responsible party in charge of killing the only woman Matt had connected with in years, well. He would not be waiting to launch himself into figuring out the next possible suspect, but he would let Jessica off the hook of helping him do it.

Once again, as if she were reading his mind, Jessica said, "What if Malcolm Ward didn't do it?"

"Do what?" he said, simply because it was ingrained in him to question.

"Set off that bomb."

"Then I'll go after the next best possible suspect or the bomb maker or the bomb setter."

"Why aren't you doing that? Going up the chain, rather than starting at what you're assuming's the top?"

He couldn't help the smile that rose to his lips. "Because I can. I'm not a cop anymore. I don't have access to the legal investigation. I'm not bound to evidence collection. I'm not bound to a step-by-step procedure that demands I climb to my conclusions. No one's going to ask me to justify my op in triplicate or demand a brief outlining my *logical progression* before I go after the person I think can give me the most answers. Maybe no one in Malcolm Ward has any involvement, but I'm pretty damn certain that because of the fear they've struck in the hearts of people who don't usually give a fuck about criminal loudmouths, that whoever's at the top will know who does." Distantly aware he'd progressed from a light-hearted answer to her question to practically spitting in fury, he calmed the slash of his hand through the air but couldn't stop the words from coming. "And if, somehow, incredibly, that person can convince me they don't know who did it? They'll know who they'd tap if they wanted a spectacular boom and the hassle of having every law enforcement agency in the region coming down on every criminal network in the city in the name of justice."

He turned his face to the window, took a needed breath, and worked to suck his anger back up.

"You don't kill cops," he finally said into her silence, emphasizing each word. He shifted so that he wouldn't be talking to the window, self-conscious now about his outburst, and dropped the tense hike of his shoulders. "Either way, for me, personally, this started with Jimmy Shad giving up the name of an organization that every idiot in the city seems aware of and somehow the cops weren't. It seems likely that if any group could weather having everyone on both sides of the law mad at them for destroying the balance, it would be this one. So that's where I'm going, either to confront a murderer or for info."

Jessica said nothing through two stoplights. A motorcycle buzzed past her side of the car and a second later she hit the brakes hard with a soft curse. She let up and drove on for a minute or so before she made a right-hand turn and accelerated back up to cruising speed before she spoke again. "You don't kill anyone, if you're a real human. Not just cops. If you find out who's at the top of Malcolm Ward, what are you going to do about it? Kill them?"

He raised his brows. He could think of all sorts of reasons to kill someone, and that didn't even include while under orders to protect national security. "I'm blind, Jessica. Blind as in, I can't see the hand in front of my face. *And* not only did Cin take my gun away, I don't have so much as a knife in my pocket. I'm hardly lethal. All I can do is call Charlie and hope DBPD can arrest the guy for something."

"Or gal," she said absently.

Matt rolled his eyes, irritated that now he knew he did that a lot, and then he was rolling them again at himself. He huffed and closed his eyes. The only reason he thought it was a man was because a woman would probably have been smarter about not bringing doom upon her head after carefully remaining under the radar for so long. Why the fuck now? Why not a quiet offing of Jimmy Shad for being a snitch and just move on?

"You haven't called Charlie to report a kidnapping," Jessica pointed out.

He laid his head back against the head rest. God, he was tired. And his head hurt. "Leaving that up to Sebastian."

"Will you trade the drugs for Carlos even if you don't have your answers yet?"

"We'll get a location. A team will get him."

"That's not an answer, Matt. You didn't see Archer's face."

"You're free to drive us to DBPD, Jess." The acid in his stomach churned, lending his next words a bitterness he thought he'd overcome until the start of this conversation turned argument. One-sided argument. Jessica never raised her voice. He didn't know whether to admire or hate her for it. "Not like I'd even know."

THE YELLOW DOG lopes through the dropping water, snapping at the thin streams. He comes to a halt directly over the sprinkler, lowering his head between his front legs to lap at the burble of water he's created. The tiny yard belongs to a tall brownstone nestled cheek to jowl with others of its kind. Cars are parked along the street. The front door opens. Matt leans out, catches sight of the dog, and whistles at him. When he lifts his head, Matt says, "Yo, dumbass, where you been?"

Matt's young, between a boy and a man, no more than twenty. Military haircut.

The dog is real now, or a real memory, maybe? He bounds over to the bottom of the stairs and shakes. Only water comes off his coat. His ears flop hard enough to whap his own face.

"Good dog," Matt says, but that only triggers the dog to rush the stairs. "Stop, wait. Stay. Sit. Sit!"

With a shimmy-slide, the dog worms past Matt and into the house. "Shit." He looks up past Cin and says it again, with a different look on his face. "Shit."

Cin scrambles up off the ground.

Doug Moultrie, wearing Army fatigues, is getting out of a cab across the street.

He slings a duffle bag over his shoulder and pays the driver before he looks Matt's way. Cin can't read the expression on his face. She glances at Matt. He's come down the steps, his hands shoved deep into his jeans' front pockets. "Where's your brother?"

Moultrie crosses the road as he says, "He's got class, couldn't come."

"Where you headed next?"

"Hunter Airfield. Georgia." Moultrie is halfway across the yard before he adds, "Got two nights. When do you deploy?"

"Next week," Matt says. Moultrie comes to a stop a foot from him, invading Matt's personal space, but Matt holds his ground. "My parents have a job over in Allentown. They're gone until Saturday."

"I've got weed," Moultrie says.

Matt draws his right hand out of his pocket and sweeps his fingers through the hair that's fallen across his forehead and lets his hand linger at the back of his head before he lets a crooked grin surface. His eyes light up with it. He's a beautiful young man. "Yeah, okay."

Moultrie answers with his own tilted smile. He's older than Matt, by three or four years, Cin thinks. His nose has yet to be irrevocably broken on some future beach exercise. Some decision's been made. They both relax and then they're piling up the steps and through the front door, Moultrie hot on Matt's heels, as they shove one another. The door slams on Matt yelling at the dog for tracking water through the house.

The veil isn't swirling in although Cin can sense it there, waiting. The house remains as solid as real life in front of her. She wills herself into the veil. Nothing happens. The sprinkler rat-a-tat-tats through its rotation. What else does Moultrie want her to see? It has to be him. Cin thinks about how it felt to drift those first few times, letting real time pass her by, and then how it's happening here, in this memory.

Matt and Moultrie walk past the dining room window, and she's drawn effortless into their wake. This time she's more aware of the moments flitting by like seconds while she's briefly in the fringes of the veil. It's after dark now and here's Moultrie lying on a twin bed in an upstairs junk room meant for the most casual of guests, lighting up a joint.

Something mellow and scratched is playing on an old turntable sitting sideways on a dresser beside a stack of scuffed and faded albums. The Lab is sprawled out across the middle of a blue throw rug in the center of the worn, wood floor.

"C'mon, man," Moultrie says, and this feels different. "Come here."

Cin sinks into the moment.

Propped up in a papasan chair, one foot on the floor, Matt raises his gaze from where he's peeling the label off a beer bottle. He studies Moultrie's face. "Yeah," he says. "Okay."

He sets the beer bottle down next to three others clustered at the base of the chair and gets up only to drop down again on the bed by Moultrie's knees.

"C'mon," Moultrie says and pats the bed on the other side of him.

Matt blinks slowly. "Was it worth it? Getting your degree?"

"Yeah. I'm gonna be Delta one day. Why, you thinking about finally hitting the books after you get out? Go back in as a CO?"

"Maybe. Maybe I'll be a cop or try NCIS."

"Maybe," Moultrie says. He wraps a fist in Matt's tee shirt. "C'mere," he says, and pulls Matt down and over him, rolling so that Matt ends up on his back with Moultrie's face over his. Moultrie sucks on the joint, the tip glowing, and then holds his breath, tilting his head back for a long moment. Leaning over again, he lowers his mouth close to Matt's and lets the smoke ease out between his lips.

Matt's lips part and he breathes it in.

Moultrie smiles down at him. "I always wondered."

"Yeah," Matt says, smoke rising with his breath.

And then they're kissing, Matt's hand coming up to the back of Moultrie's neck.

Cin's heart stutters, but she can feel it, the heat between them, the uncertainty, the longing, as the kiss deepens. A heart-breaking sound of desperate need escapes Moultrie, or maybe it's Matt, she can't tell. What she's not is surprised. She knew this about him, about them, in the Knowing, she just forgot.

Moultrie ends the kiss and flops back down on his back. They lie there, crowded together on the bed. Jammed against the wall, Matt accepts the joint with a shaky hand. They pass it back and forth a couple of times before Moultrie says, "Girls?"

"A couple. I dated this girl at Twentynine Palms for a while, a Major's daughter."

"That's dangerous."

"No, he was cool with it. Well, probably not if he actually knew what we were up to, but he didn't, so he was cool."

"Guys?"

Matt shakes his head.

They pass the joint.

"I don't want to die," Matt says on a puff of smoke. "Without knowing, y'know? I've always . . . with you, there's always been—"

"Yeah," Moultrie says. He shifts around to prop himself on his elbow so he can see Matt. "I know. But I was never here without Rick."

"I want to know," Matt says, nerves riding each word. His breath speeds up while he gathers his next words. Moultrie watches him, his gaze skimming his face and sticking on his lips. "If it's the same."

"It isn't," Moultrie says. "And it is. Pinch that out."

Matt smothers the smoldering end of the joint. Moultrie takes it from him and drops it over the edge of the bed without looking. Dumbass scrambles up.

"Oh, shit," Matt says.

Moultrie is already flipping over, reaching down.

Dumbass pounces, slobbering over the morsel. Moultrie grabs at his collar and jerks him back.

"Did he eat it?" Matt shouts, lying half on top of Moultrie to see the floor.

Moultrie falls back, laughing. Dumbass smacks his jaws open and shut, licking his lips, spit flying. Moultrie lets go of his collar. Matt's mouth is open as he stares at the dog. Dumbass grins at him and then shakes, his collar jingling. He pants in Matt's face.

"Dude," Moultrie crows, trying to catch his breath. "He's fine. It wasn't that much." Rolling up, he grabs Matt's biceps and manhandles him onto his back, their legs entangled, bringing them face to face again.

Matt's silent, holding Moultrie's gaze.

Moultrie fingers the hair from Matt's forehead and then lays his palm along his cheek. "He's okay. I swear."

Matt nods. He swallows hard and then snakes a hand up onto the back of Moultrie's neck and pulls him down into a searing kiss. When it breaks, Moultrie takes charge, straddles Matt between his knees and works his way down Matt's neck to his chest with lips and hands. He shoves Matt's tee shirt up so he can suck at each nipple in turn. He pauses there and crawls back up Matt's body for an open-mouthed kiss. He slides his hands down Matt's arms to intertwine their fingers together and lifts Matt's hands above his head. He tugs Matt's shirt all the way up, jerks it over Matt's lifted head, but leaves it tangled around his wrists.

"Stay," Moultrie whispers. Matt's breath hitches. Dumbass thumps his tail on the floor. They're both hard, their jeans not hiding anything from the other, and Moultrie carefully lowers himself to slide against Matt, once, twice. The needy whine that escapes Matt goes straight to Cin's clit, for all that she seems to be mist.

Moultrie slithers downward once more, lavishing kisses on every bit of Matt's skin along the way. He licks the taut muscle above Matt's hip bone and then lingers there to suck at the skin. Matt's hips thrust up in response, his head thrown back on a groan, hands fisting in the sheet above his head. Moultrie doesn't let up. He fingers Matt's jeans open.

Revealing the mark he's made on Matt's hip, he finally lifts his head, sliding Matt's zipper down at the same time.

Matt breaks.

They move together, Matt rising and Moultrie letting him, the tee shirt dropping to the bed. He finds Matt's mouth again as their hands scrabble to shove down jeans and briefs before they come together again on their knees.

"Wait, wait," Moultrie says, getting a hand down between them.

Matt's head is down, his mouth open, thrusting helplessly into Moultrie hand as he watches him hold them against each other.

"Let me," Moultrie says, his voice strained. His free hand is flat against Matt's lower back, restraining him. "Shhh, slow down. Hold on to me, let me."

He ducks his head down, captures Matt's mouth, and forces his head up, bringing them closer together. Matt's hands slide up from Moultrie's shoulders into his short hair. He breaks the kiss to breathe, panting open-mouthed, his forehead pressed to Moultrie's shoulder.

"We're going to take the edge off," Moultrie whispers into his ear. "And then I'm going to take all night and take you apart one cell at a time, in case this is the only time I ever get to do it."

Matt nods.

When he comes, that first time, Cin shatters right along with him, light bursting through her, aware of everything and nothing until his breath is her breath and when she comes back, the two of them are lying together, face to face, clothes finally stripped away and spilled onto the floor.

Moultrie runs his hand along Matt's flank, grips his hip, thumb circling the hickey he made. And then they're kissing again. Cin follows the heat rising off them to the ceiling and lets herself keep rising, letting the slight ever-present pull of the veil carry her away.

There's a thought she can't quite grasp. The kind of thought that breaks a case wide open. At home, she'd pour a glass of wine and read through all the case files yet again, let that thought work its way to the surface like a splinter breaking skin.

Here, she's the splinter, working her way to the surface of the veil. Having chosen to stay, to give up the Knowing, she's just as inanimate and unknowing as a shattered piece of wood separated from everything it ever knew. She breaks through, only to find herself standing yet again on the lawn of the townhouse.

Everything is gray.

Except the streams of rainbow water.

And Dumbass, the Labrador.

Glowing bright yellow, he comes bounding over to her across the gray and drops the glittery thing at her feet.

He steps back and sits, his tongue hanging out one side of his grinning mouth.

The glittery thing is Cin's Daytona Beach Police Detective's badge.

She is not just an unknowing, shattered piece of Lucinda Troy.

She's a detective.

She recognizes patterns and learns the culture of subgroups to better walk through their worlds.

The veil is no different.

She wants a case file? Here it is, all around her.

And Moultrie is giving her his statement in the only way he can.

FOLLOWING MATT'S DIRECTIONS, Jessica parked on the tree line in the lot between the Ormond Airport and the Quad at the Hull Road Sports Complex. "I've never been out here."

The Quad was just one portion of the ballfields that accommodated softball, baseball, soccer, and flag football fields. It consisted of four baseball fields nestled together with a T-cross of sidewalks dividing them and a two-story building in the center that held restrooms, concession stand, and a meeting room with a scoreboard booth.

"Ethan practically lives here," Matt said. In the last two years, he'd spent plenty of time both sweating under the summer sun and slowly freezing to death in the January wind under the buzzing night lights at these fields. The smack of a well-hit ball, the yells of the parents, the call of the ump, dust in his nose and on his tongue, the weathered boards of the bleachers under his thighs or standing along the base line, fingers threaded through the diamonds of the chain link fences while he judged how far the runner made it by the shouts around him —he wouldn't trade a minute of it. "See anybody who shouldn't be here?"

"No cop cars."

"Do you see the car the maras were driving?"

"No."

"Would you recognize the father of the shortstop, Rodrigo?"

"Absolutely."

"Let me know if you see him here, okay?"

"Do you want me to stay with the car?"

"No," Matt said, opening his door. "Walk with me."

He met her at the back of the car. "Give me the keys." She didn't protest, just placed them in his up-turned hand. He slid them in his pocket. "Just stay on my left, okay?"

Marking the bumper of the car with a sweep of his cane to the right, and then the next bumper over, he walked along the row, ready for the unevenness of the ground when he hit the grass shoulder, which he crossed to the sidewalk, turning left to follow it to the main entrance, where he turned right. Kids were screaming in delight at the little playground on the left. He slowed down and limited the sweep of his cane so he wouldn't force anyone to walk around him on the sometimes-crowded walkway to Ethan's field on the right. He veered off when he got close, headed to the chain-link fence.

"Hey, Matt," a woman said.

"Charlotte," Matt said.

"I can't believe Ethan broke his arm right at the beginning of the season. Is he still going to travel with us?"

"That's up to Lily." But she'd save a ton of dough if she just let him be disappointed. At thirteen, he had plenty of summers left to play travel ball. And here in Florida, ball was year-around anyway. It wasn't like he'd be missing an entire year of development.

"Who is this?"

"I'm Jessica," Jessica said. "We work together."

Grateful for her careful phrasing, Matt said, "Ethan in the dugout?"

"Heads up," a cheerful voice called out.

Jessica shouted, "Hey!"

Her arm hit his as Matt reached up and snagged the ball thrown at him.

"God, I never get tired of that," Dan said as he closed the distance between them. His son played on a different team, but Dan knew everyone. He worked the concession stand a lot, standing outside to grill hot dogs and talk to whoever wanted to shoot the shit.

"How'd you do that?" Jessica said.

"Reflex," Dan said. "Blind in his brain, not his eyes. Team's almost done."

They chatted with Charlotte and Dan for a few minutes, other people throwing in a word here and there as they came or went. Jessica leaned over and touched his arm. "I'm gonna hit the restroom and then buy us some water, okay?"

"Yeah, I'll be right here."

"I'm going that way," Charlotte said and left with Jessica.

"I've gotta pack up my crap," Dan said. "Looks like Ethan's coach is finishing the huddle. I'll send Ethan your way, Matt."

"Thanks. Hey, you know Rodrigo's dad's name?"

"Mateo."

"Thanks." Matt stepped all the way over against the chain link, set his back to it, and listened to the crunch-clack of cleats on the concrete walkway and snatches of conversation as the finished teams and their families left and the next wave of players, a little older, a little louder, took the fields.

"Uncle Matt," Ethan yelled, running up to him. Matt held his open hand out and Ethan smacked it with his good hand in a sideways high five. "Can we go with Rodrigo and his dad to Dairy Queen?"

"No, babe," Matt said. No fucking way was this mara asshole going to bring Ethan into the mix. Thank God they weren't hanging for an hour, waiting on Lily, or walking down Hull Road to the bus stop at US 1. "We have a—"

"Look who I found," an accented voice Matt didn't recognize said.

"Nice to see you again, miss." Rodrigo's dad, Mateo, was standing a lot closer than Matt had thought he'd be. "We were just planning on going for ice cream, would you like to join us?"

"Yes, we should go for ice cream," Jessica said promptly, her voice tight, the words clipped. "Matt."

"Please, Uncle Matt?"

"Yeah," Rodrigo piped up. "Please, Mr. Matt?"

"I love a good Blizzard," the new guy said. It wasn't the other mara from Cin's apartment, the Army Ranger, Israel Portillo. "How about you, Miss Jessica?"

"Yes. Love Blizzards. Let's go. Matt."

Shit. He had a knife or gun on her, or had shown her one.

"Bye, Matt," Charlotte called out from the walkway. "Nice to meet you, Jess!"

Matt lifted a hand in her direction. "Sure," he said to the maras. "Let's get some ice cream."

The boys cheered.

"Why don't I take the kids," Mateo said. "And the two of you can ride with Jorge."

The boys cheered again, and Ethan said, "Thanks, Uncle Matt," before they took off, running in the direction of the parking lot.

"Walk," Matt yelled after them. All he needed was for Ethan to fall and break the other arm. He lowered his voice. "Still driving that junker you had earlier?"

"No, Uncle Matt," Mateo said. "A little bird told us that car shouldn't see the light of day again."

Then MS-13 had an in, a mole, at DBPD, probably the same person who let Jimmy's name leak in connection to Malcolm Ward. "If you so much as breathe wrong on him, I will kill you."

"Easy there, who do you think I am, blind man? I'm a law-abiding baseball dad treating my son's teammate to ice cream and then taking him home." Mateo's hand brushed Matt's arm as he raised it. "I have no idea why his Uncle Matt never arrived, officer."

"Lily will pick him up at the DQ."

"I already know where she lives, Matt. Ethan will make it home when she does. You have my word on that."

Fuck.

"The boys are waiting, so let's stroll out of here, and then I'll leave you with Jorge."

CIN SITS DOWN, right there in the veil, specters and spooks drifting by with no awareness. She understands now that this is what she did, unaware of herself, when she first died. This is the *there*, as she thought of it then. Her mind tries to wander, wondering what time periods the ghosts occupy when they enter their own Here, who they haunt. An absent stroke of her thumb across the badge in her hand snaps her thoughts back to Matt and Doug Moultrie.

Resisting the pull of the veil, she focuses on her investigation.

She needs a starting point and a working theory to test.

She has names.

Matt Loose is Mark Loftin, a former Marine, NYC detective,

civilian analyst with Naval Intelligence, and apparently an operative with a private security company that must have a government contract. Any part of his resume could be false. Could that hit to the head have led to his being placed in the Witness Security program? Maybe along with his sister and nephew? The Daytona area is rumored as a long-time favored WITSEC location. He has an ex and a daughter. Where are they?

Doug Moultrie's also not a real name. She suspects he made Delta as an operations specialist with the Army. He was also with "the company". He's dead. He keeps showing himself to her, dropping her on her head in his memories. He's connected to Malcolm Ward. Did he kill Chris Bolton? Is that why Jimmy pinned his name on Matt for Bolton's murder but then said Mr. Ward killed him? Moultrie certainly fits the 'ex-special forces' part of Jimmy's description. Was he involved in Jimmy's murder? In her own? Or had he been dead already?

But Reardon also strikes her as former military. Reardon worked for RWS Motors, along with Malcolm Ward. He struck a deal with a Zeta to take over RWS's drug territory and, by extension, Malcom Ward's, by winning over the local maras with a better financial deal. The deal wasn't struck, and now Reardon's also dead. Then there are Carlos and Sebastian.

The restless movement of the specters within the veil catch her gaze. Cin's thoughts stutter and she loses her zone. Closing her eyes, she wills herself back to that one heady night. Matt dozing on the couch, looking so much younger with the tension in his face relaxed. The call from Lily, his maybe sister. She has a kid. She must really be his sister, right? She'd sent a text that night, a contact. Sebastian Ramirez. A DSC professor and apparently also "company", so it's safe to assume his name is also fake.

As is "Carlos". Cin's heart pangs. Her poor brother.

She opens her eyes to see a ghostly deer grazing nearby. It lifts its head, ears twitching. It flinches and fades, its body tattering, blown away by a strong, unfelt wind. Belatedly, Cin turns to face the direction it looked toward, seeking an unknown threat. There's nothing there.

Dumbass the Lab, back to gray and wispy, though still dog-shaped, has been sitting nearby, but now he comes over and flops down next to her. She feels the weight of him but expects her hand to go right through him when she reaches down to touch him. It doesn't. She closes her fingers in his very real fur and scratches his solid shoulders, massages the loose skin of his neck. It's grounding.

What line of investigation would be helpful right now? What can she really do? How fast does she need to do it? She's lost time in the veil, in the memories. Time progresses forward when she's with Matt, but it also keeps moving forward for him when she's here. She needs to crack the code on this timeline thing and how to manipulate it.

Now.

This all started with Jimmy Shad. "Malcolm Ward", "an ex-special forces meth-head freak", killed "his" own associate, drug-dealer Chris Bolton, and then threatened the witness to that murder, Jimmy Shad, into making Bolton's scheduled pick-up. There are at least three reasonable possibilities based on the memories she'd seen.

One, Moultrie, probably former Delta, killed Chris Bolton in front of Jimmy after their conversation on the beach. Two, if Reardon flipped Bolton from Malcolm Ward to Los Zetas, "Malcolm Ward" might have gone after Bolton. Or three, if Bolton refused being flipped, Reardon might have killed him to keep him quiet while he recruited Jimmy Shad.

One, Jimmy knew Moultrie was with Malcolm Ward. He also knew Moultrie needed to pass Bolton a message from Reardon. Since whoever Moultrie was, he was ex-special forces, he might fit Jimmy's description of Bolton's killer.

But, while not out of the realm of possibility, Moultrie was also an undercover employee of "the company", and therefore, one would assume, one of the good guys. He probably wouldn't just outright murder a small-time drug dealer, and especially not in front of a witness. Plus, Matt had, at least at some point in time, called him a friend for long enough to shag him. Although that was hardly a good indicator of character, she'd put it in the plus column for now.

Two, if Bolton had already been flipped, and that's why Moultrie had a message for him from Reardon, Malcolm Ward may have sent an MS-13 enforcer to take him out. Often former military, a mara enforcer might easily be misconstrued as an "ex-special forces, meth-head freak" by a strung-out and agitated Jimmy.

But then again, why finger Matt and call him "Moultrie" to the cops who could protect him from Malcom Ward while telling Matt it had been Malcolm Ward who killed Bolton when he thought the cops weren't listening?

Of course, once they, she, did know, she hadn't protected him. She'd used him to set up a sting instead. So maybe Jimmy was smarter than she'd always thought. Still, if a mara enforcer had killed Bolton for disloyalty, who had asked outsider Jimmy to pick up a drug drop in lieu of Bolton? Not Malcolm Ward.

Which, three, left Reardon. Reardon wasn't a Malcolm Ward insider, only another employee of RWS. Rather than risk trying to recruit MS-13 to the Zeta side in a hurry, why not use someone on the inside of Malcom Ward who knew the local mara enforcers, like Chris Bolton, to approach them? He wouldn't want it getting back to his RWS bosses if he fucked up the deal with the Zetas and needed to stay where he was. If she were Reardon, she'd want to play it safe, too. Walk the fence until she knew the Zetas were going to pull it off before she leaped.

But maybe Bolton hadn't wanted to play at all. And Reardon needed to kill him because he knew Reardon's plan and time was short. But then he had another problem. While Reardon was basically a go-between, he was also too high in the RWS chain to risk being caught transporting drugs himself. With Bolton dead, he could go ahead and rush his approach to the local maras, or he could use someone already scared of him who also happened to think he was with Malcom Ward.

Beyond Moultrie and Bolton, Jimmy didn't have any contact with Ward, so it's not like Reardon would be found out. Jimmy didn't deal, so he was a pretty safe bet not to steal the Zeta's drugs. Moultrie, already in Reardon's pocket, could keep Jimmy in line. Watching Bolton die would have also been some damn good incentive to turn courier when Reardon hit Jimmy up to do it.

Only before the "cache" is ready for pick-up, Reardon's mule is picked up by the cops after he's connected to Bolton. And being a true knucklehead, gives them his guy Moultrie's name hung on, of all people, a law professor at DSC.

Only . . . Moultrie was dead already, right? Charlie said there was no crooked nose man in the security camera footage from the scene at Jimmy's house. Did Jimmy know Moultrie was dead when he gave her Moultrie's name? No repercussion from Moultrie that way. But then he panicked and gave her Matt's description and address because Moultrie was already dead, and he knew it. Right? He'd already become part of Bolton's murder case, he couldn't risk sending her to Moultrie's murder scene.

Which made Reardon the guy Jimmy was afraid of.

The dog groans and rolls onto his back, all four paws in the air, so Cin can rub his belly. She suddenly remembers the odd dreaminess that was Jimmy and Archer standing over Moultrie's body that became Carlos, zip-tied and gagged, Reardon holding a gun on him. It wasn't a full vision like the others. Cin wasn't even sure if it was real. Was it Moultrie or Carlos on the ground? Or both?

Has Doug Moultrie been trying to show her his death? She's been aiming at him, but Matt is never far from her mind, and they have history together. She looks down at the badge in her hand. What really matters here the most? Who's the common thread if she removes Matt?

Moultrie or Jimmy Shad.

Moultrie has been her constant shadow. Hard not to think of him when he's coasting through every memory and dragging her into the veil. She's seen him with Matt and Archer and Jimmy. She died at Jimmy's house. Jimmy fingered Matt, giving them Moultrie's name. Jimmy saw someone kill Bolton. The image of Francis Duncan swims to the forefront of her thoughts. The decapitated, handless, chopped up body of Jimmy's girlfriend strewn across dog-torn, bloodied dirt.

Killed before Jimmy gave them Malcolm Ward's name. Before, not in retaliation.

The dog yips and jumps up, staring behind her into the distance. Cin rolls up into a crouch, turning as she does, steadying herself with one hand buried in the veil and the other on the dog. He barks once, pauses, and then barks several times in a row, his tail wagging. He takes off. Cin lets him go, waiting to see who or what he greets, but he's gone in the mist before anything emerges from it.

"Stop," Jorge said at the end of the Quad's wide sidewalk into the parking lot.

People flowed around him and Matt and Jessica without comment, used to gossip and info blockades in and out of the fields.

"You got a wallet, don't you, blind man? Give it to your *chica* here, phone, too."

Matt dug his rubber-banded cash, ID, and single credit card out of his front pocket and held it out on his palm. He closed his fingers around Jessica's when she took the bundle, catching her cold hand in his for a quick squeeze of reassurance. He doubted she was convinced.

"Come on, man, phone, too. And the buds."

Someone jostled Matt's shoulder as they bustled by with a muttered "sorry, sorry."

The crowd turnover had slowed to a trickle. The ritual sing-song taunts of the softball travel teams that took over the dugouts this time of day and shouts of "go, go, go" from coaches and parents drifted across the fields.

"Matt," Jessica said on a gasp, very soft.

Matt's stomach churned. His cane seemed flimsier than ever in his tight grip. How could no one see that she was in trouble? But he knew why. On surveillance video, he'd watched countless abductions and coercions and even a rape, once, in public, with bystanders wandering past. Not everyone was blind to it, there was just a certain herd instinct that meant that the perpetrator and victim were often alone in a crowd. Almost always, the crowd gave way, avoided, skirted the incidence, and closed back around them as they moved by, so they became hard to spot as they passed any one camera.

If he could just get ahold of Jorge, he could give Jessica enough space to make a run for it, cause a commotion. He slid his phone out of his back pocket, jerked his earbuds from around his neck, and thrust them both out in the direction of Jorge's voice, but Jorge didn't take the bait.

"Grab them, *chica*. You stay here and keep your mouth shut, blind man. You're being watched. You do anything but stand here without talking, your boy never gets home and this one is ours. Someone will be along to pick you up. Wait for him."

Matt nodded. He listened to them walk away. His tongue stuck to the roof of his mouth when he tried to swallow against the dryness in his throat. He thought he'd understood his vulnerability, but he hadn't. He'd badly miscalculated the situation and his own abilities. Rodrigo's presence was no guarantee of Ethan's safety, easy enough to fool a twelve-year-old boy.

Jessica . . . there wouldn't even need to be an excuse. They could both be gone. Likely to a horrible and hard end that might not come for months or years while they were trafficked until no one had any more use for them. Matt spun on his heel, sweeping his cane out. He was a familiar sight. Anyone would lend him a cell phone. He needed to call Sebastian and then Charlie.

Someone came from his left, from the playground area. Matt halted, shifting to angle his shoulders a bit toward them, but they said nothing, just stood next to him smelling of orange and Irish Spring. A couple of people ran by him, young girls, he guessed, late for practice, when their dad yelled after them and then gave Matt and his unknown companion a gruff, "Hey," as he followed.

Matt stepped forward.

"*Mala* idea," Irish Spring said.

Matt took another step.

Irish Spring tutted. "*Paciencia, hombre ciego, y estarán bien.*"

Spanish wasn't his strongest language and although his enunciation was clear, Irish Spring had a heavy accent that was more Central American than Mexican. "Patience, man," and "well" were clear enough, but MS-13 wasn't known for either, so it was hard to believe that a little patience would mean he and his would be fine.

"*No somos estúpidos, hombre ciego, tenemos algo bueno aquí en Daytona,*" the man said.

He could safely assume "not stupid" and "good here in Daytona". They had a good thing going in Daytona? They did. They were under the public radar and had a good deal with Malcolm Ward. Or maybe Los Zetas by now. Or, for all Matt knew, the local branch of MS-13 and Malcolm Ward were one and the same. Pidgin Spanish was all he could manage. So be it. "*Tú.* Malcolm Ward?"

"No. Mara Salvatrucha."

Conocer was a form of "know", whether it was the right one he had no idea. "*Conocer? El jefe*? Malcolm Ward."

The mara's phone rang. "*Sí*," he said, whether in answer to Matt's question or the call, Matt couldn't tell, and after a moment, "*Sí*." He laid a hand on Matt's bicep and urged him back towards the parking lot. "*Carlos y Jessica por las drogas.*"

Fuck. They knew Matt either had or knew about the drugs, which meant either Archer or Sebastian or both had been compromised. "What about Jessica?"

"*Carlos y Jessica por las drogas.*"

Matt stopped walking. "Carlos?"

The man shook his arm. "*Carlos. Policia.*"

"I have no drugs. I don't know Carlos. Where is Jessica?"

"*Silencio*," the man said. "*Fono.*"

"What?"

With an exasperated growl, the man clapped his phone to Matt's ear. Matt reached up and took the small phone as the mara let go of it, his fingers hard, the skin chapped and rough. "Yes?"

"We don't expect you to deliver the drugs, Mr. Loose," a woman with a cultured voice and rich Spanish accent said. "We expect you to convince Archer Troy it would be in his best interest to contact us with that information, or we cannot guarantee the safety of his lover. Or your own."

Too late for that. "You can't find Archer?"

"He never arrived at the exchange."

If Archer never got there. . . "You have no leverage if you can't threaten him."

"If you kill a cop and his lover can't hear him die," the woman said, "does it get you what you want?"

"In this case, no."

"No," she said. "Not that we can't find many, many other ways to fuck a cop before killing him, especially if we transport him to Nuevo Laredo." Cold crawled up Matt's spine, pooling in his belly, icing his heart. Nuevo Laredo, right over the border from Laredo, Texas, was a major base camp for Los Zetas. "Just like there are many, many ways to sell women and children, should you fail to convince Archer to return our cargo. We have to re-coup our loss, after all."

"Women?"

Distorted voices came across the line and then Lily said, "Matt? Matt?"

"Lily," he croaked.

"Where's Ethan?"

Matt closed his eyes.

"Matt, where's Ethan?" she all but screamed into the phone. "Where's Ethan?"

He took a deep breath and shut himself down. He opened his eyes and relaxed the muscles in his throat. "He's with Rodrigo, Lily, at a table inside. We're at the Dairy Queen. I'll go back in right now. I'll call Sebastian to come get him so I can deal with this, okay? You're going to be fine."

"Thank God," Lily said. "Thank God, thank God, thank—"

"Just do what they say, Lily, understand?"

"She will, *Suertudo*," the woman said. "Whether she wants to or not. You have two hours to locate Archer. I already have a buyer for your women and nephew. The cop's head will be discovered on a Laredo sidewalk by this time next week."

"Matt," Dan said, from a couple of steps away. "You okay?"

"Yeah," Matt croaked. He cleared his throat. *Suertudo*. Lucky One. Isn't that what Jess said the kennel workers called him? "Yeah."

He held the phone in his hand out to the side.

"You finish?" Irish Spring said.

Matt nodded.

"*Hasta luego*," Irish said, already walking away.

"*Hasta luego*," Dan called after him.

Matt swung his cane up under his arm and fingered the phone. It was small, a flip phone. He closed it. "Are you headed out?" Matt asked.

"Yes, I am," Dan said. "Someone wants to talk with you."

Matt's stomach dropped a story or two. He tried not to react, but something must've shown on his face.

"Just a friend."

"Who would that be?" Matt said, trying for casual and failing miserably. He was out of practice, but there was still a chance this was just about baseball, right?

"Someone you definitely want to talk to."

"Look, this is really bad timing. I'm waiting for someone, but he's late."

"Mr. Ward doesn't take rainchecks, Matt."

"Shit." Now what? He really didn't think playing dumb was going to help him here. "That guy was MS-13."

"I know."

Think. This was Malcolm Ward coming for him. But based on the phone conversation he just had, the local MS-13 clique had decidedly flipped on their allegiance with Ward and were busy creating bonds with Los Zetas. Did Ward already know? Did Dan? "Did you know he would be approaching me?"

"Not in particular, but I just follow orders. I'm sure he was as well."

So fucking not helpful when Matt suspected they were taking orders from two different bosses. "Rodrigo's dad took Ethan. Against my wishes."

"And there were many witnesses to the fact that Ethan and Rodrigo left together. He's fine."

"I need to contact someone." Matt waved his hand between the two of them. "Unrelated to this."

A roar rose from the ballfield to his left, parents and kids alike screaming "go, go, go" at a runner.

"If you put it on speaker, that's fine," Dan said, crowding in close to him. Matt braced himself, but he only took Matt's arm above the elbow and herded him onto the grass. "My truck's right here."

MOVEMENT MAY NOT ACTUALLY BE necessary, but Cin gets up and walks anyway. She keeps her head down and ignores the other spooks, concentrating on Jimmy Shad—his face, his voice, his surfer's slump, shoulders rounded forward, and the way his hair hung in his face.

There's a tug off towards the right and she heads that way.

He was cutting avocados in his kitchen, making poke. That annoying click was Francis on his ragged blue couch, agitated, upset. Her long fingers playing with the fat, silver lighter closed in her hand. The flame leaps up from the lighter in Cin's memory.

In its light, Francis was pretty, wholesome, but too thin. Small face, long upper lip, rounded chin. Highlighted brown hair. A click as the lighter's top flips down over the flame, extinguishing it.

She thumbs the lighter open again. Spins the wheel, the flame leaps.

Click.

Cin glances up at the actual sound in the mist ahead of her.

Click.

The veil is swirling there, slow. She steps into it, bracing against that fading sensation. The next click stretches and echoes in her head and...

Jimmy looks up, right through her, knife in one hand, avocado slice in the other.

"Frankie," he says.

Click.

Cin turns around in Jimmy's kitchen, but before she's all the way around, she's standing next to the couch. The flame leaps up from Francis's lighter.

"Francis," Jimmy says.

She snaps the lighter closed.

"Stop with the lighter, you'll break it."

Francis opens her hand and stares down at it. There's a raised emblem on it, a shield with red and white lines. A banner underneath reads "Death to Tyrants". Engraved beneath it is "183rd" and below that, "BOLTON."

"We were going to get married," she says.

"Friday, on the boat," Jimmy says, coming into the room with the bowl of poke in one hand and the plate of avocado toast in the other. He's bristling with bravado. "You're going to pay that bastard back on Friday."

"What if I can't do it?"

"I'll be there," he says, setting their dinner down on the table in front of the couch. "If you can't, I will."

Click.

Cin turns her head.

Doug Moultrie is sitting on the side of a bed in Jimmy's great room. He shoves another cartridge into the magazine in his hand.

Click.

"That's a lot of bullets," Archer says, leaning on the doorframe to the kitchen.

"I like to be prepared."

What the fuck all does that have to do with Francis Duncan and Jimmy Shad and Chris Bolton?

Cin wants to scream.

She suspects all that will do is blow her into nothingness and she can't afford that right now.

"You just prepare everything the way you practiced, and it'll be fine," Jimmy says, drawing Cin's attention back to him. "He'll be easy to take care of once he's sick. That stuff is wicked."

Click.

Another bullet into the magazine.

Cin glances over, but it's not another bullet.

It was a drawer sliding home.

Moultrie's sitting in front of a paper-strewn desk, turning a flash drive over in his fingers. He lifts a folder up and there's a laptop underneath. He opens it. It's already booted up, she guesses, because he inserts the drive.

Click.

Where Jimmy and Francis were sitting, there's now a window revealing a long hall of small offices. A woman crosses the hall from one office to another. The rooms, her attire, the way she's reading the paperwork in her hand as she walks shouts government and analyst.

Moultrie stares at the laptop screen for a second and then taps on the touch pad.

Cin swim-walks through the memory murk to peer over his shoulder.

Document after document detailing Doug Moultrie's life, his identification papers, his accomplishments, his work history, even a couple of old photos of dog-eared report cards. He has a Facebook and an Instagram account, dark hair, and Matt's bearded face.

As she recognizes him, Cin's already spiraling out of the memory.

———

As soon as Dan had them out on US 1 in his noisy pick-up truck, Matt flipped the phone open. He ran his index finger over the keypad, the slight circular depressions of the buttons. Carefully, he dialed the unique number for his ex-wife that he had memorized long ago. He had never imagined he would ever use it again, or that it would still be monitored until Cin told him Lily had called it from the hospital. It rang three times before a woman picked up.

"Hello?"

"Hey, it's Matt."

"Put it on speaker," Dan said.

Matt held the flip phone out to him.

"Matt!" the woman said, loud enough for Dan to hear. "You sound well."

He was nearly certain they had stuck to protocol by habit at Cin's apartment and not used Sebastian's name in front of the maras. Even if they had, how likely was it that the maras had passed it on to Malcolm Ward? He brought the phone closer to his mouth. "I am. Are you still kicking ass at Canardo's?"

"You know I am. You still putting bullseyes in your paper targets?"

"Only when I'm with Kennedy."

"What can I do for you, Matt?" the woman said, which was the green light for both of them, after giving the pass phrases indicating neither of them were compromised. He was maybe pushing that line, but he didn't have time for a team to come roping in.

"Can you put Sebastian on?"

"I think so, it may take a minute," the woman said. She covered the mouthpiece and Matt only heard the switch to a recording because he was listening for it. Muffled voices, faraway music, a country station on a radio.

Dan slowed the truck and stopped but didn't react to Sebastian's name. Idling. Red light. "I don't see a speaker button on that phone," Dan said.

A click and some shuffling noise and then Sebastian said, "Go."

"You got a location yet?"

"No."

"Why isn't Archer answering his phone?"

"It hasn't rung."

The truck shot forward. Matt put his free hand out to steady himself on the dash, lifting the phone to his ear at the same time.

"Why'd you get me through the ex, Matt? Where's your phone?"

"Someone asked if"—God he wished he could see Dan right now—"I'd find Archer for them. Jessica went with them."

Hopefully Sebastian would understand that.

"No phone, no Jessica," Sebastian said. "You still got the car?"

"Not exactly."

"You're in a vehicle."

"Yes."

"This a burner?"

"Yes."

"Damn. Not going to be able to locate you fast."

"Just tell me where you'll be in, say—" the maras had given him two hours to find Archer—"an hour."

The truck slowed again and then Dan hung a big, looping left. Matt leaned against the door, still holding the dash. "Sorry," Dan said.

Sebastian was giving him an address on A1A, in Ormond-by-the-Sea and then, "Tom Renick Park."

The same place Cin's ashes were to be scattered tomorrow night. Matt shoved his glasses up off his face, into his hair, and rubbed the irritated bridge of his nose.

"Matt?" Sebastian said.

"Yeah, still here."

"Who are you with?"

"Malcom Ward."

Dan batted the phone down hard. It clattered down into the truck's foot well. Matt shook his hand out.

———

CIN'S WANDERING when her awareness streaks back in. An old man is shuffling along beside her. He was once a white man, but now he's the same gray as the veil, like all of them here. She stops. Two steps later he swings back around and considers her for a long moment. He reaches out with his large paw and pats her on the shoulder. It registers as a colder sensation that ripples down her arm and then away.

Francis Duncan was Chris Bolton's girlfriend, not Jimmy

Shad's. What did she do on that boat with Jimmy to back her up? Twenty bucks on "poisoned the food." There wasn't a mass homicide reported though, so it must not have been lethal. What did they do? Tried to get revenge on whoever killed Bolton. Considering Francis's torn into pieces death, they didn't succeed, but she did get caught.

Was Jimmy's death related to that bad little plan or to his big mouth?

A stiff breeze blows the veil up all around her, until all she sees is gray. It presses into her eyes and nose and ears and mouth. Devoid of sight, in muted silence, with nothing to touch, to grab onto, Cin chokes. Trying to draw breath, she coughs the remaining air from her lungs, her throat closing.

There's a hand around her neck.

She rises, wrenching herself away with a twist of her soul, hits a ceiling, ricochets to the corner of two walls. Spreading her arms out, she sinks to the floor of a bedroom. Standing on the other side of a rumpled bed, wearing only boxer briefs, Moultrie's choking.

A fully dressed man has his button-down sleeved arm wrapped around Moultrie's neck, his other hand wedged above it, gloved thumb driving into the soft tissues under his jaw, into his jugular, his carotid. Face red, Moultrie mule kicks at the man's shins, then rocks himself back, trying to use his weight to pull the guy forward, but he only sways and steps sideways.

Moultrie is flagging fast.

"Sorry, puppy," the man says. "This is what happens when you claim one master and then answer to another. Keeps us on level ground. You understand."

Moultrie sinks to his knees. The man presses down on his head, compressing his neck even more. Moultrie relaxes into the hold, his hands drop, his muscles sag, and his joints fold. The man jerks him up one last time, steps backwards to lay Moultrie down. Now all Cin can see are Moultrie's feet.

"Shoot him," the man says.

There's a Hispanic kid watching from the bedroom doorway. His dark eyes are wide. He's not more than sixteen. The kid's hand is shaking when he draws a compact 9mm from the small of his back under his sleeveless tee shirt. He walks into the room.

"Come on, right here, where you can't miss." The man's still standing over Moultrie's head.

Staring down at Moultrie the whole way, the boy goes around the end of the bed.

"I don't want you accidently hitting me. C'mon, right up here."

The kid contemplates and then apparently walks up along Moultrie's body with a foot on each side. The man doesn't move. When he reaches Moultrie's head, the kid points the gun straight down.

"Both hands."

The kid is visibly shaking now, but he leans over, thrusts the gun closer and then pulls the trigger. The shot booms in the small room. The kid's hands lift on the recoil, but his finger is off the trigger. He tilts the barrel back down.

The man pats him on the shoulder.

A cold sensation trickles down Cin's arm.

It fills her up.

The man angles his phone down and takes a picture. "Stupid move, Reardon. An eye for an eye."

As the veil closes in on her, the kid walks by. Tucking his gun away, he flinches when the hot barrel hits the skin of his lower back.

Cin watches the man as he follows, to memorize his face. All she sees are the three dots hidden in the hollow at the back of his ear.

He's MS-13.

Before she tatters completely, she's rushing inward again, all the separate pieces of her slamming together.

She's vibrating.

The colors of the world burst and bloom and she's elsewhere, following Moultrie, the color condensing into the back of his bright red tee shirt.

He's running through a long alleyway, sweeping her along in his wake.

Past dumpster after smelly dumpster, then a man sitting in a chair outside an open doorway, a heavy spicy scent escaping into the moist, cold air.

Moultrie's breath is rising, trailing behind him in long streamers.

He doesn't appear cold.

His bare arms swing.

He's wearing fingerless leather gloves, his hands closed in loose fists.

His legs piston through each step at a measured pace.

He's not running from anything, he's just running.

A delivery truck is blocking part of the alleyway and Moultrie takes a right.

The short block dumps him out onto a four-lane road.

It's morning . . . somewhere.

All the signs are in Asian languages, not all the same. Cin recognizes Chinese and Korean.

Asian women in housecoats are dragging colored canvas shopping bags on wheels through open market stalls. Huge vegetables and massive whole fish, monster prawns fished from near a nuclear plant, she'd have to guess. Everything seems brighter and bigger than anything she's seen in Florida.

Moultrie ducks and weaves, takes to the side of the street for a few hundred yards. Traffic is light. A couple of minutes on, they're into an area of bank branches, commercial lenders, jewelry stores. He ducks left down a tree-lined side street with small shops and then further down, homes and townhomes. His long strides slow and then he stops, huffing, digging at his hip.

Grimacing in irritation, he pulls his cell phone out and taps. The text he pulls up makes his face fall flat. He closes his eyes and blows his breath out.

Hardly here in this memory, Cin crowds in close. She can't see. She tries to rise but moves too fast. Panicking, she focuses on Moultrie's red shirt far below.

She's falling.

Gray. Dark. Moultrie opens his eyes with Cin inside him.

They read the text.

Daytona. Deploy six weeks.

Dread curdles her heart at the same time that she needs to move, get there. Make sure he's okay. Gold hair, taut muscle under her hand, soft throaty laugh in her ear. A dark room behind glass. Matt stretched out on a cot. The drone of a recording, a woman's voice.

Her fingers on the touchscreen, tapping out her reply.

Have deep cover Daytona. Deploy two days.

Nodding to herself, she says, "Okay," under her breath. She tucks the phone back against her hip. Her mind's eye gives her Matt walking down a wide Manhattan sidewalk, sweeping a cane, a trainer following close behind. He walks right past the beater she's sitting in. She rolls up the window and starts the car. He turns his face towards her when she comes up alongside him. Gunning the motor, she leaves him behind, on to her next job, hoping the conditioning holds, that he never remembers.

Moultrie leaps back into his easy lope, the physical movement jolting Cin free enough to halt her next stride and fall out of him.

He runs on.

His red shirt holds her eye until a passerby walks through her and the world goes gray. The colors don't come back. She lets go this time, lets herself rise above the cityscape until she's in the veil proper.

MATT KNEW when they turned left and then headed uphill with the steady rhythm of concrete joints ka-thunking under their tires, that they were crossing the Halifax River on Granada Bridge. He didn't try to recover the phone. He relaxed a little, but left his fingertips on the dash, ready to brace as needed.

Off the bridge, Dan made a right-hand turn and a few minutes later a stop, then veered right. They were traveling along the river road. The timer Matt had developed in his head for places he'd been before dinged just seconds before Dan slowed again, pulled over to the right side of the road and parked.

"Get out," Dan said, voice lacking its earlier warmth.

The scent of the river was stronger here. A light, cool breeze dried the sweat on Matt's neck from standing out in the sun at the ball field. He pulled on the front of his damp polo and let it fall again.

Dan grabbed his bicep with no warning and Matt only just managed not to whack him with his folded cane. "Come on."

Dragging his feet even though he'd extended his cane, Matt kept his mouth shut. Hibiscus. Lemon. The river. A large house by the way it blocked and funneled sound. Dan opened a gate. The right location. Maria's house or very close to it. Dan bypassed the intercom, or maybe there wasn't one, simply knocking before he opened the door and shoved Matt in ahead of him. He shut the door, turned on his heel, and strode away.

"Mr. Loose," Maria said. "You're a man of your word and I'm a woman of mine."

From a different direction, high heels clicked across the tile floor. They stopped, and a woman said, "I'm Jane Johnson."

"Mr. Ward?" Matt asked.

"Sometimes."

What the fuck did that mean?

"You were there, at Jimmy Shad's home," Jane said. "I'm sure you've heard the same as we have regarding information that Jimmy provided to the police. It was inevitable that law enforcement would learn of Malcolm Ward eventually. Only someone who has not thought through the situation would believe we had any part in that disgrace."

"But you know everyone who might be of use to you in town," Matt said. "All I want is the name of the bomb maker."

"And of what use would a bomb maker be to us," Jane said. "If you haven't noticed, we're suppliers, service oriented. Why would we want those services interrupted by cops pounding on doors and dragging half our employees and clients in for further harassment?"

Matt held up his cane and his free hand, palms out. "It's circumstantial, I get that. Tell me who did do it then."

"Spider has told me something I think you want to be kept a secret. I'll trade a secret for a secret."

Matt lowered his hands. "You go first."

She laughed. "You made quite the enemy in New York. You have a bounty on your head."

The statement both surprised him and didn't. He'd made a lot of enemies over the years, but most of them were dead and the company would have alerted him if it were true. "Me?"

"Yes, *Suertudo*, you." She let the name sink in before she continued.

Did everyone know it? Jess had been talking to a woman in the kitchen while he was here. "Jessica?"

"She's young. We followed up. It seems you are, indeed, a lucky man to have survived. Where did you hide her?"

"Jessica?"

"Mr. Loose. Or should I say? Mr. Marcus Luznar. You are very valuable to us, but your daughter is even more so."

Okay, so she—they—did have the wrong guy. "Yeah. Not me. I haven't hidden anyone, let alone my daughter." He fingered his watch, wondering if the Zetas would wait a full two hours before calling him. "Look, I have to go get my nephew soon. I need the bomb maker."

"I know no bomb makers, *Suertudo*," Jane said. "It's just . . . not my style."

"You going to pretend you don't know?"

"Apparently, we're very similar that way," Jane said.

He sighed and lifted his chin. "My daughter lives with my ex-wife in Brooklyn. She's only valuable to me and the ex. You've got the wrong guy."

Moultrie's version of Matt is locked in Cin's head along with her own. She knows him now both young and in his prime. She knows the whole of his physical self. Closing her eyes, she concentrates on Matt's hands on her skin, his breath on her face, his heart under her ear, the sharp, musky scent of him filling her nose. She keeps her eyes closed even though it seems she can feel every cell of her non-being sifting through an hourglass and pouring out the other side.

When Matt's scent blooms in Cin's nose for real, she hears a deep intake of breath and opens her eyes to the house Maria lives in. Maria and a tall, hale, beach girl in her mid-thirties with cropped blonde hair stand in front of Matt.

Matt lifts his hand to his chest and rubs it absently.

"No, you are definitely the guy," the blonde says. "You're the father of Gustav Garcia's granddaughter and he wants to raise her."

Cin and Charlie and a few other DBPD detectives have been boning up in their spare time on El Salvador, Guatemala, and Honduras in case their MS-13 suspicions over the past couple of years became an active theory they needed to test. She knows exactly who Gustav Garcia is— he's the head of Guatemala's Los Zetas branch.

Matt shakes his head. "Gustav Garcia?"

Cin's literally nothing more than emotion right now and all of them are imploding at once. Gustav Garcia. And Matt. Matt's daughter is Gustav Garcia's granddaughter. But Matt doesn't seem to recognize the name. "Los Zetas," she says. It comes out breathy.

He brushes his hand past his ear in acknowledgement, but then brings it back to finger the scar that runs up his skull behind his right ear.

"The Guatemalan commander of Los Zetas," Maria says.

Matt shrugs.

"He's not the Zeta I saw with Reardon," Cin tells Matt.

"I don't know who that is," Matt says.

Impossible that he doesn't know with his resume.

Maria and the blonde exchange a glance. Maria lights off in Spanish, calling the woman Jane. This must be Matt's Jane Johnson, his promised connection to Malcolm Ward.

Jane is less fluent. Spanish isn't her native language, but she argues back well enough. Cin's Spanish sucks. Charlie always acted as translator if she needed one.

Matt taps his cane on the floor and says, "Look, I don't know who you think I am, but I'm just Matt Loose."

He's a good actor.

"What's your daughter's name?" Jane spits.

"Her mother named her. I was deployed."

"And her mother's name?"

"Anna."

"Just so," Jane says. "Anna Silvado. And your daughter's name?"

Matt mulls that over and then says, "I wanted to name her Sophie, but she'd have hated that. She's a tomboy, through and through. I don't know the name Silvado. Or Luznar, for that matter. You got the wrong guy."

Jane sighs. "Did Dakota choose her new name when you hid them?"

Matt shrugs. "I don't know anyone named Dakota." His tone is colored with confusion. There's no recognition in it or his eyes.

The women light off again in Spanish.

Someone's coming down the driveway, now into the small courtyard, his energy pushed out in front of him like a prow cutting through the energetic push of the river from the other side. Even as

Cin's drawn toward him, she knows it's Charlie. Everything's going to get more complicated now that he's here.

"A mara killed Moultrie," Cin tells Matt while she can. "In retaliation for Reardon killing one of theirs, or one of Malcolm Ward's, maybe Chris Bolton."

Charlie has a uniformed cop with him. He knocks on the door and then steps back beside the cop, presenting a wall of law to whoever opens the door. Maria strides over and throws it open.

"Are you Maria—" Charlie says, and then spots Matt. He throws his hands up in the air. "Just the man I need."

"Charlie?" Matt questions, turning more fully in Charlie's direction.

"Mr. Loose," Charlie says with just a hint of sarcasm.

Matt rolls his eyes.

"I'm here to inform you," Charlie says after he introduces himself and the officer with him to the women, "that the officer your son filed a formal complaint on has been arrested in connection with an incident that took place near your son's school a couple of hours ago. I have a few questions I'd like to ask you. And, conveniently, Mr. Loose."

Hard fingers close on Cin's upper arms, and she's wrenched backwards into the veil. Matt folds over with a grunt and then Cin's falling and then falling to pieces, the whole of her spread thin. She's sparking with electric shock, tangled up in someone else.

Until she's not.

Doug Moultrie's standing in front of her, the bullet wound in his forehead crusty and dry.

He lifts his chin at something behind her.

They're on a deserted playground in the middle of a heavily treed park. The leaves are rustling, the daylight dim, the sky overcast. A gray bank of clouds is heavy with rain. A dark-haired girl of about eight and a woman who is undoubtedly her mother are sitting facing each other at the center of an old-fashioned merry-go-round.

Cin concentrates on Matt. The world shimmers, but Moultrie touches her shoulder, grounding her in the memory.

She drifts closer to the merry-go-round.

". . . over you," the woman says.

"But I want to see him now." The girl wipes tears from her cheeks with one hand. The other holds a crush of wildflowers. "I didn't get to say goodbye. I don't want him watching over me. I want to see him."

"I'm sorry, sweetie."

"Why can't I go to the funeral?"

"It was yesterday, Dakota. He'd have wanted you to remember him reading you bedtime stories and watching you ride."

"Why can't I stay with Mommy at the hospital?"

Okay, not her mother, for all that they are dark-haired with similar features.

The woman only reaches out to hug the girl in response. When the girl curls up, her tears becoming heart-wrenching sobs, the woman tugs her into her lap.

MATT CAME to on his side, hands still clenched over his aching chest and gasping for air. For the longest moment, he couldn't remember anything at all, could only focus on the sensation of hands upon his face, a male body pressed against him, knees to shoulders, while Cin's heated weight lay along his back. And then it was gone. All of it. He drew in a shuddering, deeper breath and Charlie's voice filled his ears. Matt rolled over onto his back. "I'm fine. I'm fine."

"That did not look anywhere close to fine." Charlie's voice came from directly above him, and close. His warm fingers found the pulse in Matt's neck.

"Well, I'm fine now," Matt said. He lifted his right hand and Charlie caught it in his left. Matt sat up, Charlie's free hand coming to cup his elbow, then his back. "It's okay. That happens."

"It happens? Looked like you were having a heart attack."

"Do you need anything?" One of the women said. "Dan . . ."

Dan's greasy scent drifted over Matt. The man himself following it as he knelt beside Matt. "Let's get you up."

"I'm fine," Matt said again, but let them help him to his feet. It was less awkward than it could have been. Scrambling up from a prone position while blind was far from graceful in general. He situated himself and waited for someone to speak so he could orient himself. Charlie and Dan remained on either side of him. An odd pattering sound came from behind him. Rain, maybe, off the lanai.

"Officer Thompson?" Maria said.

"Has been arrested," Charlie said. "Can we sit?"

Matt suppressed the irritation that leapt up his throat, ready to announce itself.

"I'll see myself out, Maria," Jane said. "Dan?"

Charlie shifted, his clothes rustling. "Could you please give your names to my colleague here, before you leave?"

"Of course," Jane said, but she gave whoever was with Charlie a different name as Charlie herded Matt around and into Maria's wake to the couches that sat just inside the doors that opened onto the lanai. In Matt's inner eye, they were glass sliders. The pattering outside, louder now, shifted and resolved itself into a downfall of rain.

"Quite the view," Charlie said. "There's a sofa in front of you, Mr. Loose."

"Yes," Maria said. "Please go on."

Matt edged his hand along the wide back edge of the heavy fabric couch, the rough texture pleasing against his skin. He sat while Charlie talked, efficiently painting a quick picture of an anonymous call, an investigating officer's discovery of Thompson's drug-fueled and very public outing with an underage female student, and his subsequent arrest.

"Your lawyer has been called so that we can speak with your son regarding this incident," Charlie finished, directing his remark to Maria.

"And what did you need to ask me?" she said.

Charlie cleared his throat. "Did you have any knowledge of this incident before it happened?"

"How could I?"

"Perhaps you helped plan this little intervention?"

"Intervention?"

"Yes. You know Mr. Loose, obviously. He approached us regarding Officer Thompson on your behalf last week."

"Matt," Maria said, genuine-seeming warmth in her voice. "Thank you so much. Did you set this up?"

Adrenaline spilled through Matt's veins, the familiar flush rising in his cheeks. She'd caught him unawares, although he should have expected it. "Me?" he said, letting his surprise work for him. "Of course not. How would I even go about doing that?"

"How do you know each other?"

"The Poker Room," Maria said immediately. "You know, at the greyhound track? Near the speedway?"

"I know it," Charlie said, his voice tight.

"I don't go often, but it was the Kentucky Derby and some girlfriends and I went. Matt very graciously tended a private bar for us. We struck up a bit of a friendship and here we are."

"You asked for his help."

They'd used him, is what they did, Maria and Johnny Smith. They couldn't use Ward associates to help because DBPD was busy turning over every rock in town. Matt represented another layer of camouflage while they figured out who he was and if they could exploit him. In that initial meet at the Waffle House, Smith had recognized Matt's training as fast as Matt had recognized his.

"I did ask for his help. I was hoping he could utilize his network to light a fire under your Chief's ass," Maria said, delighted, and somehow making "ass" sound southern grand and genteel. "Complaints to the police were going unanswered and this man, Mr. Thompson, is a menace. I'm so glad he's finally been stopped."

Silence followed.

"So," Charlie finally said. "You believe this incident is unrelated to your request of help from Mr. Loose."

"Divine providence, Detective, that's what it is."

"You had no role in bringing about the events of this incident?"

Charlie's hands were tied. The reasonable line of questioning would be to ask if her son was friends with the girl involved, but as she was a minor, he wouldn't mention her name until a formal interview was scheduled. This visit was intended to assess Maria's reaction. But Matt was fairly certain he'd given away more than Maria had, if Charlie didn't buy his useless blind man excuse.

"No, Detective," she said.

"Would you mind coming down to the station later?"

"To pick up my son?"

"No, but I'll make inquires on him. All of Officer Thompson's arrests as a Resource Officer will be evaluated."

Maria made a discontented sound and moved. Charlie stood, rocking the couch. Trying to decide what was happening, Matt stood a second later.

"The only reason I have to come to the station, Detective," Maria said, "is to pick up my son."

"We'll have more questions for you, Ms. Hernandez, regarding Officer Thompson."

"Then we'll schedule an appointment in a civilized manner, with my lawyer present."

"Yes, ma'am," Charlie said. "Can I give you a lift, Mr. Loose?"

Matt bit the inside of his lip, tilting his head in a 'let me think' response while fingering his watch. Fifteen minutes until he could meet Sebastian at Tom Renick Park. A little over an hour until he had to answer to the Zetas. Malcolm Ward in the form of Jane asking questions about his daughter for no reason that he could fathom. Cin . . . gone. For the moment. That weird dreaminess came back to him, heat and the beat of need, Cin against his back.

Maria spoke before Matt could. "He's only just arrived—"

"Actually, I really do need to run," Matt said, holding out his hand. "Sorry to cut our visit short."

"Dan's just outside," Marie said. "He'll take you where you need to go."

Matt waved the hand she hadn't taken in Charlie's direction fairly certain Charlie wouldn't protest. "The detective can drop me off."

Out of the Ward frying pan, into the Zeta fire, right?

"Of course," Maria said. "Another time."

He nodded and managed to breathe normally until they were out of the house, and he'd slid into Charlie's passenger seat, wet from the rain, his back crawling. He panted, trying to quell the spike of his anxiety. Charlie told the uniform with him to follow them back to HQ and shut the door hard. Matt hitched in a deep breath and let it out slow.

After pulling away from the house, Charlie said, "Remember me saying Doug Moultrie was a real person? A beach rat?"

"Yeah?"

"Now he's a real dead person. You know anything about that?"

Matt held up his hands. "Why would I?"

"Matt."

"I need to be at Tom Renick Park, Charlie. Yesterday."

"Well, I need answers. Right now."

Matt sighed. "You'll get them," he said. It did no good now to prevaricate. Charlie wouldn't help him if he didn't own up to something. "I still don't know why Shad said I was Doug Moultrie, but yes, I know he's dead. A mara killed him."

"Shit."

"I need to be at Tom Renick. It's life or death, Charlie."

"Yours?"

"My nephew, my sister, Jessica, an undercover cop, more than them, if I'm not there."

Charlie slowed down and stopped.

"We better be at a stop sign, Charlie."

"I need more."

"And you'll get it. We've gotta lose the cruiser."

"You serious?"

"Los Zetas is here, Charlie. They have my sister, and I don't know why. Maria said something I don't understand. I'm blind because of a brain injury. I lost some memory. The Zetas may have a beef with me. Or maybe they just want their drugs back. I don't know."

"I need more back-up, not less."

"We've got back-up. We're going to meet our back-up." Aware he'd just committed Charlie, folded him into this craziness by choosing "we" instead of "I", Matt quieted his waving hand, placed it with deliberation on his own thigh. He loosened the grip of his other hand on his folded cane. "Please, Charlie, we don't need any more dead Daytona Beach cops. You've seen my resume. Trust me. Lives are at stake here."

"I didn't see anything about cartels on your sheet, Matt. And we have cops very experienced with both narcotics and gangs. The Volusia County Sheriff's office does, too. Some of the best in the state."

"Getting them onboard and geared up isn't going to happen without evidence. I have none. But I do have people in the cartel's hands who are going to die before we can call locals in for a briefing, let alone a coordinated effort. Drive, Charlie. Let me prove it to you. There'll be plenty of work for the locals either way this goes."

Charlie let off the brake and they picked up speed before he hit the mic. He rattled off a couple of numbers, which Matt hoped was just his ID and status. Every shop had their own version of the codes. A dispatcher answered in the affirmative.

"Cruiser's peeling off. Now talk."

ALTHOUGH THEY DON'T LOOK MUCH ALIKE, Cin puts Jane Johnson's questions, what Moultrie has shown her, and the name Dakota together, and gets Matt's daughter. She's been told Matt's dead. He's hidden them or they've run, this woman that Matt trusts. He's Matt instead of Mark because of his former job or entry into witness protection. Moultrie is trying to point Cin at Matt's background while she's trying to figure out the current issue. It's all tied together somehow, no matter how random it seemed when it started.

Moultrie is better at navigating, but he's been dead longer. Something deep inside her loosens at the thought. She prods at it. It's like a tooth you've just noticed is the slightest bit loose. It seems important, but in the long run, it's just a tooth. Maybe it's what's holding Cin back from that skill set.

The veil is swirling around her, soft and slow, the phantoms in it undefined. It pulls at her. After she died, she rested here, and for a moment all she wants to do is close her eyes and drift a bit in its comfort, be neither here nor *there* and let her back-brain work.

She does close her eyes, but when she loses her edges, Cin startles and coalesces again. Time passes while she's here. And there isn't much time. Everyone, living or dead, wants that comfort she's so drawn towards right now. She knows people who have died. Some of them died because humans have a drive to disassociate. They want to get high on their drug of choice and touch . . . the veil. Is this where souls come from? Her family isn't here, they're somewhere different.

Not different, deeper. Deeper in the veil. Nestled in it. Or . . . embraced.

Does everyone want to touch that place they come from and can't remember?

Is that what we are? Kids running back to touch home base, adults embracing the comforts of home during the holidays, returning home to live during hard times. And when we don't have a home? Or just can't absorb it, or need our spirit's home, not our earthly one? Is this what we're searching for when we need something we just can't reach or define and reach for sex or drugs or obsession instead? A salve for the open wound at our spirit's umbilicus? To touch home.

Then why do we ever leave the veil?

The answer comes with that tug again. Her loose tooth somewhere down inside. It's almost sensuous. She prods at it once more. She can feel it. Despite the fact there's no physical sensation here in the veil. No skin on heated skin. She lifts her face. No sun kisses. No chapped lips. No delicious hot water after cold rain. Or cold water on a hot day. No burgers and shakes. No hair sliding through fingers. No music sliding from maker to listener, curling up inside the inner ear to stir the thoughts lodged within our brains.

No sharp edges or startling colors or brilliant blue sky.

She's standing on the beach, arms wide, sun and breeze taking turns licking her bare skin, gulls screeing, waves rolling, and when she opens her eyes, a cornflower blue, endless, sky above. A flat raft of white clouds shows off just how high and wide it seems. The sky in the Carolinas may be bluer than everywhere else, but the sky in Florida is higher than everywhere else.

This.

This is why we come back, leave the veil.

And the comfort of the veil is why we return.

Cin wraps her arms around herself. She wants them both. She shrinks, a child shivering in the dark, looking into the bright life of a lit house from the outside. Bolton. That's what she needs to know next. Who thrust Bolton out of the sharp clarity of the living world before he was ready?

She knows what he looked like from the investigation that took her to Matt's front door. She knows Francis Duncan loved him enough to get herself killed. She knows his calling from the lighter that clicked in Francis's hand. Cin tries to feel them all, place the lighter in Bolton's hand, place Francis's hand in his, place their heads tilted together as they walk down the beach, this beach, close her eyes to the sky and her ears from the gulls and see them, hear their breath, the beat of their hearts.

The rotting fish heads and decaying human odor of the Bolton crime scene wafts into Cin's nose.

The buzz of blowflies fills her ears.

Cin's eyes snap open.

Matt kept it efficient but told Charlie about almost everything and every theory he was currently entertaining. He skipped his solicitation of Centro to set up Thompson's downfall. And he also skipped the un-death of Detective Lucinda Troy and his still very physical relationship with her. Charlie made two rights and a left, not driving as fast as Matt would've liked, but keeping up a pretty steady speed between traffic lights, and most importantly, keeping his mouth shut until Matt stopped talking.

The silence continued for longer than Matt expected though. The traffic around them had thinned out. Matt guessed from his mental map and the turns Charlie made that they must be on the two-lane portion of A1A north of Ormond, headed towards Flagler. He'd never been to Tom Renick Park, but Lily had mentioned it as a surfer's morning hangout back when she thought he might try surfing blind. Ethan had begged him to come bodyboarding with him there last summer. Who knew what would actually get him there would be drugs and murder?

"Setting the whole security-contractors-operating-in-Daytona aside," Charlie finally said, "did you or did you not know Doug Moultrie when we thought you were him?"

"All that info, and that's your first question?"

Road noise. The wobbling hum of the tires, shift of the engine. The rain had stopped at some point and Charlie had turned the wipers off.

"No," Matt said when Charlie didn't seem inclined to say anything else. "I don't know him. He's just some guy working for a former employer of mine who stole a cover I built as a safety years ago. I knew the name, but not an actual person with it. Why Shad pinned it on me, I still don't know."

"Cause he thought you could beat it."

"That's what he said, but I don't know now. Too big a coincidence."

Charlie slowed. His blinker popped on. "So you think Cin died in the first shots of a drug war."

"No, the first shots of what will be a very short argument," Matt said, bracing into the right-hand turn, "between a regional drug op and a major Mexican cartel. I don't know where the MS-13 clique stands."

"I see making a statement with Shad, even making it by blowing him up in little bits, but why law enforcement?"

The ground wasn't bumpy, but it was uneven and rough under the tires. They'd arrived. "Reardon's the only play left. I think he killed Bolton. I think Malcolm Ward had MS-13 kill Moultrie in return. Shad screwed up, talking about Ward, but the guy he described could've been Reardon, and Ward's . . . spokesperson . . . claims it wasn't them."

Charlie stopped the car and turned it off. "Jane Johnson."

"Yes."

"You believe her.

"I do. You got DNA from the Bolton murder?"

"Lots."

"Well, when you find Reardon—"

Charlie laughed. It was strangled and harsh, but a laugh. "Yeah. Like that'll ever happen now. I don't see them."

"They'll be here," Matt said. "Look, there's gotta be a leak."

"It's still a small town. We start asking around at all, and it spreads like wildfire in a drought."

"Still . . ."

"Yeah. From what you say, we've probably got Malcolm Ward members embedded in DBPD. I get it. Archer just got out of a blue Kia."

Matt opened his door, listening to Charlie do the same. "I'm going to get out, but let them come to us." After closing his door, he lifted his head. The breathy, salted breeze patted his face. That was good. Faint smell of hot rubber and a bite of gasoline. The rich, faint odor of weed. Matt unfolded his cane to full length. Children played to his right and a couple hundred yards in front of him. Their voices rose and fell and looped around one another. The constant wash of the surf was more distant. He made his way around onto a grass buffer to the front of the hood and sat on it. "Tell me what you see."

"Archer and a dark-haired man are coming over to us now. They're parked on the far side of the lot across from us."

Pop music to Matt's left, turned down relatively low, but probably coming from a car radio. "No, what do you see? Visuals."

"Oh."

Birds. Seagulls, and under them, an incongruous songbird behind him somewhere. A jet engine overhead and cars passing on A1A.

"We're three-quarters of the way back from the boardwalk," Charlie finally said. "There's a couple of teenage girls and a boy to our left with the car doors open and radio on. Smells like weed, but they've already made me, so they're trying to act casual.

"There's a few kids running around the playground area, parents standing around talking to each other. A couple of young guys on the boardwalk. Looks like a birthday party going on in the pavilion, maybe fourteen or fifteen people over there. Balloons tied all around, presents at one end of the closest table. Hi, Archer."

"I thought that was you," Archer said to Charlie, stepping in close. Pats on the back. "He tell you?"

"Yeah, he did."

"This is so fucked up, man."

"The Zetas have Jessica," Matt said. "And—"

"Los Zetas?" Sebastian said with disbelief. "Here?"

"Yes. And they have Lily. They implied they have Carlos. I don't know if Ethan is with Malcolm Ward or the Zetas."

"I thought *you* were with Malcolm Ward," Sebastian said.

"I was. Charlie here had good timing. Charlie, Sebastian. Sebastian, I assume you know who Charlie is?"

"I do."

"I managed to leave with him," Matt continued. "But I doubt it takes them long to find us, even if we weren't tailed."

"We weren't tailed," Charlie said.

"How many people you got, Sebby?"

"Enough."

Damn cagey bastard. But the company probably knew exactly where Matt's daughter was living with Anna and the banker. "Ward was asking about my daughter, but for some reason, they think she's Gustav Garcia's granddaughter. You know what that's all about?"

The teenagers broke into raucous laughter, their car doors slamming. They headed towards the beach.

"Sebby?" Matt said.

"Yeah."

"You know what that's about?"

"I do."

"How come I don't?"

"Not here, okay? Not now."

Matt clenched his teeth together, his eyes closing, and drew in a long breath through his nose. He released it slow, concentrating on the gulls wheeling and crying, before he opened them again. "The Zetas might need me to know, Sebastian."

"Shit," Sebastian muttered under his breath. Louder, he said, "It's classified."

"Is my daughter in Brooklyn with Anna?"

"That's also classified."

"Well, shit, Sebby, guess we have a problem then."

"You wanted it this way."

"*I* wanted it this way?" Matt spit.

"Yes."

Charlie said, "He wanted drug dealers to think his daughter was a Zeta higher-up's granddaughter?"

"Not exactly," Sebastian said, "but it could be misconstrued that way."

"Is she?" Archer said.

"No," Matt and Sebastian said at the same time.

"Do either of you have a plan?" Charlie asked, his tone flat.

Matt assumed he was addressing Sebastian and himself, but his plan was to roll with whatever the Zetas said when they called, so he kept his mouth shut.

"That depends," Sebastian said, "on what the Zetas want."

"They want their drugs," Archer said, which Matt thought was a pretty good answer.

Sebastian bumped Matt's shoulder as he settled down next to him on the hood. "Your glasses are on your head, why don't you put them on your face where they belong before your eyes burn up."

Matt patted his head, pulled the glasses down, and put them on. The shade across his eyes did feel better than the sun beating on them. "I agree with Archer. They want their drugs," he said.

"What do we want?" Sebastian said, his words soft.

"Our people."

"We need to know who has Ethan," Charlie said. "And which side MS-13 is coming down on."

Matt tapped his cane on the concrete parking stop his feet were braced on. "You have a number for Spider, Charlie? The IT guy?"

"I can get one."

"Please. I gotta piss. Walk me over, Sebby?"

"Yeah, sure."

Holding Sebastian's elbow, Matt counted out twenty steps in his head, the playground noise closer and closer, before he spoke. "You do know where they are, right? Anna and my daughter?"

Sebastian pitched his voice low. "No, not personally, but yes, the company knows."

"The company knows?"

"Okay, probably not. But admin will have a contact number. They can get a message to Anna if need be."

"WITSEC?"

"No. WITSEC is why you're here."

"I don't remember that. Why would I risk Lily and Ethan?"

"You needed family. They were here already. You were experiencing a lot of short-term memory loss at first. You're not in witness protection per se, but they have a lot of networking down here. Support if you needed it." Sebastian pushed through the restroom door. "Clear."

Matt let go of Sebastian's elbow and rounded on him in the musky, close heat of the concrete bunker. "That's bullshit, Sebby. This is a WITSEC dumping ground. I'm with my sister and nephew under an assumed name and she's okay with that. Why the hell did that seem like a good idea at the time?"

"She's your sister, Matt. You needed her and she made an informed choice."

Sebastian caught his fist before it landed, Matt only then aware of his action and the fury lodged in his chest, caught in his throat. He jerked his fist out of Sebastian's grasp and backed away, dragging his cane tip out in front of him. Cool metal hit his hands. He patted his left hand out. The door swung inward. He slid inside and closed it, rested his forehead against the cool inside of it.

Informed choice, his ass. He'd left his daughter behind knowing the head of a drug cartel was looking for her while under the misconception that she might be his granddaughter. Assumed a new name. But felt safe enough to risk his sister and nephew? Some thought he couldn't catch —his gut clenched, his jaw tightening—felt angry enough, maybe, to risk them? Why?

He really did need to piss.

He took care of that, trying to remember coming to Daytona and failing to find any memories there. He remembered his instructors at the school in New York. The frustration at having to learn how to navigate his new life. But it came in bursts. A car horn on the street that nearly gave him a heart attack. Folding and re-folding his money at the small desk in his room. Trying to cut a chicken cutlet in the dining hall. There were no day-to-day memories at all. He shook off and zipped up.

Did he fly to Daytona?

He remembers sitting on Ethan's bed, listening to him breathe, but he did that a lot. It seems like he was always at the ball field, there's no first-time-he-went-there-while-blind in his head. Shouldn't there be? Did he interview for his DSC job? He does remember walking into his first class. Remembers prepping for it. Remembers interviewing with Ed at the Poker Room. He'd practiced in his kitchen with water-filled liquor bottles for a couple of weeks while talking through vocal drafts of his upcoming lectures. Why had he wanted that job, though? Why can he remember being obsessed with the skills, but not why he was obsessed?

A gaggle of girls, pre-teens, were making their way down the walk to the bathroom, all talking at the same time. The restroom door banged open against the concrete and then banged shut, but the girls still created a small roar through the block walls.

The words rose on Matt's tongue. His standard answer, "My daughter's college fund." He swallowed them. He had savings, disability, and a retirement fund. He didn't need to bartend. And his in-laws, Anna's family, had gifted Dakota a trust intended to pay for her first car, first home, and at least six years of college. Dakota. Not Sophie. Why had he said he didn't know that name? Now he was just freaking himself out. Anna. Anna. Anna . . . She hadn't taken his name.

Sweat dripped down his temple, his rib cage.

What the frig was her last name?

Sebastian shut the sink off.

Matt flushed the toilet, listening to the water run out and gutter in the bottom of the bowl.

The hand blower clicked on, drowning everything else out.

Still, Matt hesitated to open the stall door. No matter how injured his brain was, he couldn't imagine a situation in which he would hide his ex-wife and daughter but put Lily and Ethan in danger. If he couldn't make his own decisions, someone else had. He swung the door open. "Was I bait?"

The silence was damning in Matt's mind, but then Sebastian said, "No, not really. We looked at the gangs here and the cartels in Florida. There were no Zetas here in Daytona. They had no foothold in Florida at all. They had their own troubles, and it didn't seem likely they'd ever show up here. No one even peripheral to either the assault or investigation had ties here."

Matt saw the first swing of the bat, Sam's head snapping back, blood flying. They'd been following up on a threat against the mayor. Walked into a trap and never knew why. "Los Zetas killed Sam?"

"You don't remember?"

Matt clenched his fist and raised it.

"Yes," Sebastian said. "Los Zetas killed Sam."

Like a true professional, he didn't offer more.

Matt weighed the importance of knowing more against the likelihood of the lies Sebastian would offer him if Matt had wanted this, wanted this Gustav Garcia to think Matt's daughter was his granddaughter. Though God only knew why the company had run with that if he'd been experiencing active memory loss. "But my sister lives here. Anyone watching for me, like say, Gustav Garcia, might spot me here."

"Always a possibility."

"Hence you."

"And others. But we had other tasks. I had been here three years already when you arrived. It's not like we were reassigned just for you."

Matt nodded.

The girls made just as much noise leaving their side of the bathrooms as they had coming in.

"When were you first aware I'd been ID'ed?"

Sebastian cleared his throat. "We weren't. We don't know that you have been."

"*Suertudo*. Both the Zetas and Malcom Ward know the dog handlers call me that."

"Lucky One. That could mean a lot of things. You know the regulars take bets on you, right? They have a full-year's calendar for days you'll drop a bottle or pour the wrong liquor or fumble that fancy credit card hand-over to the bar girls. The pot's so big, everyone's rooting for a mistake."

Now young boys on the walk, arguing over something in the surf.

"You've been to the Poker Room?"

"Sat at your bar. Changed my cologne, adopted an accent, didn't say much."

Dolphin or shark, that's what the boys were fighting over.

"In New York, was my name Luznar?"

Sebastian remained silent once again.

Matt struck his cane out and Sebastian stepped out of his way. Matt balanced his cane on the front of the sink and fumbled for the faucet handles to wash his hands. "There's a bounty on my head. The Zetas want my daughter. And everyone knows who I am except me."

The door flew open on a breath of ocean air, sun block, and a shouted "Was not!" but the boys fell silent on spotting the men. They filed in. Three or four of them. Matt splashed water on his face and over his head, letting it run cool over the back of his neck, and ran his wet hands back through his hair. Grabbing his cane, he swept out ahead of Sebastian. He did fine until he hit the asphalt of the parking lot.

Sebastian fell into step with him, shoulder to shoulder, offering guidance in silence.

Matt took it.

UNDER A CRAWLING carpet of blue blowflies, Bolton is lying in his own blood on his left side in his tiny, weedy backyard. His cloudy eyes are wide open, neck both bruised and slashed, tattooed arms sprawled out in front of him. His hands are meaty, fingers thickened by hard work, calluses, and scar tissue.

Behind him, also covered by the shift of thousands of flies, is a small wooden table positioned near the hose. Two gutted fish, a partially gutted fish, and two whole fish are rotting on its surface. Below the table, their guts are being devoured by the flies covering a bucket on the ground.

From the ME's report, she knows Bolton's trachea and larynx were crushed, his hyoid bone broken. The flies lift and resettle in a constant wave of motion that becomes the ME's hand lifting and falling, tracing the damage. Then a miasmic cloud of darkness obstructs her view.

It solidifies into the uniform of a patrol officer, his back to her. He greets Charlie, who crouches down, looking up when Cin that was walks up from the other side. She points at Bolton's neck, talking without sound.

Movement behind her becomes Moultrie and Jimmy that were, coming through the backyard fence's gate. They walk right through Cin that was, Bolton's body, the cop. Charlie turns his head as if watching them and then dissipates in their wake.

Cin steps out of their way and then turns to follow them. They walk up on Bolton gutting the first fish from a stringer of five. He flips the innards into a bucket on the ground, laughing when Jimmy jumps back a foot.

"Hey," a woman's voice says.

The word explodes inside Cin's head. Her heart bounces at the suddenness of it. Shade drops over her like the sun has ducked behind a cloud. Francis Duncan emerges from her, having walked right through Cin's chest.

Daylight and sound come roaring in.

"I got beer," Francis Duncan says, still walking away from Cin. She's carrying two large paper bags of Publix groceries.

"Grab me one, Jimmy," Bolton says, cutting off another fish's head.

Jimmy trots over and lets Francis into the house through a sliding door into the living room. He follows her inside, closing the door behind him.

"You know I've been working some with RWS," Moultrie says in a leading way.

"Yeah," Bolton says, brusque and aggressive, cutting Moultrie off from whatever he wanted to propose. "Mr. Ward doesn't like it much."

Moultrie's eyebrows go up. "Really?"

"Yeah, dude." Bolton slices into the belly of the third fish. "Questioning your loyalty."

"I thought RWS and Ward were tight."

"They are. Tight like the US and the UK."

Cin has no idea what he means, and it's clear Moultrie doesn't either.

"We don't send double agents into each other's territory," Bolton says and turns, flicking his arm out. Moultrie doesn't draw back fast enough. The tip of the gutting knife drags through the skin above his collarbone, blood welling up in its wake. Before Bolton can reverse the blade, Moultrie strikes straight forward, jabbing stiff fingers into Bolton's throat.

Bolton's hands fly up to ease the pain, but the sharp blade of the knife in his right hand strikes the left side of his neck. He jerks it away, slicing across his own jugular. Blood streams down his throat and chest. He opens his fingers and the knife falls.

Bouncing off the sand, it lands on its side among the weeds. Jaw working, mouth gaping, tears flood his eyes. He finally wraps both hands across his neck.

His knees fold.

Cin pats at her pockets for her cell phone. Seams rise under her questing fingers, reminding her of her formlessness. "Call 911," she shouts at Moultrie before she remembers Bolton died weeks ago.

His face turns dusky red before it fades to stark-white.

"Shit," Moultrie says. Supporting his upper body, Moultrie eases Bolton's slow fall as he crumples onto his side, his lips blue. "I'm sorry, I didn't mean—"

Holy shit.

Moultrie *did* kill Bolton.

He strips his tee shirt off and presses it to Bolton's neck.

Cin's glad to see he tried, but the blow to Bolton's neck had already closed his airway. Bleeding out only sped up his death. Short of a trained medic standing at the ready in Bolton's backyard, no one could have saved him.

The slider opens, Jimmy saying something Cin doesn't catch.

"Chris," Francis screams, "Chris!"

Bolton kicks out, his head jerking, eyes rolling.

Rising, Moultrie catches Francis mid-stride, claps his big, bloody hand over her mouth, and holds her back. She lifts her feet off the ground, pulling him down with her until they're huddled in a ball on the ground. Although he's talking in her ear, Cin can hear him just fine from where she stands mesmerized by the turn of events.

"I'm sorry, I didn't mean to. I didn't mean to, I'm sorry," Moultrie says over and over.

Why didn't they call 911? The cut across Moultrie's collarbone and the call would have supported self-defense.

Jimmy's frozen, standing just outside the open slider.

Blood already pooling under him, Bolton's hands flop onto the sandy ground, arms akimbo. His right leg kicks out, the heel catching, and then he's still.

Cin remembers the corpse's pose vividly.

Francis sobs into Moultrie's hand.

A mockingbird catcalls from a spindly tree crowding the fence from the neighbor's yard.

Bolton rises from his body. He's ill-formed, wispy. Noticing her, his gaze drifts to the badge on her hip before he sees Moultrie. He's standing in spirit on the other side of Bolton's body, the black and red bullet hole in his forehead the only color on him. Bolton gives him a snarl of a smile.

Jimmy stumble-runs over and hits Moultrie that was on the back with one fist while tugging on Francis's arm. "C'mon, c'mon."

They untangle themselves. Tears streak Francis's cheeks, dripping from her nose and chin, cutting through the blood Moultrie left on her face. Jimmy shoves both Francis and Moultrie towards the house. Once they're moving, he kneels and rifles through Bolton's pockets. He takes only the lighter, shoving it into his own pocket, then grabs Moultrie's bloody shirt and the knife off the ground before he jogs back into the house.

Fading more with each step, spirit Moultrie walks through Bolton's corpse directly at Cin.

Spirit Bolton smiles and then shrugs in a care-free, "life happens and then you die" kind of way. She knows it's ridiculous to read that much into a tattered, ghostly shrug, but that's exactly how it looks.

Moultrie streams through her, drawing her up and away in a disorienting swirl.

Below her, Jimmy, Moultrie, and Francis are booking out the front door to the cars, huge duffels slung over the men's backs and all of them carrying various sized and colored bags both on their shoulders and in each hand.

Moving Bolton's Malcolm Ward drug stash.

No wonder they didn't call 911.

CHAPTER
THIRTY-TWO

The birthday party in the beach pavilion wound down. The breeze off the ocean cooled. Sunset was coming. Much of the parking lot cleared out around them while they waited, making small talk for appearances sake. The burner rang in Matt's hand. Spider, he hoped, returning his call.

"The Paradise Resort." The caller was the same rich-voiced woman as before, calling on behalf of the Zetas. "Archer and you, *Suertudo*, that's all. No one else."

Resorts were all oceanfront in Daytona. Any resort would be heavily populated in June. That made no sense, but would keep any gunfire or overt violence in check. Maybe. "A simple exchange," Matt said.

The woman laughed. "The drugs for your women and the cop. Info for your boy."

Everything in him stopped. "You have Ethan?"

"He's in hand, yes."

It surprised him, but this was only confirmation of what he'd already guessed. MS-13 really was cutting ties with Malcolm Ward and giving their loyalty to Los Zetas. The info she wanted was no doubt the same as Maria and Jane Johnson had wanted from him. Maybe Malcolm Ward had been hoping to use it to make their own deal with the Zetas.

He had no idea what he'd say to them since they were all wrong about his daughter. His ex was no relation to Gustav Garcia. He'd bet his life on it. He hitched in a breath, "The Paradise is in Daytona, right?"

"You have an hour before someone pays for your tardiness," she said and hung up.

Matt flipped the burner phone closed. "Tell me about the Paradise," he said, not caring who answered.

"Go ahead," Sebastian said to one of the others, voice distant.

"It's on A1A in Daytona." Charlie said. "Abandoned after Hurricane Matthew."

Sebastian's elbow jostled Matt's arm. Matt ignored him. "Security?"

"It's chain-linked, ostensibly under re-construction since it closed." Charlie said. "DBPD can back us up there."

"Won't need them, Charlie." Sebastian said, standing up. "Google says the place was sold a few weeks ago."

Score one for the Zetas. An entire hotel gave them plenty of room for violence. "The drugs for Lily, Jessica, and Carlos. Info for Ethan."

"What kind of info?" Archer asked, his tone wary.

"I'm pretty sure they want to know where my daughter is. I don't know where this idea that she's a Zeta commander's granddaughter came from or how to convince them it's not true."

IT'S NOT true what they say about dying. It's not one minute you're alive and the next you're dead. Moultrie is literally wrapped around Cin, and she's wrapped around him. The rush of rising, the dizziness of corkscrewing into the veil with a man Cin's practically experienced sex alongside is damn near orgasmic. She never got so much action when she was alive.

But at the same time, she's loosening again, creaking out of the socket of her life like a baby tooth being pushed out of the living world. She's been slowly dying all this time and didn't know it. It's not a new thought. We're all dying from the time we're born, right? She's not quite dead yet, though. And she needs to get a move on.

Moultrie pulses, raising goosebumps on Cin's soul. She shivers, energy lighting her up. She's certain anyone watching sees sheet lightning torching the sky around them. And then he's gone, sliding right around her and away, dissipating faster than she can follow into the vastness of the veil.

Cin slows and drifts. Specters coalesce around her, coming and going, as she works her way back through the timeline.

Moultrie kills Malcom Ward member Bolton by accident in self-defensive reaction.

Like Bolton, perceiving Moultrie as an RWS spy for Reardon, Malcolm Ward sends an MS-13 enforcer to kill Moultrie in an eye for an eye move.

Reardon gang-presses Jimmy Shad because he knows him through Moultrie and Jimmy's odd man out, not strictly involved with either RWS or Malcolm Ward, but privy to the small-time ins and outs of the drug trade in Daytona. A perfect recruit to mine the Zeta stash without Reardon having to stand too close. And if he looped Jimmy's "girlfriend" into a job with RWS, it would tie Jimmy to him even tighter.

With Moultrie dead, and wanting out of Reardon's clutches, Jimmy influences and helps Francis Duncan's attempts to kill Reardon, in retaliation for Bolton's death.

Cin wonders if Jimmy ever knew that RWS and Malcolm Ward were two completely separate entities. Malcolm Ward must have caught wind of Reardon's recruitment of Jimmy. Considering MS-13's mercenary signature on Francis's murder and Jimmy's near decapitation, maybe Jimmy had already been in their sights *before* he spilled Ward's name to DBPD.

The bomb still didn't fit, though.

Too out of character for the maras, too much attention placed on Malcolm Ward.

Jimmy Shad. Pain in Cin's ass. Surfer dude, drug user, but she's gotta hand it to him. He lived in the moment. Soaked in it. Probably carried more memories of a textured physical life into the veil with him than Cin has.

The slide of skin on skin catches her unaware.

She closes her eyes and shudders with belly-tingling desire. Matt's scent lingers in her nose. Sand presses into the soles of her feet. Cin swears she can hear the rolling murmur of gentle surf. Her lungs fill with crisp, salty air. Her back settles against the leather of her Civic's racing seat, her baby's steering wheel crosses her palms. Cin closes her fingers around it. The engine's vibration purrs beneath her. A woman shouts go and the tires squeal when Cin shoves the accelerator down.

She opens her eyes to headlights picking out the white line on black asphalt. The shadows of feral palms and moss-ridden oaks pass by in a blur. She's on the Ormond Loop, a timed run so the racers don't kill each other out here in the darkest, most dangerous spot in Ormond. Cin knows already what she'll see when she hits the next curve. Gravity pushes her back as she slows and then punches the car forward, screaming around the bend.

A white light appears out in front of her, headed in her direction. Motorcycle. The closer they get to each other, the more central it seems. She hits the brakes hard, aiming for the narrow shoulder to avoid a head-on crash, but slews sideways instead, sliding along the pavement. The light splits into two and blows past. Cin's Civic spins all the way around. The lights rejoin and curve away around the bend. Her tires finally catch and the car jerks to a stop. Cin's heart gallops on.

She pants, shaking.

She's just experienced the Tomoka Lights, a local phenomenon she'd heard didn't happen anymore. Some say it's the ghosts of a local couple who died in a wreck on the Loop. Others that it's natural, like swamp gas or reflected light.

Headlights spear her car. The racer following her has come around the bend much too early. A cold waterfall of dread pins her in place. It has its own roar, deafening her to the sound of the car speeding at her.

This is it.

This is how she dies.

Cin closes her eyes.

The oncoming driver blows his horn, a long, drawn-out screech that sends her heart into overdrive. Her muscles clench in anticipation of the coming pain, the crunch of metal, the end of everything she knows.

She waits.

And waits.

The horn tapers off into the distance.

Silence.

The tentative call of one frog.

Another answers.

A chorus takes up the frog song.

A low buzz joins them.

Can Cin actually hear the marsh crickets chirping?

And something else familiar.

She opens her eyes to the veil.

A ghost car idles in front of her, a shadowy male driver behind the wheel. Could he really be the one that scared her silly that night? The source of the sometimes playful, sometimes malevolent, always mysterious balls of light that have been causing wrecks on the Loop for decades? He tilts his head in a nod, sends her a vague salute and then drives right through her. Cin spins to continue watching him.

Jimmy Shad stands in front of her.

SITTING in the passenger seat of the Civic with Archer at the wheel, Matt fingered his watch. Cin's scent remained in the car. Twenty-one after eight. According to Sebastian, who'd sent someone over, one softball team remained at the Ormond quad, still running drills. No Ethan. And no boys at the DQ.

Sunset was less than five minutes away. Getting out to the Paradise in the allotted time would be tight with traffic. A mosquito buzzed around Matt's head, and he swiped at it. The windows were down, the A/C blowing lukewarm air in Matt's face in the sweltering car.

"Fuck," Archer said, his arm swinging into Matt's space. The car swerved on the rough asphalt leading out to A1A from the park. Archer cursed again and slapped at the dashboard. Mosquito chasing.

Sebastian was already out on U.S. 1 to drive an alternate route. Charlie was stationed down on Granada Boulevard. He would fall in ahead of them and then let them pass. A company Hummer had been sent ahead to the beach. The three men inside would find a spot to tuck the Hummer in and walk up the beach from either side, trying to spot Zeta lookouts, if there were any, before they themselves were spotted.

There was no real reason to think the Zetas would suspect Archer and Matt had help.

The question marks remained the maras and which side they were backing and if Malcolm Ward was aware the Zetas were making a move on their territory at a time when they were already at odds with RWS because of Reardon. Had the maras killed Reardon for Ward or the Zetas?

Matt rubbed at the faint hollowness in his chest. The pain of Cin leaving him at Maria's house had been the worst yet, but the ache had faded fast and now he could barely feel her absence. Should he call out to her? Would she find him again? What if she didn't show? He dropped his hand and turned his face into the wind through the open window, letting it dry the sweat on his face and swirl through his hair.

On A1A, they picked up speed. Archer rolled the windows up. Matt took his glasses off and rubbed his face, then ran his fingers back through his stupid thick hair. Maybe he'd just buzz cut it after he got everyone out of this mess. He shook his head on a snort. Give him a threat and suddenly the last two years of flailing through his new world hadn't taught him anything about his limitations. He'd thought them engraved in concrete and chained to his soul.

Apparently not.

The snort stirred Archer out of his silence. "It's unbelievable, isn't it? All this? How did this happen?"

"Something I've been asking myself for a couple of years now," Matt said.

"I meant—"

"I know," he said, flapping his hand to wave off the apology in Archer's voice.

"How did you meet her?"

"She arrested me."

"Why?"

"Mistaken identity. She couldn't take me in as a murder suspect, so she made a drug arrest instead."

"Are you—"

"It was borax. I'm not big on roaches."

"Neither am I," Archer said.

Another stoplight. Another half-mile under the tires.

"How long were you with her?"

Matt pondered lying, but what would be the point? "Four days."

"Oh. But you knew her longer than that, right? You were friends?"

Wishing he could see Archer, Matt lifted his glasses and slid them back on. He'd find out later, if there was a later. There'd be debriefings and legal paperwork and gag orders and if they really fucked up, cops and lawyers and courts involved even if the company pulled every string at their disposal. But somewhere in there, Archer would find out that for three of the four days Matt had known his sister, he'd been in jail.

Probably sensing his reticence, Archer backed off just a little. "You were friends?"

Matt wondered if Archer knew what he was doing. "Yeah. We were friends."

CIN'S HEART LIFTS. Shad wasn't her friend. He made bad choices. But she knew him in life. She's glad he's here in front of her in his frayed boardies, stylized yellow suns bright on a faded blue background. The color seeps out of his shorts, swirling away in the constant current of the veil. He stretches his hand out and Cin takes it. It becomes solid in her hand as the veil thickens and stretches around them, darkness falling.

No, not falling, rising.

It's dark out. They walk the length of a wooden dock with sailboats and cabin cruisers tied along its length. Cin hasn't been here before. In death or life. She's guessing it's one of the several marinas at Ponce Inlet. Jimmy told her once the furthest he'd ever been from Daytona was Cocoa Beach in one direction and Jacksonville Beach in the other. He'd never been to Disney. Inland wasn't something that he did.

The boat at the end of the dock is a bona-fide yacht. Small white lights are strung along the rigging. They walk up the metal boarding ramp, still hand in hand. Cin opens her fingers. The scene shimmers. Vertigo lays heavy on her head. She closes her hand again on Jimmy's and they're walking on the ramp again. He glances at her sideways and she meets his gaze. His eyes reflect the dark around them, a milky way of stars bending away into the depths of him.

Cin tears her gaze away. He's more than halfway to the place of comfort she's avoiding. Is she the only thing holding him here? On deck, a crew member is stowing the padding for the deck chairs and a stack of folded tables. Jimmy drifts down the steps into the cabin. It's the yacht from the dinner party at which Francis Duncan tried to extract some sort of penance from Reardon. The cabin smells of perfumed air freshener and rotted gut and vomit.

"Yes, sir," Reardon says into his cell phone. He's standing in the spotless kitchen. "Shad's Mr. Ward's right-hand man, yes, sir." Although his voice is calm and steady, the hand not holding the phone is clenched.

Cin raises her brows at Jimmy. He shakes his head at her. Entire galaxies spin through the darkness that are his eyes.

"Yes, sir, Mr. Ward understands," Reardon says, walking through the cabin. "She'll take care of them."

Cin hears him, but she can't stop looking at Jimmy. He tugs them into Reardon's path. When Reardon walks right through them, the confused expression on Jimmy's face is comical, the dark gray shadow of Reardon's soul occluding their vision for a heartbeat. They've been dead about the same amount of time, but Jimmy's been focused elsewhere, if Cin's theory is correct.

He gives her hand a squeeze and then lets go.

There's no transition, no movement.

The veil simply surrounds her.

Maybe they never left it.

In her new world view, this memory must be important, but Cin doesn't know what it means. It implies Malcolm Ward "took care of" Francis Duncan and Jimmy Shad's spoiling of the night by killing them. Which is what she and Charlie assumed, that the maras killed her under contract to Ward. But Reardon lied about Shad's involvement with Malcolm Ward. Was he trying to put RWS and Ward at odds with each other to the Zeta's advantage? Though, since the Zetas are cutting them both out, why sow that seed of contention?

She can do this. Figure it out.

Cin recalls Reardon's face in detail, the crinkles at the corners of his eyes. The uneven line of his beard on the left side of his neck, the way his collar bones stick out from under the neck of his black button-down, the veins bulging across his clenched fist.

She's spiraling out, spinning, when the glint of silver catches her.

Blade.

She ducks.

The thwack of flat metal hitting meat rings in her ears.

She draws back as the blade slashes down again, this time hitting true, sinking halfway into a woman's thigh. Francis is dead. Her head lies to the side of her body, hair stringy with blood, one hand atop her face.

Reardon swings the blade again.

THE FLIP PHONE RANG. Matt already had it in his hand. "Loose."

"A vagrant is going to step out in front of you," Spider said. "Don't kill him."

"Watch out," Matt barked.

Archer hit the brakes hard.

Thrown forward, Matt's seatbelt locked at the same time he hit the arm Archer slung out to protect him. The hood dipped down, a thud vibrating through the Civic. The flip phone went flying into the foot well.

The car rocked to a halt.

A tap on the driver's side glass.

Archer rolled the window down. Strong body odor wafted in.

"Give me your phones," a man said. Nasal. Florida southern accent.

"No," Matt said, but Archer was already leaning past him to find the Zetas' phone on the floor.

"Turn right here on Granada. Right on Beach Street. Two miles north of Tomoka State Park. There'll be a Challenger at the old sugar mill ruins on Old Dixie Highway. Follow it."

Matt grabbed at Archer's arm, but Archer lifted his elbow and yanked free.

"Mr. Ward says to trust him, Swear-tudo," the vagrant said. "Those X3 fuckers aren't expecting us. Go."

Archer hit the gas. Less than a minute later, he slowed and turned right. Granada Boulevard. "What did he mean about Mr. Ward?"

Matt tore his thoughts from everything he presumed he knew about Spider. "What?"

"Mr. Ward?"

"That was Spider on the Zeta phone."

"Spider?"

"Your RWS IT whiz kid."

A car revved beside them, drawing Matt's attention. There was regular everyday Tuesday traffic surrounding them. Families headed for ice cream on a hot summer night, singles on dates. To them, Archer and he must look like two guys headed off beachside for drinks or dinner. How many people had he passed in distress over his lifetime and never known?

"I don't understand," Archer said.

"It doesn't matter. He's a little bit of everything to everyone. I'm not sure who he's loyal to, but he's with Jessica, who's in the same position Carlos is. He'll want her back. He had the Zeta cell number."

"Doesn't that mean he's with the Zetas?"

"No. I think he's playing both sides."

"The Zetas and . . . Malcolm Ward?"

"I guess we'll find out."

IT SEEMS Cin was wrong at every turn. Reardon framed the maras for Francis Duncan's murder, in the style reserved for the non-noteworthy —not on full public display, but not particularly well-hidden, either. He knew she and Charlie would discover Francis's relationship with both Jimmy and Bolton during the investigation and follow the obvious lead of Bolton's drug connection to Malcolm Ward as the reason she was killed.

But Reardon wasn't local. He didn't know DBPD had no idea there was a Malcolm Ward until Jimmy spilled. Jimmy himself was a Ward outsider, with minor connections, not well-indoctrinated into the "the name that shalt not be spoken" mentality and a criminal informant to boot. Jimmy was everyone's clueless Achilles heel, just happening to be there at every flex of the plot, his every move in reaction to someone else's, not plotted or planned with intelligent insight.

By the time Cin's gathered herself from scattering whatever passes for her physical being into the veil in her own uncontrolled reaction to Reardon's brutality, her drifting thoughts have already formed. She's drawn conclusions with little awareness. It's not the Knowing, but it's close.

She's close.

She turns her back on the tug of home. She sees Matt's tousled hair, the way he lifted his chin to scent the breeze of the incoming storm as he leaned against her car door at One Daytona, hands in his pockets.

Under the bloated, spoiled meat smell of the carnage Reardon wrought on the body of Francis Duncan, Matt had smelled life.

Cin can see him right in front of her.

"Cumin. Coriander. Cinnamon," he says, tapping his nose.

Under the scent of Mami's roasted chicken, sautéed onions and celery, heavy, rich butter, the mellow peach pie, are the tropical notes of Cin's Alikay shampoo when she buried her face in his neck. And the way he tasted when she kissed him? His mouth is all the heaven she needs.

Cin aims her heart and soul at him, leaping into the terrifying downward fall, willingly scattering the pieces of herself into a surge of intention.

That falls.

And falls.

And falls.

CHAPTER
THIRTY-THREE

The hole she'd left in him filled with Cin's presence like ocean surge into a dry tidal pool. Matt took his first deep breath since she left him at Maria's house. She didn't speak to him, though. Or brush a hand over his shoulder.

Somewhere not far from the old sugar mill ruins, Archer turned the Civic's idling motor off, his fear acrid and sharp in Matt's nose, his breathing fast and shallow. Even if Charlie had managed to catch their detour, it would take time for him to re-route their back-up. Cold sweat trickled down Matt's own temple and he swiped it away, hard and fast.

"Stop moving!" a man shouted from in front of the car. "Hands!"

Matt held his hands up, clutching his folded cane in one and holding the other palm out.

The latch on his door clicked. "Stay still," the same man ordered.

In one swift move, both the front doors opened. A briny tang hit the back of Matt's nose and throat, a sweet, grassy rot just under it. The muzzle of a gun pressed into his skin just under his right ear. "Out, *Suertudo*," another man said, pitched for his ears only. It was Irish Spring again, from the ballfield. Now he was coated in what must be a whole can of OFF. He'd said the maras knew how good they had it here in Daytona. Matt hoped that meant sticking with Malcolm Ward against the Zetas. Irish Spring tugged on his arm. "*Soltar el bastón.*"

Matt lurched up out of the Civic and stood in the open door.

"Drop the cane," the first man translated.

Shit.

The cane hardly made a sound when it hit the soft ground.

"*Ven*," Irish Spring said, taking him by the elbow. He walked Matt five steps out and shoved him to his knees on the shift of hard-packed sand, his jeans soaking through in an instant. Low voices drifted from where the men were speaking to Archer but, because of a whippoorwill's warbling, Matt couldn't sort the words. The gun under his ear never wavered.

A rustle of clothes and soft steps under the constant call of the frogs and tree crickets and whine of the mosquitos. A damp, earthy breeze carried off the nearby river although Matt couldn't hear the water. He couldn't hear cicadas, either, despite the heat. That meant no artificial lights and no full moon. Were they using headlights to play out whatever scenario they expected here?

There was a shuffled gathering around the Civic, the hatchback opened.

A muttered oath and a flurry of slaps on skin. "Getting eaten alive here, man."

"Told you to spray down."

"That's poison, man."

"If you'd rather get Zika or whatever the shit—"

"Shut the fuck up," the woman on the phone said from a few feet in front of Matt. "Why aren't they biting you, hmmm, *Suertudo*?"

Matt shrugged. "Never liked the taste of me. Where's Ethan?"

"Not here."

"Jessica and Lily?"

"Phone," she said, pressing it to his left hand.

Matt closed his fingers around it. Lily's voice said, "Matt? Matt?"

He got it turned the right way, Irish Spring following the movement of his head with the gun's muzzle with admirable determination. "Lily, are you okay?"

"Where's Ethan, Matt, where's Ethan?" she cried without breathing.

"I've got him, Lily."

"Give him the phone, Matt, give him the phone, give him the—"

"Lily. I can't right now. But I have him. It's okay. Where are you?"

Lily dissolved in sobbing tears, but then Jessica took the phone and said, "Matt?"

"Where are you?"

"Walking down A1A."

"By yourselves?"

"Yes, the maras dumped us out a mile or so from your sister's house, we're going there."

"Good. That's good. Don't let her leave. Don't call the cops. Lock yourselves in and stay there until Sebastian comes for you. Or that cop we talked to, Charlie. Got it?"

"I told them what I know about you, boss."

Matt closed his eyes. "That's fine, Jess. You did fine. You're alive. Throw the phone away. Hang up now." He didn't wait, just lifted the phone away from his ear. The woman took it.

Matt registered the high-pitched whine of a bullet just before a gunshot blasted through the quiet. A thump preceded the flurry of shots that followed. Matt curled up, hands over his head. Irish Spring's gun boomed in his ear. The woman grunted and fell, her hair brushing over Matt's face on her way down. "No, no, no, no," he shouted. He launched himself at her, feeling for her neck. Hot blood warmed his wet knees. He found her jaw. No pulse. "C'mon, c'mon."

Men were shouting. Someone keened, in agony. Another gunshot and the cry cut off mid-note.

Irish Spring jerked Matt up by his arm and the back of his shirt, half-strangling him.

CIN's neither here nor *there* and still everywhere.

She recognizes the familiar contours of the Loop.

On the west side of Old Dixie Highway, Matt drops to his knees on the right side of her Civic, Archer drops to his on the left. It's nighttime, but she can see the crickets and katydids in the trees, the squirrels curled in their nests, the owl above Matt's head, the whippoorwill that's calling over and over. There's a rabbit nestled at the base of a pine, a bobcat frozen with one foot lifted not thirty yards from the human on the furthest edge of a circular perimeter eleven of them have formed around the seven clustered near the Civic.

They are eighteen bright white lights, shining in the dark.

The trees glow blue with their own form of spirit light.

Across Old Dixie, the marsh swirls with a rainbow of colors and the river is a long, dark snake of living fog.

Three cars are arrayed in a fan facing the Civic. Two human lights sling Carlos onto the ground beside Archer, leaving him in an unmoving heap, but he's still there, all lit up from the inside. There are four more cars farther out, just off Old Dixie along a sandy, dead-end lane, tucked in between the large growth pines with no one left inside.

Charlie is crouched in the dense underbrush south of the group, on his phone. His car is pulled off on a rutted, muddy path that's hardly wide enough for it. There are a lot more human lights farther south, forming torches in groups, but when Cin glances over towards the beach, she knows which ones they are, Jessica and Lily.

She can hear all the human lights at once.

She listens to Matt talk to Lily and Jessica, Sebastian talk Charlie down from calling DBPD, Archer mutter platitudes in Carlo's unconscious ear while lights flitter to and away from the Civic. Brilliant fireworks of gunfire shatter the night like rocks hitting a windshield. The cracks spread wide, touching every human light affected by them. Some of the cracks spread beyond where even Cin can see. Down there around her car, lights gutter and wink out, extinguished. She can't see the five spirits rise, but feels them pass, ripples in her ocean of being.

Matt chokes, coughing out questions as he's manhandled to the Civic. No, only one question.

"Where is Ethan?"

"Where is he?"

"Where the fuck is Ethan?"

To the west, two laughing lights draw Cin's eye.

They're drinking Coke and splitting a can of Pringles.

Ethan snorts and coughs on the Coke that shoots out his nose.

The boys laugh louder.

"Stop, Rodrigo, stop," Ethan wheezes.

Bedroom. Blue sheets on bunk beds. Baseball posters. Growing boy smell.

She has to tell Matt.

She sticks to the veil.

She tugs at the tendrils that hold her back.

"Where's Ethan?" Matt says again.

The man shoves him down, clocking Matt's head on the door frame.

Cin's ocean rocks.

Inside Matt, she's dizzy.

She tumbles free.

Hits asphalt.

There's a woman lying there in front of her, facedown. Slender. Jeans. Fitted, black, down jacket.

White dust covers her.

Shapely, brown hand. Green rubber O-ring for a wedding band.

Cin kicks the gun near her open hand away.

The stiff breeze sends a crumple of plastic wrap tumbling away. There are hard white bricks scattered on the ground around them. Bullets had hit at least one. A tangle of long black hair spills from the plain black ball cap the woman is wearing.

She knows these details.

This body, this ring, the worn Doc Martins, the curve of her cheek.

Cin can't catch her breath.

Bile rises in her throat.

"Matt, Matt." A man's frantic voice.

A hand catches her vest, spins her around. Cin's legs tangle and she goes down in a heap.

No.

Matt goes down in a heap. His gun clatters when his hand hits the pavement.

Cin's feet are still inside him. She steps away from him.

Her lungs expand with no restriction. Her head clears.

His partner—it's Sam, and Cin hears Matt's panicked thoughts from another memory, *samsamohgodsam*. Sam snatches up Matt's gun and tucks it in his own waistband, then jerks at Matt's vest, forcing him upright, legs akimbo, to lean him back against a pallet of boxes marked "gypsum". He rips the vest's Velcro straps loose, gloved hands moving, trying to find the injury. One finds the bullets, three of them, center mass, the other yanks Matt's shirt up to expose the fresh red of what will be a spectacular bruise. "You're okay, you're okay."

Sam's hands continue to pat down Matt's sides, around his back, along his thighs. He pulls Matt's bent leg out from under him as Matt continues to pant. He keys his mic and asks for a medic at their end of the wharf.

But there's nothing around them from Cin's point of view.

Just Matt and Sam, a dead woman, a pallet, a few hundred bricks of powder. Cocaine or meth or heroin.

"That's one more of these motherfuckers," Sam says, his breath rising. "Makes three bodies and two in cuffs." He turns his head, lips moving. "At least fifteen pallets of coke just here. At least. Three years of work, brother. But we got 'em. We finally got 'em. Here comes the EMTs. You just keep breathing, okay?"

Matt's fingers close in the front of Sam's shirt. Sam leans over him. "Han," Matt wheezes.

Sam glances at Matt's fisted hand on the asphalt. Unlike Sam's standard gloves, Matt favors fingerless. Seeing nothing alarming, he tilts his chin down to check the hand on his shirt.

Tears roll down Matt's cheeks unchecked. He screws his face up, sucking in a deeper, painful breath. "Han, it's Han," he says, lapsing into a weak, coughing fit, twisting in Sam's grasp. The EMTs drop their gear and bodies down on either side, one saying, "We got this, sir, let us work."

Sam lets go, rising, stepping back. He frowns down at Matt and then looks at the dead woman. Steam rises from her cooling blood. Striding over to her, Sam kneels and digs his fingers into her neck. "Hey, hey," he shouts, "this one's still alive!"

One of the EMTs slams his kit shut, leaps up, and comes over. Sam helps him turn her so he can get to the hole in her upper abdomen. There's more though, another in her flank, her thigh. The EMT slaps a wad of gauze over her abdomen. "Press down hard on this. Lean on her." He rips a tourniquet from his kit and goes to work getting it tied off around her thigh.

The woman groans.

Sam turns his head to check on her. Cin follows his gaze.

Her hair has fallen from her face.

She's a stranger to Cin.

"Fuck," Sam says.

"What," the EMT grunts.

"She's his ex-wife."

"Who's?"

"My partner over there. This is his ex-wife."

Matt jerked awake.

Was he asleep?

Ethan.

Lucinda.

"Cin?" he mumbled, trying to pull himself up straight. He was slumped in a hard, leather seat. He kicked his feet out, hitting the boundaries of a small space, knocking his knee on . . . dashboard.

The Civic. The sugar mill. Ethan.

"Cin?" Matt said again because he knew she was there.

Fingers formed on his cheek.

"Cin." His muscles loosened, his lungs opened deeper, his racing heart calmed. "Thank god, Cin."

"Stay down, Matt," she whispered. "He's getting in with you."

Cars started. Matt slowed his breathing further, willed himself to relax into his uncomfortable position.

"Ethan is with a boy named Rodrigo," Cin breathed.

Matt froze, his brain a complete blank in reaction to those words.

Irish Spring slammed the driver's door shut and cranked the motor. He shoved at Matt's shoulder and Matt rocked with the motion. "*Despierta, no te golpee tan fuerte.*"

Wake up? No hit hard.

He spun the car backwards to the left, forcing Matt to brace himself.

His glasses fell off the top of his head. He groaned against the very real pain of a building headache and raised his hand to press it into the right side of his head. Irish Spring shifted into drive and peeled out, tires spinning, dirt and gravel hitting the wheel wells and undercarriage.

"Where's Archer?" Matt mumbled.

Irish Spring ignored him.

"They're leaving him and Carlos behind," Cin said. She seemed to be in the backseat, her voice coming from behind him, rather than in his ear, more like when she was physically present with him than when he was with other people.

The speedy right hand turn out onto Beach Street slung him against the door. He made a more coordinated effort to sit up. The dashboard lights seeped into sight and then the rest of the front panel, the gear shift, Irish Spring's hand, his long, tan bare arm. Redhead. Mestizo. Maybe the soap was ironic. Irish glanced over. Matt stared straight at him. Irish frowned and turned his attention back to the road.

Swaying left, Matt turned his head to survey the back. Cin sensed his eyes on her, and turned from watching the cars coming after them, headlights bouncing out onto the road. They framed her hair, throwing light all around her. Matt's breath stuttered. She looked like the angels in the stained-glass windows of the church he attended as a boy, sun pouring through her despite the darkness.

The corner of her lip lifted in a mischievous smile, breaking his trance. She lifted her finger to her lips and then pointed. "Hang on to something, I'm going to help Charlie if I can."

His vision blipped away again to nothingness. Matt straightened and threw himself right, feeling for the seatbelt.

CHARLIE IS BOUNCING BACK down the rutted track, almost to the road. A lone northbound headlight bears down on her southbound Civic and the two cars trailing it. The redheaded mara edges the Civic further to the right on the narrow blacktop. The single headlight shifts, mirrors him in a game of chicken, the pop-eyed car aiming for a head-on collision. The mara hits the Civic's brakes, tires squealing, and swerves left, placing Matt in the impact zone.

The light divides and runs down either side of the Civic, which rocks in backwash as a long horn blast peels the dark off the night. One of the two cars behind them careens onto the shoulder and the other swerves across the center line. On the shoulder, the driver avoids his brakes and hits the gas, straightening up just in time to scrape past the stopped Civic. The other car spins a complete one-eighty and slides until it kisses the Civic's driver's side, flank to hood.

A ripple of glee reaches Cin and makes her heart soar. The phantom driver of the Tomoka Lights is delighted with his own actions. From his muddy track, Charlie's headlights hit the Civic broadside, but the red-headed mara is already on the move again, pulling away, headed back towards Granada Boulevard, the car from the shoulder following. The other guns off in the opposite direction.

Charlie hits the hardtop and stops. In the wake of the Civic, not yet visible on the road, the engines of MS-13's cars echo and rebound off the swamp, the marshy grounds along the confluence of the Tomoka and Halifax rivers. He has to make a choice here, give chase, which means calling in support from DBPD, or trust Sebastian and hope that the cars he can hear are also coming from the meet. She wishes she could help him.

Someone much larger than Cin stirs in the veil, brushes a hand through the night, spreading her out. All the pieces of her swirl, but don't separate. She floats, trying to make herself a starfish the way her daddy taught her in the ocean swells off Melbourne. She manages jellyfish status, she thinks. The Timucuan chief, Cin Knows now it's him, withdraws his interest with a flush of bemusement staining his long-rooted patience as he abides over his birthright from the veil.

The cars from the original perimeter round the bend. Making his decision, Charlie flips his blue lights on, pulls his car straight ahead across the middle of the road, and stops there, straddling the yellow line. Cin doesn't know if he's a fool or a hero or even if he'll be able to feel her, but she gathers her particles and tries to muster that feeling of solidity she has when she's with Matt.

Again, something loosens deep inside her, creaks deep inside her . . .

soul. That's what's left of her, right? She loses the outer pieces of herself for a moment, but then they slam back together. Gravity pours into her, giving her weight.

The blacktop, the blue lights, the trees flashing gray-green with every circular pulse, harden. All their edges become more distinct. More real in a way Cin hadn't noticed they weren't before. DBPD tactical vest on, Charlie is standing in front of his driver side door. The first car slows.

Charlie has his hand on his gun, but it's still holstered. He walks forward as the car comes to a halt. Cin expects the driver to hit the gas and go around Charlie's Impala, but the driver just rolls his window down. "Problem, Officer?"

"We're investigating nearby shots fired. You hear anything?" Charlie says with a smooth delivery, managing casual. Cin's sure he recognizes both the driver and the passengers from where he saw them parked along the dead-end road.

The rest of the gang remains behind the lead car, but cluster up, using both lanes. Five cars total.

"No, sir, we just been cruising the Loop," the driver answers just as easily, cocking a thumb back to indicate either the Loop or the cars idling behind him. "Listening to music."

"You guys alone or is this a group cruise?"

"Just a few homies," the driver says, his voice slowing down like he's distracted. "Nothing organized."

Just Charlie's luck that the car he cut off holds a smarter mara. Then again, they probably left the obvious gangbangers in town, calling attention to themselves.

The car that squirted away earlier U-turned somewhere past the bend and now eases up in line the others.

The light's been rising during the whole conversation, but not so much that Cin really notices until the driver Charlie's talking to breathes, "Jesuchristo."

The front seat passenger says, "*¿Que es eso?*"

The backseat passenger opens his door and gets out, one foot on the road, one still inside, and stares directly at Cin.

Oh, shit, can they see her?

Doors are opening on the other cars now.

Charlie draws himself up, un-holstering his gun as he does so.

The driver of the lead car doesn't notice. He's watching her.

Charlie backs up one, two, three steps, but doesn't turn his attention away to see what they're gawking at until he's out of range of the driver's door. He raises his gun in a two-handed, ready-low grip and then glances back, his gaze roaming up. His mouth drops open.

Shit, shit, shit.

Headlights sweep the road. Cars coming from the other direction.

Cin draws her arms and legs in, wrapping herself in a tight ball with her head on her knees. As much as she'd like it to, it doesn't make her disappear any more than it ever did when she tried it as a child. Past the maras, a car charges around the curve.

"¡Mire! ¡Mire!" someone shouts, and closer to the bend, someone else, "Fuck! Watch out!"

The Tomoka Lights are bearing down on them.

Cin grins and spreads herself out.

The maras standing on the road are leaping away from their cars.

Charlie hesitates, stepping back towards the driver's side door of the lead car, but the driver is still staring helplessly into the light Cin's shedding. Charlie backpedals at the last possible second before the speeding lights hit the last two cars in the back up.

The shrieking crunch of metal on metal doesn't come, though.

In eerie silence, the headlights of the car plowing into MS-13's cavalcade split apart.

They zig-zag between the cars and buzz the scattered maras, before joining up and taking aim at Cin.

The wondrous light hits her head on.

She explodes in a shower of sparks.

Finds her feet.

Car surfs the Tomoka Lights on a wave of gleeful joy to the surface of the road and then up the other side in a wave that takes her over the top of the approaching Hummer and the car following it. Their tires screech, brake lights staining the night.

Cin lifts her arms when she sees it's Sebastian in the car, Jessica beside him, and shouts out loud, a wordless cry releasing the tsunami of triumph and gratefulness swelling inside her. She dives from the top of her phantom friend's car, knowing this time that the veil will catch her.

CHAPTER
THIRTY-FOUR

After a single turn onto what Matt knew must be Granada, they ran straight west, stopping at several lights and then driving under the hollow I-95 overpass, and off the edges of the map in Matt's head. He had no idea where they were and the nothing he saw seemed more nothing than usual. He fingered his watch. Almost ten. He didn't have the stamina he used to take for granted.

Irish Spring drove in silence. With no radio and only the steady hum of the tires, Matt drifted on his waning adrenaline, trying to stave off the inevitable crash. Knowing Ethan remained with Rodrigo, that Jessica and Lily were safe, made it harder. He couldn't maintain that much worry for himself.

His head bounced against the window, making the steady throb inside it flare. He threw his arms out, trying to steady himself, hitting the dash and Irish Spring's arm. The man didn't yell at him, though, just muttered something under his breath about how this better fucking be worth the trouble. "Couldn't agree more," Matt answered in kind, then frowned at himself. Whatever. He rubbed his face and ran his hands back through his hair.

They had turned, maybe twice, maybe more. His head hurt. He squeezed it between his hands before he dropped them with a sigh. No doubt he was being hauled to an interrogation meant to gain either the maras or Malcolm Ward the Los Zetas bounty on his head. They'd be disappointed, but lucky that they'd never gain the attention of a Los Zetas leader like Garcia must be after the move the maras just made against them.

The Zetas would slaughter them all.

Irish Spring slowed and Matt braced himself through a right-hand turn. The dirt road did his head no favors. When it seemed the jouncing, suspension-grinding ride would never end, Matt leaned forward, elbows on his knees to hold his head in both hands, a low groan escaping through his clenched teeth.

Moments later, Irish Spring bounced the car to the left, threw it into park and shut the engine off. Doors slammed. Men's voices. Matt's door opened. Hands pulled at him, forcing him out. His stomach rolled. He leaned over in their hold, gagging. Cursing, they sat him on the ground and backed off.

He swallowed the bile that rose in his throat and then the flood of saliva that followed. A rough hand grabbed his hair and pulled his head back. Another grabbed his jaw, forcing his mouth open. Two thick, bitter pills dropped onto his tongue. The unmistakable taste of Oxy. The rim of a bottle touched his lower lip. It was swallow or drown. The whiskey burned his throat. He choked. They forced another bolt down him and then let him go.

A bottle of warm water hit his lap. He fumbled to open it and then forced himself to drink several swallows before lowering it. Head propped on the heel of his free hand, Matt breathed through his mouth, willing the pills to stay down. Sweat dripped from his hair line. His polo was soaked. The men had backed off but remained nearby, subdued, and quiet. The sand he sat on was still warm from the sun. He finally identified an odd buzzing sound nearby as a bug zapper.

A mosquito whined in his ear.

He nearly clocked himself in the head with the water bottle waving it away.

The world blurred for a bit.

"How you feeling, Matt?" a man said in English.

Matt lifted his head, feeling the lessened pain of his headache rear up to greet the movement and the frown of his confusion. Without thought, he'd been listening to bits and pieces of conversation in Spanish for the past little while, having no problem understanding it.

Matt had to work to swallow. The bottle of water remained in his loose fingers. He lifted it and drank what remained while trying to pull his muddy brain together. He crushed the empty bottle in his fist. It wasn't satisfyingly crunchy, his hearing dulled still from the gunfire. He dropped it in the sand.

"You ready to meet Mr. Ward?"

Spider. Matt rolled his eyes, instantly regretting it and took a long slow breath.

"Jess said you were good at that," Spider said. His light tone was forced. "Get him up."

Hands grabbed his biceps and hauled him upright. Dizzy, he swayed forward. Someone planted a hand on his chest. How many times had the hands of strangers steadied or calmed or restrained him this way since he was blinded? "I'm fine," he growled. Sweat dripped down his temples.

Spider leading the way, the hands, and the bodies they were attached to, frog-marched Matt through the sand onto a gravel walk and then up two steps, dragging him at that point, and through a door. Cooler air. The building was large and open, the ceiling high. A large fan running at the far end. Every sound echoed. Metal walls, at a guess. Concrete under foot.

Small warehouse.

Not what he had expected. The rhythmic click of high heels wasn't a surprise, though.

The hand that had remained on his chest patted him now, as if to tell him he needed to stand on his own. The two men let him go and the outside door clicked shut behind him. How many people remained in the room?

"Mr. Luznar," Jane Johnson said, from directly in front of him. "I believe you've met my associate John?"

Matt shook his head at the use of his old name and her assumption. He shifted his feet just wide enough to steady his stance. Left his arms at his side, his hands open.

"A pleasure to meet you again." Male. Neutral tone. John. Yeah, okay, Johnny Smith. To his front right.

"And this is Israel Portillo."

"We met at Archer's," Portillo said, from the left.

A mara known to us, Israel Portillo, Sebastian had said. *An Army Ranger.* That indescribable feeling of connections locking into place washed over him. They were all Malcom Ward. Reardon and his Zeta partner never had any chance of infiltrating Daytona with MS-13 holding leadership representation in an actual alliance of criminal equals. But giving Matt, or maybe his daughter, to Gustav Garcia for whatever grief Matt and Sam caused the Zetas in New York would both serve as an apology for shutting the Zetas out of Daytona and give Malcolm Ward its very own earned connection to one of the most powerful Zeta factions in the Americas.

The trio heading Malcolm Ward were only introducing themselves because Matt was no longer an exposure threat to them. He'd be dead as soon as he gave them whatever they wanted from him. Or didn't, since he didn't know anything about his own circumstances, let alone his daughter's. He shouldn't expect rescue, no one knew where he'd been taken. Except maybe Cin. He could still feel her, but she wasn't here with him, and even if she were, she couldn't tell anyone his location.

Only one thing really mattered.

"Ethan?"

"Will disappear with you should you not help us," Jane said. "An unviolated American boy of his age and the unique sadistic pleasures that might be found with a blind man boasting your particular resume will be very lucrative. The only thing that would be better for us would be turning your daughter over to Gustav Garcia."

Not going to happen. "In that case?"

"She's reunited with her grandfather, Ethan goes home to his mother, and you are the victim of a predator, one we will make sure the cops find with enough evidence to prosecute."

A cold tingle pooled at the base of his spine. What would Garcia do to Dakota when he discovered she wasn't the little girl he wanted? Matt staved off the impending shudder. Kept his feet still by force of will. He didn't know where she was, so he couldn't tell them.

Stall. Stall. Stall.

He found his tongue. "How do I know you won't traffic Ethan anyway?"

"That's my call, Loose," Portillo said, and Matt appreciated him for using his real assumed name. "We like it here. We're not going to piss in our pond. I won't traffic him if you give us what we want."

And he couldn't do that. But he also couldn't risk Ethan. And the life Matt had, whether he wanted it or not, was far better than sexual slavery and a slow death. He shook his head, trying to clear his Oxy haze, and swayed.

Focus.

Even if he did give them what they wanted, if Ward already had a plan to traffic them, there'd be no reason to give up the money they could get for Ethan and himself on top of whatever bounty Garcia had placed on his head. "Liar," he said, pulling himself up straight and lifting his chin. "You've betrayed your service. You have no honor."

"*I've* never jeopardized my country's national security," Portillo said in a way which implied Matt had, which meant he knew entirely too much about Matt's background, even if he didn't know the whole story. "I've risked my life for my country, which is more than I can say for most Americans. And honor? I'm a man of my word. My perceptions may differ from yours, Loose, but that doesn't mean justice isn't served or life improved by my actions." His calm never wavered. His words were measured, nearly flat.

Jane Johnson had never stopped tapping her foot as he spoke, and she remained directly in front of Matt. Johnny Smith probably remained to his right. He was the wild card, especially if he was the former spook Matt suspected him of being. How long would he let Matt stall? "You kill people, Portillo, how is that improving lives?"

No one said anything. God, he'd give anything to see these people, have some body language to go from. Matt thought he'd gotten good at parsing tone, inflection, meaning, but right now, he didn't trust anything he'd learned. Someone to his right walked away. There was a shuffle from that direction, someone sniffing up a runny nose while the person who'd left returned.

"Here?" Johnny Smith said, coming closer to Matt than he'd been standing before. Turned out, it wasn't just that Waffle House had presented him with strong odors. Nothing distinguished Smith from the rest of the warehouse. No mint on his breath, no distinctive aftershave, no Fresh Rain scented deodorant. Smith set something down. If he was playing fetch, maybe the only people present were the three Mr. Wards and Spider?

Portillo strode forward. Matt blocked his hand when Portillo tried to take his arm. Portillo laughed. "That oxy helped, no?" Portillo gave him a shove, forcing Matt to step right, then crowded into him, pushing him away from the outside door towards whatever Smith had set down. "Loosened you up."

He wasn't wrong. Matt gave in, took three fast steps over to give himself some room, and turned on the ball of his right foot, planting his left heel for balance, while jabbing his right elbow up and back. He jettisoned his clenched fist straight forward at an upward angle. Fuck. Portillo's jaw was a lot harder than padding and head gear. The mara stumbled back.

Matt resisted shaking his hand out, dropping into a defensive crouch instead, both hands raised.

"Not his head," Spider yelled.

Matt ducked left from the pulled punch. He blocked Portillo's following upper cut to his left ribcage, boxed him in the ear, and then caught his neck in both hands. Raising his left knee, Matt used Portillo's own downward momentum to slam his head against it, the crunch of cartilage breaking fiercely satisfying. Portillo roared, but still grabbed Matt around the waist and bulldozed him off his feet.

Matt saved his head from the hard floor, but lay paralyzed, chest screaming. Portillo rolled off him. Tilting his head back until it finally met the concrete, Matt drew his knees up, feet flat, his lungs stuck, trying not to panic.

Finally, he drew a little breath in, moaning involuntarily with the painful release. He rocked helplessly, groaning as his breath went nowhere for a long minute before his chest finally released and air rushed in. He huffed in a couple of breaths and then started coughing. He rolled to his side and sat up, hitting Portillo in the process.

Portillo shoved him back down. "Stay down," he said, voice muffled.

Matt sat right back up.

"Enough," Jane Johnson said.

He heard one man coming under Portillo stomping away and slamming through the outside door, but the other was silent. His bulk and body heat a bare warning before the rustling of his clothes as he crouched down. Matt flinched back against the louder, musky one, his skin crawling with déjà vu. But they only manhandled him upright once again. They walked him backwards and the quiet one swept Matt's left leg out from under him, forcing him down, a hard surface meeting his butt halfway to the floor.

A chair.

A jangle of change and keys and then the whisper of something being drawn from the loud, musky one's pocket. They pulled Matt's arms to either side of the chair and zip-tied his wrists to its legs. They made six people in the small warehouse. Matt was almost certain that was all. Jane Johnson's heels clicked closer, bouncing off something stored low in the center of the warehouse. That gave him something of a layout. And something to focus on. He forced himself to stop pulling against the zip-ties already cutting into his skin and took a deeper breath.

The door swung open again, the voices of the men outside drifting in. Matt lifted his chin, expecting push back from Portillo, anger he could use to find another opportunity to assess his surroundings, find a way to turn "Mr. Ward" against each other long enough for Sebastian to discover the warehouse.

"Let's get this done," Portillo said.

"Go ahead, Spider," Johnny Smith said.

"Anna is not Garcia's daughter," Matt said. "Obviously, I'm not his son. Our daughter is not his granddaughter."

"I believe you," Jane Johnson said. "For the trouble you've caused him, I'm sure Garcia will be happy to have your head regardless."

Like, literally?

"I don't believe him," Portillo said.

"Would you like a demonstration, Mr. Ward?" Jane said. "It's quite convincing."

"Just get on with it, Spider," Smith snapped.

They were all standing closer than before. Matt tugged at the zip ties again, hands fisted. Either blood or sweat slicked his wrists. Probably both. He'd been trained by more than one agency. Spider couldn't break him, but he was only human and out of practice. Whatever they did would be painful before they killed him. He took another breath and shut down the pain of his wrists, focusing instead on the steady warm disconnect of the Oxy.

Spider dragged something else over towards him. Matt shut down his thoughts of Ethan and Lily. Packed away all stray thought of Sebastian and Charlie coming for him. Spider lifted it, swinging it forward. Matt straightened, waiting for the bat to land. It settled on the floor. Spider came around it, his hand drifting over Matt's shoulder before he let it land in a brief pat. He sat, his knees brushing Matt's.

A chair.

Matt breathed out, let go of the image of the bat, Sam's crushed head.

He concentrated on his last sight of Cin, how she looked like an angel in the back of the Civic.

Paper, maybe a wrapper, crinkled in Spider's hands.

Matt let go of his image of Cin.

Consciously looked at the nothing beyond his eyes instead.

"I'm sorry," Spider said.

Matt tensed, waiting for the slide of a needle or a knife or something else that would hurt him, something he could start building his wall of resistance against.

"Yellow," Spider said. "Creek. Mortar. Shallow."

Matt's eyelids drooped. He blinked and widened his eyes against the fog of tired settling into his brain, his limbs.

"Bullet. Ribbon. Shepherd."

CIN FILTERS THROUGH THE VEIL, already focusing on Archer, and this time there's hardly a transition at all. It's effortless.

Archer lifts his head from where he's murmuring nonsense to Carlos, who is awake and in pain. She doesn't feel the wind so much as sense it. She's more formless than when she was with Archer last. The treetops sway. Sand and pine needles stir from the ground. Dried palm fronds rattle. Above, the rotors of a helicopter chop the air. All three of them look up just as it reaches them. The black, unmarked copter lingers over them and the bodies scattered around the clearing, amazingly quiet, and then moves off towards Old Dixie Highway.

With no effort at all, Cin's on the blacktop. Sebastian and his backup have formed further barricades by parking the Hummer and Sebastian's Kia across the shoulders of the road behind Charlie's Impala. Under its flashing blue lights, two men geared out with unmarked tactical vests and rifles are taking point, and a tall sister in black, also in a vest, but wearing a thigh holster and carrying a clipboard, is just making her way to Charlie, with Sebastian in tow.

The rearmost mara reverses his ride in a wide curve as the helicopter descends to the treetops. Parts of Old Dixie are canopied and while there's some leeway here, there's not near enough room for a copter to land. The mara sees that, too. His rear tires spin, then catch, squealing, and he shoots forward.

Special operators, there's no doubt that's what they are, fast rope out of the copter's side door two at a time. The first two that hit the ground crouch and fire a line of bullets along the blacktop ahead of them. The escaping mara two-foots the brakes, the anti-skid locks up, and the car slews to a tail-wagging stop, the operators less than five feet away with their assault rifles aimed at the windshield.

Four more spread out to either side of them at a crouching run, guns up and aimed at the remaining cars. The copter is already rising. In seconds, it's high above the scene, silent and nearly invisible in the dark under just a sliver of moon.

The voice of the woman with the clipboard cracks through the confused chatter of the maras. "Hands! Let's see them!"

In short order, the maras are zip-tied for everyone's safety. Two of the operators run back to where they landed to sling stuffed red duffels sporting white crosses on them over their shoulders. The medics liberate the failed escapee of his keys. His car is already facing the right direction. Cin rides along with them north of the dead-end lane. To Archer.

Leaving the car idling with the lights on, the operators assume their positions on either side of Carlos, one lifting Carlos's wrist while the other rips his duffle open. They announce themselves to Archer with last names only. They don't ask him to move from where he's cradling Carlos's head in his lap.

When Cin places her hands on his shoulders, Archer drops his own head and groans in relief. "Told you, Carlos, my sis was watching out for you."

She never knew where Carlos was or what was happening to him, but what Archer doesn't know won't hurt him. In this case, at least. All Cin's seen instead, everything leading up to this moment, spills through her mind's eye even as she tries to memorize Archer, afraid this is it, the last time she'll have her hands on him here in the real world. Has she already had that moment with Matt?

Just the thought of him, of all he doesn't know, is a hook, reeling her constant awareness of him into a taut line. She wants to follow it, but the urge isn't demanding. She's not afraid of losing him in the same way.

They're bound together.

Like Carlos and Archer.

There's a glowing link shared between them, thin threads looping this way and that, an intricate open maze of connection from head to foot. Now that Cin's seen it, she can't look away. A shifting blue framework also loops the operators together as they work in unison, exchanging soft words, handing fluids and gauze and scissors off without looking at one another. It's different, but the same. Cin lifts her hands and watches the silver connection between her and Archer show itself. Looking up, she sees the trees are netted in gold.

Headlights hit the far side of the trees and the visible connections fade from her awareness. Charlie's Impala appears and coasts to a stop. Sebastian, the badass sister, and a mara, his hands zip-tied in front of him, get out. Jessica remains in the front passenger seat, in a black polo, her hair tucked up under a ball cap pulled low over her face, soaking the scene in, eagle-eyed and serious. Sister gives the mara a flashlight. He identifies three of the dead as X3, Sureños enforcers for Los Zetas. The fourth man and the dead woman are Zetas. The sister takes head shots with her phone and collects thumb prints on a different device. Wearing a headlamp, Sebastian takes notes on her clipboard.

The Hummer rumbles in with a stretcher and, after the corpses, Carlos and Archer are loaded into the back. All the cars have been pulled down the dead-end lane, out of sight of Old Dixie, the zip-tied maras sitting cross-legged on the ground alongside them.

Edging out onto Old Dixie, the Hummer's driver flashes its high beams. The still-hovering copter sends a basket down for Carlos and one medic. There are still no signs of DBPD. After the bodies are loaded, headlights spear the dark, coming north from town. The operators wave the copter off, basket still hanging, and beat it back to the Hummer. The driver douses its lights altogether and backs down the narrow, sandy lane a few feet, to park in the middle of it.

Cin stands in the middle of Old Dixie, mostly because she can.

A northbound pick-up truck slows, preparing to turn in. When the driver sees the parked Hummer, though, a darker-than-the-night square blocking the lane, bare hint of metal, mere outline of tires, she aborts the turn. Her headlights point into the woods as the truck idles, the four college-age girls with her still giggling and singing along with Selena Gomez about who's going to walk them through the dark side of morning until they notice she's stopped.

"Let's go to that place past the creek, then, before Halifax Plantation," the front seat passenger says, shrugging.

The driver spins the wheel and the truck lurches back onto the right side of the blacktop. The dashboard lights illuminate the driver's face from inches away when she drives by Cin. Eyes narrowed, lips clamped together, she's watching the rearview hard.

Cin reaches out and lets her fingers trail along the side of the truck. Like she's riffling pages in a book, the driver's entire future opens under her hand—graduation, commission, husband, IED, recovery, children— a boy, another boy, a girl—open water skimming under a hull, a high school graduation, retirement, driving alone into verdant green mountains, a college graduation, a puppy, a boot camp graduation, dancing in the rain, gray hair plastered to her head . . . Cin's hand comes off the end of the truck, the driver guns the engine, and she's gone, straight into the rest of her life.

The copter descends once more, to finish the clean-up.

And then Archer and Carlos are gone, too.

SOMEONE WAS TALKING. " . . . SKY. MATTRESS."

Matt's cheeks were wet, and his throat hurt. Pain shot up his arms when he tried to lift his hands to his face. He was tied to the chair he sat on. The hair on the back of his neck rose, chilling him despite the heat, his sweat soaked shirt.

"Thank you, *Suertudo.*"

"*Suertudo?*" Matt said. Why would anyone call him Lucky One?

"You don't remember?" a woman said.

And then he did.

"HEY," Charlie shouts, and Cin's no longer standing on the blacktop of Old Dixie Highway.

She's standing next to him.

Sebastian ignores him. The maras are lined up with their backs to them. Headlamp still in place, Sebastian is moving from one to the other, popping through the zip-ties with a pocketknife. Charlie has his hands fisted at his sides, a flashlight in one pointing straight down at the ground, but isn't trying to stop him.

On impulse, Cin steps into him.

Charlie's a ball of dread at the prospect of the maras being released. Nothing has been negotiated or explained to them. Without speaking to them, the remaining operators photographed and printed them while Cin was out on the road. They collected no names, asked no questions. Catch and release, Sebastian grunted when Charlie pulled him away. There's a larger operation at stake.

Without proof, without arrests, Charlie has nothing to take back to DBPD. He's no further into solving her murder, Jimmy Shad's, Francis Duncan's, Doug Moultrie's. Altogether, his team, short-staffed without her and Perez, has more murders to process than he has fingers, he doesn't know how it all fits together, and on top of that, Matt Loose is gone God knows where.

Cin tests her connection to Matt and while it's quiet, it's still there.

Charlie's anxiety drops a notch.

But hers rises.

Charlie's thinking about her. She's standing at One Daytona, the rising wind blowing her hair off her face, one hand on her hip, the other holding the evidence bag with Francis Duncan's knife roll in it, and she's watching Matt slouch against her car door. In Charlie's head, Cin's expression is utterly contented in the low red light of the setting sun. She's every inch a confident, competent detective and he admires that.

You are, too, Charlie.

What would Lucinda Troy do? The words are fully formed, a directed thought to himself.

Exactly what you would do, Cin shoots back at him.

Yeah, he thinks. *Exactly what you would do. You'd forge ahead.*

Her heart, oh, her heart. Their heart. It aches.

I love you, Charlie.

I love you, too, Cin.

He mentally shakes himself. An action plan is forming itself in his head from blurry images and words picked up and discarded, the strongest thought being cooperation with Sebastian, a partnership of sorts, using what the man knows to sort evidence, and the foremost action being to find Matt, followed by Reardon's body, then finding a way to fish for info on the bomb from the maras using today's events as leverage . . .

Cin braces herself and lets him walk away from her. Juggling the flashlight, he reaches into his pocket, and comes up with his packet of personalized DBPD business cards. He keeps his mouth shut, following Sebastian's lead, but presents a card firmly to the first mara in the line of twelve with a direct look. The man sneers, but takes it and when Charlie moves on, the mara's lips flatten.

He reads the card, flips it over. Whenever Charlie refills his card holder, he hand-writes his cell number on the back of every card.

The mara takes a long look at it and then pockets the card. The second and third maras in line take note of the first mara's actions once

Charlie continues past them and while one looks confused and the other skeptical, they tuck their cards away as well.

The longer Cin watches the maras, the faster her heart races. She can't quite catch her breath. Charlie has his back to her. She wishes he could see her. She wishes she could see his face again before she goes. Her vision fades, but it's more of a nothing than the veil . . . she's having a panic attack.

She's having Matt's panic attack.

The concrete under their knees is unforgiving, painful. They're staring down at Sam's crushed head. Hot blood drips from their fingertips, from the skin of their zip-tied wrists.

I killed Anna.

Why didn't they kill me?

"Keep your hands off," Bat Boy says. *"If she dies, he dies. Maybe he'll live and we can do this all over again."*

Matt's surprise at those words drifting from Cin's memory inserts a wedge between them.

"Is Anna dead?" Matt says out loud.

Cin can hear him, but she can't see him.

She's walking—no, Matt's stumbling—wrists pinned together in front of him, guys on either side of her half-leading, half-carrying her. Him.

She can't see anything at all.

She's being rushed into a dark void.

She's dizzy.

She stops.

Matt doesn't.

Can't.

The gangbangers peel him off her.

CHAPTER
THIRTY-FIVE

Matt's heart bucked in his chest, but then settled when light edged in. Cin hadn't gone far, then, after disrupting his burgeoning panic attack cum flashback. He dragged his feet, waiting for his brain to catch up. His executioners were apparently taking him to the Civic. Floodlights on the smaller-than-he-expected-warehouse lit up the weedy yard surrounded by old tree farm pines, which marched away in rows filled waist-high with impenetrable palmetto scrub. Several cars sat in the yard, a couple of pick-up trucks. Three men stood near the warehouse wall, in the dark, watching his unceremonious exit. Was one of them Irish Spring?

"Car," the quiet one said, opening the door. "Get in."

Biting his lip to distract himself from his torn wrists, Matt reached out to feel for the door frame. Blood seeped down his forearms from under the zip ties. Black, extra wide. He could still break them, given enough space to create the needed force. Probably.

Musky—buzz-cut, wiry, blonde—stepped back. Matt lowered himself, turning to sit. Cin stood beyond his guards, nearly transparent, her eyes brilliant white, reflecting the light from the warehouse. His breath caught on the lurch of his heart and froze. In an oddly protective gesture, Quiet One, Matt's only impression of him was big, reached out and palmed Matt's head to keep him from bumping it, blocking Matt's view.

His vision blinked out, along with all the thoughts of escape that had edged in with it. He drew his legs into the car one at a time. Quiet slammed the door. "Cin?" Matt said.

"Here," she breathed into his ear. The lightest of touches grazed his neck, raising the hair on his neck. Goosebumps rippled across his shoulders and swept down his arms.

A truck started up.

Somebody yanked the driver's door open and dropped into the seat. Matt considered his seat belt, but that would limit his options. They were pulling out when a thump came from the trunk. They stopped. The driver rolled the Civic's window down.

"Here," a man said.

The driver made an annoyed sound. "What am I supposed to do with that?" It was Quiet.

"Mr. Ward wants his head."

"Then I need a machete, too," Quiet said, making his disgust clear. "And put the damn cooler in the trunk."

He rolled the window up and the trunk opened with a thunk.

"Did Anna die?" Matt tried again, because although he doesn't know where the memory of the voice promising he'd die if she did had surfaced from, he knows, deep inside, it really happened.

"Shut up or I'll dump you in the trunk, too," Quiet said. "Don't know why I can't just kill you here. Put down a little plastic, good to go. Damn paranoid assholes."

The Matt he used to be, now that he remembered him, would not shut up. He'd needle and push. But the Matt who'd spent almost three years in the dark, in more ways than one, kept his mouth shut. If he'd kept his mouth shut back then, Sam would be alive. And Matt would be protecting Dakota from her grandfather himself.

Only that was bullshit, too. He'd been a dead man walking ever since he shot Anna.

Worse than that.

Since he'd met her.

"Anna Salvado," Not So Quiet Grumpy guy said. "Gotta hand it to you, Loose, you got balls."

The trunk lid slammed shut and they were moving again.

Matt had a damn fool heart is what he had. Anna Christina Salvado Gonzalez Garcia. He had gotten her out and the investment banker got her back in again. He hadn't liked the guy since Anna had first mentioned him a year before they split. "We have Dakota to think of now," she'd said. "And I want you to retire one day. He's just going to help us figure some financial stuff out. For the future."

When he'd found out she was moving a little of Daddy Garcia's powder to bolster their savings, Matt had drawn a line. When she crossed it the very next day, Matt walked away. He hadn't meant for it to be forever. He hadn't meant to throw her into the arms of the investment banker or back into her father's money machine. He'd thought their marriage made of stronger stuff. Or maybe he hadn't thought at all. Anna broke his heart, but it hadn't been shattered until he saw her lying there on the docks. Dead because he'd shot her.

He still didn't know where Dakota was, though, so neither did Mr. Ward. But they were going to kill him anyway. For which he was grateful. "I couldn't help you," he blurted. "What's going to happen to Ethan?"

"You gave up plenty. And we got too many guys that know your kid. Think they're going to upset their own kids by disappearing him when half the town saw him leave with one of our guys? I have a hard time believing you're who they say you are. Course, you been hit in the head, so maybe that explains it."

Maybe it did. The barrel wave of memories Spider unleashed had rolled Matt hard and left him floating in the backwash. He wasn't trying too hard to sort them considering his circumstances. What he couldn't remember now was his conversation with Mr. Ward, during which he apparently gave plenty up. And yeah, okay, Grumpy made sense, but Matt wasn't going to trust him anyway.

"You okay?" Matt said, because what did it matter if Grumpy thought he was losing it?

"Crossing, I think," Cin breathed.

Grumpy snorted. "Peachy."

And okay, yeah. Did he really think he could anchor her for the rest of his lifetime? But despite the pain every time she left him, maybe it hadn't exactly occurred to him how this would end. They rolled to another stop. This one longer, with traffic passing by at a high rate of speed. The truck from the yard pulled up behind them. Grumpy turned right and accelerated.

"Forty," Cin said. "West."

State Road 40 ran between Ormond and Ocala. He'd ridden that way for Ethan's travel ball games. Nothing good lay west. Lots of national forest land. Bears. Boars. Gators. Good place to go if you needed time to dismember and dispose of someone and dump a stripped car.

"Can you?"

"I can try," she said.

"Can I what," Grumpy said.

"Kill me quick," Matt bit out.

Grumpy chuckled but didn't answer.

Matt rolled his eyes. "Gun?"

"I'm not gonna waste a bullet on you," Grumpy said like Matt was the stupidest person ever.

And maybe Matt agreed with him. Just a little.

"Shoulder holster," Cin said. "His left. Stop."

Matt stilled the restless tug of his hands, then regretted focusing his attention there as the pain flared up in response. "Hey," he said. Gritting his teeth, he lifted his hands so he could wipe his sweaty face on his shoulder. It wasn't that bad. He needed a little more elbow room though, to free himself.

"Put your fucking hands down," Grumpy said.

"Or what," Matt said. "You'll kill me?" But he put his hands down. "Hey, tell me, what you know."

"Fuck you," Grumpy said and turned the radio on. A dance club anthem that ran the charts last year when it seemed like all Matt did besides work was lie on his bed with his headphones on, but Grumpy didn't change it.

"Moultrie killed Chris Bolton," Cin said, soft as a sigh.

Who the fuck was . . . Oh. Jimmy Shad's friend. The man Matt was supposed to have murdered. The start of all this shit. "Fuck," Matt muttered. "My head. Just wait, okay? Hold on for me."

"Not going anywhere yet," Cin said, sounding stronger. "Saving myself for you." Her mischievous tone lifted his optimism.

He closed his eyes and tried to calm his butterfly brain from lighting on one memory and then another in random bursts along the line of *what did I give them, where's Dakota, what did I give up.* He remembered standing in the lobby of the jail, Lily vibrating in outrage next to him. "You'll have to arrest me or wait until tomorrow," he'd said. "Fine," Cin whispered in his ear. Her warmth, her scent, had gone straight south and he'd nearly laughed out loud at the absurdity of his libido's timing and the choice of his desire. But then.

But then.

The car slowed.

Justin Bieber was telling his girlfriend to go love herself, Grumpy singing along.

And if he'd known then how he'd feel about her twenty-four hours later?

"This is it," Cin said.

Matt sat up.

They turned left onto a dirt road. Cin laid a hand on his shoulder, more present than she had been. When they eventually turned right, she said, "Half a mile. The truck's a quarter mile back from the turn."

Setting his feet, Matt lifted his hands again, elbows out, slowly, tilting his head away, nothing to see here, and then threw his whole body left, knocking Grumpy sideways. The car swerved right. Grumpy's body gave further under Matt's weight and momentum. Rolling up, Matt brought his left elbow up again and then down as hard as he could. Grumpy's head thunked against the driver's door window. Matt's forearm slid across Grumpy's jaw onto his neck.

"Ditch," Cin said, voice clear above the blood rushing in Matt's ears and the radio.

The front of the car tilted and then rolled sideways, helping Matt press harder against Grumpy's throat. Grumpy's arm wrapped around him, and his other fist found Matt's belly just as the car rolled almost all the way over, dumping Matt belly down on the roof, legs across the dash, feet wedged against the windshield.

Grumpy wheezed. His grip on Matt loosened, but then Matt's rib gave with a sharp stab of pain under another powerful blow of his fist.

The engine died.

Disoriented, Matt's head spun in the sudden silence.

Grumpy landed another punch.

Kicking against the dash and pushing away with his elbows, Matt squirmed out from under Grumpy and curled up around the pain, gasping. "Cin, Cin," he croaked.

The front of the chassis groaned, and the car dropped six inches.

A sharp plunk echoed from the other side of Grumpy as the window shattered from the pressure of the fall. Hard pebbles of glass peppered Matt's back. His vision came up in bits that seemed to take minutes. Grumpy labored for every noisy breath. It was fucking dark out, but the dash lights gave Matt's inner ear a break and quelled the vertigo faster than the hours it sometimes took to clear because of his blindness.

His sweaty face inches from Matt's and bright red, Grumpy hung upside down, pinned between the wheel and roof by his sheer bulk, his cheek pressed against the roof. He scrabbled at his gun. The headlights of the truck lit the ragged edge of the road and trees above them. Gritting his teeth, Matt straightened his legs and shoved off the windshield, driving his shoulder against Grumpy's chest and neck, wedging him against his seat, the swell of muddy ground behind the sagging window, and the roof, trapping his gun hand and stealing his breath.

Grumpy's free arm flailed as he fought for air. His hand latched onto Matt's hair, his grip weak.

Hot skin under Matt's nose. The ocean and a sweet coconut shaving cream.

Sweat dripped into Matt's eyes, full of nothing to see once again.

He scrunched them closed and then blinked rapidly in an attempt to relieve the burn but held his position. The truck that had been following drove by without stopping. Luck, the dark, and a deep ditch. They'd be back looking for where they lost the Civic sooner rather than later though.

Grumpy gurgled.

Matt shifted his feet and pushed harder.

Grumpy's hand fell from his hair.

All the tension in his muscles drained out. The sharp scent of urine filled the air.

Matt sunk back onto the roof, into an inch of warm, mucky water, breathing hard. He lifted his hands and wiped his burning eyes one at a time. He didn't have enough room to break the zip ties off. He held his breath and listened.

The truck had stopped, the growl of its engine faint, but steady.

"Cin?"

"Alone," she said on nothing more than a stir of air.

Grumpy's phone buzzed.

"Hold on, babe," Matt whispered.

Struggling in the small space, thoroughly soaking himself, Matt patted around above him, but the phone eluded him, stuck in some crevice he couldn't quite locate. It fell silent. With his hands still bound together and Grumpy's body weight crumpled half-way through the broken window, he also found he couldn't get to Grumpy's shoulder holster. "Fuck."

The truck crawled closer.

The phone buzzed again.

Out. He needed to get out.

Between Grumpy and the head rests, he couldn't turn around. He inched his legs across the roof until he found the passenger window, still intact. Wiggling over onto his back, the painful protest of his rib forced a wordless shout from him. With the truck still moving on the road, Matt didn't care—he let his voice loose against the breathless crush and pistoned both feet out once, twice. The low, explosive sound of the window shattering was almost lost under his shout and the approaching truck's engine. Matt kicked again. He flinched at the fresh rush of ditch water stinking of sulfur. The web of safety glass fell away from the frame. Groaning, Matt scooted closer, poking his legs out.

Up on the road, the truck stopped.

Matt's feet hit the side of the ditch. Clenching his jaw shut, he rolled over onto his knees in the mud to inch out into the ditch backward.

"*Puta madre!*" a voice yelled above the idling engine. Matt had no trouble understanding him.

Matt pulled his wrists apart as much as he could, raised his hands high, and brought them down hard on his chest. The zip tie separated.

"Hooper!" the man yelled, plunging into the ditch. "*Estas bien? Estas bien?*"

Matt cradled his torso and breathed shallow through the sharp pain of the cracked rib, listening to the man cuss under his breath from the far side of the car. Darkness wasn't much of a cover, but Matt would take it.

He steeled himself, took as deep a breath as he could, and crouched down close to the car. Splashing through the standing water, the driver rounded the back end of the upside-down Civic. Less than two feet from Matt, a startled yelp escaped him. Matt attacked, rushing forward with his arms outstretched. Hitting the man head-on, Matt wrapped his arms around him and took him down, water splashing into his open mouth. It tasted terrible.

Twisting underneath him, Irish Spring shoved Matt up by his shoulders. Matt moved with him, rising on his right knee in the mud, and let Irish sputter upright before he swung his left hand out and found the top of the man's head. Landmark. Drop ten inches to the collarbone. Hold. Punch.

Irish rocked back from the blow. Matt let him fall.

Straddling him as he fought to sit up again, Matt grabbed Irish Spring's throat with one hand and palmed his face with the other to push him back down in the mud. Irish Spring's hand landed on the back of Matt's neck, and he yanked Matt's upper body down. Fuck that hurt, but this was his only shot. If Irish broke loose, Matt was done. Bracing himself on Irish Spring's face and throat, he reared back against Irish Spring's wet fingers digging into his neck but couldn't break his grip.

Irish sunk in the mud under Matt's weight. He punched up with his other hand, pushing his fist into Matt's belly above his hip and holding it there. The punch hardly stung, the dig of Irish Spring's knuckles hurt worse, but the sudden hot warmth had to be blood, right? All he could do was hold what he'd got.

Water crept up Matt's fingers on Irish Spring's throat. The desperate man bucked up under him, trying to throw him to the side, but Matt hung on with everything he had in him. Irish shook his head. He opened his jaw and bit the heel of Matt's hand pressing against his face. Matt almost jerked his hand away, but caught himself, his hand slipping under Irish Spring's chin as the man kicked wildly, shifting his weight to try and roll them over.

Matt shoved his bitten hand forward, forcing Irish Spring's head back while still holding his throat tight in the other. Irish spread his legs and trapped Matt's ankles, giving him more leverage on the back of Matt's neck. He pulled Matt down closer, every muscle straining to keep Matt locked in place. Matt's ribs screamed against the pressure of Irish Spring's fist in his belly. Water sloshed over the top of his hand on Irish Spring's chin.

A singular image came to him. Irish Spring, body taut, holding his breath, allowing the water to close over his head to gain his advantage. The water lapped around Matt's other wrist, above his hold on the man's throat.

Digging his knuckles further under Matt's ribs, Irish Spring twisted his hand.

Fire lit Matt's belly up.

Then Irish came to frantic life under Matt's hands. Keeping his iron grip on Matt's neck, he twisted, pulling his fist away to punch Matt in the side and lower back while kicking his legs free, one of his knees thumping Matt in the back. Matt crunched his eyes closed against the pain and concentrated all his energy on pressing his weight forward into both his hands.

A lifetime passed.

Irish Spring's legs slowed and then dropped, his hold on Matt's neck loosening, his punches becoming weak slaps. His back relaxed. His head stilled. His hands slid away, fingers clutching at Matt's shirt. Matt rocked his weight forward. Irish Spring's entire body shuddered. His hands fell, splashing water onto Matt's back.

Cin's sure Matt's going to keel over into the water, but somehow he doesn't. He finds the strength to sit up, but when his hands go to where he's hurting, he dislodges the knife. It hits his thigh and slides into the ditch water. Cin tries again to be there, but nothing happens.

She's not there and he's not able to see anything through her.

When she touches his face though, Matt leans into her hand.

"There you are," he says.

"Always," Cin says, because of that promise she remembers from the Knowing.

"Is this it?" he says, placing his hand over hers.

Is it?

Cin rises just a little and lets herself see the layers all around them. Matt and Cin? Electric blue. And plenty of strands still binding them. "No, not yet," she tells him, hoping it's true.

"I don't want to lose you."

Cin doesn't want to lose him, either. She lived her entire life missing him until she met him. The time they had doesn't even come close to being enough. But she's no longer of the world, as her mami would say. Thinking about Mami conjures the comfort of her hugs. The veil, or rather what lies beyond it, tugs at Cin. "Bey," she says, trying to put everything she feels for him in that one word.

Matt closes his eyes, a slow smile crossing his muddy face. "I love you, too," he says. Cin strokes her thumb over his cheek, wiping away the tear that seeps from his eye. "I always will."

Cin's touch didn't just disappear, it faded from under his hand, leaving him cold. Her silence had been unnerving, but her touch solid, the wave of love that warmed him unmistakable. Matt shivered again, the water soaking his legs warmer than the air, and the blood leaking through his fingers on his belly warmer than the water. God only knew what was swimming in that muck. He might be seeing Cin just fine before too long. But not before he knew who had stolen their life from them. Letting out a shaky breath, Matt wiped his tears away and then dragged his fingers back through his wet hair.

The truck was still running. The woods around him remained silent. He rested his head on his upraised arm for a moment, gathering his strength, and then used both hands to search Irish for a phone. There was nothing Matt could do with the smart phone he found. And the burner in the mud near his shoulder was toast.

Pressing one hand against the burning hole in his belly, the other on Irish Spring's chest, Matt lurched up onto his feet. The pain from the stab wound was bright, but manageable. His ribs complained louder. Dragging his leg over Irish Spring's body was like climbing Mount Dora. He wasn't sure when he crested the top, only that he had done it.

He could hope for another burner somewhere in the truck, which seemed unlikely, or he could wiggle his way back into the Civic and find Grumpy's phone. Matt would bet his life on it being a burner since Irish had called him on it. A frog peeped near him. Another answered. The cricket song that had never really stopped, now that he noticed it, increased in volume. And then all of the frogs within a mile, it seemed, joined in. He waved a hand against the whine of descending mosquitos, though it made no difference.

Grinding more mucky water into the hole in his side made no difference either. The only way to make certain Ethan was safe was to send Sebastian after him. Grumpy had to have a burner.

IT TAKES Matt more than half an hour to find and dislodge the big man's flip phone in her car. Cin tries to help him, but he can't hear her now. The big man's spirit is gone, but the drowned mara lingers right outside the car. Twice, he sinks back into his body, like maybe he can put it on again. When he finally has the phone in his hand, Matt tries it while lying on his back inside the car. The keypad beeps with each number he presses, but then nothing happens. He has no signal.

Once upright outside the car, he leans against it to catch his breath. Sweat streams down his temples and neck, but he's shivering. Blood loss or the adrenaline shakes, or both, maybe. He's as pale as the mara specter standing in front of them.

"You gave me no choice," Matt snaps, although the mara hasn't said anything.

The mara throws his arms up and then waves his hands around.

Matt nods. "If I can. Were you there when Jimmy Shad died?"

The mara's face is unformed, he's drifting a couple of feet off the ground.

Cin can't hear him at all.

"You got another phone in the truck?"

His grimace is all the answer she needs.

"Who would you go to for a bomb?"

Matt shrugs at the mara's answer. Then he nods. "If I can," he repeats. "I'm kinda bleeding out here, I think. We done?"

He turns and splashes through the standing water of the wide, shallow ditch, keeping one hand on her car. Both the mara and Cin follow him. At the back end, he sidesteps, feeling for the slope of the ditch to his left and staggers up it in the direction of the still idling truck. On the sandy road, he tries the phone again. No signal.

Putting his back to the truck, he starts walking, one foot on the packed dirt road, the other on the uneven shoulder that's looser sand and rock and clumps of grass. He falls twice before he gives it up and walks on the flatter sand and clay of the road.

At the first intersection, he walks all the way across the road and only notices when he slides on the slope of the ditch on the other side and lands on his butt. After a moment, he lies back, face lit by the moon.

MATT LAY on his back and took very shallow breaths. He couldn't get lost. He didn't have time for it. He tried the phone and miracle of miracles, it rang through. He recited yet a different series of the pass codes he'd memorized years ago and waited for Sebastian to come on the line.

"Matt! Where are you?"

"I don't know. Ethan might still be at Rodrigo Romero's. It's in Hunter Ridge. His dad's place. I don't remember his—"

"Mateo Romero. Dispatching right now. Where are you?"

"Look for me on Forty, west of Ninety-five. I'm on foot."

"Are you okay?"

"No." Matt couldn't think of anything to add. "No."

"I'm on my way, chief. The sugar mill site's been wiped."

God, he was tired. "Charlie?"

"Pissed. I have him here with me, though. And Jessica, too. There's an agent with Lily."

"Could you—" His mouth was so dry. His tongue stuck to the back of his throat.

"Matt, I'm coming. Right now."

Matt worked saliva into his mouth and swallowed. "It wasn't Ward."

"What wasn't Ward?"

"Shad. The bomb. It wasn't them."

"We'll sort that later. Save your strength, Matt."

"Is Anna dead?"

Sebastian's silence told him more than Sebastian probably wanted him to know.

"How much do you know?"

"All of it," Matt said and folded the phone up in his fist.

The ground angled up beneath his feet. A warmer wall of heat greeted him. Matt stumbled to a halt. Was this finally the highway? A car passed, perpendicular to him, stirring the damp, hot air in its wake. Matt frowned. He fingered his watch, but knew it was later than it read. He didn't know how much time he'd lost in the warehouse, but Florida dawn had a moist, fecund feel to it and that rich feel lay on his skin. Maybe the watch had broken. Another car zoomed by, faster than the first. And then a semi, based on the engine noise and backwash.

This time of day, the traffic from farm country Ocala to the coast would be picking up. He needed to appear confident as he walked to give Sebastian enough time to find him before the cops were called. He could only hope that no one from Malcolm Ward happened on him first. He headed right.

The asphalt was infinitely better than sand. He walked on the shoulder, one foot on the pavement and one on the grass. Everything hurt in that way that shifted it to background buzz. He hadn't walked a hundred yards on 40 before a car slowed down. It passed him and pulled onto the shoulder. He stopped, kept his chin up, and tried not to sway too much.

"Hey, buddy," a woman said. Slight southern accent. "You okay?"

Matt lifted his hand, palm out, the southern non-verbal form of "hey".

"Hey, you okay?"

"I'm good," he said, but it came out too soft.

"Yeah," the woman said, coming closer. "I got a guy here with blood all over him. Out on Forty. Yeah. I don't know, maybe three miles west of . . . shit, I don't know, the big red barn, I think it's a feed store?"

Another car slowed.

"Yes. Yes, west of Appaloosa Lane."

The second car pulled over.

"Way before you get to Eleven. Yes. Closer to Ormond Beach. He's conscious, but he hasn't said anything."

Two doors slammed.

"Hey, buddy, hey, what's your name? Yeah, he's breathing okay, he's standing up. What happened to you?"—louder, directed at him—"No, I didn't see a car anywhere . . ."

And then, speaking over her, "I'm a doctor," a man said. He sounded young to Matt's ear. A New Yorker. "Can I help?"

Matt shook his head, but his legs decided they were done. His knees folded and then he was sitting on the warm asphalt underwater, hot hands supporting him, voices conversing somewhere above his head. A siren somewhere down the road. The warmth spread to his back. Firm fingers on his wrist. Pressure on his belly that sent the breath from his lungs. A tsunami of pain rolled upward into his chest. He caught that wave, opened his mouth, and let it go.

WHEN MATT TAKES his last breath, the veil closes around Cin.

No drama. No spinning. No shattering her into a billion points of light.

She's so confused she stands there for a minute watching a specter in a floppy hat root around in the veil with the shadow of a trowel. Bright red flowers are springing up with every turn of the fog. Two kids come from nowhere, chasing hoops, sticks in their hands. The hoops run across the flowers and roll away red. The gardener and kids blow away in wispy tatters.

Then she sees another her, on the far side of the river, fingers buried in Dumbass's fur, lost in thought. Phantoms drift by but Cin takes no notice of them. Next to her other self, Dumbass jumps up with a yip and comes running and bounding across the river right at her. Her other self rolls up into a crouch, staring past her, waiting to see why Dumbass went running off in greeting, what will emerge from the veil. Dumbass runs right past her now without so much as a sideways glance, plows through a ghostly gaggle of women in ballgowns, and disappears into the fog.

What she remembers is that nothing came out of the veil, but a happy bark has Cin turning. Dumbass gallops back out of the mist into being. He barks at her before happy dog spinning. He darts back the way he came, bouncing forward with short, enthusiastic leaps. He drops his front end, tail high, and barks. Grinning, Matt charges out of the veil and Dumbass leaps away, barking, spinning back to snap at Matt's hands and then crowding in close to him. Matt crouches down to scruff his fingers through the doggy's foggy coat.

Cin's standing beside him before he sees her.

He's only a gossamer soul, like she used to be.

His eyes widen and then she's wrapped up in his barely-there arms.

He shivers when they merge.

Although she doesn't have the Knowing to give to him, Cin gives him what she knows.

And when they draw back all the separate pieces of themselves, there's one more thing that both of them know now.

MATT WOKE WILD-EYED AND TENSE. His entire torso hated him. His head wasn't much better.

Someone laid a hand on his forearm. He startled hard, gasping in a pained breath that killed the shout in his throat.

"We got you, Matt," Sebastian said.

Antiseptic. Sharp citrus cleaner. The rapid beep of a monitor.

Hospital.

"We got Ethan, too. Ran a perimeter and—"

A draft stirred the air. The squeak of sneakers on vinyl. "I'll page the doctor," a woman said. The door wheezed shut.

"We found the scene and cleaned that up."

Matt let his held half-breath out. "Rodrigo's dad?"

"Released."

Matt huffed, immediately regretting it.

"There's nothing your cop friend could do. He claimed Lily wasn't home and you didn't answer your phone. He did what any reasonable parent would do and took the kid home with him. When they dumped his phone, it showed repeated calls to both of you. Now look, Lily's packing, but Ethan's taking it hard. You want to stay with them?"

"Yeah. If that's what they want, too." He tried to shift, get more comfortable, but he might as well have swallowed glass. "Jessica?"

A knock and then the door swung open again. Sebastian stood up, the chair he'd been sitting on sliding back. While a med tech ran Matt's vitals and fussed around him, the doctor took her time explaining the surgical repair to his gut and what Matt should expect. Matt spent most of that time, and the exam the doc inflicted on him afterward, listening to make sure Sebastian didn't sneak out.

"You arrested twice, Matt, on the way to us, and again in surgery." The doc patted Matt's arm. "Between the security, the detective that keeps checking on you, and your recent medical history, I know you've got some stress factors in play, but I'm serious when I say to take it easy."

"Yeah, Doc, I'll try my best."

"And you need rest, so your friend needs to head out. Adriana is pushing your meds right now."

"Got'cha." A warm flush crept up his arm and straight into his chest and head. "I just need another minute with him."

When they were alone again, Sebastian said, "We're transferring you out tonight. You'll be debriefed then. Try to get some sleep."

"Sebby. Jessica?"

"She's going to stay in place for now," he said, his words measured.

Matt stifled the urge to throw his hands in the air. He rolled his aching head on the pillow for lack of a better outlet. "The maras know she was—"

"She's staying. We want RWS, Matt. We need Malcom Ward on their back foot but not out of the game. All the maras know is that they were briefly detained while their identifications were verified. They were told the Zetas were in the net. We even gave them the drugs back, but they dumped the whole load in the river about ten minutes after we sent them on their way. Jessica'll be claiming ignorance. We used her, she didn't know any more than they did, if it should ever come up.

"Next of kin was notified regarding the guys you took out. They were involved in a pile-up on State Road Forty. A passenger, a certain professor of criminal justice with questionable contacts, and a second job tending bar at the Kennel Club, will be dying right here at Halifax Medical Center in a couple of hours without regaining consciousness."

Matt heard Sebastian informing him of the death of his false identity, but his brain was stuck on Jessica. He worked to grasp the thought forming from all the disconnected bits he couldn't quite pull together. "Spider. He . . . uh." Matt squeezed his eyes shut and opened them again, fighting the pull of the drugs. "He had a list of words. Shit." His eyes fell shut. Sebastian's hand landed on his head, a heavy, grounding comfort. Sebastian, who worked for the company. Who knew way more about Matt than Matt knew about him. Who had unknown colleagues and black ops back-up and years undercover, developing assets. Assets like Spider.

"Not until we had leverage," Sebastian murmured.

Shit, had he said that out loud?

"Go to sleep, Matt."

"Did Charlie know?"

"No. It was a simple insertion. A false phone record. We just wanted a way inside through Spider, but you, my friend, are quite the monkey wrench, and of course, we didn't know the Zetas were a factor. It appears they ID'ed you as soon as they hit town."

"Sebby."

Sebastian rubbed his thumb over Matt's temple. "I'm going to miss our friendship."

"Is Anna dead?"

"Yes."

"Okay," Matt sighed.

THEY'RE STILL MIXING spirit when Matt's drawn back down into his life like a reverse water jet. Cin drops to her knees, reaching for him. Dumbass is barking, deep and fierce, but when she glances at him, he's got his nose lifted. A bright light is streaming through the veil, illuminating the rush of the river, the thousands of specters milling around her.

There are so many.

Most avoid the intense light, skirting around its edges.

Some seem captivated. They wander in and wink out in bright flashes.

It's a celestial bug zapper.

But Cin can't resist its glorious pull.

She drifts forward.

Nope.

If she's doing this, it's going to be on her own terms.

Shaping her wispy self into full-blown Detective Lucinda Troy, she straightens her badge, calls Dumbass to her side, and strides into the light like she owns the place.

Charlie rubbed his gloved hands together, the slide of leather on leather loud in the cold night air. "Who wrote it for you?"

Matt wanted to play dumb, but he knew Charlie was referring to the hand-written note he'd received in a sealed envelope from Ed after Matt left Daytona. "Archer."

"You knew they'd shut me out."

"Yeah." The rural crossroads was quiet except for the ticking of Charlie's rental car's engine as it cooled. Matt's ride was long gone. There'd be snow soon, Matt could smell it gathering in the still air. "Who gave you the bomb maker?"

"MS-13," Charlie said, his tone faintly amused. "Wanted it noted that they helped the investigation."

Matt rolled that over in his head. He already knew that once they had the name, Charlie had tracked the man to his home in an upscale gated community, where he sat propped at his kitchen table, his throat slit. Still, Charlie had managed to connect the dots from the bomb maker to Sean Reardon, apparently creating as big a rift as he could between the maras and Malcolm Ward and RWS, all engineered to give the Zetas a foothold, the cops a messy, confusing distraction, and Reardon an outlet for his middle-management rage at everyone. But Reardon's body still hadn't been found, so the maras didn't admit to his murder, while they were giving up information.

Officially, Reardon was listed as a dangerous fugitive wanted by the city of Daytona Beach, Volusia County, the State of Florida, the Florida Highway Patrol, and the Federal Bureau of Investigation. Unofficially, coroners all over the state were sending samples of their unidentified dead to be matched with the unidentified male DNA found on the body of Francis Duncan and samples collected voluntarily from Reardon's distraught sister and mother, anxious to find their missing brother and son and clear his name.

Lacking the type of criminal evidence needed to block it, Veteran's Affairs allowed drug dealer and former Specialist Chris Bolton's burial in September in a National Cemetery in Virginia near his parents' home. Fingered by DNA evidence on a bloody shirt and neighborhood security cameras, a murdered beach rat named Doug Moultrie with no known next of kin was named as Bolton's killer. But there were no leads on Moultrie's killer. Not publicly.

"Portillo?"

"No evidence," Charlie answered. "Not even circumstantial. No excuse to question him. Are you sure he did it?"

Since Cin witnessed Moultrie's murder, Matt knew who pulled the trigger, but—"Certain."

"Is your kid Garcia's granddaughter?"

"No," Matt lied. The likelihood that Garcia would ever go down was nil.

"Spider went missing six weeks ago and Jessica left town two weeks later."

Matt nodded. "She's safe." And assigned to him. Spider had given up everyone and everything, including the info on what Matt had spilled, in exchange for the company's protection. Jessica was heartbroken, but she'd get over it, considering Spider was safe, and her own agreement with the company gave her mother a rent-free condo and a subsidy for the rest of her life.

"How did you know?"

Matt shrugged.

"The note you gave me, the details, how did you know all that?"

"I listen."

"Fuck you," Charlie scoffed. "Hold out your hand."

Matt considered the request. It was Charlie. He owed the man. Matt lifted his hand. Charlie pressed two tiny, cold cylinders into his palm.

"I'm sorry you and Archer missed her service."

Matt ran his fingers over the cylinders, the leather cords tied to each. "Ashes?"

"Yeah. You can keep them or scatter them. She wouldn't mind. I swear I can feel her sometimes, looking over my shoulder, telling me I'm a dumbass."

Matt couldn't help the grin that lifted his lips. He flattened it as best he could.

"What?" Wary.

"Something else in common, I had a dog we called dumbass all the time."

"Ha-ha," Charlie said. "You ready for the other?"

Matt sucked in a deep breath on the sudden stab to his heart. "Yeah."

Charlie's footsteps crunched on the gravel of the shoulder. He opened one of his car's doors and after a moment shut it again. He strode back, his steps long and confident. "Both hands."

Matt dropped the necklaces over his head and folded his cane before tucking it into the inside pocket of his wool coat. He took the wooden box from Charlie with care. It was heavier than he expected, about the size of a shoebox. Cradling the box in his left elbow, Matt traced the branching texture of the exposed grain on the top. "You chose this just for me."

"I did."

"Thank you."

"The paperwork shows Doug Moultrie's friend, Peter Davis, from Philadelphia, claimed his remains. Disposition unknown."

The crooked nose man. Matt still had a hard time wrapping his head around the fact that the brainwashing he'd endured to wipe away any knowledge that might be of use to Garcia if Matt was found in Daytona had worked that well. He hadn't recognized one of his oldest friends. The only one who knew how to access his cover identities. The man he'd trusted with his daughter's life.

Matt's throat closed on an unexpected surge of grief, his eyes prickling with unshed tears, the closest he'd come to crying over Bryan since the company confirmed the match of the two unidentified DNA samples he'd supplied to them. They wouldn't ask who the samples came from, and Matt wouldn't tell them if they did. "Thank you, Charlie."

"This is me, not asking."

"It's better this way, Charlie. For what's it worth, I didn't know who he was when you asked me, but we were important to each other once. It's why he came to Daytona in the first place, when Sebastian started hearing about Malcolm Ward in connection to RWS. You'll never understand how much this means to me."

A breeze had started to pick up. Trees creaked in the woods beyond Charlie's car. He blew out a sharp breath. "If he meant as much to you as Lucinda did to me, I think I do."

"You're right. I'm sorry."

"I saw her," Charlie blurted. "Out on Old Dixie Highway that last night. I swear I did. She was all lit up from the inside. The maras saw her, too. They came out to Tom Renick the next day. I don't know how they knew we'd be out there, but they stood there in a line on the beach while we paddled out to scatter her ashes. They were gone by the time we came back in. Sometimes I drive out there past the sugar mill when I can't sleep and just sit there in the dark. Sometimes I feel like she's sitting there in the car with me."

And there was the reason the maras gave up the bomb maker. Matt reached out, found Charlie's chest with the back of his hand, and then slid his hand up and around the back of Charlie's neck. "I don't doubt she is, not for a minute." He pulled Charlie in for a one-armed hug, then pushed him away and patted his chest. "Now. My next ride's coming and you need to get going."

"Yeah. Okay. Take care, Matt."

When he was gone, Matt stood with his face in the breeze, hand on top of the wooden urn in his arms. "I miss you both," he muttered. "And you better be taking care of Dumbass until I get there."

That place that was Cin's in his chest stayed full these days. She was always with him, though not the way he'd rather. He dreamed of her sometimes, and of the man whose ashes he held, and Anna, laughing at him over the edge of a glass of bourbon, chocolate birthday cake demolished between them. He'd wake to nothing, tears hot on his cheeks, wanting his sight, his old life, his lovers, his daughter most of all.

But then the certainty of peace, of comfort, of wholeness would seep through his skin from the very air, it seemed, sink through his muscles, into his organs and bones and soul. He couldn't quite remember dying, but he couldn't quite forget it, either. It didn't make him long for it, which kind of surprised him. There had been times before he died when he thought he'd welcome death with open arms. Now, he relished every physical sensation. Actively practiced being blind in a different way than he had before. As a challenge. As an advantage. He'd only managed to stay alive for two reasons. That last bit of sight Cin gave him allowed him to reorient himself, and the dark on that near moonless night meant nothing to him.

No amount of snapping his fingers or sorting shapes in the rain or catching things thrown at him could help him in that ditch in the woods, no matter how capable they made him feel. But now a more aggressive form of balance training was helping speed his ability to recover when knocked ass over teakettle. And he was very slowly learning to estimate distances and the placement of obstacles by the bounce of background noise, voices, music, cars, without the snapping or the rain, though he still used those, too, with better technique. After he caught something, he could now throw it back to where it came from or anywhere else with both force and accuracy.

All due to the company convincing him to return to work now that he had "stabilized." As if killing two guys and needing to run from his ex-father-in-law could be considered recovery. As if they had nothing to do with allowing Spider to hack Matt's company background and recover the trigger list to unlock his memories. As if dropping him in Daytona with his actual *sister* and letting him endanger his nephew had *never* been part of a flexible plan to eventually bring him back in.

But.

There were compensations, not the least of which was money and time and very little oversight. With Lily and Ethan, who had proven resilient, stubbornly remaining once again by his side, Matt had a lot to live for despite his sorrows. And that certainty he gained after his heart re-started out on Highway 40, that not only would he see his loved ones again, but that he already had; that they lived through him and with him, but at the same time, had moved on; that death was a looping, endless river of—

That was a car, not wind, in the distance.

His phone vibrated. He lifted an earbud. "Yeah."

"Me," she said.

"I'm here."

She pulled up a couple of minutes later. He got in, the urn on his lap. She drove a couple of miles before she said, her voice tight, "Is that him?"

"Yeah."

She sniffed and cleared her throat. "Our parents live close to me. Rick and his family are flying in next month. We're doing a family service then. Just us."

"My daughter?"

"Protected. Safe. Until now."

Matt spread his hands in reaction to her clipped tone.

"Bryan told us no one knew," she continued, "that no one would ever find us, even you. How did you know?"

Matt couldn't exactly tell her he found out in heaven. All he could do was try and reassure her. "No one knows, but me, I swear. The company doesn't know Bryan and I ever knew each other. He was so far under, I never even knew he worked for them. I ran every file I could and there's no record anywhere that even hints they know about you or Rick, or your parents, or even Bryan's real name, for that matter. No one knows I'm here."

"I lied to you about where we live. Home's a thousand miles from here."

Everything stopped in him for just a minute. He'd been happy just thinking he was in the same vicinity as Dakota, but he understood. "Good. That's good."

"Are you going to take her from us?"

"No!" he half-shouted. "God, no. She's not safe with me." They sat in silence for a long moment. Matt became aware his fingers were clenched on Bryan's urn and relaxed them. He rolled his shoulders back. "Did she know him?"

"Only as Uncle Bryan, who lived far away. After he swooped in and pulled her out of CPS when you were hurt, he was this dark hero in her head. She only knew him for those three days before he brought her to us, but he was her safety. The guy she expected to appear out of nowhere if she ever needed him again. She's pretty crushed. We all are."

"What does she know, about Anna and me?"

"That you were injured on the job while Anna was in a coma following a car wreck. That you both died in the same week. She's going by a different name. Since all of you—you and Anna and her boyfriend —had different last names from one another, she didn't seem to think changing hers was unusual. Bryan got us a birth certificate with a completely new name on it. He altered yours and Anna's, too. He made sure any paperwork trail she tries to follow someday will hold up. We let her 'discover' Dakota was just a nickname when we registered her for school. She decided to use her first name at school and now it's what she goes by. We purged every photo we had of you and Lily from when we were growing up and Dakota never had any. She went straight from school to CPS to Bryan with just the clothes on her back and her school bag."

The details were harder to hear than Matt expected.

"She's had a lot of heartbreak these last few years. I hope Bryan is the last of it."

Matt nodded, not trusting his voice.

"It's snowing," she said, and flicked the wipers on. "She's good, Mark."

His real name sounded strange to him.

"She's quiet, but she laughs more than she used to. She's serious. She's smart. We love her like she's our own."

"You keep doing that, okay?" And yeah, his words were forced and came out hoarse, but he meant them. "You keep loving her enough for all of us."

"Thank you, for bringing Bryan home, but I think from the little he told us, it's safest for Dakota if we don't hear from you again."

Her words brought a phantom whiff of sulfur to Matt's nose, made his breath catch in his throat. His latest recurrent nightmare featured Irish Spring breaking his hold and flipping Matt onto his back in the warm water of the ditch, slick with rotted weeds and redolent with a more intense stink of sulfur than the reality of it had been. In the dream, Irish Spring always laughs and pushes him down and the water closes over Matt's head, and he can't breathe until he wakes, gasping for air.

But she was right, no matter how much it was killing him to finally face the truth.

He couldn't agree out loud, though. He couldn't do that. "There'll be a pharmacy in town, an indie, on the right. You can drop me there."

She said nothing more. The car's tires hissed on the wet road. The wipers beat a steady rhythm that Matt caught himself following with his breath. Eventually she slowed the car and not much further on, hit the blinker and drifted to the right. "Will you be all right?" she said, bringing the car to a halt.

"Give me the lay of the land."

"The curb's just beside us to the right. There's a sidewalk and then two steps up to the shop door. They're closed, though. There're streetlights, but there's no one around."

"I'll be fine." Matt opened his door but wasn't sure what to do with Bryan. He lifted the box in her direction and then her fingers brushed over his.

"He loved you, you know." Her tone was hesitant.

Unsure how to take her words, Matt lifted his chin and turned his face towards her voice.

"He was in love with you."

"I know," he said.

THAT THING they both knew in the veil? That they would, without doubt meet again?

What they didn't know is that meeting again would be like this.

Cin walks in like she owns the place, only to find out that she does.

And so does every other soul.

She's the light for one brief second and for all eternity, too.

She's every living thing and none of them.

And she's everything else, too.

Her mami used to say about places she loved, "It's all that and more."

Stepping into the other side? It's all that and more. Every love affair in history, every drop of spilled blood, every kiss ever given, every fist ever raised, every baby ever born, every death ever met.

Every moment.

And she's present in all of them.

So, when she steps in, zapped and tingling with transformation, not knowing what to expect? She walks into all her moments at once.

Matt's there, walking towards her in the same moment that she's walking towards him.

Because it's all there with him, Cin Knows everything about him and the long life he lived and the kids he had and the pain he suffered and the love he shared.

But he's her Matt in this one moment that they're meeting in, thirty-five and ripped and blonde and bulldog not just in his build, but also his perseverance, his stubbornness, his desire.

This moment is theirs.

Right now, and always.

They stand a foot apart, absorbing each other.

"Cin," he says.

She can't say anything at all.

He traces a finger over her lips.

His eyes are clear and focused and intent on following the curve of her mouth.

That's all it takes for Cin to lose herself in this moment.

She cups his face, his long-weekend-in-jail-stubble is just the right amount of rough.

The chicken roasting in the kitchen smells divine, trace of cooling peach pie sweet, and Matt's skin intoxicating. He closes his eyes and inhales, a slow smile rising across his face, and then they're kissing. It's soft and chaste and perfect until it's not enough and then Matt closes what little space is left between them, demanding more.

Cin lets him in, licks into his hot mouth and surrenders her tongue and doesn't even notice he's walking her back until she hits the wall. They break to breathe, but then he's sucking on her neck and damn, just damn. His hands are hot on the skin of her lower back, her shirt rucked up, their bodies pressed together knee to chest, until he growls and steps back to rip his polo off over his head and drop it to the floor. He grabs the hem of Cin's tee shirt and strips her of it.

Catching her wrists before Cin can lower them, he holds them prisoner above her head while he plunders her mouth once more, then slides his hands down her arms to her neck to her collarbone, his hands sliding down and down until he's palming her breasts, Cin's hands on his broad, bare shoulders. His tongue circles each nipple in turn, strokes them to peaks, and then he closes his mouth on one and suckles. Heated need shoots through Cin's veins, like the strongest drug ever invented.

Maybe it is.

Her head thunks back against the wall.

She whines with wanting him. She wants him. She needs him.

One of his hands closes on hers where it's locked on the back of his neck and the other finds her hip and then he's trying to sink to his knees, but Cin needs to unwrap the leg she has around him first. Bending at his waist, he trails open-mouthed kisses along the length of her ribs in an effort to convince her, but it's not until he bites her, startling a groan out of her, that she gives it up, flinching sideways.

She needs more now. Right now.

Finally on his knees, Matt laughs and pulls back to work Cin's belt open with both hands. He pulls her badge free and slides it into her back pocket, taking the time to appreciate her butt with both hands and ravage her belly button while he does. Getting her jeans open, he pulls them down with her thong and flicks his tongue over her. Cin's hands find his hair. He abandons her jeans mid-thigh and proves there's more than one heaven.

She doesn't even try to stay upright.

He steadies their move to prone, but instead of hard floor under their hips as they kiss, there's a bed. The most comfortable, largest bed, of course, because this really is heaven. Cin's jeans are gone. The temperature is perfect. There's a light cool breeze drifting over them, dapples of warm sunlight through lush tree limbs, low Florida chorus of frogs and cicadas and birds, and from all around them, the soft roll of calm surf.

Cin only has eyes for Matt, though.

And hands and lips and tongue.

He lets her layer some of his other moments into this one, offers her the experience of his later selves on the frame of the younger self she knew. Cin touches and tastes every scar he's acquired, the tattoos he's added, and every inch of open skin between them.

His patience is infinite.

They let the heat between them simmer and build. Their fingers roam until they find all the secrets of their bodies they didn't know they were hiding. When he finally closes that final distance between them, it's slow, inexorable, and once they're joined, at this oh-so-physical juncture of souls—

—he gives himself over to her, tangles their fingers together. Cin's hips ride the rhythm of his thrusts. They breathe each other in, the solid beat of his unhurried heart her heart, his rise and fall her rise and fall, the press of his hot skin the press of her hot skin, outside and in, on and on.

Slow, so slow—

—their wave curls higher and higher, tighter and tighter, carries them along on the rush of whitewater, balanced on the edge, until they break—

—Cin falling into him into her into him, giving everything, everything to her to him to her, losing herself inside him.

"Matt," she cries out, breathless and gone.

And there he is, rising away from the physical, everything spinning away from them. He reaches for her, and Cin takes his hand, dissolute, reckless, wanting. They spin faster and faster, spiraling through the vaulted, brilliant, limitless sky above.

All the pieces of her twine through all the pieces of him.

The stars burn for them.

It's terrifying and glorious and bright.

A CAR SLID up next to him where he waited in the cold on a sidewalk outside what he knew to be a row of closed shops and stopped. The window closest to him whirred down.

"Hey, Mr. Mister!" Jessica chirped, way too bright for a deserted town in backwoods Vermont at a quarter to four in the morning.

Folding his cane, Matt slid into a purring machine that made him wonder what she'd stolen from the company's garage this time. Narrow seat, leather. "Mr. Mister?"

"I was getting bored with 'Boss'," she said.

"I'm getting kinda bored of 'May'," he muttered, fighting with his seatbelt.

"I could be 'August' for a while, that should cause some confusion."

He clicked the buckle home. "I like it."

The exhaust growled when she eased the car away from the curb, her arm brushing his. He should've asked Charlie what happened to Cin's Civic.

"Since we're so far afield already," she said, "can we go to New Hampshire?"

New Hampshire? Really? "Why?"

"I've never been there."

They rocketed away, the acceleration pressing Matt back against his seat. She shifted gears and then he was certain of the manual transmission. "Are these racing seats?"

"They are."

"What kind of car is this?"

"One of the company's engineers bought it for me at auction in Florida. They wiped it and then I arranged for some restoration. The front of the frame was a little crunched. The engine needed a little work. The interior was kind of trashed. I'm told it got a little wet when someone rolled it."

His heart *skittered* in his chest, his lungs empty of air.

"Boss?"

"Yes," he shouted, and tilted his head back on his first real laugh since Daytona. He reached out and thumped the dashboard of the

Civic. He could practically feel Cin hugging him. "Yes," he repeated, quieter. "I know where there are outlets in New Hampshire."

"You buying?"

"Hell, yes, August," Mr. Mister said. "Hit that gas a little harder, will you?"

THANK YOU
FOR READING
BLIND MICE BITE

If you enjoy mysteries with ghosts, read my three-book The Archivist
Series:
Available Now
Ghost: An Andrea Kelley Mystery (The Archivist Book 1)
Spirit: An Andrea Kelley Mystery (Thee Archivist Book 2)
Wraith: An Andrea Kelley Mystery (The Archivist Book 3)

Read on for the first chapter of
Ghost: an Andrea Kelley Mystery (The Archivist Book 1)

**To sign up for notifications of new releases, giveaways, and free
books: www.elleandrewspatt.com**

Please consider telling a friend about Blind Mice Bite
and maybe leaving a review or posting on social media. Both help other
readers find the book.

I appreciate you! ~ Elle

ELLE ANDREWS PATT

GHOST

AN ANDREA KELLEY MYSTERY
-THE ARCHIVIST-
BOOK 1

GHOST: AN ANDREA KELLEY MYSTERY CHAPTER 1

"I drownded."

Andrea eased her eyes open in the dark to squint at Billie Mae Robbins.

All of six, with flaxen hair, Billie Mae had the bluest eyes south of a sunny sky. And she glowed, just a bit, as she stood next to the bed. As usual, she wore a white cotton nightgown, the kind that only went to the knees. Today, a vivid purple bruise crossed the midpoint of her throat, thin as wire, staining the skin below it in a lighter hue until it faded above her collarbone. And today, she was drenched. Andrea's heart dropped.

"I don't think you drowned," Andrea murmured. Water dripped from the ends of Billie Mae's hair, the drops vanishing as they fell. It might not mean anything. She didn't want to wake Taka. The man lay sprawled over more than half her bed, but since he'd tracked and nailed a killer in a little over thirty-nine hours without sleep, she was letting him have more than his fair share. Plus, he was big and pretty and threw a lot of body heat, a total bonus during October in West Virginia.

"I drownded."

She had this conversation three or four times a week with a dry Billie Mae.

"I drownded all by myself," the little girl insisted.

Andrea rolled onto her side to face her. There was another

conversation they had sometimes when Andrea made bacon, which she made more now than ever simply because it was fun to see Billie Mae laugh. But this particular conversation was solemn and grave and almost always took place just before dawn broke and filled the master bedroom with muted brightness. Keeping it normal, Andrea whispered back, "I don't think you did."

"I did," Billie Mae shouted, stomping her bare foot, little fists clinched tight. Andrea flinched, even though she expected it and knew Taka couldn't hear her.

"Where?"

Billie Mae pointed out the window. Fed by a branch of the Elk River, manmade Lake Vickers lay a good half-mile away. After sunrise, Andrea knew, the lake might be visible through that window as a flat grey smudge beyond the fog-wreathed reds and yellows of the trees growing across all the yards downslope from her.

"Your mother strangled you in the bathtub, Billie Mae," Andrea whispered. She made an effort to say it as a statement of fact, to not be mean, but it had been weeks upon weeks of this dialogue already. She'd move, but she loved both the house and the fifteen-minute commute south to downtown Charleston. The steep West Virginia hills above the flat river valley city demanded narrow switch-backing roads that often slowed rush hour traffic to a crawl, but her location off Greenbrier let her bypass the worst of it. The discounted rent she negotiated after the first time Billie Mae had woken her didn't hurt either.

Billie Mae's face crumpled, tears welled and then spilled onto her baby cheeks. She shook her head, her long, wet hair swinging. Andrea couldn't ignore her. She lifted the covers, letting the cool air rush in, and got up. The hardwood floor was cold beneath her bare feet. She shivered. Taka grunted and grabbed at the blankets, pulling them back in close. There were still things she needed for the house. Throw rugs and a sleeper sofa were two of them.

Andrea padded out of the room. Sniffling, Billie Mae trailed her down the hall to the bathroom and climbed into the tub to pout while Andrea went about her morning routine for her near daily run. The claw-footed tub was not the one she died in. The landlord, Kenny, tore that one out years ago. Watching Billie Mae in the mirror as Billie Mae watched her brush her teeth, Andrea saw the exact moment she blipped out of existence, leaving behind a faint whiff of earthy damp and, Andrea already knew, a small puddle in the tub. She supposed she should be grateful that the miserable little spirit didn't leave wet footprints on the hardwood floors. She'd make bacon later and see if that drew Billie Mae out in a better mood.

Andrea warmed up on her driveway, jumping jacks and walking lunges. Frost covered the lawns lining the narrow, rural cul-de-sac, one of three lying back to back across the shallow, rising flatland above Two Mile Creek. Her stalwart little house, covered in cedar siding, looked sturdy, the white shutters bright. Taka's Yukon sat like a black monster behind her FX, snugged up in the carport. The little blue Infinity SUV was getting old, but she didn't like the newer ones as much and it suited her work just fine.

Yellow leaves from the maple beyond the carport covered her car and drive, some drifting out to join up forces with the huge leaves from the ancient oak in the front yard. Maybe Taka would rake for her while she mulched the scraggly beds around the azaleas along the front of the house.

She jogged down her street, but instead of crossing Timber Way, she opted for her longer route and turned right at the stop sign. Within a quarter mile, a cruiser whooshed past her, no sirens, but lights flashing. She slowed, hearing another coming behind and moved onto the grass of the nearest yard. Both turned left down Cooper, the twisting gravel track that ended at the public boat ramp for Lake Vickers. Could it really be happening again?

Picking up her pace, Andrea crossed the street and ran down Cooper. The Charleston Medical Examiner's van blew past her in a cloud of dust. Close to the ramp a couple of people stood in their yards, newspapers in hand as they watched the activity. Walking again, Andrea wiped the sweat from her upper lip and then her temple. The van joined the Charleston Police Department cruisers and a Kanawha County Sheriff's Bronco parked to the left of the ramp, while a yellow Hummer and a black pick-up truck, both hitched to boat trailers, crowded the right side of the small lot at the end of the road. A cluster of officers and three civilians, two men and one woman, who kept wiping tears from her face, stood in front of the center of attention, a late-model bass boat cocked sideways to the ramp in the shallow mud. She recognized a CPD patrolman, Eric, tying yellow crime-scene tape to a tree and waved to him.

He sauntered over, tape unspooling from one hand while he slid the other over his wind-blown hair to smooth it. "Hey, Andrea, you live near here?"

"Yeah, on Double Branch. What's happened?"

The lake rippled in the light breeze, the water grey and foreboding. She'd swam across it once, on a dare, but it gave her a chill thinking of it now. The lowered sky said they'd be getting icy rain later in the day. In the distance, three boats bobbed in and out of sight on the rough chop.

Following her gaze Eric said, "State stocked a good portion of the larger streams with trout a couple of weeks ago. Bass are still biting, too."

Andrea lifted her chin towards the group by the ramp as the ME van's stout red-faced driver joined them, clipboard in hand.

"Another kid. A lot fresher."

"Damn," Andrea muttered.

"Yeah," Eric said to the ground. He glanced up as he started walking again. "Heard Taka was interested."

"He is," Andrea said, walking alongside him. Just days ago, Andrea had called Taka, amazed that Billie Mae had appeared that morning literally dripping what smelled like pond water, something she had never done before, and fixated on the view downslope. Later that day, a child, nearly skeletal, had been pulled from the lake, the case assigned to another detective. "I'm sure he can't do anything now until he's cleared though."

"That was a hell of a takedown last night," Eric said. Taka hadn't said much when he showed up at her door, but she'd gotten some of the details from social media and the news. Taka had shot a suspect. It wasn't the first time. "Dave was there. Said Taka was a damn bear."

He'd be a damn growly bear this morning, too, and as mopey about this poor kid as Billie Mae... who had been soaking wet again this morning.

"Thanks, Eric," she said and left him to finish setting his perimeter. She retraced her steps home, forcing herself to run, even though she didn't feel like it anymore.

The aroma of fresh coffee soaked the air. Andrea found Taka in the kitchen, scrambling eggs, and listening to the little TV tucked into the corner near the stove, still wearing the shorts and ratty Army tee he'd slept in. She hovered in the kitchen doorway as the reporters talked about the murder of a junior at the University of Charleston.

Although drug-related murders were becoming all too common in this part of West Virginia, they didn't normally happen to pretty, young co-eds. Add in the shooting of the suspect by unnamed cops and Saturday morning viewers with no place to go. The Charleston news anchors were almost giddy.

Taka wasn't much of a morning person at the best of times. The coverage of the murder, murky video of the shoot-out, and footage of the suspect's arrival at the hospital wouldn't help today. She knew better than to congratulate him on not killing the guy.

"I'm okay," he said without turning away from the stove. She was struck anew by the breadth of his shoulders. At six feet, Taka was not much taller than her, but built on a wide frame. A result, he said, of the Cherokee blood contributed by his grandmother to a long linage of Scots-Irish-English stock. Since she could claim that heritage herself, Andrea thought it more likely the mix of Maori and African blood laid over the Asian on his father's side. He'd recently taken up the term "person of color" and seemed a lot happier when white people like her invariably asked about his heritage. Without mercy, he'd teased her about crushing on his dominant genes ever since they'd been paired up in science at Andrew Jackson Middle, up the road in Cross Lanes.

William Taka was Andrea's best and oldest friend.

"Smells good in here," she said, even as she was suddenly overwhelmed with sadness. "Was Tracy with you?" Detective Tracy

Manners was Taka's most frequent partner and workout buddy. Despite being constantly harassed for his name, he was one of the most affable, gentle men Andrea had ever met.

"Yeah. Got hit in the vest. He's bruised, but fine."

She slipped her arms around him, laying her head on his midback.

He patted her hands and finished cooking the eggs. When he turned off the stove and set the pan to one side, he turned and hugged her back hard. "What's up?"

"Kid in the lake."

Gripping her upper arms, he stepped back and held her away from him. "Another one?"

"Yeah, more recent."

"Did Billie Mae show this morning?"

Andrea nodded. "Soaked, just like last time."

"Eat up," he said, letting go of her.

"Taka," she said, but he was already down the hall, on the way to get dressed.

She pulled plates down, divided the eggs and dropped shredded cheese onto her portion. She poured coffee for both of them and then took her mug and her eggs to the kitchen table. Motion in the back yard beyond the large picture window caught her eye.

Billie Mae stood outside, still dripping wet.

Shocked, Andrea jumped. Her plate fell with a thunk onto the table. It overbalanced and crashed to the floor. Her coffee sloshed onto the table as she set it down. Ripping the back door open, she hurdled down the two low steps onto the concrete patio. Billie Mae walked through the maples, threading between the rhododendrons. Deep red leaves dropped from the dogwoods to the ground as she passed under their spreading branches.

"What is it," Taka hissed from the door. Andrea glanced back. Barefoot and shirtless, he held his raised Glock steady in both hands, the muzzle pointed towards the trees. He turned on one heel, smooth as ice, tracking Billie Mae's progress.

"Can you see her?"

"No. Who?"

Andrea pointed. "Billie Mae."

Taka lowered his gun. "No, the trees are moving in the breeze, though."

They were. They swayed in Billie Mae's wake.

Andrea stepped onto the brittle, brown fall grass.

"Wait," Taka said. "I need shoes."

While Andrea waited on him, Billie Mae faded at the rear property line, a long, wooded ditch that divided Andrea's yard from her downslope neighbor. He came back out in boots and his Charleston PD windbreaker. They crunched to the back of the yard, ducking between the trees. Andrea tracked right while Taka tracked left.

A darker spot of blue under a settle of leaves at the foot of a maple near her next-door neighbor's four-board fence drew Andrea's attention. She squatted and plucked the leaves back. The tiny blue Keds tennis shoe lay on its side. A streak of dirt stood out on its nearly new fabric. The white laces were untied, tangled with each other. She had no idea how it came to be there.

"Don't touch it," Taka said from over her shoulder, his shadow falling across her and drawing down the dread of gloom tickling her.

"Maybe it's not—"

"Ever seen Billie Mae outside before?"

Andrea shook her head no. "She was soaking wet."

Kneeling, Taka dropped a hand on her back. "I can't call it in, not until I talk to the guys at the lake. Can't tell them your ghost gave us evidence."

"You don't even believe—"

"I believe in you."

A churning ball of angst formed in Andrea's chest. She never thought it mattered to her if Taka didn't believe, but now she found the careful way he always spoke and the shuttered look he watched her with when she talked about Billie Mae did bother her. Would he rather believe she was psychic?

"Sorry," he said, not for the first time these last few months.

"I don't want to stay here by myself."

He took her elbow as they stood. "It might be nothing. If it is related, there's no reason to think anyone would know where it is and come get it, especially not during the day with the cops around the corner."

She must not have looked convinced.

"But you don't have to stay," he added.

They went back through the kitchen. Taka zipped up his windbreaker, swiped his keys from the counter, and they walked straight out to his Yukon.

***

Spectators had gathered at Eric's line of yellow tape, eyeing the emergency vehicles and the grey lake beyond them. The ME's van was gone, but two detectives, standing out in their khakis, dark shirts, and hip holsters, had shown up. Andrea stayed in the car while Taka took point and strode right into the scene without hesitation. The resulting intense huddle made Andrea nervous, with several glances being directed her way.

And then Taka was shaking his head and shaking hands and trudging back through the muddy gravel past the grim boaters who'd found the body. One of them reached out his hand and touched Taka's arm. Taka turned, listened with a small frown creasing his brows, and then trotted back to the detectives. Andrea got out of the Yukon.

The CPD dive team arrived, a WCHS news van in its wake. Eric moved to intercept the van while Taka and one of the detectives, Dan Cozner, pulled the tape for the dive team and then re-secured the perimeter. A reporter Andrea recognized from the Charleston Gazette-Mail crept along the gravel in her brown Honda and then wedged it out of the way behind the news van. Through the trees, Andrea could see half the neighborhood drive by on winding Timber Way above, but only one or two more walkers stopped to gawk.

She made her way over to the crime tape, her belly squirreling.

"Kid didn't have shoes, but boater man over there said he saw one fall from the body when they hooked and reeled it in," Taka told her when she reached him. "It sank, but he knows where. Marked the GPS for the investigation."

"You know," Dan Cozner said. "Even though TV shows get most of it wrong, they're good for teaching that kind of shit. Did you forget your shirt?"

Taka glanced over at him, the corner of his lip quirking up. "It was dark blue or black," he continued saying to Andrea. "Tony'll be over when he's done." He pushed his thumb at a tall, dark haired CSI tech Andrea had seen floating around at department functions.

"Okay," she said. "Should I go back now?"

"We're gonna wait until they launch. Make sure Eric doesn't need help with crowd control until most of the vehicles are gone."

They stood around talking about nothing while watching Cozner and his partner work. Eric poked fun at Taka for running out of the house without a shirt. Andrea wrapped her arms around herself, her sweatshirt not quite enough in the moist chill.

When the techs were done processing the boat for anything that might have contaminated or compromised the body, the fishermen loaded it up on the Hummer's trailer. Eric let them through the tape as the dive master backed his CPD Tahoe down the ramp to float the team's sleek, flat, motorboat into the water. It took twenty minutes or so for them to launch. The GPS coordinates put them quickly out of sight and the little crowd of neighbors wandered off in twos and threes. Moving over to allow the cameraman to better frame the ramp, the WCHS reporter started yet another take. Taka nodded over at Andrea. She ducked under the tape and turned, waiting for him to catch up.

"Detective Taka, a word?" the Gazette reporter called out.

He shook his head and kept walking.

"Sir, Detective Taka, about the shooting," she persisted, trotting over.

"No comment," Taka growled.

"Did you know the suspect was Councilman Miller's nephew?"

"No comment."

The reporter stared hard at Andrea, trying to place her. Andrea looked down, letting her hair fall over her face, hoping she wouldn't remember Andrea contributed research to a cold case article she wrote the previous year. Getting in the Yukon's passenger side, Andrea slammed her door at the same time Taka slammed his. He started it up and backed away, the reporter following for several strides until he gunned forward again in a three-point turn.

"Our names weren't released," he bitched.

"You aren't hard to recognize, Taka. Did you know he was Miller's nephew?"

"Not until afterwards."

Which begged another question. Taka lived with his girlfriend, Melinda. She was tall like Andrea but built on a tiny bird's frame topped with a luxurious mane of fake red hair. Also, unlike Andrea, she was frilly and girly and had a viper's tongue installed in place of her absent compassion. Apparently there were other compensating factors, but hopefully Taka would tire of them sooner rather than later.

"Why'd you come to my place last night?"

"I lost my keys," he mumbled.

No wonder he'd woken her up last night to let him in. She'd thought he was just afraid she'd shoot him for an intruder since she wasn't expecting him. Rolling her eyes, Andrea said, "Her highness wouldn't let you in if you knocked?"

"She sleeps with ear plugs and a white noise machine. I didn't even try."

Taka was a light sleeper and while he didn't tuck his gun under his pillow because he wasn't an idiot, he always kept it close. Each of his three stints in inter-agency undercover had changed him, made him a darker, edgier, older version of the Taka he used to be.

"How can you sleep with all that loud shush-shush going on?"

"I don't," he said, glancing over at her.

That explained a lot, actually, including the heavy shadows under his eyes that eight hours of unusual-for-him deep sleep hadn't even touched.

Charleston cops drew their weapons regularly, but most retired without ever discharging one outside the range, let alone to shoot someone. In eleven years with the department, Taka already had three shoots on his record, no deaths. Although they'd all been justified, the department would be worrying about his liability at this point. If anyone else noticed, if they thought fatigue had played a factor in escalating the pursuit, the CPD's internal Professional Standards

Division or PSD, Charleston's version of Internal Affairs, would use it against him.

"Does this make four?" she asked.

He turned onto her drive. "Yeah. Second highest now. Ronnie Horton has seven," he said, staring into Andrea's carport as he shut the truck off. "Must've been windy here."

Andrea craned her neck to see what he was looking at. A dented and paint spattered aluminum bucket stood upside down next to her overturned trash can. "That's not mine."

"Stay here," he said and got out, easing his door shut. He drew the concealed Glock he always carried off-duty and crept into the carport, turning his head left, right, and up. Andrea looked up, too, but the carport roof was flat—there wasn't much to see. The yards to either side were empty of people.

The can shifted. Taka leapt back, bringing his gun to bear.

Ghost is AVAILABLE NOW at your favorite bookstore.

ABOUT THE AUTHOR

Elle Andrews Patt writes speculative fiction and also works in telecommunications and data migration. In the past, she has made her living as a vet tech, pizza maker, and horse breeding farm manager among many other ventures.

Her published short fiction, novelettes, and novels have been recognized by The National Indie Excellence Awards, Killer Nashville's Silver Falchion Award, The Writers of the Future, and the Florida Writers Association.

Elle currently lives with her family in Tennessee.

Read a free story, sign up for her newsletter, connect with her on social media, and visit her website from one easy link:

https://linktr.ee/elleandrewspatt

Or visit www.elleandrewspatt.com

www.ingramcontent.com/pod-product-compliance
Lightning Source LLC
Chambersburg PA
CBHW060220030726
47499CB00004B/1131